VERA BRITTAIN

(1893–1970) grew up in provincial comfort in the north of England. In 1914 she won an exhibition to Somerville College, Oxford, but a year later abandoned her studies to enlist as a VAD nurse. She served throughout the war, working in London, Malta and the Front in France.

At the end of the war, with all those closest to her dead, Vera Brittain returned to Oxford. There she met Winifred Holtby – author of *South Riding* – and this friendship, which was to last until Winifred Holtby's untimely death in 1935, sustained her in those difficult post-war years. In 1933 Vera Brittain published *Testament of Youth*. This haunting autobiography, a vivid and passionate record of the years 1900–1925, conveyed to an entire generation the essence of their common experience of war. It was a bestseller in both Britain and America on its first publication and again in 1978 when it was reissued by Virago and became an acclaimed BBC Television serial. In 1940 Vera Brittain published *Testament of Friendship*, in which she commemorated the life of Winifred Holtby. This was followed in 1957 by *Testament of Experience* which continued her story, covering the years 1925–1950. These Testaments are also published by Virago.

A convinced pacifist, a prolific speaker, lecturer, journalist and writer, Vera Brittain devoted much of her energies to the causes of peace and feminism. She travelled widely in Europe and lectured extensively in the USA and Canada. She wrote twenty-nine books in all: novels, poetry, biography and autobiography and other non-fiction. Of her fiction Virago publish *Account Rendered* (1945) and *Born 1925* (1948).

In 1925 Vera Brittain married the political philosopher G E Catlin and had two children, one of whom is Shirley Williams.

Vera Brittain

ACCOUNT RENDERED

"Souffrir passe, avoir souffert ne passe jamais"
Leon Bloy, *Le Pèlerin de l'Absolu*

Virago

Published by VIRAGO PRESS Limited 1982
Ely House, 37 Dover Street, London W1X 4HS

First published in Great Britain by Macmillan & Co. Ltd 1945

Printed in Finland by Werner Söderström Oy
a member of Finnprint

British Library Cataloguing in Publication Data
Brittain, Vera
   Account rendered.
   I. Title
   823'.912[F]   PR6003.R385
   ISBN 0-86068-268-4

AUTHOR'S NOTE

THE CHARACTERS in this story are fictitious and their circumstances imaginary. "Halkins'", "Redhurst", and "The Welbeck Hall" are likewise inventions, and are not intended as attempts to portray any institutions of a similar type. The war 'incidents' described as occurring at the two former places have no parallel in actual events.

My apologies are due to the inhabitants of North Staffordshire for taking the same liberties with the geography of their county as I took in an earlier novel, *Honourable Estate*, which related the history of the Alleyndenes and the Rutherstons.

Thanks for valuable help are due to the B.B.C. (for kindly permitting quotation of the news bulletin in Chapter XI); the National Book Council; the Royal Observatory, Greenwich; the Howard League for Penal Reform; the Prison Medical Reform Council; Mr. Gerald Hamilton and the *Evening News*; Mr. Stephen Hobhouse; Miss Helen Mayo; Mr. Dennis Gray Stoll; and Mr. Harold Clipstone.

I also acknowledge the kind permission given me by Mr. Geoffrey Bles to quote from Nicolas Berdyaev's *Freedom and the Spirit*, and by *The Observer* and the late Mr. William Soutar for the quotation of his poem *The Child*.

V. B.

September, 1944.

CONTENTS

Part Four

CHAPTER XVIII

Prologue

THE JURY had been absent for over an hour.

In the tense gloom of the Assize Court, the waiting anxiety of witnesses and spectators had deepened into silence. Already the November afternoon was drawing towards twilight ; in forty minutes it would be time for the black-out.

Through the stillness echoed the distant voice of a boy selling the evening paper.

"La-ate Extra ! Grea-at Greek victory over Wops ! Two night raids on north-west coast ! Latest noos of Stafford tri-al ! "

Outside, through the cobbled market square, passed a little company of soldiers, whistling and singing.

> " *There'll always be an England*
> *Where* there's *a country lane . . .*"

Their confident voices sank and faded, leaving the tautness of suspense more rigid than before.

Suddenly there was a stir in the Court, followed by the clatter of the jury returning to their seats. Three women sitting among the witnesses looked intently at one another. Then, like everybody else, they turned their eyes to the prisoner standing in the dock with bowed head and hands clasped behind him, his ravaged face contrasting strangely with his sensitive musician's fingers and his immaculate clothes.

" He must be seeing all his past life now, like a drowning man," thought the young stenographer, Enid Clay. " I wonder if he's thinking of . . . her. Oh, my love, how can you bear it ! "

" If it's the worst," meditated Ruth Alleyndene, M.P.,

" I must get up a petition for a reprieve at once, based on the scientific evidence. . . ."

But Miriam Huntbach, the Quaker, heard only the excited murmur from the crowd at the back of the Court, which seemed to her to have cried for the past three days, " Crucify him !   Crucify him ! "

The Judge turned to the ten men and two women in the jury-box.

" Ladies and gentlemen of the jury, have you considered your verdict ? "

" We have, my Lord."

" And do you find the prisoner Guilty or Not Guilty ? " . . .

Part One

CHAPTER I

CHEETE

On the first Wednesday in August, 1918, young Francis Keynsham Halkin jumped from his motor-bicycle at Rough Edge, and flung himself face downwards on the hot dry heather of the moors spreading steeply upwards from Cheete.

Above him, like sentinels marking the high desolate heath where Staffordshire and Derbyshire meet, soared the queer-shaped, incongruous rocks which had so much alarmed him the first time that he saw them in his solitary childhood. Recently, from the superior standpoint of eighteen, he had excused that long-ago terror of a five-year-old, for the rocks really did resemble the fossilised remains of prehistoric giants.

But he was not thinking of the rocks today. He saw neither them nor the scythe-like curve of Ploughman's Ridge on the horizon before him, cutting the placid summer sky above Sterndale Spa lying in a fold of the Derbyshire hills. Nor did he consciously observe the clusters of harebells growing between the low bilberry bushes and the humps of tussocky grass, though later he was to find that the hardy moorland flowers, with their deceptive appearance of fragility, always recalled to his mind this forlorn island of time between the two ordeals which threatened to destroy his once secure world. Yesterday Mr. Copeland, the Rector of St. Andrew's Church at Fordham, had read the burial service over his mother ; and tomorrow, as a Second Lieutenant in the Staffordshire Fusiliers, he was going to the front. These devastating events completely overshadowed the fact that today, August 7th, was his nineteenth birthday.

In his head still sounded, intolerably poignant, the notes of George Henschel's *Morning Hymn*, which the organist had played as the bearers carried his mother's coffin out of the village church to her grave under the yews. Unconsciously his lips repeated the English words, translated by the composer from Robert Reinick's *Morgen-Hymne* :

> " *Soon night will pass*
> *Through field and grass,*
> *What odours sweet the morning sendeth !*
> *On vale and height*
> ' *Let there be light !* '
> *Thus saith the Lord, and darkness endeth.*
>
> *From heaven's expanse,*
> *Through all the lands*
> *The angels soar in rapture glorious ;*
> *Sun's light, unfurled,*
> *Flames through the world.*
> *Lord, let us strive and be victorious !* "

His mother had been so fond of that sacred song that Francis, whose remarkable musical talents were obviously inherited from her, had ordered a special gramophone record to be made of it for her last birthday, so that she could listen to it when she was not well enough to play the piano. Her last birthday ! Who would have dreamed, in spite of the cardiac trouble which had affected her so early in Francis's young life, that his pretty, dark-haired, ardent mother would die at thirty-nine !

Only in recent months, since he had left home to join the 13th Reserve Battalion of the Staffordshire Fusiliers in training at Sunderland, had Francis realised the intimate connection between his own part in the War, and the steady deterioration of the strained heart from which his mother had suffered ever since the long illness that followed the birth of his younger brother Roger when he was two years old. Roger's own death from diphtheria three years later had given a tragic irony to Catherine Halkin's vainly impaired health. Since the state of her heart made further children impossible, Francis had been an only child from the age of five.

When war broke out he was barely fifteen, but already — so the headmaster of Cheete Boys' College had told his father — he showed signs of becoming the most gifted music student ever educated at that sound if undistinguished provincial day school. Privately the headmaster, who hardly knew Catherine, found Francis's musical qualities astonishing in the son of a hard-headed Staffordshire paper manufacturer. The boy had an exceptionally clear natural touch, and his fine finger technique gave a ringing individual tone to the simplest pianoforte compositions, such as the melodies of Scarlatti and the *Lyric Pieces* of Grieg. Once, during school preparation in 1915, he was given Browning's famous poem, " How They Brought the Good News from Ghent to Aix ", to learn by heart, and instead set it to music with a vigorous theme which clearly symbolised the galloping of the horses.

Francis's father, Reginald, formerly junior partner in Halkin & Son, had been the sole owner since 1912 of that flourishing family enterprise, carried on at Fordham village between Cheete and Witnall. Like his father before him, Reginald had been educated at Witnall Grammar School before the more modern Cheete College was founded, and saw no reason why Francis should depart from local precedent. Though Catherine had pleaded for her son to be sent to a public school, such as Uppingham with its distinguished record of music-teaching under Sterndale Bennett, Reginald never seriously contemplated the possibility ; he regarded Francis as too necessary a companion for his delicate mother, with whom the busy manufacturer had so little time to spend. If Reginald was ever tempted to wish that instead of highly-strung Francis his surviving son had been the equable Roger — so much more like himself in his good-natured stolidity — he managed to conceal the fact from Francis and Catherine.

When Francis sailed triumphantly through the various examinations taken by Cheete College, and managed to pass the Oxford Senior Local with Distinction just before his sixteenth birthday, the practical Reginald congratulated himself on the money he had saved by sending the boy to a local school. He was, however, inwardly disconcerted and perturbed when Francis — encouraged by Mr. Rosenstein, the German-Jewish music teacher from Witnall who gave lessons in Cheete — won a scholarship at the Royal College of Music during his last summer term in 1917. Francis was then already acting as temporary organist and choirmaster at St. Andrew's Church during the absence of the usual organist after a major operation, and just before the term ended his first operetta, " Moorland Sunset ", was performed by Cheete College choir.

Unfortunately the War, instead of ending in six months as everyone expected, had been rolling along its cumulative course for two years when the Derby Conscription Scheme came into operation, and Mrs. Halkin began to grow apprehensive about Francis's future.

" I hope," she had said to him anxiously during the summer holidays before his final year at school, " that the War isn't going to interfere with you, darling. It's so important to study music early and get a foothold while you're still young. I know your father won't insist on your going into Halkins' when he's once convinced you're really good."

" Don't you worry, Mummy, I'll convince him all right ! I promise you I'll get started the moment I've left school and turned eighteen. Nothing could stop me but the War, and it's bound to be over by then."

No country could go on accumulating casualties at this rate for an indefinite period, privately added his sensitive seventeen-year-old perception, newly sharpened by the long lists following the first Battle of the Somme. Already they had placed on the College Roll of Honour the names of many boys who had been in the top forms when he began going to school.

There would be all the more need, he had thought even then, for men just too young for the War to revolutionise music, repudiate the lush sentimentality of Edwardian taste, and continue the vitalising work of such pioneer composers as Delius and Stravinsky. *He* wouldn't be content, like his unambitious Staffordshire father, to carry on a prosperous but undistinguished commercial undertaking from the point where his forebears had left it off. He'd be a great artist, a famous pianist and composer, who would lift his worthy but mediocre provincial family to an honoured place in the annals of British music.

It was always Mummy, and never Dad, with whom Francis had discussed these ambitions. Dad, his normal work doubled by Government contracts and his staff of expert chemists and clerks continually depleted by the call-up, had no leisure nowadays for conversation. But even if he could have spared the time, he would never have understood his son's aspirations. Music, to Reginald and his Halkin relatives, was a fancy occupation in which the women of the family dabbled amateurishly. It was not a man's job at all — particularly when the " man " involved was the only son left to inherit a flourishing concern into which Reginald, and his father before him, had put all their time and energy.

But Mummy was thirteen years her husband's junior. As nineteen-year-old Catherine Keynsham, she had married Dad straight from her Somersetshire home after their meeting on a summer holiday in Switzerland. Less than a year later, she had conferred upon her elder son that imaginative musical temperament which he fondly associated with the verdant green of the West of England, so much gentler than the harsh Staffordshire moorlands and the ugly, smoke-begrimed Potteries where men died unnecessarily from lead poisoning and silicosis. He knew, too, how closely he resembled his mother, for every stranger exclaimed at the remarkable likeness. He had inherited her light slender figure just above medium height, her creamy brown skin which flushed so easily, her tender, luminous hazel eyes, and the dark glossy hair with the crisp wave which refused to disappear however assiduously it was brushed and controlled.

And now she was dead — and it was the War that had killed her. Bitterly he recalled how, as the end of his schooldays approached but the end of the War seemed further away than ever, there had been so noticeable an increase in the anxiety associated with cardiac conditions, and hence a worsening of the condition itself. It was clear to him now that she had grown steadily frailer during the eleven months' period of his training with the Reserve Battalion, but neither he nor his preoccupied father had expected the sudden heart attack which followed his orders to go to France with a small draft of three officers and fifty men. It had come twelve hours before the end of his last leave, which had been " compassionately " prolonged in order that he might attend her funeral. Tomorrow he had to depart from home and join the rest of the draft across the Channel.

Hurt, bewildered, almost unmanned by his memories of the intimate and loving companionship that he had lost, he sprang from the heather and seized the handlebars of his motor-bicycle. Who else would ever encourage those long hours of piano-practice to which his father so much objected? Who'd really care, now, about the musical ambitions which he and she had discussed together ?

" It's just as well I *am* going to France ! " he told himself, picturing the desolate house which she had made so gracious, with its big vases of flowers, its glass-fronted bookcases where she kept her volumes of Browning and Swinburne, and the large grand piano that she had first taught him to play. " What does it matter if I never come back, now Mummy's gone ! "

He jumped on to the cycle, and thudded violently down the hill.

The next morning, Reginald Halkin went to Cheete station to see his son off by the London train. A short, grey-haired man, inclined to be stout, with a bluff, brisk manner, he had suddenly become conscious that he was middle-aged and lonely. Francis was filled with inward remorse because he could not feel greater compunction at leaving Dad, that familiar figure who had nevertheless been almost a stranger to him in childhood, and with whom he realised how little he had in common as he grew older and learned to appreciate more and more his mother's society.

They reached the station much too early, arriving at the same time as a young girl in a Red Cross nurse's uniform who was booking a ticket to Manchester. Tall, thin and pale, with auburn hair, she would not have been noticeable but for the deep-blue eyes, troubled and haunted, which added an incongruous element of tragedy to her normal inconspicuous prettiness. She hesitated for a moment, and then came up to them with her hand out-stretched.

" Please forgive me, Mr. Halkin — I don't want to interrupt, but I did want to tell you and Francis how sorry I am. . . ."

" That's good of you, Sally," answered Reginald, who

had been acquainted with the Eldridges of Rudyard Manor ever since Colonel Eldridge had bought the attractive country house on the road to Sterndale Spa at the time of his marriage twenty years ago. Catherine, he knew, had seen a good deal of the young girl; she used to play her accompaniments when she sang at local concerts, and Sally would certainly miss her. More than once his wife, giving vent to those advanced views of hers, had expressed the opinion that Sally's charming mezzo-soprano voice — so much finer than that of most amateur singers — ought to be properly trained so that she could earn her own living and have a career. But the Eldridges, of course, would never have considered such a revolutionary notion.

Seeing Francis's lip tremble at this unexpected encounter with sympathy, Reginald added hastily : " So you've joined the Red Cross, eh ? Well, time certainly moves on ! It seems only the other day that you were running about in pig-tails."

Sally drew herself up with dignity.

" I'm nearly eighteen and a half," she said. " I started taking the classes before I left school. If Guy was old enough . . ." She broke off, and her face turned crimson. " I'm just going to Manchester for the last exam.," she continued with an effort. " After that, I shall be able to start at the convalescent hospital straight away."

" Well," responded Reginald, with automatic gallantry, " I envy your patients."

" Thank you, Mr. Halkin." She turned to Francis. " Are you . . . are you going to the front ? "

He nodded, speechless, and she went on : " That's terribly bad luck for both of you, just after . . . I shall think of you often. I shall hold my thumbs for you."

" Won't you — write to me sometimes ? " begged

Francis, to his own surprise. " I shan't . . . get so many letters as I did."

" Of course I will," she replied, as a local train drew in on the other side of the platform. " I've got to go now — this is my train. But I won't forget, I promise ! "

She squeezed Francis's hand impulsively, nodded to Reginald, and hurried across the platform.

" Poor Sally ! " commented Francis's father as she disappeared into a first-class carriage. " She's still fretting about Guy. That's the worst of being a twin ! Can't think why Colonel Eldridge ever let a young lad like that go into the Flying Corps."

" She does look sad," agreed Francis. " Perhaps the hospital work will buck her up a bit. It was decent of her to say she'd write to me, wasn't it ? "

The London train came in with a roar, and Francis, walking up the platform with his father, found an empty carriage just behind the engine.

" Well — so long, Dad ! " he said awkwardly, wishing he could think of the right remark to make to the " old man " who was being left so solitary, wifeless and child-less. " I'll be back soon, never fear. Perhaps it'll all be over by Christmas ! "

" Let's hope so," echoed Reginald, who privately believed that " it " would last for another five years, and was naturally unaware of the fact that, in a bloody battle fought that very day, the Germans were being turned back for the first time in many months from Amiens towards St. Quentin. " Well — take care of yourself, son," he added, as the train began to move. " As Sally said, I'll hold my thumbs for you ! "

CHAPTER II

ÉTAPLES

FRANCIS CROSSED the Channel on a calm starry night, leaving the spectre-like cliffs of Folkestone behind him in the small hours, and seeing before dawn the shrouded lights on the long spur of harbour at Boulogne.

Neither his unsleeping apprehensions nor his sense of individual adventure was reduced by the fact that several million men and women had already passed this way, and a large proportion of them would never return by it. Nor were these feelings affected by the orders that he was given to " proceed " next day to Étaples, that base camp among the pines and sand dunes with which practically every man in the British Army had become familiar at one time or another during the past four years. Francis was as yet unacquainted with the psychological proposition that there is no such thing as the "sum" of human suffering or joy, since each person reaches, with the maximum of individual emotion, the utmost pain or enjoyment that the universe can hold. He only knew that he, Francis Keynsham Halkin, as he travelled in the slow train that took four hours to go twenty miles, was as fearful of the future, and as interested in the flat green meadows, the red-roofed French farms, and the tawny hummocks of the sand-hills, as if no young man of nineteen had ever been to the front before.

Getting out at Étaples station, he was told to report at the Infantry Base Depôt. Walking through the long narrow village with its pervasive aroma of fish and its persistent muddiness even after a succession of sunny rainless days, he skirted the back of the little harbour and, passing under the railway bridge, gazed in bewilderment at the huge panorama of camps. These, in a few hours, would sort themselves out into the Base Hospitals climbing the hill towards Camiers between the wide road and the main railway line to Paris, and the various depôts with their Mess Rooms and sleeping tents.

After four years of war the hospitals, though periodically knocked about by air raids since the great German offensive of the previous March, seemed comparatively civilised, with orange and scarlet nasturtiums decorating the doorways of the wooden huts, and clumps of budding dahlias in front of the Sisters' quarters. But the depôts, set haphazard in the sand churned year after year by thousands of trampling feet, looked colourless and dusty. Most of their occupants were temporary ; few stayed as long as the nursing Sisters and hospital orderlies, who celebrated their comparative permanence by becoming amateur gardeners. Apart from the simple but vivid flowers which they had coaxed into life, the only colour in this late summer landscape of pale sand-hills and dark pines etched sharply against the horizon seemed to come from the intense azure of the sky and the white-fringed ultramarine of the sea away to the west beyond the dunes.

Looking round for someone to direct him on his way, Francis became aware of a sudden strange vibration in the atmosphere. Trying to identify the peculiar sensation of a disturbance that he felt rather than heard, he realised that he was listening to the far-off guns echoing from the south-east and the now bitterly disputed front line beyond Amiens. So that was how one first heard them ! — those guns of France which, as surely as if she had been a battle casualty, had destroyed his mother. Black dejection was rising like a flood when he saw a military policeman, and inquired his way to the Base Depôt. Aware of his destination at last he walked there rapidly, with characteristically quick nervous movements and long energetic strides.

At the Depôt he was relieved to learn that the draft from the Reserve Battalion had not yet gone up the line.

Finding his way to the Officers' Mess, he looked round for the two subalterns who had come before him to Étaples. One, Jeremy Fielden, also a Second Lieutenant, was a boy of his own age who had gone to Sunderland from Sedbergh only a month after Francis had left Cheete College. The propinquity of war-time had made the two of them close companions, though Fielden, a cheerful uncritical youth, had none of Francis's eager ambition, and hoped only to succeed his father in a Manchester firm of chartered accountants. Both of them were years younger than the third commissioned member of the draft, Sidney Smithers, a Regular Army reservist who had spent three years of active service in the ranks, reached the eminence of regimental sergeant-major, and finally, in the desperate casualty-ridden days of the Retreat, accepted a commission which had kept him for four months in England helping to train juvenile officers. One of these schoolboy cadets, seeing the big loose-limbed man stripped in the communal bath-hut, had christened him " Nobbly Sid ", and the name had stuck.

In the Mess Room a heterogeneous collection of officers sat smoking, playing cards, reading tattered out-of-date magazines, and occasionally glancing at the notice-board where the lists were pinned of those ordered up to the line. Their ages appeared to vary from eighteen to sixty ; their ribbons and wound-stripes indicated that one or another of them had been in every battle from the Siege of Ladysmith to the present enormous and decisive conflict raging on the Somme. An atmosphere of waiting weariness pervaded the large hut. Any 1914 veteran could have told Francis how completely the psychology of that temporary company had changed from the keen confidence of the War's early months to the cynical fatigue of its fifth costly summer.

He had been there only a moment when young Fielden was beside him, followed almost immediately by the ungainly figure of " Nobbly Sid ".

" Hello, Frankie ! " Fielden addressed him by the nickname commonly used among Francis's fellow-officers in the Reserve Battalion. At nineteen Francis still looked sixteen, and had made an attractive " Principal Boy " in the regimental theatricals of the previous Christmas.

" 'Fraid you've had a rotten time, old man," Fielden continued with awkward sympathy.

" And a hell of a hot journey, I don't doubt, poor chappie ! " added Smithers, even more at a loss to find adequate expression for his fatherly commiseration.

Francis jerked out the question which had weighed the heavier on his mind the closer the dilatory train from Boulogne had meandered to its destination.

" Are we going up the line yet ? "

" Not immediately," replied Fielden. " Rumour says we've still got another two or three days here."

" You'll find yourself puttin' in more bayonet practice on the Bull Ring," Smithers informed him. " Wot's more, the sergeant-instructor knows some good 'uns that even I never heard of ; he's learnt how to swear in Portuguese. Seems there were a number of them Pork-an'-Beans at one of the 'orspitals here."

" But why more bayonet practice ? " inquired Francis, who had found this type of pseudo-ferocity the most distasteful part of his training.

" Well, it seems there's a war of movement started yesterday in front of Amiens, and the British Harmy don't know where it is with a war of movement, after sittin' in 'oles for more than three years."

" It does sound a bit different from the sort of thing we were trained for."

" It does that. Big things is happenin' up there ! They do say we've got the Boche facin' the other way at last. Why, with any luck, Frankie, it'll be finished in time for you to go back to school ! "

"Lord!" exclaimed Fielden, "Frankie left school last year, even if he does look a kid. When the War's over he's going to the Royal College of Music."

"Music, eh? Ever 'eard the Coldstream Guards' Band play *The Lost Chord*?"

"I can't say I have," replied Francis apologetically. "You see, I live in a town in Staffordshire, and there aren't many military bands round there. We do get musical festivals occasionally, but the music at those is rather a different kind."

"It couldn't be better than that there piece. It was grand — fair brought the tears to me eyes. If you can do 'arf as well when you start scrapin' the fiddle, I'll come miles to hear you!"

Francis laughed — and the sound struck him as strange after the mournful silences of the past few days.

"I'm afraid I shan't be playing the violin. I'm going to be a pianist."

"Are you indeed? Well, I hope Jerry won't damage your 'ands, whatever else he takes orf you!"

"Come along and I'll show you our sleeping quarters," interrupted Fielden, who perceived from Francis's expression that the conversation was taking an unfortunate turn. Francis followed him along a sandy path to another marquee, and deposited his pack, kit-bag, gas-satchel, map-case and binoculars in the few feet of partitioned space in which he was to sleep. While Fielden explained the routine of life at the Base, Francis put up his canvas bed and arranged his shaving kit carefully on a camp-stool beside it. He had always been exceptionally tidy, and even amid the rigours of Army life resolutely maintained that adherence to "method" which he had learnt from his mother at home.

Going back along the path to the Mess Room, he again became aware of the same tense vibration that he had noticed as he walked up the hill.

" Is that the guns ? " he inquired, though he knew the answer.

" Yes.   Our new push on the Somme seems a pretty big show.   We shall hear those guns loudly enough before we're much older ! "

Within twenty-four hours, Francis felt as though he had been at the Base all his life.   Cheete and his father faded to insignificance ;   even his mother seemed to belong to some previous incarnation, its remote perfection vanished for ever.   Only the work that he had so often discussed with her — the years of study at the Royal College, the brilliant musical career of which they had both felt so certain — remained to deprive the " supreme sacrifice " of whatever heroic attractions it might once have possessed.   Still publicly applauded in emotional accents by politicians who ran no risk of facing it, death in action appeared to Francis, not as a service to his country, but as a dark and sorrowful fate that would prevent him from offering to his generation the creative achievements of which he knew he was capable.

Coming over on the boat the night before last, he had realised how much, in spite of his mother's premature end, he still had to live for.   In his heart he recognised an overwhelming fear of the shell or bullet which would write " Finis " to his dreams of serving mankind through the composition and interpretation of music.   Well, whatever happened he must never allow that terror, that potential desertion, to become apparent to those who would share his perils.

That morning in the camp he had awakened to the sense of slight shock, the consciousness of a heavy burden rolling back upon his mind, with which a war-doomed generation was to become familiar for so many mornings of its brief sojourn in earthly time.   With the nearness of the dreaded Unknown the weight had increased, and the society of the Mess Room inhabitants, who contributed to the general atmosphere of suspense, did not help him to throw it off. Such little intellectual life as Sunderland had provided seemed here to be damped out of existence. The older officers, he noticed, showed a tendency to repeat the same old " chestnuts ", of which the small spark of humour became dimmer on each occasion. As for the Bull Ring, he never had felt anything but ridiculous while rushing to jab sacks of straw, and trying to work himself into a frenzy which his gentle nature and artistic sensibilities inevitably resented. The blood-thirsty exhortations of the sergeant-instructor fell off him like so many pellets of hail ; the grotesque idiocy of the stuffed sacks dripping straw on to the sand seemed part of a game of nursery ferocity, which offered no reply to the dreaded question of how far he would be able to endure the sight of wounds and death, or face the detestable duty of killing.

Nevertheless, he found himself seized by sudden moods of inexplicable elation, even though he felt remorsefully that this sense of renewed vitality was unfair to the memory of the mother whom he mourned. He had never been abroad before, and to the irrepressible appreciativeness of nineteen there was an unlimited fascination in the countryside between Étaples and Le Touquet. It was impossible not to be enraptured by the wide seashore, perpetually drenched with brilliant summer light, which surrounded the estuary of the Canche ; by the shops in Paris-Plage, with their vivid scarves of striped silk and miniature sample bottles of unfamiliar liqueurs ; by the *estaminets* in the woods, where one ate omelettes made with six eggs and drank black coffee or *vin rosé*. Hurrying down the wide white ribbon of dusty road between the railway bridge and the village when the Bull Ring exercises were done, he would jump like the schoolboy that he still was on to the toy tram which crossed the river and rattled along past once fashionable villas. It was a new experience, too, to be able to carry his portable gramophone into the pine woods at the top of the hill behind the Depôt, and, sitting on the dry fragrant pine-needles, listen in solitude to some of the favourite records which he and his mother had heard together. His privacy was further guaranteed by the scorn which " Nobbly Sid " displayed towards the selection.

" Got any decent tunes there ? " he had inquired the first time that Francis set out with the little case for the forest.

" Nothing out of the ordinary, I'm afraid," Francis had replied. " Just a few rather well-known classical pieces, like *The Meistersingers*, and Beethoven's Emperor Concerto, and 'I know that my Redeemer liveth', sung by a boy of the Temple Church choir." He saw no reason to mention to Smithers the George Henschel record which he always played at the end, feeling himself, in those poignant moments of sound, to be back again in full communion with his dead mother.

" Oh, that 'igh-brow stuff ! " commented Sid, disappointed. " I thought maybe you were going to give us a treat — like *The Maid of the Mountains*, or *When Irish Eyes*. Listening to those religious tunes always makes me feel like Sunday ! "

And he walked away, humming good-humouredly :

> " *When Irish eyes are smilin'*,
> *It's like the* mornin' *dew* . . ."

The evening before their orders came for the line, Francis and Jeremy Fielden walked over to Camiers to have supper at a friendly farm-house which they had discovered in a small hamlet folded into a curve of the meadows. Sitting in the pleasant kitchen, with its polished pans, its appetising stock-pot perpetually simmering, and the homely sounds of quacking and clucking coming in through the open window, they almost ceased to believe in the titanic Juggernaut grinding men to death in their thousands only fifty miles away. When they had divided the customary outsize omelette and sat smoking over their coffee, Fielden told Francis of an odd friendship that he had formed at his home on the outskirts of Sterndale with a woman palmist named " Astra ", who came to the Spa every year for the summer season.

" She's given me several lessons in hand-reading," he said. " I've tried on myself, but I can't make anything out. She says you never can ; your subconscious resistances blot out your intuitions, or something."

" Why don't you try on me ? " suggested Francis cheerfully, holding out his fine brown hands. Unlike some artists, he told himself, he was not superstitious ; it would be amusing to see what Fielden made of that queer pattern of lines and creases to which he had never given conscious attention.

" Right-o," agreed Fielden, peering at Francis's palms with a serious air. The light was fading, and he studied them for a moment without speaking.

" You've got an excellent head-line," he began. " Tons better than mine. With that and your well-marked line of success you ought to have a topping career. You've got a bumpy curve from little finger to wrist, though ; looks as if you might be handicapped by too much imagination."

" Am I going to get married ? " queried Francis, still sceptical but mildly interested. Having no sisters and, as yet, no girl friends, he had already begun vaguely to speculate about the woman who might some day take his mother's place in his life.

" Oh, yes, you'll marry ! Pretty early too. There's a clear marriage line here, see, just below your little finger. By all the signs, you ought to be a staid old family man before you're thirty. After that . . . let's look. . . ."

He peered into Francis's palm again, then dropped it suddenly with a half-stifled ejaculation.

"Well?" inquired Francis, "what have you discovered now? Am I going to keep a harem, or go in for successive polygamy, like fashionable Americans?"

But, to his surprise, he perceived that Fielden had lost the habitual rosy flush which gave a cherubic appearance to his round, good-tempered face. Uneasily Francis repeated : "What's up? Am I going to be assassinated or something?"

"Doesn't seem like it," answered Fielden hurriedly, relieved to be asked a question to which he could reply without hesitation. "Oh, no, not that . . . your life-line's quite a long one in spite of some weakish places here and there, and, as I said, your success-line's good, specially after that break in the middle. . . ."

"What is it, then?" urged Francis. "Why did you jump like that?"

"Nothing, old man, really nothing," Fielden assured him. "I seemed to go right off it for a moment and get all on the wrong track — probably mixed up your life with someone else's I've read ; one does that sometimes. . . . No, in general I'd just say, look out for one or two rather trying experiences round about forty. . . ."

"Oh, *then*!" Francis laughed, his confidence restored by the comfortable distance of forty from nineteen. "Thanks for telling me I'll make old bones in spite of all this!" And he waved his hand comprehensively at the French landscape outside the window, where a slanting light from the smouldering embers of sunset had tinted with vermilion the pale humps of the dunes.

Fielden struggled stiffly to his feet from the low wooden chair.

"That's all for today. We'd better be getting along ; it'll be dark by the time we're back, and our orders may come through tonight."

But outside, walking down the rough country road, he screened his eyes and stared at the fading sunset like a man in a dream.

" I *can't* have seen that in his hand," he said to himself, turning to look at the innocent childish features and tender hazel eyes of the boy beside him. "Old Frankie a . . .? Lord, might as well suspect myself!   Some palmist, I am!   That's what comes of meddling with things you don't understand.   Give it up, Jeremy, my lad, and learn dominoes instead ! "

CHAPTER III

ARRAS

ON HIS SECOND afternoon at the front, Francis came back from two hours' duty in the section of reoccupied trenches held by the 2nd (Regular) Battalion of the Staffordshire Fusiliers between the Ancre and the Scarpe, and began a letter to Sally Eldridge.

According to the language of communiques, this trench from which the enemy, hard pressed further south, had recently withdrawn, was situated " in the Arras sector of our line ".   A wooden placard indicated that the Germans who had occupied it since April had named it " *Sieges Allee* ", but now, for one of those reasons explicable only to the British Army, it had been rechristened " Brighton Pier ".   The dug-out, with several tunnels leading into it, which now represented B Company headquarters was particularly strong, since its German inhabitants had shored it up with three large wooden posts to correct a subsidence of the roof from a shell-burst overhead.   A ferocious anti-British cartoon from the Berlin weekly,

Lustige Blätter, was still fastened to one of these posts by a rusty drawing-pin.

Sitting down on his wire-framed camp-bed in the tunnel opposite the door of the dug-out, Francis lighted the candle stuck in the neck of a bottle on an upturned box beside him, and started his letter.

" DEAR SALLY,

I hope you are not going to forget your kind promise to write to me sometimes. I could not write earlier myself, as at the Base we were kept going with extra training, and whenever I did get some free time I was seldom alone. It seems funny to talk about being ' alone ' in the front line, but actually I do have quite to myself the underground place where I sleep. It is a kind of little tunnel running from the big dug-out which is our Company Headquarters."

He stopped, and vigorously scratched the back of his neck. More than the noise, more even as yet than the danger, he loathed this feeling of unwashed prickliness, this consciousness of peripatetic animal life on the surface of his skin. Even at the Base, he had somehow " wangled " that daily cold plunge which had been his habit at Cheete as long as he could remember.

" This part of the front," he went on, " is in country meadows between two rivers which you sometimes see mentioned in the papers. These meadows are now thick with flowers ; I don't know their names except for the meadow-sweet, which is very fragrant and manages to overcome many smells of a less pleasant character. It seems wonderful that it should go on growing after the ground has been fought over for the past four years. It also surprised me to see quite gay restaurants and smart shops in the big cathedral town which we passed through on our way here."

Conscientiously he blacked out the word "cathedral ", though the arresting beauty of the great Gothic structure, despite some smashed stained-glass windows, had been not the least of the many fascinations of Amiens, the first large foreign city that he had ever visited. Although it lay twenty-five miles to the south-west, he imagined that if he climbed up the hill at the back of the communication trench, he might still be able to see its dominant spire, rising like a sharpened slate-pencil from the mass of grey stone. It was queer how that spire appeared to sink deeper and deeper into the valley the further you got away from it.

He started up suddenly, listening to some fragments of conversation which penetrated his tunnel from the dug-out. It sounded as if the C.O. were in there, talking to the Company Commander, Captain Welland. He heard the words "big show", and realised that they were dis-cussing an impending battle.

"Then you think it's likely to be next week, sir ? "

"Yes. About the middle of the week — probably the 21st. That will give the reinforcements time to arrive."

"The moon's full that night, isn't it ? "

"Yes. It's due south about midnight. We should get an hour or so of relative darkness just before dawn."

Francis felt suddenly cold. That means our Company will be back in the line again, he reflected. Just back. We go out for four days on the 16th, Welland said.

But the conversation was continuing.

"You understand " — it was the Colonel's voice — "we've got to provide against the contingency of a counter-attack in the interval. The wire in front of us needs a great deal of attention. That raid on Saturday knocked it all to bits."

"I noticed it as soon as we came in, sir. I've got wiring parties going out every night — and burying parties too, till the place is cleaned up. No-Man's-Land isn't exactly salubrious in this hot weather. . . ."

I thought it was that, said Francis to himself. The smell of corruption was new to him, but there was no mistaking it even though he had not yet seen the cause. Resolutely he went on with his letter to Sally.

" This is a regular battalion of the Fusiliers that I am with now, but it has none of its original officers. In four years they have all gone west, or been wounded, or sent home to train cadets. Our Company Commander, Captain Welland, is a junior partner in Thomas Welland & Co., the big pot-factory at Hanley. I should think Colonel Eldridge probably knows his father, who has done business with my Dad for years. He is about thirty, a little spare wiry man with stiff hair like a brush, hard as nails and absolutely imperturbable. Percy Flower, the second in command, says that after two years in France, Welland is as good as most regular officers, and Flower is quite a fair judge, having got the Military Cross himself at the Battle of Passchendaele last autumn. You would never think it, because he was a bank clerk at Burslem before the war and he looks exactly like a bank clerk still — pale face, sleek hair, and spectacles. But I much prefer him to Bannister, the other Second Lieutenant besides myself — a fat boy from Litchfield who talks about nothing but hunting and football. The remaining officer in our dug-out is an ex-ranker subaltern named Smithers, who came out from the Reserve Battalion with me. It is rather a pity that my friend Jeremy Fielden was posted to A Company, whereas I am in B, but it might be worse as we can see each other out of the line."

The distant rumble of guns swelled to a roar from the Somme sector ten miles to the south. Creeping to the edge of the tunnel, Francis looked over the head of Captain Welland, who was sitting at the table making notes, to the slit of sky up the steps of the dug-out. After a few moments a thin wraith of far-off smoke trailed across the deep cloudless blue. Going back to the bed, he concluded his letter.

"The guns are at it again. I heard them the first time when we were at the Base, only it is not exactly true to say that I *heard* them ; it was more like a trembling in the air. But as we came nearer to the line, the noise got louder, and now there's a regular racket all the time. People who have been out here a long while say it was not as continuous as this in the days of stationary trench warfare, but there has been movement over the whole area since the German push in the spring, and at the moment both sides are in new positions which here are fairly wide apart. Between the lines are the ruins of a little hamlet — just a few remnants of houses — which we and they seem to regard with equal suspicion. You can't see what may be going on there, so both of us keep shelling it to make sure there's nothing to our disadvantage. Yesterday the perpetual racket made me feel a bit dazed, but I am more used to it today, though I can't pretend I like loud noises at the best of times. I suppose anyone who happens to be musical can't help being unduly sensitive to them at first.

"I shall have to stop now as I am going into No-Man's-Land with a wiring party tonight, and supper is nearly ready. By the time this letter reaches you the post-orderly will have carried it Under Fire. Please write to me soon and tell me all the news of Cheete, as letters mean a great deal out here, and my father is too busy to write very often."

How was he to finish up ? he ruminated. Was Sally a friend or just an acquaintance ? Even if she was more than an acquaintance he was not much wiser, since he had never had a girl friend before. "Yours sincerely" seemed a bit stiff, but "Yours ever" sounded much too presumptuous. After meditatively biting his pen and discarding several alternative endings as not quite suitable, he finally concluded his letter,

"Yours very faithfully,

FRANCIS K. HALKIN."

That night, for the first time, Francis found himself beyond the protection of the captured trench. Uncertain, as he watched the Very lights rising and falling like green stars, whether the emotion that possessed him was excitement or fear, he crept beside Percy Flower through trampled grass into the odorous dimness of No-Man's-Land. He realised, to his relief, that in spite of the late summer heat the sky was dark; a canopy of cloud concealed the young moon, and behind each descent of the green lights the night came down again like a curtain. The rest of the wiring party followed, and behind them, armed with shovels and a sack of chloride of lime, came the burying party led by Francis's platoon sergeant.

In a few minutes they reached the damaged wire barricade. For the moment the guns had ceased both north and south of them, and in the sudden tense silence they could hear the squeaking of rats which fled at their approach. Francis's instinctive antipathy to vermin made him shudder, but he realised immediately that worse things than rats were forcing themselves upon his attention. He compelled himself to confront the putrefying corpses of dead men caught on the wire.

For a second or two he thought that he would faint from the stench of bodies in different stages of decomposition, overpowering the permanent sour smell of the soil into which had been trampled, year after year, the bones and severed limbs from older battles. Accustomed now to the darkness and able to see more clearly, he found himself gazing into the wide-open eyes and twisted stony faces of men recently killed as they struggled unavailingly with the clutching relentless entanglements. Their fixed, ineffective protest against their fate seemed even more terrible than the black swollen limbs which fell rotting from corpses exposed to several days of hot summer sun.

Making a violent effort he conquered himself on the verge of vomiting, turned his back on the gruesome operations carried out by the burying party, and concentrated his attention on the wire-mending which had seemed such a normal, unintimidating task when carried out on a country training ground swept by salt breezes from the North Sea.

When the party returned to the trench two hours later the guns were rumbling in the distance, but no untoward demonstration had disturbed the sector held by the Staffordshire Fusiliers. The unseen Germans who had left their dead on the wire were not looking for trouble tonight ; perhaps they were thankful to have those obscene remains which had once been men decently buried beside the mutilated bodies of the British soldiers who had not come back from the big raid three days earlier. For the moment the still debated ground in front of B Company had been partially, as Welland put it, " cleaned up ", but Francis, as he sat in his tunnel beside the untasted cup of tea brought him by Watkins, the headquarters' batman, felt that his mind would never be cleansed from the stain of that two hours' experience. It seemed unbelievable that his mother's bright, fragrant drawing-room, where they had played Beethoven's Sonatas and Liszt's wild Rhapsodies, should belong to the same world as this dark Gehenna of rotting corpses and squeaking rats.

" Oh, God," he groaned, his head in his hands, " and they call this the Great War for Civilisation ! " Even when he had drunk his tepid tea and tumbled, tired out, on to the sacking-covered mattress, those staring eyes haunted his dreams, those dead faces gazed at him from fathomless blackness.

Two nights later, when his turn to lead the wiring party came again, he assured himself that these gruesome travesties of humanity would at least be gone. On the previous night a second burying party had finished the considerable task left incomplete by the first, and no fresh fighting had occurred in their sector to add new corpses to the old. This time the wiring party had to move along the trench to the point where it joined A Company's section, and mend a large gap which Welland had observed through his periscope that morning. It was a hazardous undertaking, and he was anxious to get it done before his Company left the line for rest billets next day. On this occasion Francis's companion in charge of the party was Sidney Smithers, to whose experienced perception he probably owed his life. They had been working for less than an hour when the moon, which had just passed its first quarter, suddenly appeared between the heavy heat clouds, and a shaft of vivid light made them all visible to the enemy a hundred yards away.

" Back at the double, lads ! " shouted Smithers. The party, with Smithers and Francis bringing up the rear, made for the nearest point of safety, which was part of A Company's trench. Before they reached it, a noisy bombardment with trench mortars began from the German line. Undoing the work of the past hour, the explosions followed the retreating party across No-Man's-Land. One of the last bombs to be thrown fell among the men crowded into the unfamiliar trench, killing four of them and wounding six. Francis, with two members of his platoon, was blown over by the blast, which loosened part of the trench parapet and buried him in an avalanche of earth and sand. Feeling exactly as though he had been knocked down by a car, he was trying to scramble to his feet when the heap of debris descended, blotting out the stars and quenching in unconsciousness the roar of explosions.

Francis came to himself in a strange dug-out. At first he was aware of nothing but an overpowering headache, like a steel clamp pressed down upon his brows. Then, with the noise of the bombardment still echoing in his ears, he opened his eyes and for a moment could see nothing but flashes of light. He had been unconscious only for an hour, though for all he knew it might have been days.

" Smithers ! " he called wildly, and immediately a familiar voice reassured him.

" You're all right — you're coming round ! Feeling better now, Frankie ? "

He rubbed his eyes, still dazed and half-blinded with dust, and looked up to see Jeremy Fielden beside him. He was lying on a camp-bed in an unknown place amid a group of strange officers.

" Hullo, Jeremy ! I'm quite all right. But what's up ? Where am I ? What's the time ? "

" It's 2 A.M. and you're in A Company's dug-out. You were buried by a bomb from a trench mortar."

" Oh, Lord — was I ? But how did I get here ? "

" Smithers and Sergeant Porter dragged you out — but you're one of the lucky ones. I'm afraid four of your men got killed, and several others wounded."

" My God ! " cried Francis, struggling frantically to sit up. " Is anyone looking after them ? "

" That's all right. We got the wounded ones down to the dressing station long ago. You've been unconscious for over an hour. The Doc's going to have a look at you, and if you're all right we'll take you back to your dug-out."

When Francis had been examined and was found to

be uninjured — except for slight concussion which, as the Medical Officer assured him, would " clear up " after a few hours' rest — Fielden and the doctor helped him along the communication trench to his own headquarters. He found Welland, Smithers and Flower awaiting him ; the sporting Bannister, to his relief, was out on duty.

Stumbling across to the table, Francis began to stammer out an account of his experience, but Welland checked him.

" I know, Halkin — it was rotten bad luck, but you're pretty fortunate to be here at all. The Doc says you'll be all right if you lie down till we go out of the line tomorrow, and then you'll have four days to pick up in. Now don't talk any more, old man ; just flop on your bed and we'll give you something hot to drink. Watkins ! " he shouted in the direction of the kitchen, " cup of tea for Mr. Halkin ! "

" Yes, sir, right away, sir," came the reply, and the tea appeared with unusual promptitude. But after Francis had drunk it he could not sleep. Lying in the darkness because even candlelight hurt his eyes and the roar of explosions still thundered in his head, he pressed his throbbing brows into the hard pillow — and suddenly found himself sobbing for his mother as he had not sobbed since his childhood.

But when he had spent two days in rest billets at a red-tiled farm five miles behind the line, he was conscious of no after-effects from being, as the men put it, " blown up ", except for a slight headache and an intermittent roaring in his ears. He found himself, it was true, quite unable to concentrate on a book or even a magazine, but that would in any case have been impossible, with the knowledge in his mind that they would return to the line for the " big show " which was likely, so the C.O. said, to play a decisive part in this new stage of the War.

An overwhelming impulse possessed him to write

again to Sally Eldridge and tell her that he had already been " buried " by a bomb, and in forty-eight hours would go into an action from which he might never return. But after all, he remonstrated with himself, he knew her very little, and couldn't send another letter less than a week after the first. Glancing at the calendar in Madame Dubonnet's kitchen, he realised with a shock that he had not yet spent a fortnight in France. It seemed more like ten years than ten days since he had left North Stafford-shire, with its dales and moors. The life at Cheete which he had shared with his mother seemed almost as remote as that unimaginable void into which she had vanished and he might follow her.

In the small untidy garden at the back of the farm, he noticed that the leaves of the chestnut which dominated the apple orchard were already beginning to turn yellow and brown. Would he still be here to see the dry branches bud into the green of spring ? When the guns began a continuous roar from the north, where heavy fighting was rumoured to be in progress near Merville, he wandered away from the farm to the country meadows now purple and blue with clumps of anchusa. Sitting beside a reeded pool which mirrored on its quiet surface the slow move-ments of the summer clouds, he asked himself how, when the hour of emergency came, he would lead the men — most of them newly drafted from England — whom he had known for so short a time. With the intuitive keenness of artistic perception, he had observed the young, raw faces — sullen, anxious, good-humoured, irresponsible — and had sensed the undeveloped but varied mentalities behind them.

" What will their reactions be to real danger ? " he meditated. " So far as their behaviour in action is con-cerned, they're just a collection of dark horses. The medical officers who passed them as fit knew nothing about their minds, let alone their souls. They might just as well have been passing cattle for the slaughter-house ! "

The too apt comparison jerked at his over-sensitive
imagination, and he shivered. He was little less, he
realised, of a dark horse himself. As the night when they
would leave their billets approached, he felt an insistent
need to combat the sense, newly awakened since the bomb
had buried him, of being uprooted and lost, detached
from all the familiar things which meant love, work and
security. The final hours before they returned to the line
he spent alone in the orchard with his gramophone,
dreaming himself back into communication with the only
human being from whom he had received real sympathy
and understanding.

Would he see his mother again if the world ended for
him tomorrow ? He realised, as he listened to the familiar
classical themes, how inadequate was her simple religious
faith to help him to face the ordeal before him. His
questioning mind instinctively repudiated much that she
had taught him, yet he had no new philosophy of life with
which to confront the noise and danger of battle, let alone
that horror of mutilation and decay which he resolutely
tried to banish from his consciousness. As though it were
the only remaining talisman to which he could cling, he
went on playing Henschel's *Morning Hymn* until the time
came for him and his men to march away. The record
was a double one, giving both the English and the German
words of the song. Feeling how strange an irony it was
that he should be about to attack and perhaps to slay the
countrymen of the poet who had so movingly expressed
his faith and hope, he ended deliberately with the German
version :

> " *Bald ist der Nacht ein End' gemacht,*
> *Schon fühl' ich Morgenlüfte wehen.*
> *Der Herr, der spricht :*
> ' *Es werde Licht !* '
> *Da muss, was dunkel ist, vergehen.*

Vom Himmelszelt durch alle Welt,
Die Engel freude jauchzend fliegen ;
Der Sonne Strahl
Durchflammt das All.
Herr, lass uns kämpfen, lass uns siegen ! "

Mingling with the rhythm of marching feet, Reinick's verses echoed through his brain as they tramped nearer to the line in the hot August twilight. When the grumbling of the guns swelled into a clamour, the symptoms of uneasiness and apprehension in his platoon became less carefully concealed. Some of the men were irritable and restless ; others made little forced jokes which aroused unnatural laughter ; yet others seemed withdrawn into themselves, morose and silent. Amid the strange patterns of light and shadow beneath the brilliant moon, they seemed to Francis like a company of pale unhappy ghosts about to cross the Styx.

Perhaps he, too, was due to cross it with them. Sitting, an hour later, with the others in the familiar dug-out, he prayed that he might not fail his school or his father, and silently waited for dawn to break.

CHAPTER IV

WINNING THE WAR

IT WAS CERTAINLY strange to find himself being carried on a stretcher without the slightest recollection of how he had got there. What made it more than ever like some feverish phantasy was the peculiar conduct of the huge red star just above the horizon. Spinning first upwards and then downwards, it behaved like a bewitched comet in an enigmatical sky. As he gazed into the deep blue-grey expanse, he found nothing to indicate whether the hour was morning or evening.

Struggling out of his dream-like trance, Francis watched the curious astronomical manifestation dwindle to the normal dimensions of the planet Mars. He perceived that he was being carried at twilight by two British stretcher-bearers to some unknown destination. But when he endeavoured to address them, his efforts to speak were defeated by the same strangling powerlessness that inhibits the victim of a dreadful nightmare.

Immediately he entered into a silent contest with his memory, which alone could explain his presence on the stretcher and the obvious injury that must have brought him there. But the harder he strove for recollection, the more thoroughly broken was the sequence of cause and effect by a gulf of emptiness in his mind. Nothing which had previously happened to him resembled this baffling experience, this sense of being completely severed from time and space. But gradually, as the stretcher-bearers tramped evenly along, their steps seemed to beat out the rhythm of a familiar musical theme—

> " *Bald — ist — der — Nacht —*
> *Ein — End' — ge-macht . . .*"

Suddenly he remembered that, very recently, he had been playing the *Morning Hymn* on his gramophone at the rest billets. Then someone told him it was time to go . . . where? Yes — there was to have been an action . . . a big show. What had happened? Had he been in it? Something, certainly, must have taken place, to put him on this stretcher.

Tramp, tramp, tramp. " *Bald — ist — der —Nacht . . .*"

A roaring in his ears, like the sound of flooding water, quenched the notes of the song. The bumping landscape and the sinister planet faded. When Francis again recovered awareness, he was sitting on a camp-chair being given an anti-tetanus injection by an orderly. All around him was darkness, illumined only by a guttering night-light in a saucer which threw odd shadows on to the canvas roof.

" Where on earth am I ? " he asked, relieved to have found his voice, which at least established his identity with himself. The stifled groaning that came from recumbent figures on blanket-covered stretchers surrounding him on the floor answered his question in advance.

" Why, you're at No. 172 Casualty Clearing Station," the orderly told him, surprised by the inquiry.

" But why's it so dark ? "

" Air raid warning. We always have to put the lights out here when the Jerries are over. It wouldn't be 'ealthy to show them so near the front line." Seeing that Francis still looked troubled, he added : " Them raids don't usually amount to much. If you'll stop there just for a bit, sir, we'll find you a bed in a few minutes."

By the time that he was undressed and lying in an iron cot at the further end of the big marquee, Francis's consciousness of the present was diamond-clear, but the immediate past still eluded him. At any rate he had located his injury, for a downward glance from the camp-chair had revealed that his left foot was thickly padded and tightly swathed with bandages. Trying to sit up in order to read the label over his head when the lights were switched on again, he felt for the first time a pain like a red-hot needle shoot through his foot. More cautiously levering himself up by his arms, he succeeded in ascertaining the extent of his injuries.

" 'Sec. Lieut. F. K. Halkin. G.S.W., left foot'," he read. " Only a gun-shot wound ? Well, I'm not likely to lose my foot for that, at any rate."

He dismissed his wound as trivial, compared with the strange vacuum in his mind. He could recall now the four days in billets, and remembered playing his gramophone just before they went up the line. That was on Tuesday evening. They were going to attack on Wednesday at dawn. Did they go up the line? They must have done, but he could not remember. . . .

It was nearing midnight before the over-driven Night Sister, occupied with more dangerously wounded patients, came to Francis's bed. By that time the long struggle for memory, barely interrupted by a late supper of bully-beef stew, had drawn lines of strain and agitation upon his face.

" Sister ! " he called desperately, " what day is it today ? "

" Why, Friday," she replied, in a pleasant reassuring voice. " Anything wrong with Friday ? "

" But it *can't* be Friday ! " he cried in dismay, gazing at her with dark troubled eyes. " Why, the attack was to start on Wednesday, and . . ."

She looked at him more carefully, noticed his damp forehead, and laid her fingers upon his swiftly beating pulse.

" Got a bit mixed, have you ? " she commented cheerfully. " Well, it's not surprising, after what you boys go through ! I'll just give you something to quieten you down."

She went across to the table, and came back in a moment with a half-filled medicine glass.

" Now, Mr. Halkin, you drink this and go to sleep — and stop worrying about what day it is. You won't have to think about going up the line for several days, so get all the rest you can and make the best of it."

" All right," said Francis, thankful to find that the medicine was already diverting his energies from the futile but agitating quest after the events of three days which had, apparently, escaped from his consciousness. He fell into a light doze, and began automatically to mutter words of command. In the morning the Night Sister, giving her excessively long report to the Day Sister, indicated his bed.

"And you might keep an eye on that boy at the far end," she suggested. "I mean the one with the flesh wound in his foot. It isn't much of a wound, but he's fairly got the jitters over something; I've had to give him a bromide. Seems worried to death because he's mixed up the days of the week. It can't really be that that's bothering him, of course, but there's something or other on his mind."

That afternoon, Francis had a visitor. By this time he had become almost accustomed to the blankness of the immediate past, and his first sense of fear and bewilderment had changed to a feeling of shame. Somehow or other, he concluded, his mind must have given way under an unknown strain — perhaps a considerable one, judging by the colossal fatigue of which he was aware now that his initial perturbation had worn off. Whatever happened, nobody must suspect the existence of this unaccountable blank. He learned, with a satisfaction which he would not normally have felt, that it was Sidney Smithers who had come to see him.

"I'd rather it had been Jeremy," he thought, "but though he's not exactly brainy, he picks things up more quickly than old Nobbly. I may be able to find out what's been happening without giving myself away."

In a few moments, the big ungainly man was sitting beside his bed. The battalion — or what was left of it — Smithers told him, was already out of the line again.

"Welland seemed a bit worried about you, so I said I'd just trot over to the C.C.S. an' look you up. It's nice to see you're alive, anyway, if not exactly kickin'."

"And you too, Smithers. Have we . . . had an awful lot of casualties?"

"We have that. The battalion's 'ad a lousy time. Me

and the Skipper's the only officers left in our Company, and your platoon's all gone but five. Sergeant Porter and young Wardle only turned up this morning."

He cleared his throat and went on with an effort.

" Rotten business about poor old Fielden. I'm damned sorry, Halkin. A nice lad if ever there was one."

Francis felt as though cold fingers were exploring his vitals.

" Jeremy ! He's . . . he's not been killed, has he ? "

Smithers looked at him curiously, concerned and bewildered.

" Why . . . surely you knew ? You was up there in the old Boche dug-out at Ervillers when Corporal Ridgeway from A Company told us about 'im."

Francis clasped his hands tightly beneath the bedclothes.

" I . . . don't know what's up with me today. I'm all . . . sort of dazed. I don't seem to have taken things in properly."

" Well, there's no wonder," said Smithers reassuringly. " It was a hell of a big show for a lad like you — almost the first time in the line too, and after gettin' knocked over by that toch-emma bomb. . . ."

Yes. That had happened, Francis remembered. I was buried by a bomb and made unconscious. But that, surely, was before the show began . . . ?

" An' you did fine," Smithers was saying. " Kep' at it, you did, all the seven mile an' after, and never turned so much as a hair."

" Seven miles ! " Here, at last, was some definite information. "Do you mean . . . we advanced *seven* miles?"

" That's right. Seven mile all told, in the three days. Pushed the old Hun all the way back to Ervillers, and then consolidated. A few more days, and we'll get Bapaume." He looked at Francis again, still puzzled by his apparent ignorance of an action in which he had played a con-

spicuous and creditable part. Meditatively he added :
" They do say we've got more than twenty thousand
prisoners in our sector. Lucky thing for you that snipin'
Jerry among them only got your foot ! When you first
went down, we thought you'd gorn west as well as
Fielden."

So that was it. A sniper, being taken prisoner. Was *I*
trying to take him ?

" What happened to Jeremy ? " Francis whispered.

" Machine-gun bullet through 'is head. Killed him
outright, so at least he didn't suffer. . . . I wouldn't take
on, old chap. It ain't no good gettin' too fond of people
in this bloody war — we're 'ere today and gorn tomorrow.
Maybe the lad's better off than you nor me. After all, we
don't know what's goin' to 'appen to either of us."

Francis bit his lip. " What about the others ? " he
managed to inquire after a moment's silence.

" Flower's out of it for good — right leg blown off at
the knee on the first day. Bannister got a Blighty one
through the shoulder, lucky devil. Pity the Boche
couldn't 'ave done a bit more for you while he was about
it ! We're likely to be out of the line now for a matter of
weeks while we refit, so the Skipper said."

That evening the overworked Medical Officer stopped
beside Francis's bed. If he saw anything abnormal in
the boy's unaccountable pallor and dark haunted eyes,
he determinedly ignored it. Instead he concentrated his
attention on the label above the bed as though that, and
not Francis, were the patient.

" Not much wrong with you, eh ? " he observed cheerfully.

Francis agreed energetically. Later he heard the
doctor talking to the Sister about his immediate future.

" We've got to get these lightly wounded cases back to
the line as soon as we can. Every man jack of them will
be needed for the final push. . . . I'll send him down to

Abbeville for a couple of weeks — the wound should be quite healed by then."

At Abbeville, as the Medical Officer had prophesied, Francis's foot mended quickly. But his dazed and bewildered mind did not. Lying in bed for the first few days, he saw again the wide staring eyes and blackened limbs of men caught on the wire . . . and now Jeremy Fielden was among them, his round cheerful face shrunken, battered, stained with blood from the bullet through his head. Francis felt weighted down, oppressed with the sense of inevitable death ; a new bitterness rose in his mind towards his own epoch and the historical events which had trapped him. The notes and words of the *Morning Hymn*, so long cherished for their associations, beat through his tired brain with a frequency that became maddening in its persistent irony :

> " *Der Sonne Strahl*
> *Durchflammt das All.*
> *Herr, lass uns kämpfen, lass uns siegen !* "

At night, overwhelming shadowy figures rose from the dark abyss of his dreams ; he saw monstrous shapes, heard demoniac voices telling him that he had done all that could be expected of a gifted and sensitive man, urging him to abandon the struggle. " *Lass uns kämpfen, lass uns siegen !* " prompted his memory, and mockingly the voices answered : " *Kämpfen ! Siegen !* Why ? For what ? "

" I won't give in ! " he answered them, until sometimes, it seemed, he had cried aloud. " You haven't conquered me — and you shan't. I'll fight on ! I'm not a coward, and you won't make me one ! "

Before long, his impression of arguing aloud was confirmed by his fellow patients.

" You *do* talk in your sleep, young Halkin," complained the Major in the next bed. " Is that the effect of the 21st ? "

"Oh, no!" Francis protested, hastily and mendaciously. "It's an old habit. I've done it ever since I was a kid."

But it was on this very day, hobbling on crutches through the little town on the River Somme — here brown and swift-flowing, as though in a hurry to carry seawards the alien blood which had mingled with its waters — that he had seen a company of khaki-clad girls from the Women's Army Auxiliary Corps. Some of them, he thought, looked no older than Sally Eldridge, and he wondered whether the Colonel would ever allow her to come to France. By one of those war-time coincidences which happened so frequently, he returned to his ward to find a letter from Sally awaiting him.

"DEAR FRANCIS," she wrote,

"I was thrilled to hear from you, and almost on the top of it came the news that you were wounded. What a pity it wasn't more serious so that you could have come home! I don't want you to be seriously wounded, of course, but you know what I mean. Your name was in the casualty list two days ago. When Daddy rang up your father, Mr. Halkin said people had been inquiring about you all day. I do hope you didn't have too awful a time, and that you are being well looked after.

"The convalescent hospital here is full of patients now, and I am on duty all day, but they are mostly light cases, and the work is not as hard as I should like. I do wish I was old enough to go to France.

"Last week there was a concert at Witnall in aid of the Witnall and Cheete Red Cross. I sang three songs — 'Absent', 'Melisande in the Wood' and 'There's a long, long trail'. The elder Miss Bates played my accompaniments — oh, so badly! I can't tell you how much I missed your poor dear mother. Every time I think of her, Francis, I think of you, and what a dreadful blank she must have left in your life. I know what it's like, because of the blank Guy left in mine.

" The concert was got up by Mrs. Alleyndene of Dene Hall. I had heard of her, of course, but never actually seen her before. She was very pretty and well dressed and I thought her rather frightening, but Mother says she can remember her when she was only the Alleyndenes' governess. Her daughter Ruth has been nursing in France for nearly three years ; I wonder if you will come across her.

" The war news seems to be getting better after being bad for so long. Won't it be wonderful if we really do beat the Germans and have peace for the rest of our lives ! The Rector said last Sunday that if we win it will be a victory for truth and righteousness, and the beginning of a new world order. I wish it could be over before you come out of hospital, but I suppose that really would be too good to be true.

" With best wishes for a not *too* quick recovery,
                    " Always your friend
                              " SALLY ELDRIDGE."

Francis folded the letter carefully and put it in his pocket-book.

" I've got to get fit again," he told himself firmly. " I've got to get back to the line. She believes in me — and I can't let her down."

Before the end of September, Francis returned to the front. He found his much-depleted regiment still out of the trenches ; by the time they returned there, the collapse of Bulgaria had occurred. Turkey, too, was already shaken to her foundations, and rumours of an Austro-German peace overture flew excitedly from camp to camp.

On October 1st, the Staffordshire Fusiliers took over a sector in front of Cambrai, while the French to the south of them captured St. Quentin. Although Francis assured everybody that he felt perfectly fit, Welland insisted that he did not look up to the mark, and sent him down to be Transport Officer after the former T.O. had received a "Blighty" while taking up the rations to the advance units of the Company.

This position had become anything but a sinecure, for the Army, so long stationary, was now perpetually on the move. The roads were congested with lorries carrying artillery and supplies, struggling constantly to keep pace with the guns booming ever further eastward. Companies marching back from the line slept as best they could in the dripping woods or the damp autumn fields; those moving up protected themselves by surface dug-outs hastily constructed in sand-pits or quarries. Parties of "walking wounded" or processions of prisoners frequently interrupted the steady surge forward of the long infantry columns. The whole Army advanced across derelict wastes broken with ditches and craters, and littered with barbed wire and discarded ammunition. Only a few days after the tramping feet had passed over the long-occupied ground, weeds, thistles and tussocky grass half-hid the rusty rifles of the hurriedly buried dead. Already the Hindenburg Line itself had collapsed, and with Germany's allies out of the War, the end seemed, at most, a matter of weeks.

Before the middle of October the Staffordshire Fusiliers were north-east of Cambrai; by the beginning of November they had reached Valenciennes. To the young Transport Officer striving to keep up with the advance, most of the casualties were unfamiliar names. After lasting out nearly the whole of the War, Smithers had his elbow smashed by a shell outside Valenciennes, and was sent back to England. Only Welland seemed invulnerable, and was ultimately to receive a D.S.O., as he said, for " persistent survival ".

So new was this type of warfare after the prolonged stalemate, so constant the motion forward and so comparatively small the numbers of killed and wounded, that Francis was hardly perturbed by a brief repetition of the mental eccentricity which had accompanied him for three days through a major battle that he still could not remember. It was certainly odd to sit down to a cheerful sing-song in the Mess during a twelve hours' respite, and to hear the joyous strains of a *Chu Chin Chow* chorus change to the solemn notes of the *Morning Hymn*, followed by the roaring of an unseen torrent and then silence. But this time the disturbing experience of blankness lasted only for an hour or two, and the worst that happened was a mock scolding from young Baxter, a new officer fresh from Oundle, for getting so " tight " while celebrating the advance. This occurrence, in any case, was all but eclipsed by a day which in Francis's recollection seemed to follow immediately afterwards.

One November morning, just before midday, the Commanding Officer, his usual imperturbability transformed into an unmistakeable air of eager anticipation, entered the ornate dining-room of the recaptured château which was now the Fusiliers' headquarters. A small crowd of officers stood there waiting, for rumour had outstripped the C.O. and brought them together.

" Well, gentlemen," he announced, " I've got some real news this time. The War's over ! "

" It's not a false alarm again, Sir ? "

" No ; we've finished with false alarms. The Germans signed an Armistice at Compiègne this morning. I'm going out to announce it to the men."

A long silence followed his departure as the little gathering of officers tried to realise the incredible fact. For nearly all of them, peace had its problems hardly less acute than war ; readjustment, domestic dilemmas, financial difficulties, the uncertainty of employment, confronted one or another in the now imminent future. But for Francis, driven out into the large empty garden of the château by the rapture of excited relief, the years to come seemed to hold no dark shadows. Now, after losing no more than fifteen months, he could go up to the Royal College of Music, equipped with his scholarship ; he could study the piano, become a great composer, fulfil his own and his mother's dreams. He did not see the dreary day or the leafless boughs of the sodden trees ; through his mind ran a sequence of familiar lines which he was too preoccupied to recognise as a memory from a bygone school Shakespeare class studying *Macbeth* :

> " *Tomorrow and tomorrow and tomorrow,*
> *Creeps in this petty pace from day to day*
> *To the last syllable of recorded time. . . .*"

This, he told himself, meant the end of war, at any rate for the period of his working life. It couldn't come back for at least fifty years, after all that the world had been through. Whatever tomorrow might bring, it could never be so bad as yesterday.

He threw back his head with a characteristic nervous gesture newly acquired during the past few months, and shouted to the dun sky above him : " There's going to be a future ! Tomorrow and tomorrow and tomorrow. . . . I can count on tomorrow ! "

Part Two

CHAPTER V

INDUSTRIAL ACCIDENT

At four o'clock on the windy afternoon of March 20th, 1939, a summons went out for Mr. Francis Halkin, Director-in-Chief of Halkin & Son, Ltd., to come at once to the Red Cross Room.

The agitated young messenger took some minutes to find him, for Halkins' had grown from the small family business of the early nineteen-hundreds into a modern factory employing a thousand workers. Its machine sheds and warehouses extended for nearly half a mile along the banks of the River Checkley at Fordham, the Staffordshire village straggling upwards from the marshy valley to the low rugged hills three miles from Cheete and eight from Witnall on the edge of the Potteries. Eventually the head of the firm, who had acted as chief Air Raid Warden at the factory since the Munich crisis of 1938, was discovered inspecting a new consignment of stirrup pumps with Samuel Sugnall, the Deputy Warden, at the A.R.P. headquarters.

" Beg pardon, Mr. Francis, but you're wanted at Red Cross Room. Nurse Warslow said, would I please tell you t'urry."

" I'll come right away. Accident, I suppose ? "

" Yes, sir. It's Ted Locke — 'im what tends rag-cutter Number Five. They do say 'is 'and's 'arf off."

As Francis hastened across the muddy concrete yard to the Welfare Department with quick nervous strides, he struggled irritably against an overmastering sense of repugnance. Why had this mischance to occur on the very afternoon that he was hoping to get home early, and look through the A.R.P. shelter plans for which he was responsible ? He had been pressing for the completion of those plans for the past five months, and today, when the Prague crisis of the previous week had finally galvanised Witnall's only firm of architects into producing them, he was going to be held up by one of the few serious accidents for which his factory was now responsible !

At the Red Cross Room — so-called from the familiar symbol on the packages of cotton-wool and bandages which filled the surgical cupboard — he found that the groaning, apologetic victim had already been given First Aid and rescued from the verge of collapse by voluble Sylvia Warslow, the nurse in charge of the Welfare Department. From her he learned, greatly to his relief, that the boy who summoned him had exaggerated the machine-tender's injury. Two fingers of the right hand were crushed, said Nurse Warslow, and the third almost torn away, but though this finger might have to be amputated, the risk of losing the hand itself was negligible. Nevertheless, tired and harassed as he felt that day, Francis found himself obliged to check a surge of exasperation at the sight of the injured man's colourless lips and the tin bucket of gory dressings beside the fitted wash-basin.

" I suppose you've asked Mrs. Rushton to telephone for the ambulance and notify Dr. Biddulph ? " said Francis. " It's Witnall Infirmary for you, I'm afraid, Locke."

" Yes, Mr. Francis," the nurse replied. " She and Miss Clay came round to help me as soon as they heard of the accident. They're in the sick bay getting a stretcher ready. I thought he ought to go along on one."

" That's right," said Francis. " He'd better lie down there till the ambulance comes."

Mrs. Rushton, the middle-aged secretary, came into

the room as he spoke. His father's secretary for many years before she became his own, she was the buxom, capable widow of a chief clerk twenty years older than herself. Her assistant, a young stenographer, Enid Clay — a slim fair girl with large grey eyes set wide apart, and beautiful even teeth — followed her, and told Nurse Warslow that the stretcher was ready.

" I expect he'll feel better when he's lying down, poor man ! " she said, as the nurse helped Locke into the adjacent room. " But it does seem queer, his getting caught like that by a machine he's been tending for years."

" That just shows your ignorance, my dear child," observed Francis. " When you've been longer at Halkins' and learned a bit more about Dr. Flint's work here, you'll realise there's nothing surprising in such cases, once you know their history." He turned to his secretary. " You'll check up on his domestic circumstances, of course, Mrs. Rushton ? We mustn't let that side of the work go just because Dr. Flint's too busy to visit us."

The colour had ebbed from Enid's delicate face, but she pursued the subject with an unshaken determination to ignore the tone of contempt in which Francis habitually addressed her.

" You mean, Mr. Francis, he wasn't giving his mind to what he was doing ? "

" Do you really imagine, Miss Clay, that these accidents are caused by inexplicable fits of carelessness, in men who have been reliable mechanics for years ? It's been the job of experts like Flint to discover a direct connection between certain types of accident and the patient's mental condition. In nine cases out of ten, they've found out that these mischances are not acts of God, but the result of emotional maladjustments. I suppose you think that Dr. Flint and other psychological specialists are nothing but crazy cranks ! "

" Indeed I don't," began the young girl, but Mrs. Rushton interposed.

" You forget, Mr. Francis, she's only been here a month, and Dr. Flint stopped coming before she started. She knows next to nothing yet about our research section."

" Well, the sooner she begins to learn, the better," said Francis abruptly.

" But I *want* to learn. . . . What sort of research is being done, and who's doing it ? " Enid persisted.

" There aren't many experts in industrial psychology at all, particularly in this part of the country," explained Francis wearily. " We were lucky to be near enough to Birmingham to have one of the few available."

" Dr. Flint began directing the Welfare Department soon after Mr. Francis became a partner here," added Mrs. Rushton. " When the doctor was first appointed his ideas seemed a bit outlandish to me, I confess, but I understand them better now. And he doesn't go quite so far as some of the others."

" That's true," Francis agreed. " Last time he was here, he was telling me about one of his colleagues on the Medical Psychologists' Association, who claims to have discovered a connection between accidents to eyes, or spectacles, and a preoccupation with marital relationships. Flint showed me a most stimulating paper on the subject in the *Psychologists' Monthly.*"

As he spoke, Francis walked to the window to see whether the ambulance was coming, so he did not notice the sudden crimsoning of Enid Clay's face and neck beneath the soft curls of her short ash-blonde hair. That time last week, she wondered, when she ran into the gatepost and bruised her eye — could it have been caused by her too graphic picturing of her employer's reunion with his wife after Sally Halkin's absence for a month spent with relatives in London ?

But Francis, his eyes on the main yard where the

ambulance would appear, was oblivious of her embarrassment.

" I tell you," he added, " people may make fun of
these pioneers now. But some day, when cases which are
still operated on as a matter of course get taken to the
psycho-analyst instead of the surgeon, as Flint prophesies,
they'll recognise them for the human benefactors they
are ! "

He looked at his watch, and again turned upon Enid.

" Look here, Miss Clay, that ambulance ought to have
come. I can't hang about here all day ! Ring up again
and tell them to get a move on — and if the message
wasn't clear enough last time, see that you make them
understand now. When you've done that, get me Dr.
Biddulph at the Infirmary. I'll have a word with him
about this case."

Bullying her again ! — what's up with Mr. Francis
today ? Mrs. Rushton asked herself as Enid, her face once
more pale and crestfallen, hurried from the Red Cross
Room to the telephone. At least a dozen young steno-
graphers had worked under her during the thirteen years
in which she had acted as confidential secretary, first to
Mr. Reginald Halkin and then to his son, and to each
Mr. Francis had been courtesy and consideration itself.
All except this one, of whom his treatment was — well,
almost . . . sadistic. Yes, that was the word. She was
the keenest worker of them all, too, tidying up the files
in her off-duty time, and staying on hours after the office
had closed to finish outstanding correspondence. And of
her devotion to Mr. Francis and his theories there could
be no doubt, whether one regarded him as a new-fangled
type of employer with all sorts of revolutionary ideas about
Socialism and psychology, or as a well-known composer
who gave all his spare time to music. Perhaps she was a
little *too* devoted . . . maybe that was it ? Everybody in
North Staffordshire knew how whole-heartedly Francis

Halkin adored his fragile, elegant wife, with her pretty mezzo-soprano voice and her charming appearance. He wasn't the sort to seek outside diversions, however mildly platonic they might be.

" To my mind you're a sight too hard on that girl, Mr. Francis," she remarked. " You can't expect a new stenographer to know all about the factory in a matter of weeks."

" Oh, she's competent enough, I grant you," said Francis abruptly. " It's probably her upbringing that makes her get on my nerves."

Well, I never, thought Mrs. Rushton, taken aback. As if the fact that her father was Mr. Norman Alleyndene's chauffeur had anything to do with Enid Clay's qualifications for her job ! And fancy Mr. Francis, of all people, making such a remark !

" Since when did *you* learn snobbery from your in-laws, Mr. Francis ? " she inquired, permitting herself the frank asperity of long association and ten years' seniority. " If the girl didn't start with the same advantages as others, it's the more to her credit that she got a scholarship from Hanley Street School to the High School, and then did so well at the Technical College. She's the best short-hand typist we've had here, bar none, and it's not right that . . ."

" Now, my dear Mrs. Rushton, for God's sake don't scold me ! What with all this A.R.P. on top of everything else, I get too damned tired nowadays to listen to scoldings."

" Well, I daresay Miss Clay's tired too," pursued Mrs. Rushton, undaunted. " She helped Nurse with Locke when he was first brought over — and a nice mess the poor fellow was in ! But she didn't turn a hair — she's been taking First Aid at the classes here — and they'd stopped the haemorrhage and given treatment for shock, all before you arrived on the scene."

" And I'm nothing but a looker-on at my own factory, of course ! I don't share any of the responsibility for my employees ! Oh, well, have it your own way ; your stenographer's your funeral, not mine ! All I ask is, keep this particular paragon out of my sight as much as you can. I'm not strong enough for so much efficiency, and I can't stand the way she follows me round with those great serious eyes. . . ."

The subject of their discussion reappeared in the doorway.

" Dr. Biddulph on the line, Mr. Francis, and the ambulance is here."

" Right you are. Perhaps you'd both help Nurse to get Locke fixed up, and when I've spoken to Biddulph I'll be off. Jim Frampton's brought those shelter plans at last, and I want to look through them before dinner."

When the ambulance had gone and Francis had departed, Enid Clay accompanied Mrs. Rushton back to the office and put on the kettle for a cup of tea. The young girl still looked so downcast that Mrs. Rushton launched forth upon a strenuous attempt at consolation.

" I don't know what's wrong with Mr. Francis today. He's had some strange moods lately ; you mustn't pay too much attention to what he says."

" Oh, I don't, Mrs. Rushton ! " Enid answered, her pale face lighting into animation. " I know he's terribly over-worked. I don't think he ought to have added the job of Chief Warden on to everything else, do you ? "

" Well, this A.R.P. does seem to take it out of him more than most things — which is natural enough, I suppose, in a musician like Mr. Francis, who never meant to go into business at all. Look, dear, the kettle's boiling ! "

" My father once mentioned something about that," observed Enid, making the tea. " Didn't Mr. Francis study in London a long time ago, with the idea of taking up music altogether ? "

Mrs. Rushton sat down at her desk with a tea-cup beside her, and took out the Record Book to enter Ted Locke's admission to the Infirmary.

" Yes," she said. " He went to the Royal College of Music for some years, just after the War. It was before my time here, but Ben — my husband — was senior clerk at the factory then, and he said Mr. Halkin used to go on like anything about his son studying music instead of entering the firm."

" You mean old Mr. Halkin who died last year ? "

" Yes. Mr. Reginald Halkin, the son of Mr. Jeremiah who founded the business. He — Mr. Reginald — never rested till Mr. Francis was back here, but at least he'd the sense to let the lad have his way for the time being, and find out what he could do and what he couldn't."

Enid drank her tea in silence for a few moments ; then she resumed the conversation.

" Why did Mr. Francis come back in the end ? He seems to spend all his spare time on music now, so he must have been tremendously keen then."

" I've never known the real reason to this day," Mrs. Rushton replied. " I only know it wasn't by any means all his father's doing. Something happened in London to make Mr. Francis change his mind, but exactly what it was people never found out. There were rumours, of course. According to one — so Ben told me — Mr. Francis was supposed to have had some kind of wild love-affair with a titled lady who was promoting his work. He was studying to be a pianist then, as well as a composer, but he never touches the piano now."

" Do *you* believe that story — about the love-affair, I mean ? " inquired Enid, looking intently at her tea-spoon.

Mrs. Rushton shook her head.

" It doesn't seem likely to me. After all, he and Mrs.

Halkin had only been married a few months when they gave up living in London, and everybody knew he'd been head over heels in love with her. I don't know when I've seen a young man so bowled over by his feelings as Mr. Francis was at his wedding."

An almost imperceptible note of relief had crept into Enid's voice as she continued her questions.

" And you've no idea what else it could have been ? "

" None at all. You must remember it's a long time ago ; there aren't many people here now who were at Halkins' then. I didn't begin to work for Mr. Halkin myself till two years later, when my husband died, and by that time everyone took Mr. Francis for granted as his father's partner." She put the Record Book back into the drawer, and added : " I must say I didn't expect him to be much use to the firm, knowing what I did about his musical ambitions and the way he'd resisted his father. But I soon learned to take back my thoughts."

" He made a great many changes here, didn't he ? "

" He certainly did. He brought Dr. Flint over from Birmingham on weekly visits when the doctor was still quite a young man, and between them they turned the social side of the place upside-down and started the Welfare Department. What's more, they got Mr. Halkin to accept their schemes, which wasn't by any means the easiest part of the job. But Ben used to say that Mr. Halkin was so thankful to get his son into the firm, he was ready to agree to almost anything."

Enid handed Mrs. Rushton a second cup of tea.

" Wasn't it rather unusual, Mr. Francis being so keen about the workers here, and psychology, and welfare, when his real interest was music ? "

" Oh, I don't know. I shouldn't think he was ever the narrower sort of artist — one-track-minded, they call it nowadays. He's always been very conscientious and what I should call responsible in his outlook ; he seems to think of everything, even music, in terms of how it's going to affect humanity at large. But it was Dr. Flint who got him all worked up about industrial psychology after their first meeting somewhere abroad. Mr. Francis is like that — once an idea appeals to him, he gets thoroughly possessed with it. If it doesn't appeal, it becomes a sort of bogy — like A.R.P."

"Perhaps," suggested Enid, "it was having to look at the new shelter plans that put him out this afternoon, as well as the accident. He hasn't any . . . home troubles, has he?"

"Oh, no. He and Mrs. Halkin are still as devoted a couple as you'd wish to find, though I don't doubt she's a bit of a strain on him at times. Highly strung, you know, just the same as he is, and I should say rather given to worrying. Last time she was here she was talking to me about the chances of another war, and she seemed all wound up over it. It's not as if they had any children to worry about either — but perhaps they'd be better if they had."

Enid rinsed her tea-cup under the tap, and carefully keeping her back to Mrs. Rushton as she dried it, inquired: "Do you know why they haven't? I mean — didn't they want any, or what?"

"It's odd you should ask that," said Mrs. Rushton, as she stamped the afternoon correspondence, "because only the other day I was thinking how many human problems I've discussed with Mr. Francis in this room, yet we've never so much as mentioned one of his own. But people do say that two of Mrs. Halkin's aunts died in childbirth, and she got the idea that she might take after them. I shouldn't wonder if there weren't something in it. They're a high-and-mighty lot — Colonel Eldridge was first cousin to Lord Silverdale — and I daresay the family has more blue blood than red. Anyhow, she decided that having children was too much of a risk, and as she'd only to express a wish for Mr. Francis to grant it, he just agreed."

"What a shame ! " exclaimed Enid, with unexpected vehemence. " He *ought* to have children — a wonderful person like him ! "

Mrs. Rushton, half rueful and half amused, looked with shrewd appraisement at the young girl.

" Oh ! So you think all that of him, do you ? — in spite of the rough treatment you generally get ! "

" Of course I do, Mrs. Rushton. What he says and does to me doesn't affect what he *is* ! If I'm stupid I deserve to be told off, and even if I'm not, it doesn't make any difference. Mr. Francis has been a kind of god in our family ever since I can remember."

" And how long is that ? " inquired the secretary. " How old are you, my dear ? "

" I'm twenty-one — twenty-two in September. But my father used to talk about Mr. Francis when he began to make all the changes here, and I was still a small child. My father's very keen on Socialism, and he says no one in the Potteries has ever done so much for the workers as Mr. Francis — except, of course, for Ruth Alleyndene."

" Well," said Mrs. Rushton, wondering the more at Francis's contemptuous and quite uncharacteristic reference to Enid's social status, " I've certainly always voted for *her*, ever since she first stood for Witnall about ten years ago. To my mind there ought to be more women of that sort in Parliament, whatever Party they belong to. But I don't get much time for politics. Those case-sheets Dr. Flint started get more, not less, as the years go by."

Enid walked over to the table and spoke eagerly.

" Why don't you let me give you a hand with them ? I should just love it, and I'm certain I could do them all right."

" It would be a help, I'm sure. Nurse Warslow never

has cared for the record side of the Welfare Department, and it would be a change to give it to someone who liked it. But have you done anything of the kind before ? "

" Well, yes . . . I have. Before I came here I took on a temporary job with Davy, Son, & Hollins, the solicitors at Cheete, and Mr. Davy let me write up some of his legal cases."

" I never did ! " exclaimed the secretary admiringly. " You'll be telling me next you're going to read for the Bar ! "

Enid blushed.

" As a matter of fact," she said, " that's exactly what I've always wanted to do. But there's no money to spare at home for a profession that doesn't even pay when you've trained for it. I've got a younger sister and two little brothers, so I had to earn as soon as I could. Only sometimes . . . I do dream a bit about the future, and think that perhaps when I've saved up enough, I shall be able to study law. I wouldn't care how late it was, so long as the chance came in the end."

" You've certainly got some pluck, my dear, and pluck's one of the things I like to see. We must get Mr. Francis to take an interest in your career, instead of being so down on you. He's ever so good to young people as a rule."

She got up, and switched on the light. High-powered and vivid, the white gleam leapt through the naked first-floor window, throwing into clearer relief the long dark lines of engine sheds, and beyond them the grey twilit hills with the rows of workmen's cottages climbing almost to their summit. Somewhere amongst them, Ted Locke's wife would be waiting for her husband's return.

" Look here, Miss Clay," said Mrs. Rushton. " What about you going along to see Mrs. Locke instead of me, and then writing up the case ? Mr. Francis will think none the worse of you for taking an interest in Dr. Flint's work."

Enid jumped up excitedly, all strain and fatigue forgotten.

" Oh, thank you, Mrs. Rushton ! I'd just love to ! I'll find out everything I can, and try to be really intelligent this time. There's nothing I want so much as to please him ! "

She flung on her hat and coat with the zest of a schoolgirl setting out on a holiday, and hurried through the door. Mrs. Rushton, her benevolent heart wrung by the spectacle of a young woman's idealistic passion for a talented and preoccupied employer who thought of her only to wish her out of his way, heard her running down the stairs outside the office. A moment later she watched her cross the wind-swept yard to the towing-path beside the river, and hasten along the banks of the Checkley towards the darkening hills.

CHAPTER VI

A YOUNG MAN MARRIES

OUTSIDE THE GARAGE at the gates of the factory, Francis started up his Buick and drove home. A rapid though careful driver, he covered in less than ten minutes the five miles of downhill road between Fordham and his pleasant modern house overlooking the dark industrial ridge of the Potteries.

When Halkin & Son opened an office in Witnall in 1933, and set up there a new branch factory which specialised in pottery transfers, Francis and Sally had moved to this house from their bungalow at Fordham in order to be half-way between the two sections of the business. It was the farthest from the main Cheete-Witnall

road of a terrace of nine houses built upon a site formed
out of the Dene Hall estate, once the ancestral home of
the prosperous Alleyndenes. The fantastic Hall with its
turrets and pinnacles, built by Ruth Alleyndene's great-
grandfather Enoch in the year of Queen Victoria's
accession, had fallen beneath the house-breakers' tools
ten years ago. Its last occupants, Stephen and Jessie
Alleyndene, were the parents of the present M.P. for
Witnall and her brother Norman, who had directed
the Alleyndene Pottery Company since Stephen's retirement.

By 1939 the suburbs of Witnall had finally swallowed
the magpie-haunted meadows which once stretched between Dene Hall and the outskirts of the town, and had
now reached the bottom of the hill on the side of which
Dene Terrace stood. In front of the nine red brick houses,
long narrow gardens divided by low walls sloped downwards until they reached the banks of the River Checkley,
slow here and deeper than at Fordham as it neared its
junction with the Trent. In the Alleyndenes' day a copse
had concealed the narrow river from the windows of
Dene Hall, but the copse had now been cleared. Francis's
garden was bounded by a steep public footpath leading
downhill from the main road to a stone bridge which
spanned the deepest part of the stream.

Francis locked up his car in the private garage at the
back of Number 9, and glanced, as always, at the familiar
ridge which today had been almost stripped by the March
wind of its canopy of smoke. More clearly than usual, its
dark outline cut the evening sky, tinted rust-red where the
darting tongues of pot-factory furnaces met and mingled
with the gathering fires of the early spring sunset. Again,
as at the paper mills, Francis became conscious of an overwhelming fatigue. Locke's serious accident had tired
him, he realised, but his weariness had a deeper origin
in the shock and apprehensions of the Prague crisis the

previous week. This in itself was a disconcerting sequel to the Munich crisis, which had followed so soon after the death of his father and his own assumption of the chief responsibility for Halkins'. Although he had lost no time in converting the firm into a Limited Liability Company, and had now the assistance of three co-directors, Francis had never quite recovered from the tension of the previous autumn, with its mingling of public and private pre-occupations. Hitler's recent annexation of Czecho-slovakia had revived the host of sinister, half-formulated fears which six months ago had begun to prey, like mordant vultures, upon his mental and physical vitals.

As he stood outside his front door with his head thrown back, looking upwards from the sunset to the hurrying clouds, Francis was clearly recognisable as the eager boy who had saluted the future from the November garden of a château in France. His dark hair, with its persistent tendency towards an unruly waviness, was hardly less abundant, and as yet untouched with grey. His hazel eyes looked as vulnerable as ever ; his slim figure was straight and hard in its athletic fitness. But he carried with him now an indefinable dignity which had not been his in 1918, and an unself-conscious awareness of distinction which was oddly interrupted by an occasional jerkiness of movement, and by the anxious frown which now and again distorted his brow.

When he opened the door, Sally's clear, musical voice called down to him from the bedroom above.

" Is that you, darling ? "

Even after nearly fifteen years of marriage, Francis could never hear Sally summon him without a vague stirring of the emotion to which her singing always moved him. Especially vital still was the feeling of protective love so deeply aroused in him twenty years ago by the young girl who had comforted him in his first bereavement after her own loss of a twin brother destroyed by war.

She came down the stairs now to greet him, wearing a favourite powder-blue dress which enhanced her willowy elegance and the blue-grey of her eyes. Her auburn hair, faded to the madder brown of fallen autumn leaves, was neatly coiled at the back of her long, graceful neck.

" I'm so glad you're early," she said. " We've got a visitor coming to dinner ! "

" Oh, who ? " asked Francis, surprised. For the past two years he had accepted, as a regrettable but apparently unavoidable fact, Sally's increasing nervous dislike of receiving guests and her growing reluctance even to sing in public. This, he felt, was one reason why life of late had seemed to be narrowing, to be shutting him in like the terrifying Edgar Allen Poe story of the prison whose walls closed upon their captive and finally crushed him to death. That she had asked someone to dinner was a welcome break in this gathering concentration of life upon themselves in which he was compelled reluctantly to share — but he did wish that it had not happened tonight. He felt so tired . . . the need for controlling the fathomless dejection which oppressed him had exhausted him even more than he realised. And the A.R.P. plans were waiting for inspection.

He was relieved when Sally replied : " It's Ruth Alleyndene. She rang up to say she was in Witnall and would like to see us, so I could hardly do less than ask her, could I ? "

For several years now, Francis had been friendly with the nationally famous Witnall M.P., who had won the formerly Conservative borough for Labour by thirty-seven votes in 1929, lost it in 1931, and won it back by another narrow majority in 1935. Her opponent in the three elections, Sir Harrison Talliner, had recently died, and her reputation — gained by hard work, a trained intelligence, a humane heart, and an outstanding gift of eloquence — had now reached a point at which her former opponents as well as her supporters were talking about the possibility of an unopposed return at the next General Election.

" I'm glad she's coming," said Francis. " It's about six months since she last visited the factory. What time did you ask her for ? "

" Eight o'clock. She told us not to expect her much earlier. She's got a Women's Cooperative Guild meeting in the Town Hall at six."

" Good. That'll give me time to glance through these shelter plans ; they've come at last. It looks like being a necessary job, I'm afraid, if not exactly an enthralling one."

Sally shivered suddenly.

" Oh, Francis, do you really mean that ? Do you think we're bound to have war ? "

" No, no, my darling, I wasn't saying anything of the kind. I only meant that the more we prepare for war the less likely we are to have it, because that's just the cussed way things go. . . . Look here, Sal, are you doing anything before dinner ? "

" Nothing special. The Kiddemores can manage one guest all right. Why ? "

" Only that if you'll sing while I'm working, it'll help me to tackle this job. I don't exactly take to A.R.P. like a duck to water."

Her thin face brightened.

" Of course I will ! What would you like ? Do you know, darling, I was looking yesterday through a pile of your mother's old music, and I found that German song you and she were so fond of during the War. I mean the one by George Henschel, the *Morning Hymn*. Would you like me to sing it ? "

Francis half turned from her and looked through the window of the lounge hall at the sunset embers glowing sullenly through the driven clouds.

"No. Don't sing that, Sally," he said. "I never want to hear that thing again. Mother liked it, it's true, and it's a fine enough song of its conventional type, but it would only remind me of things I want to forget — her funeral, and those months at the front, and especially . . . No, sing me some of the old-fashioned things with tunes — "*Where'er you walk*", or one of the solos from *The Beggar's Opera*. I don't want to be intelligent when I'm tired."

"All right," she answered, "I know. There's a fire in your study, and I'll find something to help you through those wretched plans."

Francis sat down in an easy-chair by the hearth in the little first-floor room, where the books and magazines clearly testified to the divided interests of his complicated life. Current issues of technical journals lay side by side on tables and window-ledges with volumes of country dance-tunes and Welsh folk-songs. On the bookshelves which covered the wall opposite the windows, the *Lives* of great composers, and such well-known classics as Berlioz's *Instrumentation* and R. O. Morris's *Contrapuntal Technique in the 16th Century*, stood incongruously above heavy manuals on the art of paper-making. One deep shelf was reserved for the leather-bound original compositions of "Francis Keynsham". There did not seem to be much room for the further preoccupations, responsible and disturbing, of an A.R.P. Warden.

He was putting on the carpet slippers which Mrs. Kiddemore, the cook-housekeeper, had laid out for him, when he heard the notes of his wife's light but lovely mezzo-soprano voice ascending from the drawing-room below. And she was singing neither Strauss nor Gay, but the tuneful, familiar song she had sung on the night that he had asked her to marry him — "Drink to me only with thine eyes". He laid down the plans on the table beside him and, forgetting all about sandbags and blast walls and concrete flooring, gazed dreamily at the fire as her voice carried him back into the past.

Francis had been demobilised from the Army and a student at the Royal College of Music for more than a year, when he and Sally became engaged. Before he went back from France he had known that he loved her, and had believed that she loved him, but with respite from the prospect of imminent death there came a return to normal peace-time standards of prudence and hesitation. Strange as it might appear, Sally Eldridge had seemed more easily attainable to a Second Lieutenant whose life might be terminated by a machine-gun bullet at any moment, than to a future pianist and composer with years of valuable work before him.

He was not entirely dependent upon his unmusical father, for his mother had left him a small income which would be sufficient, with care, for a young couple to live on. But how could a twenty-year-old music student, with a long climb in front of him before he could hope to support a wife in relative comfort, present himself to the aristocratic Colonel Eldridge as his daughter's suitor? So he and Sally wrote to each other in term-time, played games together and went for walks on the moors between Cheete and Sterndale in vacation — until the night of the concert at Cheete Memorial Hall in aid of the North Staffordshire Fund for Rebuilding Devastated France.

Francis had, of course, been invited to add lustre to the programme of local talent, and had contributed not only the *Moonlight Sonata* and three Chopin *Preludes*, but a pianoforte setting by himself of Elgar's *Lament for the Fallen*. Sally too had thought it appropriate, that evening, to sing some of those familiar war-time songs which had acquired a poignant significance for her when first Guy, and then Francis, went to the front — " Keep the home fires burning ", " Sweet Early Violets ", and " There's a long, long trail ". Francis, filled with the peculiar nostalgia aroused by these melodies in the ex-soldiers of the nineteen-twenties, wondered as he sat in the audience after his own much-applauded performance how many years he must wait for the long, long trail to go on awinding into the land of his dreams. But when Sally responded to the *encore* which followed this last of her war-songs, he knew that he did not intend to wait any longer.

> " *Drink to me only with thine eyes,*
> *And I will pledge with mine ;*
> *Or leave a kiss but in the cup,*
> *And I'll not look for wine* " —

she sang ; and it seemed as though the words were a direct challenge to himself. It was intolerable to go on behaving towards her with brotherly restraint, when all he wanted to know was whether she cared as he did, impatiently counting the hours whenever he left her until he could arrange to see her again. As she came out of the artistes' dressing room with a pale blue cloak over her white satin dress, his sudden inability to wait another second had almost choked him.

" Sally," he gasped incoherently, " how are you going home ? "

" Why, in the car, of course," she replied, for Rudyard Manor was a good three miles along the main road from Cheete to Sterndale Spa. " Father's just gone to get it from the parking place."

" It'll take him some time, with the crowd that's here. Could you — couldn't you come into the square for a minute or two, till he's ready ? It's such a lovely night."

" Why, yes, if you like, Francis," she answered, telling herself firmly that his agitation might not be due to her songs at all ; that it might have a meaning quite different from the one that she hoped for. So they crossed the road between the thronging cars to the park-like tree-shaded square opposite the Memorial Hall. It was commonplace enough by day, with its green-painted urban seats, its gravelled paths and asphalted playground adorned with swings and see-saws for the juveniles of Cheete, but now the warm perfume of night-scented stock and the light of the August moon glancing vividly through the dark heavy trees gave it an unwonted atmosphere of mystery and romance.

Francis almost dragged her along the empty paths to the corner farthest from the concert hall, and then, caressing her hand, lifted it passionately to his lips.

" Sally, darling ! " he burst out impetuously, " you were too much for me with your lovely singing ! I've tried to be sensible, to wait till I had something to offer you, a place in the world worth having — but it's no good. I can't wait any more. I must know. I love you ! I adore you ! I've never so much as looked at another girl since I saw you on the station the day I went to the front. . . . Will you marry me, Sally ? "

" Oh, Francis ! " she whispered, half dazed by his vehemence and the exquisite pain of his unconscious pressure on the fingers he still held, " I've never looked at anyone but you since that day either ! I seem to have been waiting for tonight as long as I can remember. If you'd asked me a year ago, I'd have said yes ! "

" Darling ! " he cried, almost unmanned by the un-affected sweetness of her capitulation. " Oh, darling — let's make up for it now ! "

And in that first spontaneous embrace, oblivious to everyone and everything but themselves, they had indeed made up for it, lost in the perfect simplicity of reciprocal emotion which they would reach again but never surpass. And when, coming back to earth, they went penitently to seek the waiting Colonel and his car, the opposition that they had feared did not arise. Instead, Francis was invited to come for the night to Rudyard Manor and discuss his proposal.

Francis, like Sally, was very young, it was true, but the Colonel had an esteem for Reginald Halkin and had taken a liking to Francis himself. He was glad, too, to see his daughter so happy after the many months of war in which she had been pale and subdued, fretting inconsolably over her twin brother's death. As soon as they arrived at the Manor he went upstairs to talk over the situation with his wife, who had gone to bed with a sick headache which she immediately forgot, while Francis sat in the drawing-room with Sally in his arms and her soft copper-coloured hair against his cheek.

The Halkins were not " county ", of course, admitted the Eldridges, but they were a highly respected family long established in the district, and there was no doubt that their business was flourishing. Old Jeremiah, and his son Reginald after him, had been sound conservative financiers who took no risks ; on the other hand, they had proved themselves to be open to new ideas when finally convinced of their value.

And it wasn't, put in Mrs. Eldridge, as if Halkins' made manure — or even margarine. Paper was not only a reputable but an aesthetic commodity, especially when it was used for putting those pretty patterns on cups and plates. . . . Moreover, the landed estates of the Silverdales were now a liability rather than an asset. There wouldn't be much to leave Sally when the Colonel's time came. On the whole, a marriage into a well-to-do commercial family looked like a solid proposition. True, young Francis had repudiated all intention of becoming commercial, and the musical career which he proposed to follow was quite unlikely to be remunerative. But potentially, music offered even more prestige than the manufacture of paper, and as an only child, Francis would in any case inherit his father's substantial estate.

By midnight the Colonel had consented to their engagement, stipulating only that Francis must finish his period as a student at the Royal College before he and Sally were married, and that he should fulfil his father's wishes and enter the family business if he found no opening in his own profession within, say, twelve months afterwards.

To Francis this proposition appeared to present no difficulty. Enchanted as he was by Sally, he would probably have agreed to any arrangement; but the possibility that he could fail in his chosen career seemed so unlikely as to be quite negligible. The reports of his teachers had been so uniformly favourable; his powers were so exceptional, his energy and determination so great. Colonel Eldridge could hardly, indeed, have imposed a condition which Francis felt more certain that he could fulfil. . . .

The plans for the A.R.P. shelters at Halkins' slid from the table to the floor, but Francis did not notice them. He was back again in those four years of waiting — years of hard work and assured happiness, despite the perpetual argument between the father who still believed that his only child ought to join him and eventually take his place at the factory, and the son with his unshaken determination to combine the profession of a pianist with that of a composer.

" Like Rachmaninoff," he explained earnestly to his unconvinced parent. But Reginald — to whom Rachmaninoff was simply a foreigner with an outlandish name — thought it much more suitable for his son to follow in the well-trodden footsteps of the reliable Halkins, than to emulate the feverish career of some temperamental Russian or Pole.

Thanks to his mother's legacy, Francis was able to live in London without drawing upon his reluctant father's banking account, and to study at the Royal College under

Sir Hugh Allen, Gustav Holst, and other famous musicians of the nineteen-twenties. In March, 1920, he had gone to the first public performance, at a Philharmonic Concert in the Queen's Hall, of Holst's *Hymn to Jesus*, and thereafter became a yet greater admirer of his music — clear-cut, downright, pungent, unsentimental ; sometimes remote and austere with a colourless radiance which seemed to combine the quintessence of both heat and cold.

At a performance by the Bach Choir shortly afterwards, Francis heard the great *Requiem* of Verdi, whom he had hitherto regarded as a pure sentimentalist. Carried away by the disturbing staccato wrath of the *Dies Irae*, he spent the rest of the night half-consciously wandering between the West End and his lodgings in the King's Road, Chelsea, until sunrise found him on the Embankment, and he watched the dawn break over the river below Chelsea Bridge. That night was surpassed in its strange excitement only by the totally different but even more exhilarating experience of hearing a concert performance, conducted by Eugene Goossens in 1921, of Stravinsky's *Le Sacre du Printemps*, with its wild theme of nature worship among primitive peoples expressing itself in the adoration of spring as symbolising the renewal of fertility. Haunted all night by the fierce revolutionary music, he plunged early next morning into Battersea Park, and pacing beside the empty ornamental lake where a few exotic birds were fluttering, felt himself longing for Sally and marriage with an all but unbearable tension of the flesh, and wondering whether he would have a son or a daughter to carry on his work and his name.

With one or two of his fellow-students, Francis also found time for occupations other than music. In the limited hours during which he was not studying or practising, he read Dante, Ibsen, Dostoievsky and Tolstoy, and attended lectures by distinguished members of the Fabian Society. After listening to Bernard Shaw, H. G.

Wells, G. D. H. Cole, and Mrs. Sidney Webb, he decided that he was a Socialist with a mission — in any spare hours left over from his profession — to convert Fordham in general, and Halkins' in particular, from the feudal conservatism of his forebears to Fabian ideals.

It was through these lectures and the discussions which followed them that he became half conscious of disquieting events — the Allied occupation of Germany, the conflict over Reparations, the French march into the Ruhr — happening in that international world which had once rudely interrupted the classic progress of a life so carefully shaped by his mother and himself. Reluctant as he was to leave Sally when he might be with her, he went to Central Europe during the summer preceding his marriage, and tried to make some first-hand estimate of political events in the intervals of listening to Haydn conducted by Bruno Walter in the Vienna Opera House, and the enthusiastic performance of *The Bartered Bride* and other Czech compositions in Prague. Later, in Leipzig, he heard Bach's music played in the churches of St. Nicholas and St. Thomas where Bach himself had been organist and musical director two centuries earlier, and in the Royal Opera House at Dresden sat excitedly through *Der Ring des Nibelungen* which Wagner began to compose there. Returning towards the Rhine, he spent three nights at the *Ritterhaus* in the two-mile-long main street of Heidelberg. And it was there, on the second evening, that he met David Flint.

Young Dr. Flint, three years Francis's senior, was the recently-qualified son of a pioneer psychologist who had spent much of his time upon research in psychotherapy while working as a general practitioner in Edgbaston, Birmingham. Six months earlier the elder Dr. Flint had died ; and with the sum contributed in honour of his memory by some of his wealthier patients, David proposed to start a clinic for psychological ailments in the heart of the city.   He intended, he said, to specialise in industrial psychology, and in the mental and nervous troubles of factory workers.

The two young men sat up talking until far into the night, discussing the pioneer position that Halkins' might occupy in post-war industry, and the important part that music — which had, David explained, its own peculiar therapeutical effects — could play in the prevention of psychological breakdown.   When David left Heidelberg, Francis, who had intended to go straight back to England, instead spent a fortnight with him investigating Cologne. In return for the hours in which David accompanied him to the ancient Dance Hall of the Gürzenich, the Wallraf-Richarts Museum, and the choral celebrations in the twin-spired Gothic Cathedral, Francis went with David to the slums and hospitals where the child victims of blockade and famine were still suffering from rickets and dying of tuberculosis.

Coming back convinced by David's passionate belief that psychological understanding between nations was rooted in the adequate nourishment of minds and bodies, Francis wondered for an uneasy week what type of adult would develop from the starved and stricken youth of this sullen Germany.   But his apprehensions had then been banished — all too irresponsibly, he often thought in the decade ahead — by the fascination of his chosen work in a rapidly recovering England which, as soon as she had forgotten the War, overlooked the fact that other countries remembered it.

Francis and Sally had been married at the village church of St. Andrew's, Fordham, on an early afternoon of September in 1924.   Even before he had taken his final examinations at the Royal College, Francis knew that he had been chosen for the coveted opportunity offered annually by a wealthy musical patron, Lady Floria

Ledburne, who every year selected a College student for special promotion through her money and influence. Already she had sent him proofs of the poster advertising the Welbeck Hall concert, financed by herself, which in mid-November was to launch him upon his career as a pianist.

His wedding, and the honeymoon at Cheddar in Somerset which followed it, still stood out in Francis's memory like a golden climax after month upon month of musical triumph and official congratulation. Even his discovery that the establishment of satisfying intercourse in marriage was less a matter of emotional zeal than of technical skill, had not been able to spoil that honeymoon. Sally had been so patient, so full of tender understanding, that he still recalled with gratitude her gentle determination to spare him embarrassment. He would never forget the perfect night when the consummation of their union was finally achieved, the soft warmth of her naked body against his, and beyond the open windows of their bedroom the harvest moon, shining from the indigo sky above the tall rock-chimney of the Cheddar Gorge.

That fortnight had been almost too promising a preliminary to the months ahead. He had finished his period as a student — delayed for so short a time in comparison with that which men two or three years his senior had suffered, though it had seemed so long — and the Welbeck Hall concert would be but the beginning of a career which he knew that he could make outstanding in his day and generation. He was only a month past his twenty-fifth birthday, and the alluring future — freed now from war, and filled with endless possibilities of love, and music, and creative achievement so valuable that it would finally free him from occasional uneasy twinges of conscience about Halkins' and his father — stretched indefinitely before him, a magic pathway.

One day as they sat above the waterfall in the warm strip of garden at the back of the Rock Hotel, Francis had turned aside from their serial conversations on music and modern composers, to tell Sally about David Flint and his idea of the part which psychology could play in the development of industrial welfare. Although September was more than half over, Red Admiral and Tortoiseshell butterflies still flitted with summer animation about the clumps of golden-rod and Michaelmas daisies, and dragon-flies darted from the mountain stream across a dew-soaked stretch of emerald lawn.

A hundred yards up the road began the Gorge, that gigantic gash in the Mendip Hills where the chattering jackdaws wheeled in circles about the summits of the rocks until Francis and Sally felt dizzy. To the surprise of Francis, who liked dramatic scenery, Sally was frightened by the Gorge and refused to go through it a second time. She was afraid of stones falling on her head, and pointing to the fragments of rock by the road-side, declared that the huge cliffs seemed to sway and threaten to close in upon her. She would soon have reached the verge of panic had not Francis gaily seized her arm and hurried her up an artificial stairway to the top of the cliff, where she could see the normal mild Somerset country undulating gently towards the south, and the clouds tranquilly reflected in the silver mirror of Axbridge Reservoir.

They looked down at the verdant plain, divided by small cultivated fields like strips of carpet in numerous shades of green and brown laid carefully side by side, and by orchards where luscious apples now hung ripe for picking. Like toys scattered haphazard by a giant hand, little grey and white houses with red gabled roofs half hid themselves beneath clumps of comfortable trees. To the right of this agricultural chequer-work stretched the reservoir ; to the left the tall grey tower of the Church, its one soaring pinnacle crowned by a weather-vane, dominated the cluster of buildings round the village post-office and the old stone cross.

Francis gazed affectionately at the lovely undisturbing scene.

" Doesn't it make you realise," he said, " what Blake meant by ' England's green and pleasant land ' ? I never feel that line's true of Staffordshire — or even of Derbyshire, with so much rough moorland and so many stone walls."

" You've never quite belonged to Staffordshire, have you ? " observed Sally.

" I don't think I really have," agreed Francis. " You know, darling, whenever I was feeling heroic in the War, and telling myself I was going to die for England, it was always this bit of England that I pictured myself dying for."

He laughed, but there was deep emotion in his face and voice.

It's because all this part of the country is connected with his mother, Sally thought. I do wish I had known her better. And I wish Francis had told me more of what really happened to him at the front, and especially about that time after the battle when he " went queer " for several days.

" Never mind, my love," she assured him aloud. " That's all over now. You don't have to think about dying any more. We're not likely to have a war again in our lifetime."

" No," he said, " thank God ! "

One mild evening they sat on the cliff-top and watched a sunset of such surpassing beauty that Francis remembered it all his life. It was to be for ever associated in his mind with a conversation in which, years afterwards when he was responsible for Halkins', he realised that Francis the musician had first put into coherent words the social ideals which Francis the employer was to follow. From the deep violet haze where the orange lantern of the sun had disappeared above Axbridge Reservoir spread a huge herring-bone formation of pink-tinged cloud, till it extended right across the immeasurable vault and seemed, like a roof, to be just above their heads. Gradually, as the sun sank farther behind the bank of mist, the purple canopy brightened to pure translucent flame, and the bone-shaped clouds, separated by the deep azure of the sky, softened into flamingo-hued feathers till the whole heavens seemed on fire.

Half fascinated and half terrified by the contrast of height and depth intensified by the dramatic loveliness of the sunset, Sally looked down over the cliff edge to the twilight already shrouding the narrow road and the doll's-house roofs of the little cluster of houses in the valley below.

" I do wonder," she mused, " what caused this enormous ravine ? It looks quite unnatural when you compare it with the rest of the country."

" Isn't it queer," speculated Francis, " to think of the huge convulsions and cataclysms which were happening on this earth before any men were there to see ? Imagine these Mendip Hills all solitary, covered with thick forest, and no human being to hear the sound of the tremendous force which tore open this deep gorge ! "

" Perhaps it frightened the jackdaws, and they've been protesting ever since," she suggested, watching the restless circular movements of the jabbering birds which seemed to go on perpetually flying without alighting anywhere.

" There wouldn't have been any jackdaws either. . . . In a way, it seems symbolic of our own times. I mean, the War tore just the same kind of terrific rent in our social and economic fabric — and yet hardly anyone, no more than a handful of people, saw and heard that rent or understood what it signified. But some day, a race of men who'll think of us as half-blind intellectual pigmies will understand and sum it all up. To their mental eyes, the historic catastrophes of our age will seem as clear as this great cleft in the hills looks to the physical eyes of you and me ! "

He flung himself down on the turf at her feet and, folding his hands behind his head, gazed up at the fiery sea of the sky.

" You know, Sal," he said, " although I've no right to interfere at Halkins' when I'm not going to work there, I do wish I could make Dad a bit more modern in his outlook. Flint says we ought to start a welfare department, and have somebody advising us who isn't content just to nip disease in the bud, but intends to go out for preventing it altogether."

" You mean, realising a patient is susceptible to something and treating him for it before it begins ? "

" Yes, he says that's the most valuable side of medicine. According to him, its object shouldn't be mainly to cure disease, but to get the utmost possible, both mentally and physically, out of every human being. He told me that long before psychology was accepted as a science, his father had come to the conclusion that the roots of illness don't lie in the body at all. He described them as the fruit of maladjustments in the relationship between the individual and the community."

" I don't quite understand," she said.

" Well, to put it more simply, he says you have to look for the origins of disease in the mind, not the body. People like Dad's employees are much more often ill because they're miserable, than miserable because they're ill. They're pent up, thwarted — what psychologists call frustrated. And this leads to diseases of all kinds, social as well as physical. My father, like my grandfather, has always taken for granted that things like poverty, and malnutrition, and unemployment, and war, are just ' acts of God '; but Flint says they're diseases, and curable. He puts them down to a wrong relationship between the individual person, and society as a whole. Medicine, to him, means the science of the entire man and the total community — not just a part of either."

" It seems a tremendous idea for a young man like Dr. Flint to tackle," commented Sally, smiling tenderly at the unlimited range of Francis's enthusiasms.

" But it isn't, darling. Nothing's too big to tackle ! You can't do it all at once, of course. You have to start by learning more about the human mind itself. At present we hardly appear to know the first thing about it, and even that knowledge has to be fought for. When Flint's father started his research work at Edgbaston, he suffered the fate of every pioneer and got derided as a crank — like Adler and Freud."

Sally knelt down beside him, ruffling his dark hair.

" I wonder what Father would say if he could hear you talk like that ? He hasn't even suspected you're a Socialist yet — and as for Freud, he just regards him as a dangerous foreign lunatic ! I'm afraid my parents still think the world was made for families like the Eldridges and the Silverdales."

Francis put his arms round her neck, and drew her lips down to his.

" There are plenty of people in the world like your parents, my sweetheart. I've still got to convince Dad that Stravinsky isn't a dangerous foreign lunatic too — and as for me, he thinks I'm just such another ! But you mustn't mind. It'll be worth while in the end. You'll see ! " . . .

A lump of coal crashed into the hearth, startling Francis for a moment from his reverie. On the mantelpiece, the chromium electric clock struck seven.

CHAPTER VII

EPISODE IN THE WEST END

When the honeymoon was over, Francis and Sally had moved into their studio flat in Church Street, Chelsea. They took with them the possessions collected during their youth, Francis's music library and manuscripts, the necessary minimum of new furniture, and a large stock of useful wedding presents contributed by Eldridge relatives and Halkins' old customers.

Francis, to whom Chelsea with its tree-studded Embankment and tall eighteenth-century houses was already familiar, settled down immediately to six weeks of strenuous work before the November concert. Although he had officially left the Royal College equipped as pianist and conductor with a recognised talent for orchestral writing, he still visited South Kensington several times a week for more advanced studies. He was also composing a new selection of dance music for the Russian Ballet, and had optimistic expectations of being invited to conduct the first performance at the Ballet's next visit. But by far the greatest part of his time and energy was occupied in practising the piano for his *début*.

He spent many hours of each day alone in his studio, mastering the pyrotechnics and massive harmonies of Tchaikowsky's *Pianoforte Concerto in B flat minor*. Thanks to Lady Floria, he was to be accompanied by the Welbeck Symphony Orchestra, conducted by Sir Marcus Mitcham — for whom he occasionally played pianoforte at Covent Garden Opera rehearsals. But for his now rare prickings of conscience regarding his father and Halkins', where so many changes of organisation were overdue, Francis would have found his daily routine a near approach to heaven. As it was, he had constantly to remind himself that he now ranked as an executive solo artist who had been offered an exceptional opportunity to display his powers, in order to prevent himself from running like a schoolboy through Chelsea and Kensington to the familiar building in Prince Consort Road.

In their ground-floor apartment with its three small rooms and commodious studio, Sally was equally happy. The front door, flanked on either side by flat period windows, opened straight on to the pavement, but at the back of the studio was a lilliputian garden now filled with asters and bronze chrysanthemums. The size and fascination of London seemed illimitable to Sally's twenty-four years, in which she had never left Staffordshire except for occasional visits to Manchester and her brief period of education at a private school in Sterndale Spa. Mistress of her own life at last, Sally rearranged their furniture several times a day. Whenever Francis was absent at the College, she herself dusted the studio, and tidied his music on the baby grand piano given to them as a wedding present by her parents.

Domestically, Francis was not a critical husband. Brought up by a mother whose own interests had lain outside the normal household routine, he was quite content with the simple meals that Sally planned for him and usually left to be cooked by the more expert skill of Mrs. Turner, the daily woman from Battersea who " ran in ". Sally had plenty of time to practice her singing when Francis was out, to study the classical songs which had not appealed to the untutored taste of Cheete concert audiences, and to accompany Francis in his half-hours of leisure for walks along the Embankment or round Battersea Park. On mild October evenings they would cross the Albert Bridge hand in hand, and from the other side of the river watch the sun set in autumnal splendour behind the dark-red silhouette of Chelsea Old Church.

There seemed to be no reason why this satisfying life

of hard work and tender companionship should not continue uninterrupted until Francis had established his reputation as both pianist and composer. Instead it ended, with the abruptness of a thunder-clap, in a fashion that neither of them, in their now rare nightmares, had remotely foreseen.

Three days before the November concert Sally was summoned by telegram to Rudyard Manor, whence her mother had been taken to Cheete Cottage Hospital for an urgent appendix operation. In spite of the now closely impending test of his powers, Francis accompanied her to Staffordshire for the night. When the operation was over he left her and Colonel Eldridge at the hospital and spent the evening with his father, whose resignation to Francis's choice of a career was still far from complete.

"I'm not exactly old bones yet, but I don't get any younger," Reginald Halkin had remarked as he and his son sat smoking on either side of the dining-room hearth where the elder Halkin passed so many solitary hours. "The place wants new blood," he added, "and some new notions. You realised it right enough yourself, after talking to that young Flint. If only your brother had lived . . ."

In the silence that fell between them, the unfinished sentence completed itself. The double domestic tragedy which had deprived Reginald of a companion at home, and Francis of a substitute for himself at the factory, seemed to darken the air of the house in which the "old man" now lived with an elderly cook and her daughter as his only companions. Finally, moved to compunction by Francis's expression of conscience-stricken dejection, Reginald concluded : "It's not that I doubt your ability, son, even if piano-playing doesn't look like a real job to me. I know you did well at your London college, and this concert you're playing at seems a rare chance to show what you're made of. Don't think your old father doesn't want you to succeed. If the affair turns out well and you make a splash, I'll never say a word about the mills again."

Francis went back to London next day with the sense that his father had given him a challenge. Afterwards he could never decide whether it was this, or Sally's continued absence owing to her mother's post-operation exhaustion, which led to the sudden and violent increase in his feeling of tension as the critical evening of " Francis Keynsham "'s *début* drew near. The performance for which, in the few remaining hours, he practised so feverishly, seemed to have become a final test of his power to justify his decision to Reginald. As a taxi took him to the Welbeck Hall with the fiery chords of the Tchaikowsky *Concerto* ringing through his head, he wondered when he had felt this half-excited, half-terrified apprehension before — and suddenly recalled the night before he went into action between the Ancre and the Scarpe. . . .

At the Welbeck Hall he passed through a momentary outburst of light and noise into the artists' waiting-room. Sir Marcus Mitcham, with his waxed moustache and bushy eyebrows, was already there talking to Lady Floria Ledburne. As usual, Francis found her both fascinating and alarming. Her sheath-like sapphire-hued dress, sparkling with sequins beneath her mink coat, seemed to add a blue sheen to her smooth raven hair. From her white, heavily powdered face her dark eyes, keen and inscrutable, looked appraisingly at Francis. As he tried to return her glance with gaiety and confidence, the distant sound of the orchestra tuning up began, inexplicably, to take on the rhythm of a long-neglected but once familiar theme which he struggled to recognise.

When he went on the platform to the sound of polite, expectant applause from the considerable audience which had gathered to hear Lady Floria's protégé, the theme had transferred itself from the now silent orchestra to his own brain. It swelled and roared in his ears like a torrent, extinguishing the rhapsodic flights of Tchaikowsky. Quite unexpectedly, the brilliant lights and waiting up-turned faces seemed to strike him like a blow, and the heavy indoor air gave him a strange feeling of oppression. The place suddenly appeared to him as an illuminated cave . . . a trap — yes, that was it . . . a glittering trap, drenched with that powerful, searching light. As he sat down at the piano, he became aware of a peculiar sensation. It was akin to faintness, yet it was less that than a failure of concentration, a sudden inability to grasp what he was doing, a feeling that the ground beneath his feet had turned to shifting sand and that everything around him was losing reality.

"Tchaikowsky. Concerto in B flat minor," he repeated to himself, struggling to recover the ringing tone of the challenging chords. But the words and the sounds had no meaning because they were replaced by others, beating through his brain to the insistent lilt of a remembered tune.

" ' *Bald ist der Nacht* ' . . . Concerto in B flat minor . . . ' soon night will pass ' . . . there are the horns . . . brass . . . ' *ein End* ' *gemacht* . . . dark massive chords . . . Concerto . . . B flat . . ."

His head began to swim and his hands to tremble. He struck a few chords at random, only to realise that they had no coherence . . . and then everything about him went blank. . . .

In his Dene Terrace study, Francis sat up suddenly. The memory of failing sensation had been so vivid that he grasped the arms of his chair tightly to assure himself of consciousness. For after that strange repetition of a war-time experience which he had done his best to forget, complete awareness had returned to him only when he found himself lying on a sofa in a warm, faintly-perfumed, unfamiliar room. Somewhere, floating on a disconnected island of recollection, the words "sudden collapse", impressed upon his memory by some unidentified person, explained his astonishing presence in a green and gold boudoir.

"It's all right," a voice beside him said drily. "You're not in Heaven — nor even in Hell. This is only my suite at Claridge's."

Still half-dazed, he looked up to find himself alone with Lady Floria Ledburne. She had discarded the sequin-trimmed evening dress for a violet velvet house-frock, and a brandy bottle with soda water and two glasses stood beside her on a silver tray. As she poured out a drink and handed it to him, her own emotions struggled between the romantic attraction which the young man with the sensitive face and springing hair had originally inspired in her, and her exasperation with the dejected musician who had disappointed her confidence and wasted her money. The first sensation won, and she said more kindly : "You needn't worry about this getting into the Press. I've seen to that."

Francis gazed at her gratefully but despairingly. Inexperienced as he was, he took her ability to control the Press as much for granted as her power to finance concerts and launch unknown musicians. What could not be taken for granted was the full significance, as it gradually dawned on him, of his unforeseen failure ; the fact that something devastating and decisive had occurred, in the light of which he could not continue his promising career without taking some action. Some action, yes . . . but what kind ? What exactly did the situation require ? The answer to these questions depended, surely, upon what he had done . . . and that was a vague nightmare about which he could remember no details, and felt a violent reluctance to inquire. From that day, indeed, to this, he had never learned precisely what happened in the

Welbeck Hall on a November evening of 1924.

Lady Floria was not the woman to enlighten him, even if she had judged the moment appropriate. With an imperious wave of her hand, she cut short his struggling, bewildered apologies.

" Sir Marcus urged me to send you to hospital, but I said I'd risk bringing you here. However, I'm taking his advice in one respect. He thinks you ought to see a nerve specialist without delay, so I rang up one who's a friend of mine — Dr. George Gifford — and made an appoint- ment for you tomorrow morning at 10.30. His consulting rooms are in Wimpole Street ; you'll find the number in the telephone book. You don't have to keep the appoint- ment unless you wish, of course. But I think you'd be well advised to do so."

After Francis returned to his empty flat, he had passed a sleepless night of mental conflict in which he faced the fact of his public unreliability with an anguish which almost made him groan, even now, to remember. At 10.30 next morning, after a long struggle to overcome his fathomless, apprehensive distaste for the visit, he presented himself at Dr. Gifford's consulting rooms in Wimpole Street.

Dr. Gifford was obviously expecting him ; Francis even believed that he detected an expression of concern on the specialist's grave, kindly face. Across the years, scraps of their conversation — for him so momentous — floated back into his mind.

" I believe Lady Floria Ledburne has told you of my . . . collapse at the Welbeck Hall last night ? " he had begun abruptly.

" Yes, Mr. Keynsham. I had a conversation with her on the telephone before you recovered consciousness. Has anything of the sort ever happened to you before ? "

Francis seemed to be dragging out his very vitals and

exposing their innermost secrets to the cruel daylight as he answered painfully : " I'm afraid it's no use pretending it hasn't. In the War I had one or two . . . strange lapses of consciousness. . . ."

Dr. Gifford looked up with a newly awakened understanding.

" I see. Was this following shell-shock, by any chance ? "

Reluctantly Francis replied : " Yes. . . . I was buried by a bomb from a trench mortar and made unconscious. I thought I'd completely grown out of it, but last night in the concert hall it seemed to come back. . . . It was due to the feeling of tension, I think — the sense of having to bring something off in front of a large number of people. At least, that's the only connection I can think of between this experience and . . . the other."

" You had what appeared to be a sudden fainting attack, Lady Floria said." He inquired more gravely : " Are these conspicuous public appearances really essential to you ? I mean, is there any part of your career which does not involve them ? "

" Well," said Francis, his voice inarticulate with distress, " I've been studying to be a pianist. One can't exactly go in for that without public appearances. Do you mean I . . . ought to avoid them ? "

" I'm afraid the facts do seem to suggest that conclusion." Perceiving the despair on Francis's face, Dr. Gifford added immediately : " You mustn't look on this as a major tragedy, Mr. Keynsham. Lady Floria said you had a brilliant record at the Royal College. Surely there are other departments of music in which your gifts could find expression, apart from the concert platform ? The organ, for instance — or composition. Are you obliged to work for your living ? "

" Not exactly *obliged*. I'm not a wealthy man, but I've got a small private income." He continued with a sense that the words were being dragged out of him by force. " My father's pretty well off, though. He's a Staffordshire business man — a paper manufacturer. I . . . I could always join the firm if I wanted to."

" Well," said Dr. Gifford slowly, " I should consider that last possibility very carefully before you reject it. Business isn't exactly congenial to you, no doubt, but it need not cut out your music altogether. And it would have the advantage of enabling you to go in for, say, orchestral composition without any financial anxiety or public strain."

Throwing back his head with an expression of renewed determination in the eyes which had been so full of misery, Francis held out his hand.

" Thank you for the advice, doctor. I shall probably act on it. But I've still got to adjust myself to the situation."

" Of course you have. It's particularly hard when your preliminary studies have been so promising. . . . But I was in the War myself, at Ypres, and I've seen what it did to men much tougher than you. Some day, perhaps, the human race will stop submitting itself to that kind of barbarism — but not in my time, I'm afraid, nor even in yours."

Grim and humiliating though he knew that the immediate future must be — he had to confess failure to his father, to say nothing of Sally's parents — Francis realised that he owed Dr. Gifford a debt of gratitude for showing him, without circumlocution, the road which he ought to take. Even in those moments of desolation, he reflected that this unlucky mischance might ultimately prove to be a blessing in disguise if it compelled him to exchange the rôle of executive artist for the more creative work of a composer.

Slowly and painfully, at his desk in the studio, Francis

composed a short letter to Reginald. It was no use
pretending, he wrote with a deliberate mixture of candour
and vagueness, that his Welbeck Hall concert had been a
success. His inability to carry through the programme
with the skill and vigour that he had hoped for, had made
it clear to him that the part of a *virtuoso* pianist was one for
which he was unsuited. He would not, he felt, be justified
in making another such experiment, for this would simply
be courting failure. He now intended to concentrate his
special abilities on the writing of music, particularly for
orchestra. And, since this work was not incompatible
with business in the same way as the career of a pianist,
he had decided to fulfil his father's wishes and join him at
Halkins'.

Feeling as though he were underlining the sentence
which Dr. Gifford, for all his tactful consideration, had
passed upon him, Francis addressed the envelope and
sealed it. Then, facing the most painful of all the consequences of his collapse, he wrote a letter to Sally at
Rudyard Manor.

" MY OWN DARLING,

" I am afraid that what I have to tell you is more
painful than words can describe, but it just has to be
faced. My performance last night was worse than a
failure ; it was a complete disaster. Before I even
started to play the Concerto I had a kind of fainting
fit, and knew nothing more until I found myself in Lady
Floria's rooms at Claridge's. Considering the way I had
let her down she was more than kind to me ; she kept
me there till I felt quite myself again, and then sent me
home in a taxi.

" By her advice I went to see a West End nerve
specialist, Dr. George Gifford, in Wimpole Street this
morning. After asking me various questions about the
War, etc., he told me that I ought to avoid any work

which involved the strain of public appearances. He advised me to stick to composing, and suggested that I could combine this with business. So, after thinking it over for a long time, I have just written to Dad to say that I will do as he wishes, and join him at the factory.

" I am afraid, my darling, it will be a great disappointment to you that I have to give up the career from which we both hoped so much. But these consequences of the War only affect one aspect of my music. Now that I understand my own limitations better, they are never likely to trouble either of us again.

" I don't know how to ask your forgiveness after the way you have helped me and all the work you have put into our charming little home, which reminds me of you every moment of the day. Never mind, we will make another one just as good.

" I do hope Maman is better, and that you won't have any more anxiety about her to add to this new distress which I have so unintentionally brought upon you.

" Ever with most devoted love, my own sweetheart,
                    " Your adoring husband,

                                        " FRANCIS."

Sally had come back to London next day, of course, immediately after reading his letter. She was kind and patient and understanding as always, struggling for his sake to hide the anxious disappointment which he remorsefully perceived that she felt. It was she who wrote a charmingly tactful little note of thanks and apology to Lady Floria, and her helpful inventiveness in dealing with their respective relatives surprised him by its ingenuity. She managed to reassure and pacify the perturbed Reginald, who, despite his thankfulness for Francis's decision, was half consciously aware that some distressing mystery had involved a blow to their family pride. And she composed the skilful letter to her parents by which, without any actual untruth being told, the Colonel and his now convalescing wife were left with the desirable if surprising impression that a few weeks of flat-life in London had convinced both Francis and Sally that Staffordshire was a far better background for his music.

Now that this unexpected turn in their fortunes had been faced and accepted, Francis and Sally tacitly agreed never to mention even to each other the strange, half-explained shadow which had so suddenly fallen across those happy, active weeks of their early married life. Without further delay they let the flat, packed up their furniture, and returned to Staffordshire.

That was in December, 1924, fourteen years and three months ago.

CHAPTER VIII

PROGRESS COMES TO HALKINS'

LOOKING BACK upon those fourteen years, Francis realised how closely the factory and the village which was its background were now woven, despite his early attempts at escape, into the stuff of his life.

Every day, walking from the garage at the gates to his office in the centre of the long series of sheds and warehouses, he passed the great stores of raw materials which never ceased to fascinate him with their colour and variety. Piles of rags and cotton waste, stacks of bamboo canes, esparto grass and reeds, wood shavings, barks of trees, heaps of old bagging, ship rope and canvas, tarpaulin, waste paper, worn and filthy rope-soled shoes from Arab territories — what scenes and climates were not suggested by that strange, heterogeneous collection ! If he closed his eyes and sniffed the predominantly nautical smells of tar-encrusted rope and sail-cloth, he could imagine himself on a voyage of exploration through the many countries whence the picturesque ingredients of Halkins' world-famous fine papers were gathered.

Close to the storehouses stood the disinfecting apparatus, a tribute to David Flint's initiative and his employers' collaboration. Quite early in his career as visiting welfare specialist, Dr. Flint had suggested that the preliminary disinfection of the raw materials at the port of entry was not sufficient to safeguard the health of the workers. So disinfecting machines were installed, into which all the raw materials were passed before they embarked on their complicated career through sorting-rooms, rag-cutting machines, willowing and dusting apparatus, and the various processes of boiling, washing and bleaching in the rag-engines.

Only the eye of imagination could recognise the clean pulp in the rounded cast-iron troughs of these engines as the refined relative of the coarse, dirty stuffs waiting in the storehouse. In appearance this pulp resembled curds and whey ; to the touch it felt soft and slimy, like wet cotton-wool. Even at that stage its metamorphosis was barely half completed ; it had still to be beaten, pressed, dried, smoothed and calendered, before it was wound on to reels at the extreme end of the machinery. Farthest from the main Cheete-Witnall road, and beyond the sheds where special types of paper were " loaded ", " sized ", or coloured, stood the finishing house in which the flat paper from the cutting machines was carefully examined by women in starched white overalls. Standing at long trestle tables, they cast aside all damaged or defective sheets with an amazing deftness of touch.

Francis had only been a week with his father at Fordham when he decided that, if he must be a manufacturer, he would bring the factory up to date, and introduce music and colour into the lives of its employees.

"We ought to start a welfare department," he announced to Reginald. "And I'd like to give David Flint a job here as a sort of visiting adviser. He opened the Gilbert Flint Memorial Clinic in Birmingham over a year ago, and he's already begun to visit some of the more progressive factories — Sedbury's at Edgeville, for instance, and one or two of the heavy industries as well. Ours would be quite a little job, of course — but even if we're only a small firm, we can still be one of the most enlightened."

And now, in fact, they were. The memory of bitter frustration had gradually faded as positive achievement in another sphere began to take its place. Twelve months after Francis had settled at Fordham, the oldest inhabitants were saying that, in spite of his interest in music and his totally different appearance, the young man had obviously inherited the sterling qualities of his conscientious and respected grandfather.

From 1887 to 1912, Halkins' had been run as a partnership between father and son. Although there was little in common between old Jeremiah Halkin, the tall, shrewd, cadaverous chapel-goer, and his stocky genial son Reginald, the business, besides prospering, had kept well in line with contemporary industrial developments. Physically spare and tough, morally rigid and unbending, Jeremiah had regarded the growth of industrial legislation as a form of progress in which he had no choice but to cooperate. But Reginald, though habitually deferential to his autocratic parent, was apt to break loose in the company of his contemporaries ; he had a fondness for bawdy stories, and lacked old Jeremiah's ironclad Gladstonian notions regarding the obligations of employers to workers. Despite the rural surroundings of the factory, David Flint had found that the rate of tuberculosis was relatively high, while absenteeism due to minor illnesses and small accidents amounted to hundreds of hours of lost work in a twelve months' period.

"We ought to tackle this first — and drastically," he commented on his first visit, as he studied the sickness records conscientiously kept by Benjamin Rushton. But he soon discovered that the easy-going but well-intentioned Reginald required little persuasion to adopt the innovations which his son desired. He realised, he said, that Dr. Flint was justified in his view that health depended, not so much on the work that their people did, as upon the conditions under which it was done. And no doubt Dr. Biddulph of Witnall Infirmary, a contemporary whose collaboration David Flint proposed to invite, would be of the same opinion.

"I realise we've got to take the long view," Reginald had assured the young doctor whose appearance and manner attracted him at first sight. "I daresay Callum's and some of our other competitors will be able to undersell us for a time, because of the overhead costs that this new department will mean. But judging by what you say, industrial welfare seems to be the coming thing."

"You'll be in the van of a great movement, sir," David asserted eagerly. "In ten years' time there won't be a commercial enterprise worthy of the name that will be able to carry on without a department of this kind."

"I daresay you're right. On a long view, good conditions and employees who are well and happy may mean an increased output all round. And if you can make the Welfare Section a sound proposition, that in itself will advertise the concern in the best sense of the word. What Francis and I want you to do is to look at the medical needs of our folks and then at the conditions they're working under, and help us to fit the two together. Halkins' have always had a good name for looking after their employees, and we want them to keep it."

Within five years, helped by Dr. Biddulph, a full-time

resident nurse, and the records kept first by Ben Rushton and later by his widow, David had established a welfare department which became a small model for factories throughout the Midlands. Its reputation spread beyond Staffordshire, and led to visits from the representatives of industries in neighbouring counties.

Tackling first the problem of tuberculosis, David and Biddulph began by improving the ventilation of the sheds and workshops, and by instituting suction plants for the removal of dust with the minimum of disturbance. They persuaded Reginald to substitute electricity for the gas which had caused respiratory infections among some of the workers, especially those engaged in the transfer of gold-leaf designs to pottery. In the sheds where work on fine papers meant shutting the windows to keep out smuts and smoke from the distant Potteries, they had electric fans installed to keep the air on the move. After a few conferences with Reginald and Francis, they eliminated excessive overtime, established a preliminary medical examination which enabled them to exclude applicants with a tubercular family history from indoor processes, and instituted a system of holidays by which workers whose health appeared to be failing were sent away before rather than after their period of sick-absence had occurred. They encouraged the organisation of outdoor sports and games, until Halkins' had a football fifteen with which few Staffordshire teams could compete. Long before 1939, the tuberculosis record at Fordham had become the best in the Potteries.

Side by side with the mastery of this physical enemy, David began a series of reforms and innovations which catered for the minds as well as the bodies of Halkins' employees. He established an optical department where eyes were regularly tested by the Witnall Infirmary specialist, and a First Aid Unit for which Francis picked ten of the most intelligent workers. Believing also that good music, his own favourite form of relaxation, was restful even for men and women without musical abilities, David urged Francis to share with his employees the advantages of those talents which — for reasons unexplained to David, but doubtless sufficient — the younger Halkin had evidently decided not to use for a concert platform career.

Francis required no persuasion. Once the first shock of disappointment was past, he had resolved that, since his obligations compelled him to remain in Staffordshire, he would make Staffordshire the centre of his musical inspiration. Already he was planning a three-act opera, "The Old Wives' Tale," based upon Arnold Bennett's famous novel ; and had begun to compose a *Five Towns Concerto* for piano and orchestra. Now, encouraged by David, he arranged a continuous series of lunch-hour concerts at which local talent was gathered from a wide area, and Sally often sang folk-songs and ballads. He also started a factory orchestra which twelve months later gave the first performance of his own one-act operetta, *The Potters* ; and a massed choir which he planned someday to enter for the singing competition at a Staffordshire Musical Festival. One year, the orchestra and choir had tackled a Haydn Symphony ; the next, they gave selections from *Tannhäuser* and *The Meistersingers*. They touched their high-spot in 1935 with a Bach Cantata and parts of the *B minor Mass*.

In the autumn following his return to Halkins', Francis had arranged for the composer, Stewart Hailey — a fellow student at the Royal College — to give a series of informal talks on famous musicians. These began with Francis's own favourite, Brahms, continued with Beethoven, Mozart, Mendelssohn and Chopin, and concluded with the rarefied and spiritual Bach. After the talks, Francis started a harmony class in which he taught three-part counterpoint to a dozen enthusiasts, and urged them

to attempt composing for themselves. Thenceforward a
" worker's composition " was always included in the
programme of the annual factory concert, and one of these
— a short Overture by Joe Bullock, a rag-cutter — was
ultimately performed at a Manchester recital for Midland
musicians.

In addition to these musical innovations, Francis
adopted another suggestion made by David, and started
a Day Continuation School at the factory. For this he
put the main syllabus into the hands of Morgan Roberts,
the local lecturer for the Workers' Educational Association.
Once a week, on the afternoons of his periodic visits for
suggestions and supervision, David himself gave lectures
to Halkins' employees on the care of their health and that
of their families. These lectures were open to the general
public, and within a year had extended to Staffordshire
the reputation as a psychological specialist which David
had already established in Birmingham.

The file of case histories in Halkins' Welfare Department soon became unique. Within a remarkably short
period, Francis had come to know, and to pass on to
David, the family stories and backgrounds of the great
majority of his employees. He discovered their tendencies,
their mental aptitudes, their aspirations and their potential
delinquencies, and he shared, with the passion natural
to an imaginative man, David's own enthusiasm for the
elimination of accidents and the prevention of all unnecessary injuries.

The speed and intricacy of modern machines, David
explained to Reginald, took a heavy toll from fingers and
thumbs as well as causing an increase of eye-strain. No
test, of course, could prevent the accidents due to emotional upheavals in otherwise normal workers, but the
" incidence " of industrial accidents could be greatly
reduced by confining the less reliable workers to relatively
safe occupations. That was why he had instituted a

psychological test for the elimination of " accident-prone " workers from certain processes. He also proposed, with Mr. Halkin's permission, to interview and correspond with representatives of the firms which supplied Halkins' machinery, and impress upon them the need for incorporating adequate guards, safety-stops and fencing into the machine-designs. Already, when even a minor accident occurred, David had the machine inspected to see whether a repetition could be avoided, while the injured worker was visited by the nurse or secretary to ascertain the possible origin of some emotional disturbance, and was asked on recovering to submit to a psychological test.

One of the pleasantest recollections of Francis's early years at the family factory was the semi-official visit paid to the Welfare Department in 1929 by Ruth Alleyndene, the newly-elected Labour M.P. for the Witnall Division of Staffordshire, which included Fordham. On polling day in May, Francis had voted for her in company with most of Halkins' employees — who had hitherto automatically voted Conservative for no better reason than that Fordham was an isolated village still twenty years behind the current political trends of the Potteries. But he had been too busy to go to her meetings, and until she visited the factory had never seen the tall, beautiful, serious young woman a few years his senior, who was to become one of the strongest supporters of his innovations at Halkins'. He only knew, with the rest of Staffordshire, that she had resolutely departed from the feudal Conservatism of her own well-to-do, pottery-owning family, and was married to Denis Rutherston, a Professor of Philosophy at London University. To the Potteries she was still Ruth Alleyndene, and always would be.

Francis, accompanied by David Flint, escorted her round the Red Cross Room and the sick bay, took her to see the improvements in the workshops, showed her the disinfecting plant, and even the soda-recovery apparatus — which had been his own suggestion to his father as soon as he had mastered the technical details of paper manufacture. The three of them had talked, he remembered, as eagerly as though they had known one another for years. Francis had started by raising a matter which had recently begun to weigh upon his mind — the exploitation of women by modern industry and commerce. Ruth Alleyndene was an eager feminist, he knew, and he hoped he could persuade her to ask a question on the subject in Parliament.

" But surely," she had said, stopping, like all visitors, by the trough of a rag-engine and testing the consistency of the smooth white " half-stuff " with her fingers, " women aren't exploited at Halkins' ? Even in my father's time at the Pottery, they were supposed to work here under exceptionally good conditions, and now your workrooms are models of what such places should be. You ought to see some of the factories I visit ! "

" Oh, we do our best," he admitted. " But we can't act alone — and anyhow I'm not really discussing the arrangements here at the moment. I'm thinking of the way demands on women as consumers are created by modern advertising. The trouble even with intelligent women seems to be their extraordinary imperviousness to most forms of education."

" That's true enough," agreed Ruth Alleyndene. " That's why women haven't yet achieved much power in politics — or in stopping war. All but a few are still far behind men in the sense of being educated, as distinct from merely taught. The consequence is, they simply accept masculine values wholesale."

" War," he took her up, stopping suddenly at the entrance to the machine sheds. " War " — he repeated, as though the word had been the cue which started an unseen process of thought. Dragging himself out of it, he asked her a relevant question. " Have you any hope that the new government will get down to this business of war fundamentally ? I mean, will it really try to organise peace, instead of just talking pious platitudes ? "

" Well, with Arthur Henderson as Foreign Secretary we ought to get somewhere. But it all depends on how much *time* we have. You can't change the atmosphere of Europe and organise peace in two or three years."

" And meanwhile, what does the well-meaning citizen do ? "

" A great deal," she replied. " I was going to say that people in key positions, as you are, can help to check precisely that general acceptance of power-policies at the top which is the main ingredient of all modern wars. You can do it by making people more conscious and therefore more critical — as well as healthier and therefore saner."

" The trouble is that general medicine and industry and psychology are still all fenced into their separate compartments," put in David Flint, eagerly riding his hobby-horse as they walked back from the warehouses to Francis's office. " You've got to look at all three fields as parts of one picture, each having some relation to the man or woman you're dealing with. Health isn't just a state of not being ill. It's a vital, positive aspect of a man's total personality, the measure of his powers both mental and physical."

" I'm glad that's the outlook you're creating here," said Ruth. " When I was nursing in the War it always seemed to me that the assumptions of medicine were far too negative ; that it oughtn't to be just the science of healing, but a means of helping people to do their work. It wasn't till I started taking my children to a Babies' Welfare Centre that I realised how pioneer specialists like you, Dr. Flint, are trying to get just this conception of medicine taken for granted by the medical world."

" You must come and see us again ! " exclaimed Francis fervently, as she picked up her dispatch-case

from his office chair. "There are literally thousands
more things I want to talk to you about ! One doesn't
often find your sort of understanding among Members of
Parliament ! "

She laughed, sympathetically noting the flung-back
head, the springing hair, the luminous, vulnerable eyes of
this progressive young employer who was also a composer
with a rising reputation.

"You're right ; we're a poor lot ! But so far as I'm
concerned, I shan't need any persuasion to visit the
factories in this constituency. I was mentally reforming
my father's pottery when I was thirteen ! Long before
I've finished coming here, you'll be wishing I'd stop in
Westminster and stick to making speeches ! "

But, after all, she had only been back once or twice on
brief inspections, for two years later she had lost her seat
in the Socialist débâcle of 1931. And though she was
re-elected in 1935, the swift downhill slide of international
events had kept her more and more in London, working with the small Parliamentary Peace Group which
endeavoured to persuade the British Government to save
Europe from chaos. In spite of several invitations, she
had never yet had time to come to his home. That was
why he felt specially glad that he and Sally were seeing
her tonight.

By the time that he had been in partnership with his
father for a decade which seemed but an infinitesimal
moment, Francis found that musical composition, once
to have been his life's main purpose, had become a side-
line, though successful and gratifying so far as it went.
His work, it was true, was gradually making an international reputation ; his *Aria for Three Strings*, for example,
had been performed at the Ann Arbor Festival in Michigan in May, 1932. And three years later he had been
invited by the German Government to tour Germany

with a small party of British performers and composers, and had repeated his visits of 1924 to Berlin, Dresden, Leipzig, Nuremberg and Cologne.

Some of his more politically-conscious friends, such as Alfred Huntbach, the Witnall bookseller, who was watching the Nazis with a vigilant eye, had questioned the wisdom of making this particular 'trip under official German auspices. Far more popular locally had been his invitation, in 1938, to visit New York as the guest of the American Academy of Arts and Sciences at their thirtieth anniversary celebrations.

But since that occasion on which he had scaled, for the first time, the stimulating heights of American hospitality, Francis had found his opportunities for creating music, and even for listening to it, growing steadily fewer. His father's death in the summer of 1938, which increased his responsibilities as an employer, had been quickly followed by the Munich crisis, which emphasised his obligations as a citizen, and caused him to assume the rôle of chief A.R.P. Warden at the factory. Worst of all, it had robbed him — he hoped only temporarily — of the services of David Flint, who wrote regretfully that national strain and international tension had so greatly increased the work of the Gilbert Flint Memorial Clinic, that it had developed into a full-time job which compelled him to cut out his visits to factories.

And now the annexation of Czechoslovakia had come to increase that international tension, which threatened to eclipse the social innovations at Halkins' — just as Halkins' had once eclipsed the musical career of which Francis and his mother had dreamed. His mother ! How immense was the period of time which today separated him and her ! She seemed to belong to another century, a totally different epoch ; he realised with a shock that if she were alive, she would even now be barely sixty. He himself was not yet forty — an age at which a man's life was still of interest to war-making governments. Shivering a little as the study fire sank low, he wondered if the pressure of events and responsibilities would ever relax sufficiently to allow him to complete his *Somerset Symphony*, or begin the projected Choral Fantasia inspired by Shelley's *Adonais*.

Sometimes, to Francis's best friends in the neighbourhood, it seemed that in his over-burdened life, with its diverse objectives, he made time for everyone's interests but his own. He and Sally had never cultivated a large social circle, for he was always too busy, and she by nature too reserved. But they had a small group of intimate companions, the chief of these being Alfred Huntbach and his Quaker wife Miriam, who lived in Witnall and ran a well-selected book and music store which had been a second home to Francis ever since his return to Staffordshire.

The Halkins were also on friendly terms with Wesley Bates, the tall, bespectacled son of a Witnall bank manager, who was one of Francis's co-directors at Halkins'. His cheerful young sister often accompanied Sally on shopping expeditions to Manchester, though these had become less frequent with the growth of European crises. For some time after he returned to the district Francis had avoided, without being able to explain precisely why, the renewal of his war-time acquaintance with Walter Welland, now Chairman of Thomas Welland & Company, the Hanley potters. But the long-standing business connection of the two firms had brought Francis into touch with his former Company Commander almost against his will. When they did meet, Welland showed none of that disposition to discuss the War which Francis had dreaded, and the prosperous bachelor potter was now one of his closest acquaintances.

" It's a pity Francis and Sally never had any children," Miriam Huntbach often remarked to her husband. She herself could not now picture life without her two school-girl daughters, the cherished offspring of her late marriage, as a thirty-five-year-old school teacher, to the middle-aged bookseller.

But Francis had never expressed any regret for his childlessness, and within the last few years he had told Alfred Huntbach that he was definitely glad of it. During the early years of his partnership with his father, when he and Sally had lived at Fordham, he had been, he said, too busy to think of a family, and there was no room for children in the bungalow even if Sally had wanted them. In 1933, when they moved to Dene Terrace, they had for the first time in their married life plenty of space for nurseries. Yet it was 1933 which now seemed to Francis to mark the final, irrevocable stage of their decision to remain childless. For in that spring Hitler had come to power in Germany, and the shadow of war, growing persistently darker the more they tried to disregard it, had begun once again to creep over Europe.

CHAPTER IX

ENTERTAINING AN M.P.

As SALLY OPENED the study door, Francis jumped half guiltily to his feet. The hands of the clock on the mantelpiece pointed to seven-thirty.

" Miss Alleyndene's just telephoned," announced Sally. " The meeting's over, and she said she was starting at once."

" That means she'll be here in a few minutes. She makes that little Austin Seven go like a twin-engined racer."

" Did you finish the plans ? "

" To tell you the truth," admitted Francis apologetically, " I hardly glanced at them. It's ages since I felt so
fagged out as I did this evening. I must have been half
asleep ; I've actually been dreaming about the past,
instead of preparing for the future."

Sally knelt on the hearth-rug and carefully raked
together the embers of the dying fire.

" Was it so much better than the present ? " she
inquired.

" Not where you're concerned, darling. You've never
looked lovelier, and I don't know when I've heard you
sing more beautifully than you did just now. It was really
that which started me thinking. ' Drink to me only '
always reminds me of Cheete, and the square outside the
Memorial Hall."

" Me too, Francis. In those days," she added ruefully,
" we never thought you'd have to worry about A.R.P.
and that sort of thing again, did we ? "

" Well," he said, pushing back the armchair, " perhaps
I shan't have to do more than worry ! I daresay Ruth
Alleyndene will be able to tell us something about the
situation. Her views on it will be interesting, anyway.
. . . I'll be down in a moment."

" All right. I've put the sherry out. It wouldn't do
you any harm to have a glass before she comes."

Ten minutes later, the rush of a small car along the
Terrace and a ring at the front door bell announced Miss
Alleyndene's arrival. The heavy wind, breaking into the
house as Kiddemore, the gardener and occasional butler,
opened the door, seemed to blow her through the hall and
into the drawing-room where Francis and Sally awaited
her.

Ruth Alleyndene was now a slender, handsome woman
in the middle forties, with a gracious manner and the
beautiful speaking voice of the successful orator. Always

externally self-possessed, she had acquired an unmistakeable air of authority and a poise seldom shaken. As a
child and a young woman, she had lived on the very spot
occupied today by Francis's house when the present Dene
Terrace had been part of the ornate hall built by her
ancestors. He guessed that, even though it was ten years
since Dene Hall had been demolished, it must still be hard
for her to revisit the transformed scene once hallowed by
so many memories. But he did not know that it was the
story, gleefully related by her father to his in Dene Hall
garden, of an erring cook turned out of the house by
Ruth's grandmother in the hour of childbirth, which had
inclined his guest of the evening towards Socialism from
the moment that she overheard the conversation as a child
of thirteen. He was only aware that she had passed
through many tragedies before she was elected Labour
M.P. for Witnall in 1929. The thought of the sorrows she
had survived, the lessons she had learned from experience,
always gave him a feeling of confidence, even though the
subjects of which they spoke might be disturbing.

Over the sherry they talked of her crowded meeting organised by the Witnall branch of the Women's
Cooperative Guild. Then, as they went into dinner,
she told them that she and they would soon be near
neighbours.

"I've just bought a cottage at Fordham," she
announced. "Ever since I was re-elected, I've been
feeling I ought to have a house in the constituency and
not simply exist on the Alleyndene tradition. It's all the
more important now that Father's getting too old to come
often to the pottery — especially as Norman's uncom-
promising Toryism doesn't diminish with time."

Francis mentally recalled the occasional visits to
Fordham of the saturnine Norman Alleyndene. The
Alleyndene Pottery Company was one of Halkins' best
customers for pottery transfers.

" I've always thought it odd your having him for a brother," he confessed. " Except for a certain family likeness, the two of you seem to have absolutely nothing in common."

" We never did have, even as children," said Ruth. " He was three years older than I, and always seemed to stand rather apart from the rest of us." She added, as Kiddemore cleared the soup and went into the kitchen to fetch Mrs. Kiddemore's fried chicken, " It was my other brother, Richard, who was my constant companion. He was only fifteen months my junior, and we were more like twins."

" He was killed in the War, wasn't he ? " asked Sally gravely. The conversation had stirred her own unsleeping memory of her brother Guy.

" Yes. In Gallipoli, when he was only twenty. As a matter of fact," Ruth continued, a little surprised at her readiness to respond to the sympathetic interest of these two in her family history, " there seems to be some evidence that he went out of his way to get shot. A great friend of mine . . . an American . . . was there at the time, and he told me about it afterwards. I met him when I was nursing at Hardelot Plage."

To Francis a shadow seemed momentarily to fall across the table in spite of the brightly-lit room and the genial glow of the fire.

" Why did your brother do that ? " he asked in a low voice. " Was the War . . . were things too much for him ? "

" Not so far as the actual fighting was concerned. Although he was a painter, and temperamentally quite unsuited to war, I understood from my American friend that he was a good officer, and never gave in however tough the job was. . . . Apparently," she continued, wondering why it was so easy to talk to Francis on topics not usually discussed at the dinner-table, " it was discovered that he had homosexual tendencies — and just before the action his commanding officer was kind enough to tell him that he was likely to be cashiered and expelled from the Army."

"What a damned shame!" exclaimed Francis. "Especially as I read recently in one of Flint's text-books that homosexuals nearly always make efficient and enduring soldiers. According to the writer, they don't suffer from sexual deprivation in the same way as the rest ; hence they're less liable to nervous strain."

"That does seem probable, though I've never heard anyone suggest it before," commented Ruth. "For years I couldn't talk about Richard to anyone but . . . the American — and then he was killed too. After that I talked to no one till I met Denis. Some of us were pretty abnormal for a time when the War ended. I suppose you were both too young to experience that particular phase of desperation ? "

The reappearance of Kiddemore with the chicken created a diversion, and the Halkins did not reply. Once, they tacitly if half-consciously agreed, their part in the War was acknowledged, all kinds of admissions best never made would be dragged up from the secret depths of sleeping awareness.

"Well," continued Ruth, when the chicken and vegetables had been served, "all that egotistical reminiscence is just to explain what I'm doing here now. Those years made me determine that whatever happened, my own children shouldn't suffer from war if I could help it."

"They actually are twins, aren't they ? " inquired Sally.

"Yes, two of them. They're thirteen at the end of April. Jack's at Westminster and Jill's at St. Paul's. The other one, Timothy, was an afterthought when I was out of the House ; he's only six. It's even more for them than my constituents that I've taken the cottage."

A chill ran through Francis as he guessed at the political judgment which lay behind her action.

" You mean . . . war ? "

" Perhaps. Anyhow, I can't chance it after Chamberlain's warning speech to Hitler at Birmingham on Friday. If war comes, our house in Barton Street won't be exactly a healthy spot ; it's only a stone's-throw from the House, and I couldn't let the children stay there. I don't suppose Staffordshire, with all its industries, will escape air raids altogether. But Fordham's still only a village, and a safe area compared with London."

A good deal safer than Witnall, thought Francis, determinedly pushing back into his subconscious mind the dastardly wish that he and Sally had remained at the little bungalow in Fordham, instead of moving to a fine modern house on the edge of a great industrial district. Absorbed in thoughts of her children, Ruth Alleyndene did not for once observe her neighbours, or notice that Francis was trembling and Sally had turned pale despite the normal reassurance of her presence, and her calm acceptance of the fact that if dangers did come she would be in the midst of them.

Sally was the first to find her voice.

" But, Miss Alleyndene . . . do you think war's inevitable ? I mean . . . don't the Munich talks count any more, now Hitler's taken Czechoslovakia ? "

Over the ice-pudding Ruth began to discuss the current situation as seen inside Parliament. Neville Chamberlain, she declared, was a sincere but short-sighted man, and no real peace-maker. His Munich agreement had proved to be a house built upon sand because it was based on expediency rather than principle.

" He's one of a long line of politicians without constructive courage or imaginative wisdom," she explained. " Their only conception of international relationships was to keep on staving off disaster by one ignominious ex-

pedient after another. Whether they called it ' Safety
First ' or ' Non-Intervention ', it all amounted to the same
thing. It was nothing but a running away from funda-
mental economic and political issues, and a hope that when
the inevitable crisis came, the responsibility for handling
it would fall on somebody else."

" But Chamberlain's flight to Germany did look like a
courageous gesture," said Francis. " I mean, it suggested
something rather better than just an attempt to save his
own political skin."

" Oh, I grant you that. But all he was concerned with
was saving England — and he saw England as an enlarged
Birmingham, full of sick and needy people to whom a
conscientious Conservative social reformer could do good.
He sold the Czechs because they really didn't matter to
him, compared with slum mothers unnecessarily dying in
childbirth for lack of maternity benefits."

" Then you never thought the Munich agreement
would last ? " faltered Sally, as they returned to the
drawing-room for coffee.

" I didn't see how it could. Chamberlain's only idea
of keeping peace is superficial pacification — or appease-
ment, as it's now rather stupidly called. He's as incapable
of making a generous imaginative gesture and initiating a
share-out of material advantages, as I am of making a
boiler. All he wants is to be left undisturbed in the safe
familiar world of British imperial privilege. To him,
' Peace with Honour ' meant ' Peace without Sacrifice '."

" But," said Sally, pouring out the coffee, " you surely
don't think we ought to give in to Hitler ? "

Ruth took her cup and turned to them both, her mobile
face alight and her dark eyes shining with the intensity of
her vision.

" I'm not talking about ' giving in ' to anybody !
Sharing your privileges isn't the same thing as surrender,
though most people in this country still seem to think it

is. Just imagine what might have happened if the Prime Minister had given a great magnanimous lead to the whole world as soon as war was averted — made an offer to take the initiative in disarmament if the so-called aggressors would follow! Suppose he had coupled it with the suggested cancellation of the Ottawa Agreements, in return for decent treatment of the Jews in Germany! Instead of that, his one idea when he came back from Munich was to speed up rearmament. You could hardly expect the Nazis to allow both that and our privileges to go on uninterrupted. We haven't a divine right to dominate the markets and trade-routes of the world in perpetuity."

"The trouble is," Sally interposed, "you couldn't be sure the Nazis would carry out such an agreement even if you made it. Would it be any use giving a magnanimous lead to a man who doesn't keep his word?"

If Ruth had heard this argument before, her responsive smile betrayed no sign of weariness.

"You can't trust any government to keep its word unless honesty is made worth its while," she replied. "Governments are not philanthropic institutions; they're usually self-interested and aggressive, though they show these qualities in different ways. The point about Munich is that it could *only* have succeeded, or been justified, as the first step in a courageous, revolutionary programme. To make the Munich agreement and then come home and begin frantically to rearm, was the final and worst stage of the weak provocation which has served this country as a policy since 1931. It wasn't only inconsistent, but terribly dangerous."

"Dangerous?" echoed Sally apprehensively. Even after Kiddemore had entered and carried away the coffee-tray, the sinister word still seemed to hang poised upon the air.

"Yes, dangerous," said Ruth decisively. "What

happened in Prague last week has made it clear that
Munich was just the last of Britain's collection of lost
opportunities. Unless a miracle happens, I don't see how
war can be avoided now."

This time the silence lasted so long that Ruth wondered
whether her host and hostess had taken in the significance
of her statement. Then, all at once, both Francis and
Sally began to ply her with questions about preparations
in London. Was it true about the strengthening of ware-
house basements, the digging in the parks, the sign-
posts in Kensington and Knightsbridge marked with the
incredible words : " To the trenches " ? After she had
given as graphic a picture as she could, Francis talked
about his own increasingly heavy work as chief A.R.P.
Warden at Halkins'. He brought the half-inspected
shelter plans from the study, and asked for her advice.
By the time that the evening was over, Ruth realised that
for three hours she had talked of nothing but war and
A.R.P.

Hitherto, she reflected, driving back in the little car to
her room at the North Stafford Hotel opposite Stoke-on-
Trent station, her conversations with Mr. Halkin had
turned on music and books, or the present and future of
Staffordshire industries. But tonight he seemed to have
lost all desire to discuss his work either as musician or
manufacturer ; he could think and talk of nothing but the
possibility of war.

Well, she supposed, it was only natural ; war would
destroy the unifying internationalism of music and put a
stop to constructive social developments, as war always
did. It might even remove Francis Halkin, who was still
a comparatively young man, from his vital work as artist
and pioneer employer to those anonymous military
levelling camps whence the gifted were summoned as
remorselessly as humanity's misfits to be broken on the
Juggernaut wheels of force. But the relationship between

industry and human welfare would remain. War would not alter, but would probably intensify, the need for a creative approach to social problems.

It was a pity, she thought, as the car bumped through the cobbled streets of Witnall and Hanley, that Mr. Halkin had got things so much out of perspective. Was it because she had seen him for the first time at his home, instead of in his office ? Did the fault perhaps lie with Mrs. Halkin ? She was graceful, and even, in a quiet way, rather beautiful, with her limpid blue eyes and soft copper-brown hair, but she was obviously an anxious, highly-strung type of woman, who would begin to worry long before the occasion arrived.

How odd it was, Ruth reflected, undressing slowly in the pleasant warmth of the modernised bedroom, that people's private lives should so often belie their public endeavours ! Mr. Halkin had talked not only to her, but to his employees who had been in Dr. Flint's charge, about the importance of a well-balanced mind in a perfectly adjusted body. Why didn't he present himself to Dr. Flint as a patient, she wondered, recalling Francis's tired, harassed face, and Sally's nervous movements as he talked about his air raid precautions.

But even she did not guess that Francis had gone to bed to sleep restlessly and to dream about the dreaded return of war, which he saw as a monstrous Frankenstein whose clutching hand stretched like a cloud from a far horizon, and gradually lengthened till it blotted out the sky.

CHAPTER X

SEPTEMBER CRISIS

LESS THAN six months after Ruth Alleyndene's visit to the Halkins, the war which dominated Francis's dreams had already become imminent.

On the last day of August, rumours darted like swallows from one end of the factory to the other. The Poles were said to have attacked a wireless station ; fighting on the Polish frontier was reported to be developing ; all Americans were returning home ; the German liner *Bremen* had vanished on her way back to Europe. When Francis tried to ring up Halkins' agent in New York, he discovered that overseas telephone calls had been suspended.

On September 1st, the news included a Berlin announcement that the door to negotiation was not yet closed, and the commentator reporting it remarked encouragingly that so long as it was not closed, it was still open. But the Halkins felt less optimistic. Their copy of *The Times*, which they always read assiduously, announced that naval mobilisation had been completed and the remainder of the Regular Army Reserve called up. It also instructed local A.R.P. controllers to assume duty, and reported arrangements for the evacuation, during the next four days, of over three million children and adults from crowded towns and industrial centres, including parts of North Staffordshire. The threat of war and aerial bombardment seemed to be coming very near to Witnall.

Shortly after six o'clock that evening, Francis came back from the factory to find Sally crouching miserably in the drawing-room while the final sentences of the B.B.C. news bulletin echoed with incongruous urbanity into the silence.

" What's up, darling ? " he inquired immediately, distressed by the pale tension of her expression.

" It's only the news," she answered listlessly. " It gets on my nerves. . . . I've heard all the wireless reports today. They've talked about nothing but frontier skirmishes and the breakdown of negotiations . . . and now it seems that Germany has actually invaded Poland. The announcer said general mobilisation's been ordered, and Parliament was meeting at six o'clock to discuss the situation."

Francis did not speak for a moment. Then he said slowly : " I shouldn't worry yet, Sal. We've had so many crises, and each of them looked like causing war at the time. This one may blow over just the same as the others."

" But general mobilisation hasn't been ordered before," she protested.

" The trouble is," he continued, " you're alone too much nowadays. It was rotten luck losing both your parents so soon . . . and old Dad being gone too. Why don't you go and see Miss Bates or the Huntbachs when you feel depressed ? "

" Perhaps," she said, ignoring his suggestion, " we shall have some more news at nine o'clock."

" We might, but it'll only mean more details about what's already occurred. I shouldn't even listen-in if I were you ; it'll only upset you. Much better wait till the paper comes tomorrow and we can see the whole thing in perspective."

But when *The Times* arrived in the middle of breakfast next morning, it was still less reassuring than the previous day's wireless. Their coffee and bacon went cold as they pored anxiously over the news in black type beneath the ominous headings. Poland had indeed been invaded by German forces, and many towns, including Warsaw, had already been bombed. . . . The British and French

Governments had sent a *démarche* asking Germany to withdraw her troops from Polish territory. . . . In the central London area the hospitals had been cleared, and stretcher cases removed to outer districts. . . . Nearly 500,000 children and teachers had been evacuated the previous day. . . . The Government had announced steps to ensure maintenance in repair of essential buildings that might suffer war damage. . . . President Roosevelt had appealed to Britain, France, Italy, Poland, and Germany, to refrain from bombing unfortified towns or civilians from the air.

Francis turned to the editorial, but neither its heading, " One Man's Crime ", nor its solemn contents had any comfort to offer.

" The long period of international tension, never appreciably relaxed throughout the summer, was ended yesterday by an act of naked aggression, which by itself exposes the hollowness of all Nazi declarations of peaceful intent and Herr Hitler's clumsy sophistries. In the early hours of the morning German troops crossed the frontier in strength along most of its length and proceeded to bomb a number of towns. . . ."

" And . . . what's this country going to do ? " faltered Sally. Glancing hurriedly over the article, Francis showed her the crucial paragraph.

" This nation has never in its history been so unanimous in support of any decision taken by its leaders as it is now, on the eve of entering upon the war that must be waged. In coming to the help of Poland we have no material interest of our own to maintain. None the less shall we be fighting for that which is vital to our life, and to the life of all civilised peoples. For we know that, in a world where respect for the rights of the weak and for the plighted word can be overridden by the high hand of military power, there is no tolerable life for nations and for individuals ; and they who most whole-heartedly repudiate the use of force, or the threat of force, as an instrument of policy have no choice but to answer force with force when it is invoked against the ideals by which they live."

Observing the acute distress in Sally's face, Francis drew her attention to a letter on the editorial page which struck a somewhat brighter note. It was signed " Guy P. Dawnay ", and had been written from an address in Hampshire.

" I must be only one of thousands," it ran, " who thank you for the words of your leading article today. Great Britain is prepared . . . her strength adequate to resist the great shock . . . and solid enough to outlast any aggressor.

" The French are magnificently united. In a year their organisation has been perfected ; their air power improved and strengthened out of all knowledge. . . . On every side we see the vindication of the Prime Minister — *cunctando restituit rem*. . . ."

" Well," commented Francis encouragingly, " at least we do seem to be ready for anything this time. . . . Look, here's a whole paragraph about A.R.P. ! "

Urgently he scanned the instructions under the head-line " What Everybody Should Know " :

" Make sure you know the way to the nearest shelter and fire post." " Carry your gas mask with you every-where." " Listen regularly to wireless news bulletins." " Make sure you know what the warnings sound like." " Black-outs will last from dusk to dawn." " If you have a car or motor cycle, obscure the lamps at once." " Clear all inflammable material from attics." " Men are needed for the dangerous A.R.P. services. . . ."

"'The dangerous A.R.P. services'," Francis muttered under his breath. Throwing down the paper, he hurried into the hall and picked up his hat. "Look here, darling, I've got to go — there's all this to see to ! I'm late already, and I don't suppose I shall be back for lunch ; it isn't like an ordinary Saturday. If I were you, I wouldn't stay at home by yourself. Run over to Witnall and have a talk with Miriam ; she always does you good."

Sally's fears would be quietened by their tranquil, well-balanced Quaker friend, he felt certain, trying to view the international situation calmly while he hurried to the factory as fast as the Buick would take him up the hill. But in spite of his efforts to remain detached and rational, the phrase "displacement of population " came into his mind from some prophetic story that he had once read.

Suppose, in a second World War, that England were invaded like Poland ? Or suppose that the Potteries were raided so heavily that the packed populations of its adjoining towns had to flee, and seek refuge elsewhere ? In imagination he saw the wide empty road from Witnall to Cheete packed with a distraught crowd of refugees, men, women and children struggling beneath the burden of their goods and chattels, frantically making their way from Staffordshire through Derbyshire towards Cheshire and the distant sea.

At his office he found Mrs. Rushton, with the Staffordshire *Sentinel* in front of her, discussing the news with Nurse Warslow and Enid Clay over an early cup of tea.

"Good morning, Mr. Francis !" Mrs. Rushton addressed him with a cheerfulness that seemed to him infuriating after Sally's apprehensions and his own hectic imaginings. "Well," she added, "so that Man's been and gone and done it again ! "

"Haven't you girls got anything to do but drink tea and read the paper ? " inquired Francis, with a forced jocoseness which he hoped might conceal his deep-seated irritability.

"We've only just begun," pleaded Nurse Warslow. "After all, we don't get a war every day of the week ! "

"War ! What makes you so certain England's going to be involved ? Whether there's a little crisis or a big one, you all seem to think it's bound to affect us."

"But, Mr. Francis, the newspapers do say we're going to war," urged Enid Clay. "Isn't it a good thing Dr. Flint started the First Aid Unit ! If we do get air raids and casualties here, we shall know how to look after them ! "

So they'd been discussing air raids, had they ? — and as lightly as though aerial bombardment were in the same category as a snow-storm or a thunderbolt.

"If you'd ever seen war-time casualties, Miss Clay, you wouldn't anticipate them so eagerly," said Francis. "You simply don't know what you're talking about ! "

"But indeed I do, Mr. Francis ! " Enid answered with spirit, though her knees went weak and her heart thumped as it always did when he spoke to her severely. "I'm an officer in the Girl Guides, and we often have to help with accidents."

"My dear girl, the kind of thing you've seen is a picnic compared with war ! Wait till you get a case that's all damage and no man. Then you'll begin to understand a bit better what casualties mean."

"Well, I never, Mr. Francis, are you trying to frighten us ? " exclaimed Mrs. Rushton. She was perturbed by a strident note in Francis's voice — a note which, if he had been an emotional woman, and not a responsible business man on the verge of forty, she would have called hysterical. What had come over Mr. Francis lately ? she wondered. Through all the years that she had known him, he had been eager, strenuous, over-conscientious, always inclined to drive himself too hard, but never harsh or irritable with his secretaries.   Never until the past five or six months.

" To my mind," she continued, " it's better to cross bridges when you come to them.   These girls'll stand up to horrors all right when they've got to face them, never fear !   Now, what about a nice cup of tea, Mr. Francis, and give old Hitler the go-by for half an hour ! "

A week after Neville Chamberlain's guarantee to Poland in the House of Commons on March 31st, Francis and his co-directors had held an emergency meeting to discuss A.R.P.   The first time that the firm had considered the advisability of taking such precautions, in 1935, Francis had opposed them.   To prepare for war, he argued, was more likely to foster the war spirit than to achieve anything of practical value ; it made people take war for granted, instead of rejecting it as abnormal and evil.   But the Nazi reoccupation of the Rhineland the following spring had shaken him, and after Hitler's annexation of Austria early in 1938, he reluctantly accepted A.R.P. as necessary for the factory.   When the Munich crisis occurred, he had agreed to add the responsibility of Chief Warden to his other obligations.

Now, with the new commitment to Poland, Halkins' directors were obliged to concern themselves about the possibility of aerial attack and the safety of their workers. The menace of war had become so real, and the need to prepare for emergencies so urgent, that it looked as though the function of Chief Air Raid Warden would soon overwhelm every other that Francis endeavoured to fulfil.   He had left that meeting five months ago with a weary sense of depression and distaste.   Never once had he questioned his ability to maintain the double rôle of musician and manufacturer, whatever demands upon his time and energy the unusual combination might involve.   But he seriously doubted his efficiency as an Air Raid Warden.   If war did come, how would its return affect him?   Would he be able to bear the strain, or would he play the coward, and disgrace himself and Sally? His fear of fear and of confusion weighed upon him, an ever-increasing load, as the days went by.

Nevertheless, he had characteristically flung himself into A.R.P. preparations with all the vigour that he could still command. Calling on his contemporary, Wesley Bates, to help him, he had discussed the measures which ought to be taken, while constantly insisting that the actual outbreak of another war was incredible and impossible.

" I daresay these precautions are inevitable now. That is, they've become so. With all this talk of air raids, our people wouldn't feel safe without them. But . . ."

" But you don't like them, Francis — any more than I do."

" Of course I grudge the time and money spent on something so essentially unconstructive. But it's more than that. Air Raid Precautions seem to me just another part of the ' War of Nerves '. After all, the one thing the dictators hope to achieve is to work everyone into a state of alarm, and then get their way by threats — and all this preparation is simply playing into their hands."

" Then would you put the Prime Minister's guarantee to Poland into the same category? " Wesley Bates had inquired.

" To my mind it's another major mistake," asserted Francis. " If Poland were attacked, what practical help could we give? No, the Polish guarantee and A.R.P. have one serious feature in common — their main consequence is to increase tension in Europe."

As spring moved on into summer, and a brilliant June gave place to one of the wettest Julys on record, Francis had spent more and more of his time upon shelters and stirrup-pumps, sandbags and fire buckets, the organisation of fire-fighting teams and the training of First Aid parties.

When the persistent rain gathered into streams which splashed down to the sunk floors of the reinforced shelters, he arranged for their drainage, heating and ventilation. At home, too, he laid in a store of emergency supplies in case raids should come, not to Fordham, but to Witnall or Hanley, and he, as an accessible Air Raid Warden, should be called out to help with casualties. His music was all but crowded out by these new responsibilities ; like the rush of wind before a thunder-storm, the inexorable momentum of Europe's catastrophe seemed to sweep away his last solace, his only remaining consolation.

And all the time his inward feeling of fear and distress had increased. Exactly what he dreaded, he could not have explained in words, but it was something monstrous . . . horrific . . . a chaos of panic and wounds and death. Just as he had set himself an exaggerated standard of thoroughness in his A.R.P. preparations, so he visualised situations for which only an unattainable ideal of fortitude would be adequate. He began to sleep badly and became increasingly obsessed by terrible dreams, in which the half-submerged recollections of the Arras battlefield mingled with nightmares of gruesome damage to familiar people and places. Vividly, in the silence of the small hours, memories had come back to him of men on the wire . . . men with blackened limbs, or sightless eyes staring fixedly at the sky ; disembowelled men ; men without faces. As the wet summer dragged on against the rumble of war rumours and the clash of " incidents " in the Danzig Corridor, these phantasies had no longer been confined to the long-dead soldiers on the Western Front, nor even to Halkins' employees for whose safety he was responsible. The pictured casualties began to wear the faces of his intimate friends — of Wesley Bates, of Alfred Huntbach, of his faithful servants the Kiddemores.

Then, one August midnight, the ultimate nameless horror which he had incessantly tried to combat, suddenly

took form and identity. He had no idea how long he had
been sleeping, when his dream shaped itself into the
incommunicable terror of a noiseless air raid. There was
no sound, yet he saw the bombs dropping, watched the
leaping tongues of fire, could almost smell the acrid fumes
of charred bricks and burning timber. . . . All at once,
when this soundless nightmare was at its height, he
seemed to feel a thud, and a headless body came down
upon his bed. Shuddering, he examined the mutilated
form . . . and found that it was Sally's. . . .

He awoke with a stifled shriek — to hear the steady
drip-drip of the trees in the garden ; to feel Sally asleep
and warm beside him. But the sense of suppressed horror
had gone with him throughout the following day — and
for a seemingly endless succession of days. He fought
against sleep, because sleep now threatened him with
these dreadful phantasies of a mutilated wife ; yet the less
he slept, the more heavily his responsibilities at Halkins'
weighed upon him.

Again and again he had found himself overwhelmed
with fatigue, and irritable with his employees. More than
once he had observed significant glances passing between
Mrs. Rushton and Enid Clay as some sharp word of
criticism or reproach escaped him. He realised that he
was smoking cigarettes to a degree which he knew to be
bad for him, yet he seemed unable to stop himself. At the
end of each day his feet felt as leaden as though he had
walked for miles through a heavy swamp, instead of
sitting in his office. He caught himself starting at every
small sound ; a renewed habit of semi-conscious listening,
added to his fear of sleep, produced a now habitual
insomnia which was rendered the more unbearable by
feverish reconstructions of daytime problems.

The deeper these fears and apprehensions became, the
less Francis felt able to communicate them to anyone else.
Least of all could he discuss them with Sally, for he knew

from her strained expression and her habit of lying in wait for the newspaper, that she too was carrying an intolerable burden of dread. It was not until Sunday, September 3rd, when the Prime Minister's broadcast announced that England was actually at war, that his inability to endure any longer his own society or his secret thoughts drove him over to Barlaston for a talk with his erstwhile Company Commander, Walter Welland.

Welland, comfortably looked after by an elderly housekeeper, lived in an attractive country house three hundred yards from the road at the end of a tree-shaded drive. Perhaps it was due to this peaceful bachelor existence that the twenty years since the Armistice had hardly changed him. His small wiry figure was sparer, his dry skin more lined, his stiff fair hair now thickly sown with grey. But from a distance he appeared exactly the same man as the Captain Welland who had once ordered a distressed and bewildered boy to lie down in his dug-out after a bomb had buried him.

The perpetual rain had now given way to a late summer of ironic loveliness, and the two men walked up and down the gravel path beside Welland's tennis-court comparing the preparations made in their respective factories against aerial warfare.

" Now that it's come, you know, Francis, it's going to be a mighty different war from the last," Welland concluded.

" Yes," agreed Francis, a little less weary than usual owing to the reassurance of Welland's presence. " We believed in something then . . . It gave the whole affair a kind of glamour — thinking you were really fighting the powers of darkness. It made you stick what now seems impossible."

" They'll be the same old Huns, when we run up against them," Welland observed.

" That's part of the tragedy ! " exclaimed Francis

vehemently. " More than once, as you know, I've been to Germany on musical expeditions — and I liked most of the people I met there immensely. It seems just crazy that for the greater part of your life and mine, we've been at loggerheads with a nation that's given more music to the world than any other — to say nothing of its organising efficiency."

" If only they'd stick to music, we should all have reason to be thankful," said Welland. " But you must admit that nowadays they do try to dominate the world."

Francis slashed at the rhododendron bushes with his stick. " They only try to do what we've done for generations," he asserted. " We're non-aggressive simply because we've got everything we want already. And we're just as keen on defending what we've got as other people are on taking it. Everybody who thinks at all knows that ! "

Welland smiled.

" You don't grow less . . . dynamic as you get older, do you, Francis ? "

" Well, Walter, if I can't tell you what seems to me the truth, where can I tell it ? We all know that the darkness is in each one of us ; the Nazis may be a gang of criminals, but they haven't got a monopoly of evil. To conceal that fact from one's self means deliberate self-deception — and though the people of this country are often unconscious hypocrites, they don't like being hypnotised by the Press into believing lies. And the worst of it is, now that war's come they'll all be in it, prepared and unprepared."

" That's certainly the grimmest aspect of the whole thing," agreed Welland. " In an Army you do at least try to train people for what's coming to them. With civilians, it's nothing but the survival of the fittest — and the luckiest."

" Of course," Francis went on, " they'll be doped, not only in Germany, but here, with the idea that it's their duty to die as quietly as possible, without asking why. After that, the politicians will bully them into irrational hatreds. They'll pin their naïve faith to official false-hoods, and anyone who questions the wisdom of his political leaders will be treated as a Fifth Columnist ! "

It was not until they had gone in to dinner, and Francis sat opposite his friend with the evening light on his face, that Welland observed his unusual pallor and the lines of strain round his eyes.

" Almost as if he took drugs," Welland meditated. " I hope he hasn't acquired the habit, after all these years of remaining unspoiled by success."

Aloud he said : " You know, old man, you're looking absolutely done-up. Don't you think you're overwork-ing ? "

Reluctantly Francis acknowledged the correctness of Welland's observation.

" I'm feeling just about dead-beat, Walter, and that's the truth. A.R.P. added on to increased work at the factory leaves hardly a moment for music ; and then I've been sleeping very badly the last few weeks. After all " — he laughed without mirth — " our daily doses of broadcast news haven't been exactly cheering lately, have they ? "

" You ought to have taken a really good holiday. When was it due ? "

" It was fixed a bit late this year, unfortunately. I promised Wesley Bates I'd wait till he came back from the Isle of Man, and then he was going to carry on as Chief Warden for a month while I got a change. Sally and I were going to Cheddar in October, but things don't look much like a holiday anywhere now."

" Well," urged Welland, with real concern, " do take it as easy as you can. If I were you, I should get Biddulph or your friend Flint to overhaul you."

When Francis left — relatively early, for Welland had begged him to take a sedative and turn in soon — the sanguine remnants of sunset trailed their ragged banners across the darkening sky. All of a sudden, as he drove slowly homewards, something in the lie of the land, the time of the year, the faint vermilion light shining through the canopy of cloud, brought back a memory which had vanished for many years beneath the level of his consciousness. With a start he recalled Jeremy Fielden, and his amateur attempts to read his hand and predict his future.

" He said ' Round about forty ' — and I was forty last month. . . . Could he really have foreseen the threat of another war, with all its anxieties and problems ? Was that what he meant ? Is it possible for the lines on an individual hand to indicate the coming of a complex political situation ? "

But the cheerful boy who had told his fortune in a French farmhouse two decades ago had long been dust, and the dark Staffordshire countryside resting in the illusive tranquillity of the September twilight vouchsafed him no answer.

CHAPTER XI

THE FOURTEENTH OF JUNE

" I see they're evacuating more school-children from London," said Sally, looking up from *The Times* at breakfast as the clear yellow sunshine of another summer flooded the newspaper from the tall French windows which opened on to their garden.

" Yes . . . it'll take the best part of a week from such a big area. We ought to get our own evacuation over sooner."

" Ours ! Francis . . . you didn't tell me. . . . Are they going from Witnall ? "

" Yes. Over two thousand have registered. They're moving out into Derbyshire and Cheshire." Seeing how pale she had gone, he added reassuringly : " Don't worry, darling ! It mayn't mean a thing. It's just that you've got to take maximum precautions where children are involved."

It was the 14th of June, 1940. Besides announcing the evacuation of 120,000 school-children, to continue for five days, *The Times* contained many other pieces of disquieting information. Fighting was increasing in violence on both sides of Paris, while a strange stillness reigned over the capital itself as an unending procession of refugees from the city streamed southwards, blocking the roads. *The Times* special correspondent with the French Government at Tours reported that no news-papers, except for one composite sheet, were appearing in Paris, and that the wireless was reserved for guarded announcements. It was feared that about 6,000 British troops had been surrounded and captured near St. Valéry-en-Caux.

Sitting beside Sally and looking at the incongruous beauty of the summer morning, Francis could hardly believe that little more than a month had passed since Mrs. Kiddemore reported the Nazi invasion of the Low Countries as she brought in their early morning tea. In spite of his previous apprehensions, the last four months of 1939 and the first three of 1940 had brought to North Staffordshire none of the terrors which he had anticipated. The main changes at Halkins' during the period known to American commentators as the " phoney war " had arisen from a sudden avalanche of those Government contracts which had kept his father so busy during Francis's boyhood in World War No. 1.

But the Nazi occupation of Norway and Denmark had notified Staffordshire, like the rest of England, that the War had begun to change its character ; and with the invasion of Holland, Belgium and Luxembourg at dawn on May 10th, came that violent acceleration of events which took Britain's breath away, and started the House of Commons on an orgy of panic-stricken legislation. While the Government, for day after day of pitiless unbroken sunshine, faced successive calamities of a speed and magnitude hitherto unknown to English history, Halkins' awakened to the realisation that the aerial bombardment which had been expected the previous September might now come to Staffordshire in a matter of days or even of hours. The dropping of German bombs on Yorkshire, Norfolk and Essex at the end of May showed that this time Francis's conscientious precautions were taken against no illusionary peril.

As the familiar French citadels which had once withstood the German armies for four interminable years fell one after another in a few weeks, and the advance mechanised units of the enemy forces reached the Channel ports, Francis redoubled those efforts to construct additional shelters, establish First Aid posts, and train fire-fighters, which had already made such heavy demands upon his time and energy. During the tense period in which the trapped British armies made their dramatic escape from Dunkirk, he had again been tormented by the harrowing dreams of the weeks preceding the outbreak of war. After June 6th, when an extensive German night raid over England caused the sirens to be sounded from Hampshire to Durham, he found himself haunted by the old recurrent nightmares of casualties which wore the familiar faces of his closest friends. He also became obsessed by the conviction that he too would be one of those victims before his life-work was half done. Even his music could not now be relied on as a refuge; sometimes an indefinable dread seemed to be associated with it, a reminiscent horror waiting just round the corner, as though a seed of chaos were latent in the creative side of his life. Three days ago, in a mood of bitter frustration, he had sat up late to write the first draft of a short Funeral March in A minor, and beneath the title had added the words : " Dirge for the death of a failure."

Sally abandoned her barely tasted breakfast, and spoke insistently.

" If the children are being evacuated from Witnall, it means that we're definitely a danger area, doesn't it ? "

" Well . . . yes. Compared with the heart of the country, any industrial district's a danger area," Francis admitted.

" And we're on the edge of it. We might get bombs here, and casualties, and then invasion, as soon as France falls ? "

" It would be unlucky to get bombs three miles from the centre of the town, but we might, of course. . . . Still, France hasn't fallen yet."

Sally faced him resolutely.

" Perhaps not — but if Paris goes, it means the end of their resistance, and *The Times* says the Germans have crossed the Seine. Francis . . . have you made any kind of arrangement, in case we're both killed ? "

Francis rose rather stiffly from his chair.

" Well, as a matter of fact I have . . . just to be on the safe side. I made sure my Will was in order when I was in Claude Fontaine's office on Tuesday, and he gave me one of the three copies to bring home."

As he spoke, he pictured the half-ironic look of dismay at the state of the world on the face of the small dark-haired solicitor, himself a descendant of the Huguenot refugees who settled in Staffordshire after the Revocation of the Edict of Nantes. Intelligent and popular, he was always addressed by his humbler local clients as " Mr. Fountain ".

" Is that all you've done ? " asked Sally.

"Not quite. Last night I drafted a letter to Fontaine, giving him further details."

"Won't he be rather surprised to get a letter like that?"

"Oh, no. Why should he? I shall seal it up — and anyway it's quite customary to leave a letter of instructions with one's Will." He laughed uneasily. "They're usually just about one's funeral. . . . I'd rather like you to look at it some time, before I actually send it."

"I'll look at it now. After all . . . we may get raids here any moment, and I expect you'll have a busy day?"

"Yes; I don't think I can get back to lunch. I've been over the preparations again for weeks, and put the First Aid and fire-fighting teams through their paces — but naturally one's got to do a bit extra in a crisis like this."

"Very well, then, let me see the letter before you go."

Francis went up to his study, and came back with an envelope in his hand. Taking out a folded letter, he laid it before her, and she read it carefully.

"MY DEAR FONTAINE,

"Life is very uncertain for everyone at the moment, and it is likely to be no less so for us than for others.

"If, therefore, you should ever be notified that my wife and I have both fallen victim to the present situation, I should be grateful if you would make yourself responsible for seeing that all my musical compositions and manuscripts are given into the possession of my friends Alfred and Miriam Huntbach, 157 High Street, Witnall. I shall have spoken to them on the subject before this letter is posted. I am asking Mr. Huntbach to act as my executor so far as my musical work is concerned. He is familiar with my publishers, whose addresses he knows, and I shall give him the names of musical colleagues from whom he can seek advice.

"I am also anxious that the Kiddemores, our gardener and housekeeper, should not be left stranded by any catastrophe from which we might suffer. So would you kindly make sure, in such an event, that they receive their National Insurance cards, which are in my desk, and £20 in cash to cover their immediate expenses, in addition to their legacy under my Will.

"As regards funeral arrangements, I should like these to be carried out very simply, and with as little publicity as possible. We should both prefer to be cremated, and to have our ashes buried close to my parents' grave in St. Andrew's churchyard at Fordham.

"Thanking you for your many services to my firm and myself,

"Yours sincerely . . ."

"It seems all right," said Sally. "But what will happen if Mr. Fontaine's office gets destroyed? It's right in the centre of the town."

"Oh, I shall leave a duplicate letter in my desk with the Kiddemores' insurance cards and the copy of my Will. That's the place where anyone would look if we got done in. Anyhow, darling . . . the chances are we *shouldn't* both catch it at the same time."

She laughed, with an hysterical break in her voice.

"Heaven help me if you caught it and I didn't! If you went, I wouldn't want to go on living. There's no one else who matters a row of pins!"

Francis stroked her hair, passing his hand tenderly over its glossy copper-brown smoothness.

"Well, dearest, there's no need to be so tragic about it yet! The only point now is, do you agree with this letter? If so, I'll sign it, and send it as soon as I've spoken to Alfred."

"All right," she said. He signed his name, "Francis

K. Halkin ", added the date, " June 14th, 1940 ", and took the letter upstairs again.

" By the way," she told him a moment later as he went out to start the car, " I've promised to go to the Huntbachs directly after lunch. Miriam wants some of the check material I bought at Croxton's sale for the kitchen curtains. They suggested I should have tea and wait till you come. Would you be able to pick me up there ? "

" Of course. I'm glad you're not going to be alone all day, and it'll give me a chance to talk to Alfred. It's really remarkable how little he and Miriam worry. I wouldn't like to be in the middle of Witnall myself at the present time — with two young girls at home, too. But it doesn't seem to bother them at all."

" Shall I post your American letter in Witnall ? " Sally inquired.

" My American letter . . . ? Oh, you mean the one to the Pennsylvania Symphony Orchestra, about the special Concerto they've asked me to write ? Yes, by all means post that. The news had sent it right out of my head."

" Do you suppose their autumn concert for the work of British composers is likely to come off now ? "

" I don't see why it shouldn't. If by any chance it's our swan-song as a nation, they'll be all the more likely to do it ! Anyhow, I mean to have a shot at that Concerto." He stooped down from the car and kissed her. " Now don't you worry, my darling. I'll pick you up in Witnall as soon as I can get away."

At the factory a number of strenuous duties awaited him, and he had time only for his more urgent correspondence. No one was drinking tea today, and each of the female members of his staff reacted differently to the sense of crisis in the atmosphere. Mrs. Rushton, he noticed, was very quiet ; a shadow, as of foreboding, had quenched her usual cheerfulness. Nurse Warslow, excited and talkative, roused his attention to the contrast between herself and Enid Clay, who seemed almost to burn with a smouldering intensity of passion. Her air of rapt self-dedication impressed even while it exasperated him, and he hurried through the dictation of his letters with a sense that he was racing against the march of history.

Late that afternoon, Francis drove over to Witnall to pick up Sally at the Huntbachs'. Tired as he was after a day of renewed precautionary preparations which had barely left him time to eat his lunch, he was half afraid to find them all listening to some new and devastating piece of broadcast information which he felt unable to endure. But though the clock struck six as his car turned the corner by the church, he found the house quiet, and his wife and Miriam sitting over the remains of tea in the small back garden while the elderly bookseller ran the lawnmower over the soot-darkened strip of grass as placidly as though the German armies were a thousand miles away.

"Look here, Alfred," Francis began, putting down his belated cup of tea, "I've just drafted a letter to Fontaine, nominating you as my music executor in case of . . . some accident to both Sally and myself. It's a great service to ask — but, in the circumstances, would you be prepared to undertake it? None of my friends know the publishers and their ways as well as you do."

"Of course, my dear boy — but oughtn't you to ask someone more your contemporary? After all, I'm eighteen years your senior. You'll still be writing symphonies and concertos when Miriam and I are pushing up the daisies."

"It's just to cover the present situation. Modern war doesn't take much account of chronological age . . . and Sally and I might be blown to blazes as early as anyone else."

" In that lamentable but improbable event, Francis, you can count on me."

" It's awfully good of you, old man. I'll post Fontaine's letter as soon as I get home."

Through the brilliant, inexhaustible June sunshine, Francis drove Sally back to Dene Terrace. Outside the door of their house, each of them looked without speaking across the suburban valley to the great industrial ridge, which seemed as though it must offer so irresistible a target to a would-be destroyer. Francis guessed that Sally, like himself, was hearing in imagination the roar of bombs descending upon those closely packed houses, listening to the pitiful cries of trapped and shattered children, watching a leaping crescendo of fire turn the pot-bank furnaces to dwindling candles.

The two of them ate their dinner almost in silence. Even Mrs. Kiddemore, usually affable and loquacious, could not penetrate their mutual reserve. Each knew what the other was waiting for ; as they sat in the quiet drawing-room over their coffee, their forebodings seemed to gather visibly, and focus themselves upon the loud-speaker in the corner. What would they learn from it about that day's critical events ? Was the doom of France certain, or was hope still left ? How actually near to England were the catastrophes against which Francis had been preparing all day ?

" Shall I turn on the wireless ? " he finally asked, five minutes before nine o'clock.

" Yes, of course."

" Are you sure it won't upset you, darling ? "

" Oh, Francis, what's the good of always saying that ! " she cried sharply. " We've got to know. . . ."

He turned on the knob of the battery, and almost immediately the resounding boom of Big Ben echoed through the waiting stillness. They both sat tense as the voice of the announcer followed.

"This is the B.B.C. Home and Forces Programme. Here is the news. . . .

"German armoured cars, motorised units and infantry have been entering Paris since about seven o'clock this morning. From the little information that is available about events during the night, it appears that the German advance guards reached the western suburbs about midnight from the district south of Rouen. German columns were known to be pouring over the bridgeheads to the west of the capital about eleven o'clock. No more evacuees were allowed to leave the capital, because, as the German troops began to move into the suburbs there was a danger of collision and confusion. German machine-gun posts were already established within the city boundaries. Actually German troops appeared to be under orders not to penetrate any further and it was not until seven o'clock this morning that the march into the capital began.

"An Exchange correspondent in Paris was able to send this short message about the atmosphere in the capital just before the German entry. He said : ' Every house, every shop is closed, and the shutters are up. On the streets, no one is to be seen except the police and civil guards, and they have handed in their weapons, and are a rigidly civilian body '."

The cultured tones went inexorably on, as blandly impersonal as if they were giving the results of a football match, instead of announcing the fall of a great capital which had been the symbol of Western civilisation :

"Reuter's correspondent reports that last night, explosions could be heard in the centre of the city as big armament factories in the suburbs were blown up. All important buildings and bridges were left intact. Those people remaining in the capital included officials and workmen in the essential services, the Prefecture, mobile guards and firemen, Cardinal Suhard, Archbishop of Paris, Mr. William Bullitt, the United States Ambassador, and a number of American journalists.

" The French High Command announced this morning that as the enemy push on both sides of Paris had again increased during the night, the troops covering Paris had been ordered to retreat. ' In refraining from direct defence of the capital,' said the French communiqué, ' the French Command aimed at sparing it the devastation which defence would have involved. The Command considered that no valuable strategic result justified the sacrifice of Paris.' "

Through Francis's brain ran a sequence of remembered words : " The French are magnificently united. In a year their organisation has been perfected ; their air power improved and strengthened out of all knowledge. . . ." Incongruous sentences ! Where on earth had he read them ?

The B.B.C. announcer turned from the fall of Paris to the increasing threat to Britain which the French collapse would accelerate :

" On the vast front in Champagne, the French say that the enemy is progressing towards the south. His most advanced troops are directed towards Romilly, on the Seine, about 70 miles south-east of Paris, and St. Dizier, on the Marne, about 40 miles south-west of Verdun. The movement of the Allied armies continues in good order."

At this point, Sally's taut semblance of composure snapped.

" Turn it off ! " she cried, and suddenly burst into tears. " The Germans'll be over here in no time and you'll have to go and fight again — I know you will ! "

" Sally, darling, don't cry ! — it only makes things

worse," Francis implored, and seized her twisting hands to quieten her. " After all, I've got a very responsible job, and there'll be more than enough to see to here. . . ."

Perhaps tomorrow, his insistent apprehensions prompted. Perhaps tonight. . . . What would she do if the air raids which preceded invasion began to harass Witnall before he could get her away to some safer place ?

There was a knock at the door, and Mrs. Kiddemore, who lived with her husband in a cottage nearer Witnall, tentatively put her head into the room.

" We're going now, Sir. Ten o'clock tray's all ready in kitchen."

" Thank you, Mrs. Kiddemore. You've heard the news, I suppose."

" Yes, Sir. Looks as if we'll be gettin' it proper before long, don't it ? "

As Sally, mopping her eyes, struggled to regain her self-control, Francis went with the Kiddemores to the front door. The midsummer evening light, slanting across pot-banks and chimneys to the suburban fields, showed a group of men taking down the crossroads sign at the bottom of the hill. The sun's dying gleam turned to twin beacons the lamps on Francis's car, still standing where he had left it outside the front door.

" I shall have to take it to be overhauled tomorrow," he explained to Kiddemore. " The engine's knocking. And I want to be sure I know how to put it out of commission, just in case . . ."

" That's right, Sir ! When Jerries come, we don't want 'em runnin' round pickin' up anythin' on wheels, like Tories on election night. Shall I have a word with Tom Coppenhall if he's down at garage ? "

" Yes, if you wouldn't mind. Let me see — it's Saturday tomorrow. Tell him I'll bring it round just before lunch, as soon as I get home from Fordham."

Sally looked up wearily as he came back.

" I feel stifled in here. Can't we get some fresh air, and then go to bed early and end this awful day ? "

" Of course," he agreed. " I'm pretty tired too. We'll have a turn in the garden and then go up. But let's put on a little music first, to take away the taste of the news."

There was certainly no doubt of his fatigue. Now that catastrophe, so long anticipated, seemed really to be about to descend on them, he felt more than ever doubtful of his ability to bear the increasing strain that he would have to carry. Already, even since the news bulletin, a strange feeling of unreality was coming upon him. For a second, moving towards the loudspeaker, he forgot what he was about to do. Then, remembering, he twisted the knobs mechanically until, through truncated fragments of news in different languages from various stations, he cut into the middle of a musical programme. Where the music came from he did not know, but he found himself listening to German voices . . . and seemed all at once to identify the words of a familiar tune :

> " *Bald ist der Nacht ein End' gemacht,*
> *Schon fühl' ich Morgenlüfte wehen.*
> *Der Herr, der spricht : ' Es werde Licht ! '*
> *Da muss, was dunkel ist, vergehen.*"

He shuddered violently. A feeling of breathlessness seized him ; an unwonted pain cramped his chest, and for a few seconds he became conscious of palpitation. Putting up his hand, he found his forehead damp with sweat as the music continued :

> " *Vom Himmelszelt durch alle Welt,*
> *Die Engel freude jauchzend fliegen ;*
> *Der Sonne Strahl durchflammt das All.*
> *Herr, lass uns kämpfen, lass uns siegen ! *"

Was he really hearing a musical programme coming over the air from some unknown station on June 14th, 1940 — or was he listening to a gramophone record played on the Western Front just before an attack in August, 1918? It was one of the things that he would never know; for, with the gesture of a man trying to stop an express train which is rushing him over the edge of an abyss, he switched off the wireless, and turned to Sally.

"I don't think I even want to listen to music. We'll go out — unless you'd rather make tea first?"

"No; I don't want any tea. I feel more like a whisky and soda." She dragged herself out of her chair, went into the dining-room, lifted the tantalus from the sideboard cupboard, and fetched two glasses out of the kitchen. Pouring a liberal measure of whisky into each, she added a small quantity of soda-water, and handed one to him.

"Be careful what you're doing with the whisky," he enjoined her vaguely. "After all, you don't often take it. . . ."

She laughed hysterically, draining her glass.

"Careful! What's it matter now! What's anything matter, when we may be dead in a week! If I can't forget the War any other way, I'll use this one!"

With a hand which now shook a little, she half-filled her glass from the decanter, and this time drank the spirit neat.

"That's better!" she cried wildly. "Now for some air!" And throwing open the French windows, she jumped into the garden and stumbled down the sloping, sun-baked lawn.

Francis followed her mechanically, hardly knowing what he did. The sense of unreality, of gradually dissolving into space, which he had noticed indoors, seemed to be growing upon him, eclipsing memory and dulling

awareness. As he gazed fixedly at the copper-red ball of
the sun just disappearing behind the pot-banks on the
horizon, the words of the *Morgen-Hymne*, first German,
then English, hammered out their familiar tune in his
brain. They had begun to drive him almost crazy, when
a faint scream penetrated his failing consciousness.
Struggling towards the sound across the dry grass, he
perceived that Sally had fallen headlong down the flight
of stone steps which led from the lawn to the narrow gravel
path bounded by their garden wall.

She lay in a pale heap at the bottom of the steps, a thin
stream of blood trickling slowly down her cheek from a
gash where her temple had struck the wall. Confused and
bewildered, he knelt beside her. He thought he called
her name loudly, but though he could see that she was
still breathing, she did not reply. Some vague memory
whispered : " Concussion ! " and as he looked up from
her ashen face to the vivid rim of the vanishing sun, the
words " telephone " and " Biddulph " spun round in his
head like tops. They turned into scarlet circles of revolving consciousness which gradually lost all meaning until
they disappeared. . . .

He seemed hardly to have watched them spin for a
moment . . . and yet it must have been longer, for when
he again perceived his surroundings, it was almost dark,
and he was standing up, shrieking aloud . . . shrieking
because the old nightmare, the indescribable horror of a
noiseless air raid, had come upon him . . . and with a
thud Sally's body, mutilated and bleeding, seemed to
descend in front of him on to the ground. . . .

Looking wildly round, his eyes wide open and his face
distorted, he saw her unconscious form, fragile and lovely
in its quiet oblivion, lying at his feet unimpaired save for
the tiny gash at the edge of her hair where the blood had
dried. For an incalculable period of time — perhaps
seconds, perhaps minutes — he stood staring fixedly at her

as she lay gently breathing in the fathomless peace of deep unconsciousness. Then, suddenly, he stooped, and lifted her up. Clasping her convulsively in his arms, he carried her along the edge of the lawn, and began to run down the steep footpath which skirted his garden.

Part Three

CHAPTER XII

STAFFORD ASSIZES

MURKY AND WAN, the light of the rainy November morning penetrated with difficulty into the Shire Hall at Stafford, where the quarterly Assizes were in session. Throughout the hearings the electric lights, like a bunch of incandescent harebells, continued to burn above the reporters' table, illuminating its baize cloth scattered with pewter inkstands and untidy piles of paper. Mackintoshes and umbrellas rustled and rattled from the benches crowded with spectators at the back of the Court.

That day, less than forty miles distant, the bereaved of stricken and smouldering Coventry were burying their dead. Standing between the bomb-craters in the cemetery, they watched coffin after coffin lowered into a common grave. The previous night, as a reprisal for British attacks on " residential districts " of Hamburg, Birmingham had been battered by the heaviest raid that it had yet received. Sleepless and miserable, the inhabitants of Stafford had listened for hour after hour to the sound of heavy bombers roaring like overhead railway trains above the quiet country town.

In a large oaken chair with a wooden canopy above it and a heavy red curtain behind sat Mr. Justice Dannefroy, who had just opened the Stafford and Staffordshire Assizes with an address to the local magistrates assembled in the gallery and the numerous members of the legal profession seated opposite the reporters at the baize-covered table. Within the past few days, he reminded them, the citizens of a neighbouring county had suffered heavy blows and terrible casualties. The men, women and children who had died at Coventry and Birmingham were innocent victims of a war fought to demonstrate that principle of equality before the law which was the essence of British justice.

" I ask you to stand for a moment in their memory," he said, a sudden emotion illuminating his strong tired face, with its humane eyes and thin ironic lips. The Court rose, its occupants remembering for the hundredth time that week the adjacent tragedies which no one could forget.

Amid the groups of witnesses and spectators on the right of the Judge, three women of different ages and types sat close together. Ruth Alleyndene, Miriam Huntbach and Enid Clay had been brought to the Assize Court by the prospective trial of a friend, and by the possibility that each might be called upon to testify on his behalf. Just behind them, waiting also for this case which was to come up later that morning, Mrs. Rushton and Nurse Warslow sat with Wesley Bates.

They all remained taut and expectant as the Clerk of Arraigns read out the small preliminary charges, and one humble prisoner after another stood in the dock before the Judge. These cases were various and mostly un- savoury — wounding with intent to kill, perjury, arson, bigamy, child assault. Would they never be finished ? impatiently wondered Enid Clay, her fingers tightening in painful anticipation on the edge of the bench where she sat. But Ruth Alleyndene, less emotionally involved and therefore more mentally detached, found attention to spare for these poor prisoners. How much dignity they showed even in the most sordid cases, she reflected, watching the fair-haired young husband charged with bigamy stand upright before the Judge without a glimmer of fear on his pale impassive face. What a demonstration of human courage it was, in circumstances where every influence conducive to high standards of behaviour would seem to be lacking !

She was still thinking about the bigamous husband and wondering how far nine months' imprisonment with hard labour would diminish his experimental interest in matrimony, when ten men and two women filed into the jury-box. Then the name that they had all been waiting to hear seemed to rend the stillness with the effect of a bomb explosion.

" Francis Keynsham Halkin ! "

From the steps below, Francis's slim familiar figure came up into the dock between two warders. With quiet dignity he too confronted the assembled magistrates, as though he were standing on a concert platform and they represented his audience. But to Ruth, who had not seen him since the evening she dined with the Halkins at Dene Terrace in March, 1939, the face half turned for a moment towards his friends seemed all but unrecognisable.

He looked about him incredulously, and she felt in her own nerves his sense of being in a nightmare which was bound soon to end. It alternated, she suspected, with the illusion that he was taking part in a play in which he was both the chief actor and the critical audience. Intuitively she perceived in him the sensation, common to most men and women in similar periods of abnormal crisis, that to be the prisoner at the bar on a capital charge is the type of experience which happens to other people, but never to one's self.

While Francis remained standing, Ruth noticed that his back was bent and his shoulders crouched like the shoulders of a hunchback. Only the hands clasped behind him — the delicate musician's hands with their long slender fingers — appeared unaltered.

" Oh ! " she breathed. " I wouldn't have believed anyone could change so much in eighteen months ! "

" He looks much better than he did at the hearings in

the Guildhall," Miriam Huntbach told her. " The first time of all, you wouldn't have known who it was. He looked like an old man of eighty."

Enid Clay did not speak. She continued to grip the wooden bench as the Clerk read the charge.

" Francis Keynsham Halkin, you are charged that you did wilfully murder your wife, Sarah Dorothy Halkin, at some time between 9.15 P.M. on June 14th and 7 A.M. on June 15th, 1940. Do you plead Guilty or Not Guilty ? "

" Not Guilty," said Francis, with a firmness which his appearance had not led them to expect. The warders instructed him to sit down, while his senior Counsel, Sir Lancelot Prettyman, K.C. — internationally renowned as much for his red hair and Mephistophelian eyebrows as for his legalistic eloquence — informed the Judge that the murder charge against Mr. Halkin could not possibly finish that day. The Judge then told the twelve members of the jury that they would not be permitted to go home for the night.

" Facilities will be given you," he added, " to explain to your husbands or wives the reason for your absence."

Ruth examined the jury with some curiosity, wondering how much understanding it was possible to hope for. The foreman, a white-haired cadaverous man with black spectacles, resembled a sexton, or perhaps an undertaker. Number Two was probably Jewish ; he had a large aquiline nose and dark hair, emphasised by a light sporting suit. Number Three could have been his brother, though his suit was darker and his appearance rougher ; he might be a gardener. Number Four, small, neat and dapper, with large horn-rimmed spectacles, suggested a chemist. The two women jurors presented a marked contrast ; one, whom Ruth afterwards discovered to be the owner of a local sweet-store, was plump and looked emotional ; the other, a quiet, plain, mouse-like little woman, belonged to the teaching staff at the Council School.

Their collective appearance suggested a slightly bewildered worthiness; it strangely combined conscientiousness and scepticism. They gave less reason for optimism than the Judge, but at least they appeared to possess more responsiveness than Francis's impassive solicitors, Messrs. Davy, Son & Hollins, of Cheete, who were conducting the case because his own solicitor, Claude Fontaine, was perforce a witness for the prosecution. Perhaps, she told herself, she was prejudiced, since she had good reason to believe that the senior partner, Mr. Theodore Davy—a tall elderly man with thinning white hair who lived in Fordham—had always voted for Sir Harrison Talliner in General Elections.

But the prosecuting Counsel, Alaric Franklyn, K.C., young, dark-haired, dynamic, superficially a little hardened, was beginning to open the case for the Crown. The charge, he said, was a grave one in so far as it involved questions of law. These questions would be settled for the jury by the direction of the Judge. In order to establish a charge of murder, the prosecution had to satisfy the jury that accused unlawfully committed a voluntary act which brought about the death of his wife; and that, when he did that act, the prisoner intended either to kill his wife or to do her grievous bodily harm.

Mr. Halkin, explained Counsel, was a director of Halkin & Son, Ltd., a highly respected firm of paper manufacturers which had been founded by his grandfather. He was also well known in musical circles as a composer, whose works had been performed, not only in Staffordshire, but in different parts of the country, and even abroad. Though he and his wife had no children, they had always lived happily together. Their gardener and cook, a married couple named Kiddemore, would testify to the deep affection between them, and everyone else who knew them had received the same impression.

" On June 14th, a date which will be famous in history

as that of the fall of Paris," Mr. Franklyn continued, " the
accused and his wife were known to have been considerably troubled by the serious threat to this country, which
became acute at that time, and, indeed, still continues.
Mrs. Halkin, in particular, was greatly upset. When
the Kiddemores left as usual soon after 9 P.M., the news
that the Germans had occupied Paris had just been
announced on the wireless, and Mrs. Halkin was in tears.
No one but the accused saw her again until her body was
taken from the River Checkley the following morning."

The jury, their interest stirred by this dramatic statement, began to look expectant as the young Counsel
went on.

" Throughout the day in question," he said, " Mr.
Halkin was exceptionally busy with preparations arising
from the state of crisis, and had his lunch at the factory.
At that time he was quite normal in manner and appearance ; indeed, as his secretary will tell you, he dictated
his letters with unusual speed and concentration owing to
the pressure of other work. He supervised the completion
of air raid precautions throughout the afternoon, and at
six o'clock drove in to Witnall to pick up Mrs. Halkin, who
was having tea with Mr. and Mrs. Alfred Huntbach. The
Huntbachs, who own a book and music store in Witnall,
were close friends of the Halkins, and during this visit the
accused asked Mr. Huntbach to act as his music executor
in certain eventualities. Mr. Huntbach agreed, while
protesting that the prisoner was many years his junior, and
Mr. Halkin explained that he made the request because
he feared the war situation might cost him and his wife
their lives."

" About ten minutes past nine that evening," continued Mr. Franklyn, " just after Mrs. Halkin had been
seen crying about the fall of Paris, the accused went to the
door with the Kiddemores. He seemed rather distressed
by the news himself, and told Kiddemore he wanted to

make sure that he knew how to put his car out of commission in the event of a German invasion. He also stated that it needed overhauling, and asked Kiddemore to mention the matter to the local garage proprietor, Mr. Coppenhall, on his way home. That was the last time Mr. Halkin was seen in his normal health."

The Court was now so silent that, each time the prosecuting Counsel paused, the busy scribbling of the reporters could be heard above the stillness. In the dock the prisoner appeared to listen with weary indifference, as though he were hearing an old story unfolded about somebody else.

" At seven o'clock on Saturday morning, June 15th," Mr. Franklyn related, " the Kiddemores arrived as usual at the Halkins' house, Number 9 Dene Terrace. As they turned into the Terrace from the main road, Mrs. Kiddemore thought that she heard a distant splash. It did not impress her at the time, but she realised its significance a few minutes later. At the house they found that the black-out, which was usually over the windows when they arrived, had either been already drawn back or had never been done. Immediately afterwards they also discovered that the French windows of the dining-room, which led into the garden, had been left wide open."

Counsel then described how the Kiddemores, considerably disturbed by the unusual appearance of the house, had hurried up to the bedroom to look for their master and mistress. Not finding them there, they had searched through all the rooms, but discovered no trace of them except for a tantalus and two glasses, which had obviously contained whisky, on the dining-room table. The Kiddemores were impressed by this, because Mr. Halkin and his wife hardly ever touched spirits.

" It was then," continued Alaric Franklyn, " that Mrs. Kiddemore recalled the splash which she had heard as they entered the Terrace. Although it seemed unlikely that this could have any connection with the deserted house, she urged her husband to go down to the river. So Kiddemore went along a public footpath which led past the Halkins' garden from the main road to the banks of the Checkley, and started to look in the water. He had not gone far when he saw a half-submerged form lying against the bank, and found it was that of his employer. Mr. Halkin was fully dressed, and apparently dead. Kiddemore pulled him on to the grass, and shouted to his wife, who had followed him, to telephone for the police. Later that morning, when the police dragged the river, the body of Mrs. Halkin was found in the deepest part of the stream, close to the stone bridge where the public footpath ended."

As Counsel described the discovery of Sally's dead body, a flicker of emotion, transient and elusive as the wind passing over a field of grain, broke for a moment the waxen rigidity of Francis's face. But when the story continued, it became once more immobile and set.

" As soon as the police arrived, a constable gave Mr. Halkin artificial respiration, and this was successfully continued by Dr. Shelton, who arrived soon afterwards. After treating the accused, who appeared unaware of anything that was happening, he took him to Witnall Infirmary and handed him over to Dr. Biddulph. The body of Mrs. Halkin was discovered about nine o'clock, soon after Dr. Shelton had returned to Dene Terrace, and he came to the conclusion that she had died from drowning, in spite of the fact that her head was cut and severely bruised by a blow or a fall. He also estimated that she had been dead from nine to twelve hours ; that is, she must have died the previous evening between 9.30 and midnight. Dr. Shelton had already formed the opinion that if the husband had been in the water only a little longer, he would not have survived his wife."

How vividly Enid Clay, her eyes fixed upon Francis, recalled that painful morning ! In the golden incongruous sunshine of 9 A.M. on June 15th, she, Mrs. Rushton and Sylvia Warslow had been discussing the news and the possibility of invasion with Wesley Bates at the office, when the telephone bell rang. Mrs. Rushton had answered it, and Enid remembered, as though it had all happened an hour ago, the sudden ashening of her face and her stifled exclamations.

" Something serious. . . . Oh, doctor ! Oh, *no* ! . . . Yes, Dr. Biddulph . . . yes . . . I'll ask Mr. Bates to go to the house at once. . . . Yes, I'll come to the hospital. . . ."

She sat down heavily at the desk, and for a moment, while Wesley Bates and the two young women stood beside her in breathless suspense, she was unable to speak. Then, in low monotonous tones quite unlike her customary cheerful voice, she had given them the news.

" It's Mr. Francis. . . . The police were called to the house early this morning. . . . He was discovered in the river, and they're dragging it to find Mrs. Halkin."

Enid could still feel the crimsoning flow of blood to her face and its equally sudden ebb, leaving her white and shaken. She could hear her own passionate cry : " Oh — he's deserted us ! "

But Mrs. Rushton, with quick realisation of her anguish, had removed that misconception immediately.

" No, my dear. . . . Maybe he meant to, but he didn't succeed. They gave him artificial respiration and brought him round. . . . The police doctor took him to the Infirmary. Dr. Biddulph rang up from there just now."

For a moment of silence they all waited motionless, trying to realise the tragedy. Then, very gravely, Wesley Bates spoke.

" I think, Mrs. Rushton, we've had our first invasion

casualty. . . . We'd better go to the house now, and then on to the Infirmary. Will you come with me straight away ? "

The voice of Alaric Franklyn, crisp and slightly metallic, broke into Enid's meditations.

" In the accused man's study," he narrated, " the police made one or two discoveries which seemed to bear upon the situation. On his desk, fastened by a new elastic band to the Kiddemores' insurance cards and a copy of his Will, they found the duplicate of a letter addressed to Mr. Claude Fontaine, the prisoner's solicitor, and dated June 14th. You will hear later from Mr. Fontaine that this letter contained the expression of the accused's wishes with regard to his musical compositions, and also gave explicit instructions concerning funeral arrangements — not only for himself, but for his wife.

" Later the police examined some of his manuscripts, and almost immediately came upon one which had evidently been recently written, as it appeared to be unfinished. This manuscript was the rough draft of a Funeral March, and beneath the title, in the accused's handwriting, were the words : ' Dirge for the death of a failure '. . . ."

Enid could hardly recollect how she had spent the rest of that nightmare morning. She remembered the onerous pile of letters, mainly from civil service officials who wanted everything in triplicate, or from customers, perturbed by the crisis, to whom she devised ingenious answers which were as non-committal and uninformative as the government departments themselves.

At lunch-time Mrs. Rushton and Mr. Bates had returned, tired and distressed. They had found the police in possession of 9 Dene Terrace, and learned that Sally Halkin's body had just been taken from the river. They had then driven on to the hospital.

" Did you see . . . him ? " Enid had breathed.

" No," Mrs. Rushton replied. " He hasn't come round yet. They're keeping him under drugs."

" They don't want him to return to full consciousness till he's fit to face the charge," added Wesley Bates.

" The charge . . . ? "

" Yes, I'm afraid so. If two people make a suicide pact and the attempt fails in the case of one, the survivor is usually charged with . . . murder."

Murder ! Oh, then let me hang instead of him ! cried her sorrowful heart. But she schooled herself to speak quietly.

" Do they know it was a suicide pact ? "

" No. He alone can tell us the truth. But it seems the most likely theory. No one doubts his devotion to Sally."

That was true. No one had ever doubted it. How often she had told herself that, flagellating her vehement nature for its undesired, unrequited passion !

" He's been working much too hard for months," she said, frantically seeking to account for the terrible predicament which no one, as yet, could explain.

" Yes, indeed," agreed Wesley Bates. " That's certain enough. I realise now that a person of his artistic type should never have taken charge of A.R.P. — especially on top of all his other work. I blame myself for not paying enough attention to some of the things he said. He loathed all those preparations to the bottom of his soul. He didn't want to believe there *could* be another war ! "

" You're not the only one, Mr. Bates," Mrs. Rushton insisted. " We've all been to blame, not seeing evidence which it was part of our job to notice. There was his irritability, and his impatience with Miss Clay here, after he'd shown us the temper of an angel for years. Why didn't I ask myself what it meant ? "

" Do you remember," corroborated Nurse Warslow, " how angry he was with Miss Clay just before war broke out — all because she suggested it was a good thing we had a First Aid Unit to look after casualties ? "

Enid remembered only too well. She could still hear Francis's voice, with its strident note, scolding her.

" Wait till you get a case that's all damage and no man ! Then you'll be able to understand a bit better what casualties mean."

Oh, why, why hadn't she understood ? She loved him so much, yet she had been as dense, as stupid as the rest ! The pain of that realisation was still with her when she and Mrs. Rushton accompanied Wesley Bates to the sad little service at St. Andrew's Church which had followed Sally's cremation. Except for a brother and sister of the late Colonel Eldridge, only the three of them stood in the country churchyard, where the persistent, inappropriate sunshine poured down upon this strange evidence that England was threatened with bombardment and invasion. The small urn with its ashes, into which Sally's fragile elegance had been so grotesquely transformed, united with the shadow of the years ahead to convey even to Enid's youth the full realisation of mortality.

She returned to the present to hear the King's Counsel winding up the case for the Crown, damning and grim in its appearance of tragedy unrelieved by mitigating circumstances.

" When Mr. Halkin finally came to himself in hospital," he related, " it seemed quite clear that he did not understand why he was there. Nor did he realise that his wife was dead, because he kept on asking Dr. Biddulph to see that she was sent from Witnall to a safer area. When he was finally told of her death by Mr. Huntbach, on June 19th, he had great difficulty in accepting the fact, and appeared not to have the least idea how it had occurred. On his discharge from hospital he was taken to the police station and charged with murder. He said that he wished to reserve his defence."

Mr. Franklyn paused, and the scribbling of the reporters again sounded busily until he continued.

"When Dr. Biddulph asked Mr. Halkin what was his last recollection before recovering consciousness in hospital, Mr. Halkin replied that he could recall nothing after listening to the news of the fall of Paris, except for hearing a certain piece of music some time after that hour. This alleged loss of memory is especially strange in view of the fact that Mr. Halkin's brain appears to have been quite uninjured by his immersion in the river or anything that happened before it ; and though we do not doubt that his return to life did not mean an immediate return to full consciousness, there is nothing in the facts before the prosecution to explain a continued inability to remember. The evidence of the prosecution will be that, just before hearing this music, Mr. Halkin accompanied the Kiddemores to the front door, and made those references to the examination of his car which I have already mentioned. You will learn from Kiddemore that he spoke to Mr. Coppenhall, the garage proprietor, at his employer's request.

"No one can say exactly what happened after that, except from circumstantial evidence. Mr. Halkin alleges that he can recall nothing after about 9.15 P.M., and Mrs. Halkin is dead. The post-mortem has established the fact that, although her head was injured severely enough to cause concussion and unconsciousness, she died, not from this blow, but from drowning. You may hear a plea of insanity put before you by the defence, but if all the facts before us are true, it is clear that Mr. Halkin had envisaged not only his own imminent death, but also that of his wife, for some considerable time. The two empty glasses on the dining-room table present a complicating factor, especially in view of the subsequent injury to Mrs. Halkin's head. Having ascertained that the husband and wife seldom touched spirits, the prosecution has had to contemplate the possibility that a quarrel occurred between them when both were in a state of semi-intoxication, and that the accused struck Mrs. Halkin down in anger and then threw her body into the river. This possibility must still be taken into account ; but apart from the head injury, there is no sign of any struggle in either the house or garden. Having regard to the affectionate relationship between the prisoner and his wife, and to the evidence of premeditation which will be put before you, the prosecution inclines to the belief that Mr. and Mrs. Halkin agreed to die together, and that this unhappy lady injured her head in jumping from the stone bridge close to which her body was found."

The young Counsel drew himself up and confronted the listening Court, flinging back his gown with a histrionic gesture.

" In view of the distress which the threat of invasion caused to both this talented musician and his wife, the jury may well think that there was consent on Mrs. Halkin's part to the termination of her life by drowning. They may believe that the two glasses of whisky meant no more than a natural attempt on the part of the unfortunate couple to reinforce their courage before taking the fatal plunge. The jury may also conclude that, after helping his wife to carry out this decision and perhaps witnessing her death, Mr. Halkin's own resolution failed, until his act was precipitated by the appearance of the Kiddemores in the distance, and the realisation of the inquiries which he would have to face."

Mr. Franklyn paused for breath, and then concluded :

" The case for the prosecution, however regrettable it may be, and whatever reluctance to press it we may feel in view of Mr. Halkin's responsible position and distinguished musical career, is this : That he and his wife resolved to die together by drowning themselves in the River Checkley ; or, alternatively, that the husband struck down his wife in a quarrel, threw her while unconscious into the water, and then decided to follow her. Whichever of these theories may be accepted does not matter from the point of view of the law. If the first theory, as we believe, is correct, the law directs that when two persons agree to commit suicide, and one of the parties dies and the other recovers, the other is guilty of murder. If the second theory is accepted — that the prisoner, intoxicated by an unusual dose of spirits, attacked his wife, injured her head, threw her into the river, and then decided to join her — this is murder even more definitely.

"That is all, my Lord, that I have to say for the present."

When Counsel sat down, the Judge dismissed the Court for the luncheon interval, and a sudden buzz of conversation began as spectators and witnesses crowded into the corridor. Ruth and Miriam, followed at a short distance by Enid, passed through the light-brown doors together.

"What's *your* opinion about Mr. Halkin's motive, Mrs. Huntbach?" Ruth inquired. "Do you think this suicide pact theory is sufficient to account for everything?"

Miriam considered the question with her grave Quaker exactitude.

"It's possible," she said at length. "One thing I'm sure of; if Sally had known that Francis intended to die, she wouldn't have wanted to be left behind. She was very anxious about the War — very anxious indeed — and she was too reserved by nature to have many friends to discuss it with. My husband and I thought she was far too much alone through Francis being preoccupied with so many different kinds of work and responsibility, and whenever she was worried, we used to persuade her to come to us. My two girls did her good. It's a thousand pities she had none of her own."

" Isn't it just as well, now, that she hadn't ? "

" Miss Alleyndene, if Francis and Sally had had children, this awful thing would never have happened. People don't make suicide pacts when they've young life to consider."

" That's true enough," assented Ruth. " Nothing on earth would make me leave my own three to their fate."

A child, thought Enid, stepping quickly across the muddy cobbled square. A child would have saved him from this . . . even an illegitimate child perhaps. If only I could have borne him a child ! But he never cared about me . . . not even enough for that stolen half-hour which might have given him something to live for. He despised me, and I'd have died for him. . . . Oh, Francis !

Leaving Ruth and Miriam to continue their walk to the Dove Hotel, where both were staying, Enid turned up a side street. She hurried towards her humble lodging for a meal that she knew she would not eat as the November rain, grey and cold, came down upon her from the dun-coloured sky.

CHAPTER XIII

THE CROWN *v.* HALKIN

WHEN THE COURT reassembled after the luncheon interval, the first witness called by the prosecution was Alfred Huntbach. His wife, regarding him with grateful affection, surveyed the loose-limbed untidiness, the drooping, old-fashioned moustache and the tall spare figure, which for so long had typified companionship and un-demanding kindness. His benevolent countenance now appeared troubled as he looked at Francis's weary, impassive face. Miriam sympathised deeply with her husband's distaste for the position in which he found himself.

"He doesn't care about giving evidence for the prosecution," she whispered to Ruth. "It's no fault of his, of course, but he does wish he could have been called for the defence instead."

In reply to Counsel's questions, Alfred agreed that he was the owner of a book and music store in Witnall, which he had inherited from his father. He had known Mr. and Mrs. Francis Halkin since they settled in Staffordshire at the end of 1925. A more devoted couple it would hardly have been possible to find. On the afternoon of June 14th, Mr. Halkin came to his house to fetch Mrs. Halkin, who was having tea with them. He was then in his usual health, though both he and his wife seemed worried about the threat of invasion.

"Just before he left," Alfred continued, "he asked if I would act as his executor in relation to his musical compositions, in the event of his death."

"Did he tell you that he had recorded this wish in any other way?"

"Yes, Sir. He told me he had written a letter about it to his solicitor, Mr. Fontaine."

"And did you agree to do what he asked?"

"I did — but not without protest. I reminded him that I was many years his senior, and suggested he ought to ask someone younger."

"Can you remember what he said after that?"

"Yes. He indicated that his request was only intended to relate to the international emergency."

"Did anything he said suggest to you that his wife was involved in these fears and preparations?"

Alfred paused, perceiving the significance of this question. At last he replied : "In a general way, he saw the situation as threatening his wife just the same as

himself. So far as I recollect, his actual words were :
' Sally and I might be blown to blazes as soon as anyone
else '."

Sir Lancelot Prettyman rose from his seat to cross-
examine.

" Did you see Mr. Halkin when he was in Witnall
Infirmary ? "

" Yes, Sir. Dr. Biddulph asked me if I would try to
help him adjust himself to his actual position. Even when
they stopped giving him drugs, he didn't seem to understand where he was or what had happened."

" What did he say when he first saw you ? "

" He didn't appear to know me to begin with. Then,
when we'd been talking rather at cross-purposes for about
ten minutes, he suddenly said : ' Why, it's you, Alfred !
Do you know who I thought you were ? ' I said I had no
idea, and then he told me that he'd taken me for his old
music teacher, Hermann Rosenstein, who died just after
the last War."

The suppressed titter that rose from the Court ended
immediately with the next question.

" Did he seem to be aware of the death of his wife ? "

Alfred paused again. He looked anxiously at Francis
before he replied : " No, Sir. I had a good deal of trouble
in making him understand that it had occurred. He
appeared to have assumed that she had not visited him
because Dr. Biddulph had sent her away from Witnall to
a safer area."

" What happened when you finally persuaded him
that Mrs. Halkin was dead ? "

" He fainted. He was very weak at the time. I was
not allowed to see him again that day."

" Is it within your knowledge that before the tragedy
he had been seriously overworking ? "

" It is indeed, Sir. More than once I said to my wife
that, what with his music and the extra work which the

war caused at the factory, he'd no right to make himself responsible for A.R.P. as well."

" From your acquaintance with him extending over many years, would you say that he had a tendency to attempt more than his strength could bear ? "

" He certainly had. He used to get tremendously carried away by his musical compositions, and then worry for fear he was failing in responsibility towards his firm and his employees. Consequently he tended to take on himself all kinds of jobs which other people could have done just as well."

" One final question, Mr. Huntbach. Is it not a fact that when Mrs. Halkin came to see your wife on June 14th, she brought some material she had purchased at a sale, and asked if she could have part of it back ? "

" That's so. It was for the kitchen curtains. My wife promised to return what we did not need."

The next witness was Claude Fontaine, Halkins' solicitor, who had been obliged to hand over the case to his rivals in Cheete because he had been summoned to appear for the prosecution. He testified that, on the 13th of June, Mr. Francis Halkin had called at his office, and said that he wanted to inspect his Will.

" Did he seem at all agitated ? " asked Alaric Franklyn.

" I wouldn't say exactly agitated, Sir. He was a good deal troubled by the situation, as we all were. I wasn't particularly happy about it myself."

" On the day of the tragedy, did you receive a letter from him containing some supplementary instructions ? "

" I did. It arrived by the second post."

Alaric Franklyn passed an envelope across to the witness, who glanced at his own name and address.

" Is the letter in your hand the one that you received that morning, after the police had already discovered a copy in Mr. Halkin's desk ? "

" Yes, Sir."

" Would you kindly read it to the Court ? "

The witness read the letter aloud, beginning with Francis's reference to the uncertainty of life, continuing with the request that his manuscripts should be given to the Huntbachs " if you should ever be notified that my wife and I have fallen victim to the present situation ", and concluding with the instructions about the Kiddemores and the burial arrangements for himself and Sally. When the reading was concluded, the witness handed back the exhibit to the prosecuting Counsel.

" Is it a fact," inquired Mr. Franklyn, " that in the accused's Will, the person whom he had made responsible for his manuscripts and his musical interests generally, was Mrs. Halkin ? "

" That is so," replied Claude Fontaine reluctantly, endeavouring by his rueful expression to convey his apologies to the impassive Francis.

" Did the Will contain any instructions regarding his funeral ? "

" Yes, Sir."

" Was his wife included in these instructions, or did they refer only to himself ? "

" Only to himself," the witness answered, more reluctantly still.

" Thank you, Mr. Fontaine," said the prosecuting Counsel. Consulting his notes, he called the next witness.

" Thomas Coppenhall."

The smart, well-groomed garage proprietor stepped into the witness-box. He was the owner, he said, of a garage about half a mile from Dene Terrace on the way to Witnall, and was accustomed to look after Mr. Halkin's car. About 9.30 P.M. on June 14th he received a message from Mr. Halkin's gardener, Kiddemore, to the effect that the Buick needed an overhaul. Kiddemore had said that Mr. Halkin seemed rather distressed about the fall of Paris, and wanted to be sure that he knew how to immobilise the car in case of invasion.

"He was a good driver, but not very handy with mechanics," Mr. Coppenhall added.

"Is it not a fact," inquired Sir Lancelot, cross-examining him, "that Mr. Halkin promised to bring the car round on the following day?"

"That's so, Sir. About lunch-time, Kiddemore said."

"Are you aware that Mr. Halkin gave a good deal of time to A.R.P. work?"

"Oh, yes. He was Chief Warden at his factory. We sometimes talked about A.R.P. when he brought in his car."

Slowly and emphatically, Sir Lancelot put a final question.

"Did he ever mention his experiences in the last War?"

Tom Coppenhall looked surprised.

"Why, no," he answered. "I never knew Mr. Halkin was in the last War. We often discussed this one, but I don't remember a word about the other."

Ruth Alleyndene, equally surprised, explored her memory for the conversation that had taken place when she dined with the Halkins. Surely they had discussed the last War that night? . . . Yes — of course — she had told them about her brother Richard . . . and the death of Eugene Meury, her American lover . . . though naturally she hadn't mentioned that he was her lover. . . . And, after that, she was sure she had said something about Mr. Halkin and his wife being too young for the War . . . and they hadn't answered. Then there had been an interruption of some kind, and the conversation had changed.

She leaned over to Miriam.

"That's new to me, about his being in the last War," she said quietly. "I suppose you were aware of it?"

"Yes," whispered Miriam in reply, "but I didn't

discover it for quite two or three years."

" Wasn't that rather odd, when you knew them so well ? "

" It was, very. When I did find out, it wasn't from him, but from Sally. I was having tea with her one day, when we discovered in conversation that we'd each preserved all our husbands' letters. She took me upstairs to show me where she kept Francis's, and I saw the first one he ever wrote her."

" How old was he then ? " asked Ruth.

" Only about nineteen. The letter was in a careful schoolboyish handwriting, not a bit like his present illegible scrawl. It had the Active Service Censor's mark on the envelope, and Sally said he wrote it in a dug-out near Arras."

" What date was that ? "

" So far as I remember, about three months before the end of the War."

I was still at Hardelot then, thought Ruth. Not so very far from Arras. I'm sure I told the Halkins I was nursing there. Why didn't he mention that he'd been in France ?

He hadn't even told her, she recalled, after she wrote to him when he was first in prison, offering to help him in any way she could, and saying that her experience in the last War had given her some idea of what it meant to touch the deepest depths of sorrow. He had replied in a brief, restrained note, in which he had expressed his admiration for her work in Parliament, and, writing of his love and grief for Sally, remarked how completely the fear of death disappeared as soon as one had no more to live for.

" I understand now," he concluded, " why you went to Russia to care for the victims of famine and typhus after the 1918 Armistice. Did you ever recall those words from the *Pilgrim's Progress* which my mother read to me when I was a child, and which I have thought of so often in this place — ' How welcome death is to them that have nothing to do but to die ' ? "

In answer to that, she had written again :

"You probably cannot realise it now, but you certainly have much more to do than die. Even if you are never able to return to Halkins' — and even that is not inevitable in these days of swift events and short memories — you have still your symphonies and sonatas to write, and a new understanding, most dearly bought, to put into them. Though Sally's life may be ended, music is not ; it is one of those things that go on for ever, needing its interpreters all the more in such an age as this." . . .

An important witness, in response to the call for Annie Kiddemore, had now entered the box. Miriam regarded with compunction the plump familiar figure, and the anxious expression on Mrs. Kiddemore's amiable rosy face. She was the last person, Miriam ruminated, whom one would ever have connected with tragedy, murder and death.

" Were you and your husband employed by Mr. and Mrs. Halkin as daily cook and gardener ? " Alaric Franklyn began.

" Yes, Sir. We worked at 9 Dene Terrace for close on five year."

" Was Mr. Halkin on good terms with his wife ? "

" That he was," affirmed the witness eagerly. "Me and Kiddemore often said, he'd kick th' bucket for Mrs. Halkin and think himself lucky t' 'ave chance to do it."

" Did they spend much time in each other's company?"

" As much as they got the chance to, Sir. When the

master wasn't busy at factory or writin' music, they was always together at home and on holidays, exceptin' once or twice when Mr. Halkin went to foreign parts."

" Oh, he travelled, did he ? Where did he go ? "

" Different places, Sir," answered Mrs. Kiddemore vaguely. " He went t' America for some sort o' music festival — and once he was a long time in Germany."

That won't do Francis Halkin any good, thought Ruth, noticing a slight stir in both the jury-box and the Court as Annie Kiddemore uttered the unpopular name. We're not in a state of hysteria yet, but it's mounting with the heaviness of the raids. Before this trial's over, half the spectators will have him listed as a Nazi agent.

The K.C. continued his examination.

" On June 14th you were at Mr. Halkin's house as usual. What time was it when you last saw Mrs. Halkin ? "

" It was just after nine in th' evenin'. Th' master and mistress had been listenin' to th' wireless."

" Was Mrs. Halkin in her normal health ? "

The witness's brow wrinkled in perplexity.

" She wasn't ill," she answered after a pause. " But she wasn't so to speak normal, neither."

" What was the matter with her ? "

" She was cryin' about th' goin's-on in France," said Mrs. Kiddemore reluctantly. " Th' master was tryin' to comfort her. He was holdin' her hands."

Enid, endeavouring not to see too vividly the domestic picture that Mrs. Kiddemore's words called up, looked swiftly at Francis, but his eyes were closed. Was he living again through that sorrowful little scene at his vanished home — or was it beyond endurance to confront this friendly and troubled witness face to face ? She glanced at the witness-box to see that Mrs. Kiddemore had been replaced by the grey-haired gardener, who, with his stocky frame and red, good-natured countenance, might have been her twin rather than her husband.

" Did Mr. Halkin have any conversation with you before you left ? " Counsel was inquiring.

" Yessir. He came with me to th' door, and asked me to see Tom Coppenhall at garage about his car."

" Tell the Court what happened when you came on duty next morning."

Kiddemore launched out upon his narrative in a low, anxious voice.

" Me and th' missus arrived at th' house at seven o'clock as usual. As soon as we got there, we noticed th' black-out hadn't been done, and then we saw both th' dinin'-room windows had been left wide open. We went upstairs to see if anything had happened to th' master and mistress, but their bedroom was empty and th' bed hadn't been slept in."

" Did you find anything which might be connected with their absence ? "

" Yessir. Th' decanter was on dinin'-room table, and two empty glasses that smelt o' whisky."

" Were your employers in the habit of taking spirits ? "

" No, Sir. Th' master only drank whisky once in a blue moon, and I never knew the mistress touch a drop at all."

He continued with an effort.

" It was when we was in dinin'-room, th' missis remembered hearin' a splash as we came into Terrace. I hadn't noticed it meself, but I'm gettin' a bit hard o' hearin' on left side. She said it sounded as if 'twere down by river, and wi' things so queer at th' house, she thought I'd better step that way an' see."

" And what did you find when you reached the river ? "

" I saw what looked like heap o' clothes, half in water and half on bank. When I got closer I found it was th' master. I pulled him on grass, and shouted to th' missis to telephone for th' police."

" Did you give your master artificial respiration ? "

" No, Sir. I was fair meythered," said Kiddemore remorsefully, " and I didn't know th' master was still alive till later. When th' police came, they brought him round, and then Dr. Shelton put something in him with a syringe."

He looked apologetically at Francis, and this time, Enid noticed, Francis's eyes were open, and the faintest gleam of an expression appeared in their depths. I'm grateful to you, he seemed to be saying to Kiddemore. At least you didn't interfere like the others.

Sir Lancelot Prettyman stood up to cross-examine.

" Would you say that Mr. Halkin was more anxious about the war situation than his wife ? "

" They was both meythered by it, but th' mistress was the one to get upset. She was always listenin' to news on wireless."

" What sort of an employer was your master ? "

" First-rate, Sir. He was a grand employer, was Mr. Halkin."

" Would you say", inquired the Judge, leaning forward, " that he was considerate and responsible towards those in his charge ? "

" That he was, Your Worship. Very considerate and responsible indeed."

" Thank you," said Sir Lancelot, to Kiddemore's relief. Before leaving the witness-box, he looked with pleading perturbation at Francis's face, unable to gather from its renewed impassivity whether his testimony had done harm or good.

When Kiddemore retired from the Court, two police officers in succession took his place. The first, Inspector Henshaw, testified that he had photographed a section of the River Checkley, and later, when Mrs. Halkin's body was discovered, the stone bridge beneath which it had lain. The second, Police Constable Myatt, described how he had been called to 9 Dene Terrace, and had been taken through the garden to the river-bank, where the body of a man who appeared to have been drowned was lying.

" When I learned he'd only been in water a short time, I thought there might be life in him yet, so I knelt down on grass and gave artificial respiration till Dr. Shelton came."

At this point Enid observed a minute rekindling of interest in Francis's eyes as he turned his head towards the constable. Was he reflecting on the series of chances which had made this burly Staffordshire policeman into an instrument of destiny, spoiling his carefully-laid plans, interfering with his will to accompany Sally into the hidden hereafter, and exposing him instead to the unforeseen ordeal of a murder trial ?

" Did you find anything in the house which appeared to throw light on the tragedy ? " inquired prosecuting Counsel.

" Yes, Sir. There was a decanter on dining-room table, and two empty glasses which 'ad hobviously contained whisky."

" Anything else ? "

" We found some papers in th' prisoner's study," reported the constable. " One was copy of th' letter which Mr. Fountain read to Court just now, put with a copy of th' prisoner's Will. Then there was some sheets of music, with ' Funeral March ' on top and words written in pencil underneath."

" Can you tell the Court what they were ? "

" I don't rightly remember them now, Sir. Somethin' about bein' a failure. I know they give me the himpression that Mr. 'Alkin 'ad been thinkin' a good bit about 'is death, and th' Inspector agreed."

" Did you observe any evidence of a struggle between the couple, either in the house or garden ? "

" No, Sir. None whatever. Th' open windows in dinin'-room was th' only sign of anythin' out o' the way.

It's true th' garden was too dry for footsteps to leave any mark, but somethin' was bound to 'ave showed if they'd 'ad a scuffle."

" Would Dene Terrace be in a danger area in the event of an air raid on the district ? " asked Sir Lancelot, cross-examining.

" Well, not exactly in itself, Sir," the witness replied. " Them gardens cuts it off from Witnall proper. But it's right on th' edge of a danger harea. Mr. 'Alkin would likely have been the first warden called if the 'Uns had perpetrated a raid on that end of town."

The early shadows of the dark, rainy evening were already closing upon the Court when the two doctors, following the police officers, gave the final evidence for the prosecution. Dr. Shelton testified that he had found the prisoner unconscious but living, and had speeded up the process of revival begun by the constable. Later, when Mrs. Halkin's body had been recovered from the river, he calculated that she had been dead from nine to twelve hours.

" Did you find any injury on the body ? " inquired Alaric Franklyn.

" Yes. The right side of the head was severely bruised, and there was a small gash on the right temple."

" Was this injury consistent with the infliction of a blow ? "

" Yes. But it could equally well have been caused by a fall."

" Did it appear to you to have been a contributing cause of death ? "

" No. I formed the opinion — as the post-mortem later proved — that Mrs. Halkin had died from drowning."

Sir Lancelot rose to cross-examine.

" Would it have been possible for her to inflict this injury on herself ? "

" Only by falling. I hardly think that she could have

struck her own head with sufficient force."

Dr. Biddulph affirmed that he had known Mr. Halkin for several years in connection with the work of the Welfare Department at Fordham. He was a sensitive and conscientious man, but not more highly-strung than was consistent with his musical talents. The doctor had never before known him in a mental condition which in any way resembled his state of mind at Witnall Infirmary.

" Can you describe this mental condition ? " asked the defending Counsel.

" Not easily, Sir. It struck me as quite peculiar in my experience of the patient. He appeared, even when he had recovered from virtual drowning, to be totally unable to grasp the sequence of events or the fact of his wife's death."

Alaric Franklyn jumped up.

" Could this inability have been feigned, do you think ? "

" I don't believe so. It was not until I had called in Mr. Huntbach that the patient seemed able to recognise me, or anyone else he knew. He appeared to confuse us with acquaintances from the past."

Again the Judge leaned forward in his chair.

" I want to get this matter of the head injury straight. Could the husband have caused it if he had struck his wife by accident ? "

" Quite impossible, I should say," Dr. Shelton replied, returning to the witness-box. " The post-mortem revealed that it was a very heavy blow, sufficient to produce unconsciousness, though not to cause death. In my opinion, it could only have been inflicted deliberately, or else as the result of a headlong fall, of the kind that might occur if the lady had thrown herself over the bridge into the river. In the former case, one would have expected to find some signs of a struggle."

" The case for the Crown is now concluded, my Lord,"

announced Alaric Franklyn ; and the Judge adjourned the Court until the following day.

That evening, hour after hour through the long November black-out, Enid Clay sat alone in her lodgings staring into the dead remnants of an economical fire. Outside the shabby old-fashioned house, the stillness of the night was early broken by the sinister wailing of the air raid siren and the sound of German bombers clattering portentously overhead, followed by the distant booming of heavy guns. At midnight, restless and unhappy, Enid went out into the damp, dark street. A dull red glow in the sky to the south suggested that Birmingham, twenty miles away, was again the object of the main Nazi attack.

" If Mr. Francis is hanged," she thought, " I'll get a job in some dangerous place like Birmingham or London, and try to follow him."

For that possible means of exit, at least, she had the War to thank. All through the night, as she lay on the hard bed in her small cold room, her wakeful sleep was haunted by his changed face, and by the blank indifference which seemed to possess him towards the struggle being waged on his behalf between life and death.

CHAPTER XIV

HALKIN *v.* THE CROWN

THE FOLLOWING MORNING, Ruth Alleyndene and Miriam Huntbach arrived early to hear Sir Lancelot Prettyman open the case for the defence. The atmosphere of the Court was subdued by rumours of a second heavy raid on Birmingham, where many of those present had friends, which had lasted for nine hours of the night.

Anxiously concerned for the safety of Dr. Flint and his clinic, Mrs. Rushton and Wesley Bates had little attention to spare for the news that Hungary had joined the Axis, or even for the compensating triumphs of the Greeks, who were defeating the Italian armies in Epirus.

What mitigating explanation, Miriam wondered, as she watched the spectators queueing up for the seats on the public benches, could there be for a mutual decision to run away from life, with its burden of war and peril? What excuse would the defence find for Francis's failure to confront those dangers which must be borne by every humble employee who had looked to him for help and protection? These workers were no more responsible than himself for the disaster which had fallen upon the world, except in so far as they had permitted, by their acquiescence, the leadership of politicians whose blind complacency and lack of psychological understanding had so largely contributed to the return of war.

" I can't help wondering," she remarked with apparent inconsequence, " how the people responsible for our politics can bear to think of their share in bringing catastrophe on everyone else."

" If they'd felt like that, there wouldn't have been any catastrophe," responded Ruth, as though she had read her thoughts. "And then Mr. Halkin wouldn't have been in the dock. A few of us in Parliament did what we could to make them realise how things were going, but we were mostly out of the House in the critical years between 1931 and 1935. And now, just because we belong to the Parliamentary Peace Group, they pay no attention to anything we say."

Enid Clay, who was sitting immediately in front of them, turned suddenly round.

" Some people *must* hear the voices crying in the wilderness," she said, glancing at Miriam. " Otherwise societies like the Quakers wouldn't exist."

Ruth smiled warmly, encouraged by this appreciation from a young voter in her own constituency.

" That's our hope — that a few more people will hear the voices in each generation," she said. " It's the best hope we have."

The Court had now assembled and Francis came up the steps into the dock, giving to each woman, for different reasons, the same sense of shocked incongruity that she had felt the previous morning. But they all noticed that today both his demeanour and his expression had changed. His back appeared more upright, and a tense expectancy had replaced yesterday's impassive weariness.

As soon as the Judge was seated, Sir Lancelot Prettyman rose to open the case for the defence. He would have, he said, to discuss an unfamiliar topic at some length, but this, he hoped, would not prevent the jury from realising that before any answer was demanded from the accused, it rested with the prosecution to establish that the prisoner was guilty of the murder of his wife.

" Mrs. Halkin, it has been stated, died from drowning some time between 9.30 P.M. and midnight on the evening of June 14th." He leaned impressively forward to emphasise the next point in the minds of the jury. " This case is confused by the fact that the unfortunate lady, just before or at the time of her death, received a severe head injury, which, it is suggested, might have been inflicted by her husband in a fit of passion. But — apart from the affectionate relations between the couple, and the absence of any signs of a struggle which the evidence for the prosecution has confirmed — I want you to understand that this blow, though sufficient to produce unconsciousness, did not cause the death of Mrs. Halkin, or even accelerate it in the slightest degree. If the prosecution could establish that Mr. Halkin was responsible for the injury, it would throw some light upon his conduct, but it would not prove that he put his wife into the river.

We can, therefore, dismiss it from our minds so far as the charge of murder is concerned."

The attentive faces in the jury-box looked vaguely puzzled, and the crowded spectators, scenting the development of some unexpected line of defence, stopped coughing and shuffling, and settled down to a listening immobility.

"The evidence indicates," continued Sir Lancelot, "that Mr. and Mrs. Halkin were last seen in each other's company on June 14th, just after the nine o'clock news bulletin reporting the fall of Paris. After that, there is nothing to prove that they acted together. We know that Mr. Halkin accompanied the Kiddemores to the front door, leaving his wife in the drawing-room greatly distressed by the impending collapse of France and the consequently increased threat of invasion to this country. It has been suggested to you by the prosecution that the empty whisky glasses found on the dining-room table were in some way connected with the tragedy, and might even provide evidence of a quarrel due to intoxication. But we have no proof that this whisky was consumed *after* the couple were seen together listening to the wireless. What could be more natural than that Mr. and Mrs. Halkin — depressed, as we all were, by the critical events of that day — should depart so far from their usual custom as to have a glass of whisky *before* the news, or even immediately after their evening meal ? "

The Judge had now begun to make notes, and the reporters' pencils skimmed the white pages of their notebooks under the incandescent harebells as the famous Counsel's narration proceeded.

As the jury knew, he said, the accused had apparently been in his usual health, and taking part in a conversation with his gardener, up till about 9.15 on the night of June 14th. They would have noted from Mr. Coppenhall's evidence that the prisoner intended to take his car to the garage to be overhauled at lunch-time the following day.

Yet within an hour or two of that suggestion his wife was dead, and he himself was found in the river early next morning.

Again Sir Lancelot leaned significantly towards the jury.

" I put it to you that the real inference from these facts would be that, when the accused returned to the drawing-room from talking to the Kiddemores at the front door, he found that his wife was missing, or perhaps saw her running or walking towards the river. After searching for hours and finally realising that she was gone, he attempted in desperation to destroy himself also. You are aware that Mrs. Halkin died before midnight, whereas her husband did not even enter the water until Mrs. Kiddemore heard the splash about 7 A.M., and was taken from it within ten or fifteen minutes. These are features of the case which, as they stand, form no proof at all that the death of the wife was caused by any act of the accused."

Throughout these opening passages of Sir Lancelot's oration, Ruth, Enid and Miriam had listened with undivided attention. None of them could quite perceive in which direction defending Counsel was leading the Court ; the points he made seemed to confuse rather than clarify the issues. But now, as he continued, a growing enlightenment began to dawn upon their minds.

" If, however, it *was* an act, or a series of acts, on the part of the accused which terminated his wife's existence, we have in this case some remarkable factors to consider which, while not unfamiliar in the history of crime, will present you with problems which will doubtless seem unusual. My friend spoke of a defence of insanity, but that is not the ground on which we propose to take our stand. It is a defence of automatic action performed in a state of amnesia arising from a loss of control by certain vital functions of the brain. In considering this aspect of the matter you will have the advantage of evidence by important psychological experts, of whom one has long been familiar with the life-work and character of the accused, and has assisted him in carrying out the socially valuable changes which he introduced into his factory."

So at least Dr. Flint isn't dead ! thought the listeners from Halkins' with relief. The twelve brows in the jury-box knit with painful concentration as the learned Counsel began to discuss the various forms of amnesia and their causes. It was a phenomenon, he said, which the suffering and strain of the last War had brought into prominence, and which was already far more common in this one than most of them realised. The stress and anxiety due to the present air raids were, unfortunately, likely to lead to its increase.

" It is only in a small proportion of these cases that any act of a criminal or tragic nature occurs. Such an act is due to the same cause as the minor acts of apparent eccentricity which are more common: namely, the exist-ence, as it were, of a gulf or barrier between the control-ling functions of the brain, and the executive actions performed by the body. That is why no one can foretell how the victims of this psychological phenomenon are likely to behave. My learned colleague has stated that evidence exists of premeditation on the part of the accused, regarding not only his own death, but that of his wife. I put it to you that this evidence indicates anxiety rather than premeditation. One of the facts not yet fully under-stood by psychologists is the manner in which a condition of apprehension experienced by a person in his rational state, may influence his behaviour when his normal control is lacking, in such a way as to suggest intention. A man thus afflicted is not, however, insane. He is merely turned by his previous fears in the direction of actions which he has temporarily lost the power to appreciate.

" The expert witnesses whom I am calling will give evidence relating to the mental qualities that control the body, and will also discuss the phenomena that ensue when this control is absent. Their judgment will not only be based on present observations of the accused, and his actions with regard to the pitiful tragedy that we are here to consider. The story of Mr. Halkin's liability to loss of memory begins with the closing months of the last War."

Ruth Alleyndene started. She and Miriam Huntbach exchanged significant glances, while a peculiar sound, like a strangled sigh, came from the now excited listeners on the public benches. Ignoring it, Sir Lancelot continued.

" On August 21st, 1918, the accused was involved in the great offensive action conducted by General Sir Julian Byng between Albert and Arras. At that time he had been less than two weeks at the front. He is, as you are aware, a music composer of considerable distinction, and it is obvious that he would be more sensitive to musical influences than most young men of his age. Just before going into the battle, he was listening to a piece of music — a sacred song — played on his portable gramophone. From the time that he heard this piece until he found himself being carried on a stretcher to the Casualty Clearing Station — a period of more than three days — the prisoner's mind was a blank."

There was no noise in the tense Court now. Enid Clay, her hands locked tightly in her lap, sat with her eyes fixed on Sir Lancelot for fear of missing a word. She felt as though she were seeing a faint glimmer of light after groping for days through a long black corridor. For the first time since she had come to Stafford, the certainty that Francis would be condemned to death began to recede a little.

" In this connection," said Counsel emphatically to the jury, " it is important for you to remember that, four or five days before the battle, the accused was blown over and buried by a bomb and remained unconscious for an hour. He was wounded, though not seriously, in the action itself, but he had, and still has, no recollection of receiving this wound. He did not fully recover awareness until he found himself at the Casualty Clearing Station being attended by an orderly. On another occasion a few weeks later, when the War was almost at an end, his mind became a blank during a regimental concert. But this time the loss of memory — of which evidence will be put before you — lasted only for a short period."

Sir Lancelot bent impressively forward.

" Those months of war provided his first experience of the state that doctors call ' amnesia ' — meaning a failure of awareness, combined with loss of control by the mind over the executive functions of the body. But the prisoner's liability to this loss of control did not end with the War."

He paused a moment before continuing.

" Towards the end of 1924, when Mr. Halkin was living in London with his newly-married wife, he was selected to perform at an annual concert arranged by a well-known musical patron, Lady Floria Ledburne, as a means of launching promising musicians. At that time he had only recently completed his period as a student at the Royal College of Music, and intended to be a pianist as well as a composer. You will be told by Lady Floria herself how his power of memory and concentration suddenly failed when he was actually on the platform at the Welbeck Hall, about to begin his performance."

The three women gasped simultaneously. For a second, Enid turned her head.

" I never knew that ! Did you know it, Mrs. Hunt-bach ? "

" No, my dear. He never told us why he gave up the idea of being a pianist."

" Now I understand — oh, several things that have puzzled me ! " whispered Enid, suddenly remembering the conversation in which she and Mrs. Rushton had discussed Francis's reasons for leaving London and joining his father. One of the things that puzzled her had been his reticence about his early years. It would not have been surprising if it had extended only to her ; but Mrs. Rushton, so long his confidential secretary, had known next to nothing of his life in London, apart from the rumours which circulated the factory before she began to work there. Enid listened intently as Counsel concluded his opening speech.

" From that time onward the accused abandoned his proposed career as an executive musician, and returned home to become his father's partner in the family business. He gave it up — and indeed ceased to play the piano altogether — because his mind had become a blank at the critical moment of his public performance, and he had been advised by a specialist that, under similar conditions of strain, his liability to lose control over himself was likely to recur.

" Therefore, ladies and gentlemen of the jury, you are not dealing with a man who, looking for something to explain his actions, puts forward the defence that his mind, or memory, suddenly failed. The witnesses whom I shall call will prove to you that, from the time of his earliest manhood, the accused was subject to this condition. The defence therefore holds that there is no proof that Mrs. Halkin's death was occasioned by the prisoner, but that, if it was, he was the victim of unconscious action, and cannot be held responsible in law for anything that he did."

Counsel turned towards the dock, while the Court waited for the next move in this extraordinary drama. The spectators held their breath as he announced firmly : " I call the accused ! "

When Francis went to the witness-box, Enid realised at once the truth of her impression that he was a changed person from the man of the previous day. His eyes were resolute and vigilant ; his head was held high. It seemed obvious that he was going to defend himself with all the vigour and vitality still at his command — a decision, she thought, which was foreshadowed in the note he had written from prison in reply to her tentative letter wishing him well. His answer had been brief, almost curt — but it was not the letter of a defeated man.

" DEAR MISS CLAY,
" Your sympathy is appreciated. It was good of you to write.
" Next week I shall be called upon to explain the events of last summer. I can only say that I shall try to do so with honesty and courage.
" Yours sincerely,
" FRANCIS KEYNSHAM HALKIN."

She realised now that what she had taken for the impassivity of despair had been merely a conservation of strength. His life still meant something to him ; he still believed that he could make good use of it, and he meant to fight for the right to live it. For Enid, the reference to the Welbeck Hall episode had thrown a new light on Francis's history. It showed her that already he had confronted failure, and snatching his energy and skill from the very jaws of defeat, had built with their aid a doubly distinguished career. If he had done that once, he could do it again ; he could carry his life back to its pinnacle from the utter depths into which it had fallen.

Counsel for the defence began now to put the first formal questions, and Francis replied without hesitation. Yes, he said, he had studied at the Royal College of Music after the Great War. Before that, immediately after leaving school, he had joined the Staffordshire Fusiliers. He arrived in France on August 9th, 1918, and took part in the offensive of August 21st. All but five of his platoon became casualties.

" Do you recall anything of the battle ? " inquired Sir Lancelot.

" Nothing whatever," answered Francis promptly. " I remember listening to my portable gramophone in the orchard at our billets, and knowing that we were going up the line for a big show. The next thing I recall is lying on a stretcher carried by two R.A.M.C. orderlies. I remember looking at an enormous red star and thinking I was having a nightmare, until it suddenly shrank to the size of an ordinary planet."

" What happened after that ? "

" I had another fade-out. This time apparently it was quite brief ; my memory began to function again when I was sitting on a chair at the Casualty Clearing Station being given an injection by an orderly."

" After you recovered from your wound, did you have any repetition of that experience ? "

" Yes. It must have been just before the Armistice, as it was late autumn and we were constantly on the move. I remember sitting down for a regimental sing-song after supper one night, and then came a gap till the whole thing was over. I tried to explain to a young subaltern who had just joined our Company that I wasn't drunk."

The spectators relaxed for a moment while Sir Lancelot consulted his notes. He started then on a different line of inquiry.

" Did you and your wife become engaged after the War ? "

A shudder seemed to pass through Francis — almost imperceptible, yet visible to Enid.

" Yes," he replied. " In 1920."

" And when were you married ? "

" September, 1924."

Sir Lancelot paused. Then he inquired : " Were you and your wife quite happy together ? "

But this time Francis could not reply at once. He

turned very pale, while Enid gripped the bench, sharing
his anguish, and the Court appeared to hold its breath
as he struggled for self-control. Finally, in a toneless
voice which seemed to have been squeezed dry of all
emotion, he answered : " More than happy. She was life
itself."

His Counsel again changed the subject.

" Were you chosen by Lady Floria Ledburne to play as
soloist at a concert in November, 1924 ? "

" I was."

" Do you recall your item on the programme ? "

" Yes. It was Tchaikowsky's Pianoforte Concerto in
B flat minor."

" Tell the Court what happened when you started to
play it."

Francis stood still for a moment, remembering. Then
he said slowly : " Before I sat down at the piano, the
atmosphere of the concert hall made me feel faint. Then
the music went out of my head, because a . . . song I
used to play on the gramophone in the War seemed to
drown it. My hands began to tremble, and then everything went blank. My next recollection is of sitting in
Lady Floria's room at Claridge's."

" So *that's* the origin of the supposed love-affair ! "
said Enid to herself. Sir Lancelot turned from Francis to
the jury.

" It was reported to the defence," he said, " by Mrs.
Alfred Huntbach that Mrs. Halkin had kept all her
husband's letters in a box in her bedroom at Dene Terrace.
I propose to read one of these to the Court. It was
written on November 20th, 1924, the day after the
occurrence at the Welbeck Hall."

He unfolded a sheet of paper and began to read aloud.

" ' My own Darling ' . . ."

Again Francis went deadly pale, holding on to the

edge of the box while an almost hypnotic silence surrounded him.   When he hid his face in his hands, Enid
closed her eyes.   Inexorably the reading continued.

"'MY OWN DARLING,
"'I am afraid that what I have to tell you is more
painful than words can describe, but it just has to be
faced.   My performance last night was worse than a
failure ; it was a complete disaster.   Before I even
started to play the Concerto I had a kind of fainting fit,
and knew nothing more until I found myself in Lady
Floria's rooms at Claridge's.   Considering the way I
had let her down she was more than kind to me ; she
kept me there till I felt quite myself again, and then sent
me home in a taxi.
"'By her advice I went to see a West End nerve
specialist, Dr. George Gifford, in Wimpole Street this
morning.   After asking me various questions about the
War, etc., he told me that I ought to avoid any work
which involved the strain of public appearances.   He
advised me to stick to composing, and suggested that I
could combine this with business.   So, after thinking it
over for a long time, I have just written to Dad to say that
I will do as he wishes, and join him at the factory.'"

Sir Lancelot cleared his throat, and went on more
slowly and impressively.

"'I am afraid, my darling, it will be a great disappointment to you that I have to give up the career
from which we both hoped so much.   But these consequences of the War only affect one aspect of my music.
Now that I understand my own limitations better, they
are never likely to trouble either of us again. . . .'"

"*Oh !*" cried Enid, gripping the bench once more.
The tears started to her eyes as she heard a similar stifled
exclamation from Miriam Huntbach behind her.   Un-

moved by the stir of emotion which had swept across the Court, Counsel read the letter to the end.

"'I don't know how to ask your forgiveness after the way you have helped me and all the work you have put in for our charming little home, which reminds me of you every moment of the day. Never mind, we will make another one just as good.

"'I do hope Maman is better, and that you won't have any more anxiety about her to add to this new distress which I have so unintentionally brought upon you.

"'Ever with most devoted love, my own sweetheart,
        "'Your adoring husband,
                        "'Francis.'"

Enid looked up to see the man who had written those words standing erect, with his head once again held high. As handkerchiefs were put back into pockets all over the Court, Sir Lancelot took up his examination.

"According to this letter, the specialist you saw advised you to discontinue executive music?"

"Yes. He thought I ought to keep to the creative side. So I decided to join my father in business, and give all my spare time to composition."

At this point the Judge made one of his rare interventions.

"Where is this Dr. Gifford, Sir Lancelot? Are you not calling him?"

"We naturally intended to do so, my Lord," Counsel answered regretfully. "Unfortunately, we were informed that he died in the South of France in 1935. But Lady Floria is here to give evidence."

"I see," commented Mr. Justice Dannefroy. "Let the accused carry on with his story."

Francis described how he had left London almost at once, and returned to Staffordshire to go into partnership with his father at Halkins'. He and Dr. David Flint had introduced many changes into the factory for the benefit of the employees, who numbered about a thousand. All the time that he could spare from these responsibilities was given to musical composition, which he had endeavoured, whenever possible, to relate to the life and interests of the Potteries. In addition to Staffordshire Musical Festivals, works of his had been performed by the British National Opera Company, the Royal Philharmonic Society, the Russian Ballet, the Welbeck Symphony Orchestra, the Boston Symphony Orchestra, and the Michigan Opera Company at the Ann Arbor Festival. He had travelled extensively for the purpose of making musical contacts, both on the Continent and in the United States.

"What were your reactions towards a second World War?" inquired Sir Lancelot.

"I was very unhappy about it, especially just before its outbreak. During the first six months, I hoped and even believed that extreme violence might be avoided. But when the invasions began, the months of respite made them seem all the more sinister."

"Did you personally expect to be much affected?"

"Yes," answered Francis slowly. "I saw the War as wrecking both the international side of my music, and the attempts I had made to give new ideas and standards to our workers. After all the time I'd spent in trying to interpret our community to other countries through my compositions, the nations of Europe were going to be at loggerheads again just as though the years of peace had never occurred."

"You expected that the last War really would end war — at any rate for your lifetime?"

"Yes. I believed that it *had* ended it — until 1933. Then I gradually realised that the first War, and the Treaty which followed it, had made the second inevitable."

Again there was a stir in Court. Was the war-time

public agreeing or disapproving ?   Rather hurriedly, Sir
Lancelot abandoned one controversial topic for another.

"What did you feel about air raid precautions ? "

" I wasn't at all keen on them at first.   In fact, when
the idea was first discussed by our firm about five years
ago, I began by opposing it.   It seemed to me that these
preparations would cause people to take another war for
granted in advance.   But when the international situation
became worse, I realised that our factory couldn't do
without them.   So I tried to get enthusiastic about my
work as Warden, but I'm afraid I haven't the right kind
of temperament."

" In what way do you regard yourself as unsuited to
such work ? "

Francis considered, and then replied :   " I suppose my
imagination operates too vividly.   Instead of concentrat-
ing on the precautions themselves, I began to think more
about the disasters they were designed to prevent.   This
made me sleep badly, and I began dreaming about the
last War — and then about air raids.   In these dreams I
imagined I was looking for corpses in burning buildings —
or dragging people I knew out of ruins."

" Can you tell the Court which of those imagined
corpses was the most familiar to you ? "

Shuddering from head to feet, Francis closed his eyes.
Almost inaudibly, he replied :   " Yes.   Once I thought I
saw my wife's dead body — and it was headless."

Sir Lancelot resolutely disregarded the stifled exclamations that burst from the Court.   He passed a document
over to Francis ; it was the letter that he had written to
Claude Fontaine.

" Do you remember writing that letter ? " inquired
Counsel.

" I do."

" What was your purpose in leaving directions for
your musical compositions to be given to Mr. Huntbach,

when you had already made your wife your music executor in your Will ? "

Francis paused, understanding all too clearly what a weapon these alternative instructions had proved in the hands of the prosecution.

" When I left those directions," he finally said, " we were facing the fall of Paris, which in a short time was likely to mean the collapse of France. Most people thought that the next development would be the invasion of England — with whole families getting annihilated, or taken prisoner, and relatives never seeing one another again."

" Had you ever thought of committing suicide in those circumstances ? "

" Certainly not." He meditated, and continued : " I was responsible for the factory, and the protection of our workers. It would have been my last thought to leave them in the lurch. But we knew what invasion had meant to Holland and Belgium. I did picture Witnall suffering the fate of Rotterdam — and my wife and myself being killed without trace. There seemed to be a chance, though, that if we went, the Huntbachs might escape. That was the whole explanation of the instructions. Since then, after all, whole families have been wiped out in the air raids."

" Did your wife know you had written this letter ? "

" Certainly she did. I showed it to her before I signed it, just after breakfast on June 14th."

Sir Lancelot made an impressive pause. Then he inquired : " Do you remember writing another letter, of some importance to yourself, the previous day ? "

This time Francis answered eagerly.

" Yes. I wrote to Mr. Wilson P. Taft, the conductor of the Pennsylvania Symphony Orchestra, agreeing to write a concerto they wanted for this autumn. They were arranging a special programme of the work of British composers."

" Did you ever post your letter ? "

" My wife posted it in Witnall when she went to tea with the Huntbachs."

Sir Lancelot turned to the Judge.

" I have a deposition here from Mr. Taft, my Lord, confirming that letter's receipt."

The Judge nodded, and Counsel continued.

" On June 14th, did you hear the six o'clock news on the wireless ? "

" No," said Francis. " I was driving into Witnall to fetch my wife just at that hour."

" And your wife did not hear it either ? "

" No. She was with the Huntbachs, and they never followed the news as closely as we did."

" Then you did not know the day's events for certain till you listened-in at 9 P.M. ? "

" The wireless bulletin was our first intimation. Hearing the news of the fall of Paris is the last thing I remember that evening — except for one other incident."

" What was that ? "

Francis hesitated. Then he replied resolutely : " I remember turning on a musical programme, and thinking I heard a particular piece of music."

" Was that piece familiar to you ? "

" Yes. It was a song called the *Morning Hymn*, which I had played on my gramophone in France just before we went up for the attack."

" Had you ever heard it since ? "

" In a sense, yes. It was the piece that put the Tchaikowsky Concerto out of my head when I collapsed at the Welbeck Hall."

This time the exclamations were audible. Again ignoring them, Counsel proceeded.

" What next do you recall after thinking you heard that song on the wireless ? "

" I remember," Francis replied, " waking from what

seemed like a sleep to find my old music-master at Cheete College sitting beside my bed. I tried to ask him what he was doing there, and he gradually turned into my friend Alfred Huntbach."

" Had you any idea at that time that your wife was dead ? "

" None whatever. As soon as I realised where I was, I spoke to Dr. Biddulph about her leaving Witnall, in case the raids started. All my ideas were very confused, but I had a general impression that I'd persuaded her to go."

" Until you were charged with her murder, then, you had no notion of the circumstances of her death ? "

" No. Before Alfred Huntbach convinced me, I was not aware that she had died at all."

Francis then described how, while he was in Witnall prison, he had been examined by a number of doctors. Among them was the Medical Officer of Kingsport Prison.

" Do you remember any incidents connected with the day that you saw him ? " asked Counsel.

" Yes. We were talking in a waiting-room next to one of the sink-rooms, and all through our conversation a tap which needed attention was splashing into an enamel basin."

" Did Dr. Slaithwaite notice it ? "

" He did. He asked me to turn it off, but I couldn't stop the water."

To the now tensely expectant listeners, the pause before Sir Lancelot's next question seemed long. Slowly, impressively, he continued his examination.

" Did the noise of the running water remind you of anything ? "

" Yes. It seemed to have a queer sort of connection with the sound I always heard echoing through my brain before a loss of consciousness. It was like a rushing torrent. I kept on thinking about that sound all day."

" Tell the Court what happened after you went to bed that night."

Francis hesitated, trembling all over and now very pale. At last, throwing back his head, he forced himself to utter the next few sentences.

" Some time after I went to sleep, I had an unusually vivid dream. I seemed to be standing in my garden gazing down at someone lying on a path. The light was rather dim, and I had to look closely to see who it was. I realised then that the person was my wife. Her eyes were closed and she seemed to be asleep. I knelt down and tried to call her name, but found I couldn't utter a word."

As he stood gripping the edge of the box, his face turned a yellowish white like the face of a corpse. The Judge leaned forward.

" If you wish, you may take a short rest before you continue."

Coming out of the trance into which he had almost fallen, Francis faced the Judge.

" Thank you, my Lord, but I should prefer to go on. I'd rather get it over."

" As you will," said Mr. Justice Dannefroy, and the hearing proceeded.

" Do you remember anything more about this dream?" inquired Sir Lancelot.

" Yes. The dim light in my garden went dark, and suddenly I seemed to hear a tremendous splash. I woke up to find myself out of bed at the other end of the cell, with my pillow clasped tightly in my arms. I felt confused, and very cold. At last I found the bell, and rang it, and an officer came in. He helped me back to bed and gave me a sedative, but I didn't go to sleep again." He shuddered, wiped away the sweat that trickled down his forehead into his eyes, and added, stifling a groan, " I was afraid to sleep. I lay listening to the sound of water for the rest of the night. Next morning I saw Dr. Slaithwaite again, and related my dream."

I can't endure this much longer, thought Miriam. It's exactly like watching a crucifixion.

But in the same moment, she knew that because Francis had to endure it, she must and would. And suddenly she realised that his ordeal was indeed a crucifixion in the deepest sense. By his suffering he was expiating not only his own terrible though perhaps unintentional act, but the guilt of those whose national policy had made use of him to his undoing. He was paying part of the heavy cost of errors which had again plunged the world into sorrow ; he had taken upon himself the sins of his contemporaries, and in his own person was bearing their afflictions. . . .

This is what happens when a civilised community goes to war, thought Ruth Alleyndene. Every great war renders its account to the society that made it, but those responsible are seldom the ones who pay. It's civilisation itself, not Francis Halkin, that ought to be in the dock. It evolves these highly sensitive, creative types, and then sets them to do the work of barbarism . . . and years afterwards we get maladjustment, resulting from shock, showing itself in mental disorganisation. He's like a man in a Greek tragedy, the sport of circumstances which he couldn't control. When he talked about one country interpreting itself to another through music, he was giving expression to the civilised principle in face of the organised forces arrayed against him . . . . Yet how strange it is that the same society which drives thousands anonymously into battle, will also spend three days patiently examining a man's personality and discussing his future ! . . .

But Enid Clay only thought : " I wish I were there in the dock beside him ! I wish I could take his hand, and make him feel by holding it that none of this makes a scrap of difference ; that I'm his whenever he wants me, any way, any time."

Her reflections were interrupted by the metallic tones of Alaric Franklyn, cross-examining.

" You have told the Court of a collapse you experienced at a concert where you had been specially chosen to perform. Doesn't this indicate an unusual shrinking from situations demanding courage and presence of mind ? "

Francis dragged himself out of the semi-coma of exhaustion, and faced the young Counsel steadily.

" I have dealt with many situations in my factory which required presence of mind — and even courage," he said with dignity. " But the one thing I cannot do, and have never done since that day, is to play a musical instrument at a public performance."

Sir Lancelot jumped to his feet.

" If my learned friend will forgive me, I should like to ask accused to elucidate that point."

With weary patience, Francis explained.

" I have already told the Court that when I saw the nerve specialist, Dr. George Gifford, he advised me to avoid public appearances. The reason was that the feeling of tension somehow became associated with the battle where my memory first ceased to function. It was tied up with a fear of failure . . . of letting people down."

" A fear of quite a special character ? " asked the Judge, intervening.

" Yes. Quite different from anything else in my experience."

" Did you ever have this reaction to playing in public before the last War ? "

" Never, my Lord. I used to perform regularly at school concerts, and for some months before I joined the army I was acting as temporary organist at Fordham Church."

"Surely you must have been called on to play publicly while you were at the Royal College of Music?"

"That's true. But they were either student perform-ances, or amateur concerts at home. Nothing vital, or final, depended on any one of them."

Mr. Franklyn resumed his cross-examination.

"Did you tell Dr. Slaithwaite of Kingsport Prison that when you dreamt of your wife lying on the garden path, you noticed a trickle of blood running down her cheek from a cut in her head?"

"Yes," said Francis. "I remember that. I didn't omit it on purpose. The dream was confused in spite of its vividness, and I can't recollect every detail all the time."

"Are you not aware that when your wife's body was taken from the River Checkley, her head was found to be injured?"

"Yes. I am aware of that."

"Then do you not agree that this part of your dream — or recollection — has peculiar significance?"

"I suppose it has."

"It suggests, does it not, that the injury to your wife's head preceded her fall into the river?"

"Yes," said Francis, while the three women watching him, perceiving the direction of the prosecution's questions, felt their hearts sink within them.

"Yet you ask the Court to believe that you have no recollection of the way in which this injury occurred?"

"I have no recollection whatever."

The young Counsel flung back his gown, resolutely aggressive.

"I suggest to you that you quarrelled with your wife, struck her in anger, and, fearing the consequences of your deed, threw her while unconscious into the water."

Francis confronted him steadily.

"I do not recall anything of the kind," he reiterated with determination.

Dexterously Alaric Franklyn diverted the line of inquiry.

" You have told my distinguished colleague that when you left instructions for your musical compositions to be entrusted to Mr. Huntbach, you visualised your wife, as well as yourself, being killed without trace ? "

" That is so."

" Why, then, in this same letter to Mr. Fontaine, did you leave such precise instructions regarding the burial arrangements for both of you ? "

" I couldn't be sure there would be no trace of us. The instructions were similar to the ones I left in my Will, which was made long before the War."

Counsel leapt into the breach which Francis, in his growing weariness, had unwittingly made in his own defences.

" But is it not a fact that the funeral instructions in your Will referred only to yourself ? "

" Yes.   That's true."

" Why, then, did you add your wife's name to the new document ? "

Francis was silent for a moment.   Then he replied, in a voice almost toneless with fatigue : " I have told you. The whole letter was due to the general threat of invasion."

Again Counsel slightly shifted his ground.

" Do you remember composing the first draft of a funeral march ? "

" I do."

" At what date was that march composed ? "

" About three days before the fall of Paris."

" Did you write beneath the title these words : ' Dirge for the death of a failure ' ? "

" Yes," Francis admitted reluctantly.

" Do not those words suggest that you regarded yourself as a failure, and were contemplating death ? "

" Not necessarily.   One can have moods of self-disgust, and even wish one were dead, without any real idea of ending one's life."

" I put it to you that this manuscript and your letter to Mr. Fontaine, taken together, provide irrefutable evidence of a determination to end not only your own life, but that of your wife."

For the first time, Francis's self-control gave way.

" My Lord ! " he exclaimed passionately, turning to the Judge, " have I no claim on your protection ? He's putting forward, as evidence of premeditation, fears and precautions which must have been common to half the population of this country six months ago ! Ever since the last War I've always tended to be apprehensive about disasters, but that doesn't mean I was plotting to murder my wife ! "

Quietly the Judge rebuked him.

" You must answer his questions as he puts them. It will be the responsibility of the jury to decide whether his presumptions are justified. That is what they are here for."

Francis bowed his head humbly.

" I apologise, my Lord," he said.

Enid clenched her hands impotently, feeling in her own nerves every surge of Francis's exasperation with the professional obstinacy of the prosecuting Counsel, every effort to achieve the strenuous discipline which alone could avoid the pitfall of self-justification.

" Oh, Francis ! " she breathed, " you've been a magnificent witness ! Even with everything — your life, your work, your future — at stake, you're more clear-headed and downright than any of them. Sir Lancelot was right to call on you ! "

But at the very moment that she sought for a self-control which would rival Francis's own, she realised that the cross-examination had ended, and Sir Lancelot Prettyman was on his feet.

" Was this funeral march the only piece of its kind you had written ? "

" No, Sir. I wrote a short dirge for the organ after the death of my father. It was played at the village church when he was buried."

The Judge bent towards him, pencil and notebook in hand.

" Was there any connection in your mind between the draft of your funeral march, and the piece of music that you believed you heard on the wireless on June 14th ? "

" So far as my memory goes, my Lord, none whatever."

" And to the best of your recollection, there was no struggle between you and your wife after you heard that music ? "

" No, my Lord."

" Not even in the dream in prison which you have related to the Court ? "

With slow emphasis, Francis replied : " I remember nothing of the kind."

" Thank you ; that is all," said the Judge.

Francis stood still for a moment. He looked at the Judge, then at the jury, and finally round the Court ; his mind seemed closed to the realisation that his ordeal was over. For a second he trembled and swayed, as though his knees were giving way and he was about to crumple up. Then, with a last backward gesture of his head, he drew himself erect and walked resolutely down the steps to the dock.

He had been in the witness-box for two and a half hours.

CHAPTER XV

OLYMPIAN EVIDENCE

THAT AFTERNOON the Court met in a subdued atmosphere of anti-climax to hear the remaining evidence for the defence.

Francis, tired and pale, had relapsed into his former attitude of impassive fatigue. Ruth and Miriam shared the sense of emerging, severely buffeted by storms, from a turbulent ocean on to an island which offered temporary security, though it was not yet the farther shore. The anxious, benevolent faces of Wesley Bates and Mrs. Rushton gave the same impression of watchful respite. But Enid Clay felt that she understood for the first time the words of Isaiah : " When thou passest through the waters, I will be with thee ". They sustained her when, for a brief moment, she followed Mrs. Rushton into the witness-box to testify that on the morning of June 14th, Mr. Francis Halkin had dictated his letters with speed and efficiency.

The Court reawakened to attention when Lady Floria Ledburne appeared to give evidence. Across the gulf of years in which they had never again met, the wealthy society woman and her former protégé confronted each other. Her shiny raven hair was now an immaculate white, but the same intelligent dark eyes looked keenly round from the same heavily powdered face, and her mink coat was a duplicate of the one she had worn at the Welbeck Hall in 1924.

" Do you recognise the accused as the performer at the concert you arranged ? " Sir Lancelot asked her.

" Yes," she replied, with a small inscrutable smile as her eyes seemed to penetrate through the haggard face before her to the spirit behind it. " I should say that, fundamentally, he hasn't changed much. I should have known him anywhere."

In response to Counsel's questions, she admitted with imperturbable frankness how greatly Francis's personality had attracted her when she first heard him play at the Royal College of Music. She then described the arrangements for the concert at which she had selected him to appear.

" Can you remember what occurred on the evening of the performance ? " Counsel inquired.

" Very clearly. It isn't the sort of thing that happens repeatedly in a lifetime."

" Would you kindly describe your recollections to the Court ? "

Without pause, she began her narrative.

" I was talking to Sir Marcus Mitcham when Mr. Keynsham arrived. The piece he had selected was Tchaikowsky's Pianoforte Concerto in B flat minor, and I had arranged with Sir Marcus for the Welbeck Symphony Orchestra to take part — very fortunately, as things turned out. As soon as I saw Mr. Keynsham, I noticed that he looked rather pale and perturbed — which didn't strike me as unnatural, though I hoped he'd get over it quickly. It wasn't till he sat down at the piano that I realised something was seriously wrong. Instead of playing the Tchaikowsky, he struck a few haphazard chords which had no relation to the piece at all, and then collapsed over the keyboard."

" What happened next ? "

" An attendant gave him some sort of first aid and he walked into the artists' room, but he didn't seem to be exactly *compos mentis*. Sir Marcus very kindly treated the audience to a short orchestral concert instead."

" Did any report of this occurrence appear in the Press at the time ? "

" No. I saw all the critics who were present, and

requested them, as a personal favour to me, not to give the mishap publicity."

A faint flicker of interest appeared in Francis's rigid face at this revelation of facts which had been hidden from his knowledge for sixteen years. Sir Lancelot continued his questions.

" Did you take charge of the accused in any way, after his retirement to the dressing-room ? "

" Certainly I did. Sir Marcus wanted me to send him straight to hospital, but I preferred to risk taking him back with me to Claridge's."

" Had he come to himself by the time you returned to the hotel ? "

" No. He was like a man in a dream — or perhaps a sleep-walker, though I've never seen one. I persuaded him to lie down on a couch in my boudoir, and after about an hour he recovered his normal consciousness."

" Did he remember anything of what had occurred ? "

" Not a thing from the time he arrived at the concert hall. He seemed very much upset and confused, so I gave him a drink and tried to reassure him. When he appeared to have recovered, I persuaded him to see a nerve specialist the next day, and sent him home in a taxi."

" Have you ever seen him since that date ? "

" No, Sir Lancelot. I know his work, of course — in the circumstances I've felt rather a special interest in it — but we never met again." She looked at Francis with faintly smiling appraisement, and added : " I still think that the loss was mine."

" Thank you," said Counsel. He glanced over his shoulder and summoned the next witness.

" I call on Walter Welland ! "

The former Company Commander walked across the Court into the box, and looked at Francis with the air of dismayed incredulity that he had worn throughout the trial. The lines on his sensible friendly face seemed deeper ; his light bristly hair appeared to stand on end, as though it shared his troubled surprise at finding his erstwhile Second Lieutenant in such a predicament. He took the oath more slowly and precisely than any other witness, and faced Sir Lancelot with an expression of solicitous vigilance which clearly betokened his fear of inadvertently saying something that would damage his friend.

" Are you Chairman of Thomas Welland & Company ? " Counsel began.

" I am."

" In 1918, were you an officer in the Staffordshire Fusiliers ? "

" Yes, Sir. I commanded B Company in the Second Battalion."

" And was the prisoner a subaltern in your Company ? "

" Yes. He joined us straight from England about the middle of August."

Enid leaned eagerly forward, her face cupped in her hands as these new and vital facts of Francis's unknown past emerged from the mists which had concealed them.

" What opinion," asked Sir Lancelot, " did you form of the accused ? "

Welland wriggled uncomfortably. He could not immediately adapt himself to the social behaviour of lawcourts, which appeared to regard human beings as laboratory specimens without personal feelings or reactions the moment that they entered the dock. This request to analyse a friend's character in his presence struck him as highly disconcerting. At that moment, intuitively perceiving Welland's embarrassment, Francis caught his eye and almost smiled. Assured of forgiveness in advance, Welland plunged awkwardly into description.

" Well, he was only a lad of eighteen or nineteen, and it's difficult to remember after all these years. . . . He was a thoroughly conscientious young officer, and very plucky. But most of us were tough old veterans by that time, and of course we didn't know he was a musical prodigy. So I daresay we thought him a bit highly-strung and over-sensitive now and again."

" Did something happen to him soon after he joined your Company ? "

" Yes . . . it was very bad luck . . . he got blown up and buried by a bomb when he'd only been three or four days in the line."

" Were you present yourself at this occurrence ? "

" No, Sir. Two officers from another company brought him back to the dug-out. We understood he'd had a nasty experience, but life was pretty cheap just then, and I'm afraid we didn't worry very much about him."

" Did he tell you he had been unconscious for over an hour ? "

Welland paused, struggling with his memory.

" I don't recollect him telling us that," he said at last. " He looked pretty rotten, but he didn't complain. The battalion M.O. told us he'd been concussed, but said he'd be all right after a few days in billets."

The jury listened attentively now, and the Judge was again making notes. Sir Lancelot resumed his examination.

" On August 21st, did you take your Company into action ? "

" Yes, Sir. We advanced seven miles, to a place called Ervillers."

Mr. Justice Dannefroy leaned forward.

" It was in the Arras sector, was it not, Mr. Welland ? "

" Yes, my Lord. My regiment was mostly round Arras."

The Judge smiled. I know that sector, his expression seemed to say. Sir Lancelot continued.

" What happened to accused in the battle ? "

" He was slightly wounded on the third day, and sent down to the Clearing Station."

" How did he acquit himself during the action ? "

" Very creditably, by all accounts. I'd something more to do than keep an eye on him ! But it was a pretty tough show for a young boy just over from England. Nearly all his platoon went west, so as soon as we came out of the line I got one of my officers to go down to the C.C.S. and look him up."

" Did you get a report on his condition ? "

" Yes, Sir. My officer said he seemed dazed and worried, as if he'd got something on his mind. But we never found out what it was."

Again the Judge intervened.

" Where is this officer, Sir Lancelot ? Surely the defence should call him ? "

" We certainly would if we could, my Lord," replied Counsel. " He was an ex-sergeant-major named Smithers. But our information is that he emigrated to Australia soon after the War, and we have not been able to trace him."

" The defence seems to have been unfortunate in the loss of important witnesses," remarked the Judge. " Carry on, Sir Lancelot."

In reply to Counsel's questions, Welland continued by describing Francis's return to the battalion, which was then in rest billets, towards the end of September. Although his wound had healed, said Welland, he seemed anything but fit ; and when they went back to the line he made him Transport Officer.

" Since the War, have you seen anything of accused ? " inquired Counsel.

" Certainly I have. I got to know him again after he joined his father at Fordham, and everybody was saying what a good job he made of it. People were rather surprised at his keenness, because he'd previously given all his time to music. I've seen him quite frequently in recent years."

" When was the last occasion ? "

" On September 3rd, 1939, the day war broke out."

" At that time, did his health strike you as normal ? "

Sure of his ground now, Welland answered emphatically : " No, far from it. He seemed worried about the war situation, and altogether in a thoroughly abnormal state. When I suggested he was working too hard, he admitted it. I told him he ought to have taken a holiday, and he said he'd meant to, but the War would probably prevent it."

" Thank you, Mr. Welland," said Counsel, but, before he left the box, Walter again looked anxiously at Francis. While he had stood there giving evidence the years seemed to evaporate, and he was once more the Company Commander, retrospectively concerned for a wounded subaltern just out from England, and remorsefully aware that he might have shown more sympathy after the boy's first isolated encounter with death. Have I helped you at all, old man ? his eyes pleaded earnestly ; and it seemed to him that, almost imperceptibly, Francis nodded.

The next witness was a pleasant-faced, young-looking man of forty, who gave his name as Eric Anthony Baxter. In reply to Sir Lancelot he stated that he was a schoolmaster by profession, and was now on the staff of Hailborough College.

" Were you a subaltern in the Staffordshire Fusiliers towards the end of the last War ? " asked Counsel.

" Yes. I joined them in October, 1918."

" Have you any recollection of the prisoner at that time ? "

" I have, Sir. He was an officer in our Company, and was then looking after the Transport. But he was a quiet sort of young chap who kept to himself a good deal, so I didn't see much of him." As he spoke, the witness looked intently at Francis, as though to fit the strained features of a distinguished composer involved in catastrophe on to the half-remembered immature countenance of the boy whom he had known twenty-two years ago.

" Do you recall anything at all peculiar in the conduct of the accused ? " inquired Sir Lancelot.

" Yes. At least," Baxter corrected himself, " I remember thinking it peculiar afterwards. At the time I hardly knew Mr. Halkin. I'd only been out from England a few days."

" Can you tell the Court what you recollect ? "

The witness paused, mentally reconstructing the long-vanished scene. Finally he said : " We were having a sort of impromptu musical show to celebrate the advance — the kind of thing that's now called community singing. The regiment must have been somewhere between Cambrai and Valenciennes at the time. I was sitting beside Mr. Halkin, and I noticed he wasn't taking any part in the songs. He was staring straight in front of him like a man in a kind of dream."

" Did you speak to him at all ? "

" Yes. I made several remarks of the facetious kind one indulges in at that age, but he didn't reply. I assumed he'd had a bit more than was good for him. It wouldn't have been surprising, as we were all both tired and jubilant, and a little liquor went a very long way. It was only later I realised he hardly ever touched spirits. In the Mess he had a reputation for being a bit ' pi ', as we called it."

" Have you come across him at all since the last War ? "

" No, Sir. Not till today." Again looking at Francis's immobile face, he added : " Of course I know his musical compositions. We all do. Our school orchestra often plays them."

" Thank you, Mr. Baxter. We are much obliged to you," said Sir Lancelot, and the amiable figure from

Francis's past retired into the pleasant oblivion from which it had emerged.

A very different type of witness now took the oath, in the shape of a tall handsome Scotsman of commanding presence, with penetrating grey eyes the keenness of which did not wholly conceal their benevolent humour. With his fresh complexion, small pointed grey beard and erect knightly carriage, he resembled a figure of Elizabethan chivalry rather than the popular conception of a college don from a Northern university. Only a handful of the spectators present recognised the distinguished Aberdeen psychologist, Professor Hamilton Maclaren, or understood that they were about to listen to expert testimony on the little known, much feared, and still widely distrusted subject of psycho-pathology.

Professor Maclaren gave a brief account of his own qualifications. He then stated that the mental phenomena associated with the prisoner, as they had emerged from the evidence, were of a type familiar to him in patients afflicted by psychological disturbances, both in the last War and in this. These men — and in this War, owing to the air raids, a number of women too — suffered from an acute state of emotional anxiety. They were liable, particularly when they were of a conscientious, responsible type, to resist this condition until its stresses overcame them, and their normal stream of consciousness was suspended.

" What happens to them then ? " inquired Sir Lancelot.

" They usually perform acts which are not in the least typical of their ordinary character. Fortunately these acts, though sometimes eccentric and even ludicrous, seldom threaten the safety of other people."

" How long do such periods usually last ? "

" Sometimes for weeks, sometimes for days, and frequently only for hours. During their incidence, the person is unable to exercise his normal judgment and will."

"And when these periods are over, does the patient recollect them?"

"Usually not at all. It is possible to restore his memory by treatment, sometimes completely."

Sir Lancelot made a gesture towards Francis.

"In your opinion, is the prisoner's evidence consistent with the picture of abnormal behaviour that you have drawn for us?"

"Yes, Sir. Mr. Halkin's description of his periods of unconsciousness is strictly consistent with many cases within our knowledge. A man in this state of suspended awareness is driven in spite of his normal self by impulses which he has previously tried to exclude from his consciousness."

"Would a man of his musical, highly-sensitive disposition be more liable to become the victim of this condition than someone tougher and less gifted?"

"Not necessarily. Gifted people sometimes have an almost limitless capacity for subconscious self-protection, particularly where the exercise of their talent is concerned. I would rather say that Mr. Halkin's musical disposition rendered him peculiarly liable to be disturbed by the precipitating causes of the original amnesia — in this case the bomb explosion, and the strain of going into action so soon afterwards."

Sir Lancelot put his next question slowly and impressively.

"Would a man subject to this abnormal condition be capable, when in such a state, of forming an intention to kill somebody without his ordinary self being aware of it?"

"He would find himself doing it without appreciating the nature of his action," replied the Professor.

Alaric Franklyn jumped to his feet.

" Could a man suffering from this affliction persuade his wife to die with him without her even realising that his mentality was abnormal ? " he inquired.

" The situation would be unusual," answered the witness, " but such cases have been known. The one abnormality gives rise to the other, producing a phenomenon known as *folie à deux.*"

Mr. Justice Dannefroy looked up from his notebook.

" Do you really suggest, Professor Maclaren, that a condition of this kind is catching, like the measles ? "

" I wouldn't put it quite so simply as that, my Lord. The nature of psychopathic influences are as yet very imperfectly understood. We only know that such cases exist."

Sir Lancelot resumed his examination.

" You suggest, Professor, that on the evening in question the accused was the victim of some mental abnormality ? "

" Yes. Judging both by the evidence and from my own experience of other cases, I should judge that at a certain stage his normal stream of consciousness became suspended."

" Assuming that a set of abnormal ideas or motives did possess him, when would you say that the transformation took place ? "

" I should say that it occurred when he was listening to the wireless, and thought he heard a piece of music which had been closely linked with his early life."

Alaric Franklyn rose to cross-examine.

" With the accused's mind in that condition, would he be able to give instructions to Kiddemore about his car, and then forget that he had ever done it ? "

" The rational instructions are not inconsistent with the total picture. At that stage, the transformation into his second, or alternative, personality would not be quite complete."

"And from that time onwards, the accused would become the victim of automatic action directed by·a kind of devil which temporarily possessed him?"

"Scientifically, Sir, your description is not strictly accurate, but the picture you present is substantially true."

The young Counsel placed his hands on his hips, swaying slightly as he voiced the professional lawyer's suspicion of expert medical testimony.

"I want to grasp thoroughly this question of automatic behaviour, Professor Maclaren. Suppose I left this Court under the influence of your learned discourse without being aware that I had done so, and returned to consciousness to find myself in my hotel room surrounded by textbooks on psychology which I had just purchased. . . ."

"Tha-at would nae be automatic, mon," said the Professor decisively, relapsing into broad Scotch. "Tha-at would be a r-rational attempt to r-rectify your ain eegnorance."

A gust of appreciative laughter swept away the tense atmosphere, and the Judge looked up sternly.

"If there is any more disturbance of that kind, I shall have to clear the Court. Proceed, Mr. Franklyn."

Somewhat subdued, Mr. Franklyn proceeded.

"In your view, would such a state of mind account for the episode at the Welbeck Hall?"

"There is a connection between the two phenomena." The Professor went on to explain that the prisoner's collapse at the piano was probably due to tension, related in his mind to the tension preceding a military attack. In both cases the tension resulted in a period of unconsciousness, the first lasting much longer than the second. The return of a similar state of tension, whatever the cause, would be liable to lead to a similar phase of unconsciousness. It was doubtless this calculation which induced the specialist, Dr. Gifford, to advise the prisoner to avoid work which involved the strain of public appearances.

" Would the accused be conscious when he composed his funeral march just before the fall of Paris ? " inquired Mr. Franklyn.

" Certainly. The period of automatic action which produced the final tragedy had not then begun."

" And would he be conscious when he wrote the letter to his solicitor, giving instructions about his musical compositions, and the burial of himself and his wife ? "

" Yes. He would be conscious then."

" Don't you think it strange that almost immediately after these actions, which most people would interpret as signifying a particular intention, he should be discovered with that intention carried out in his wife's case, and barely prevented in his own ? "

" No," insisted the witness. " There is a basic psychological connection between all these phenomena."

" But," pursued the Counsel, " if he was fully conscious when he composed the dirge and wrote the letter, why don't you think he was fully conscious on the evening that his wife's life was terminated ? "

The Professor looked at him with the patient expression of a distinguished teacher instructing a dense and impertinent pupil.

" It's all part of a conseestant picture," he said.

Sir Lancelot got up. " We are much indebted to you, Professor Maclaren." He added in slow, significant tones : " I call upon Sir Wilberforce Morley."

There was a stir in Court as the famous brain specialist, a big man with a florid complexion and an impressive coronet of snowy hair, rose to his feet. As he walked to the witness-box the reporters busily scribbled their little paragraphs of description, for every journalist present knew that Sir Wilberforce must be allowed to steal the maximum publicity from that afternoon's proceedings. He had been a popular celebrity ever since the occasion, now many years ago, when he had saved a highly-placed

Minister of State from blindness and possible insanity by an emergency operation performed under dramatic conditions after a serious accident.

" Have you any personal knowledge of the accused, Sir Wilberforce ? " inquired Counsel for the defence.

" Yes," answered the specialist. " I met him for the first time about two years ago in New York, when we were both the guests of the American Academy of Arts and Sciences at their anniversary celebrations. We also happened to return home together in the *Queen Mary*. Mr. Keynsham — I mean Mr. Halkin — had been the guest of the Beethoven Society while I attended a State Convention of Mental Specialists in Massachusetts."

" Had you any opportunity of forming an opinion about his character and capabilities ? "

" Certainly I had. He seemed to me a brilliant young man, and though I am not a musical expert myself, the general opinion appeared to be that he had a great future before him as a composer. The one disappointment our hosts experienced was his refusal to perform any of his own compositions."

Turning towards the dock, he smiled at Francis with avuncular benignity. This time, his pale face now lifted to the witness-box as he listened to the evidence, Francis achieved an answering smile. Tears again threatened to fall from Enid's eyes as she noticed it, and a glow of warmth towards the benevolent specialist comforted her anxious heart.

In reply to further questions from Counsel for the defence, Sir Wilberforce explained the connection between various types of mental phenomena, such as somnambulism, automatic action, and periodic amnesia. When Sir Lancelot's inquiries were concluded, the cross-examination developed into a competition between Sir Wilberforce and the prosecuting Counsel for the floor of the Court, with Sir Wilberforce an easy winner. He was accustomed to respectful attention, and was determined to have it. For fifteen minutes, blandly disregarding Mr. Franklyn's endeavours to question him, he lectured the Court on eccentricities of the brain as though it were a conference hall full of students. The Judge, patiently taking notes, listened without interference. Occasionally a humorous glint appeared in his eyes as they lighted upon the worthy, bewildered faces of the jury. It was obvious that they were going to need from him the most explicit direction that he was able to give them.

Finally, drawing a long breath, Alaric Franklyn jumped headlong into a momentary pause.

" Sir Wilberforce," he persisted, " if a man leaves letters, and documents, clearly suggesting that he anticipates the death of himself and his wife, and then achieves, or attempts to achieve, the very catastrophe that he has expected, does not that indicate an intimate connection between premeditation and performance ? "

" Not necessarily," was the reply. " There may be a general apprehensiveness which only translates itself into executive action when the automatic, or secondary, personality has taken control."

The young Counsel turned to the Judge with a half-gesture of despair, and Mr. Justice Dannefroy now pursued the inquiry further.

" If any importance is to be attached to the accused's dream in prison," he said, " it would seem to indicate that he found his wife unconscious, or reduced her to unconsciousness by a blow, and then threw her into the river. Do you think, Sir Wilberforce, that this man, or any man, could carry out such a deed without knowing what he was doing ? "

" I admit that the action was drastic," commented the specialist, " but such cases have been known to medical science."

" You may have heard," continued the Judge, " that

one theory of the prosecution is that there was an agreement between the husband and wife to end their lives.
I am not saying that this is correct. But supposing it
were, do you agree with Professor Maclaren that these
two people could both be moved by automatic impulses
together ? "

"It is impossible to say what mental condition existed
in the case of the wife."

"Yes, but there is no evidence that the wife was in any
way abnormal. If the husband fell into a state of amnesia,
would you not think that his wife would be the first to
recognise it, and to summon help ? "

"I could not say," responded Sir Wilberforce serenely,
as though this domestic aspect of the tragedy held no
interest for him. "I have not sufficient knowledge of the
matrimonial relations between the two."

As he completed his evidence, the exhausted reporters
flung down their pencils with a sigh of relief. There was
a stir among the watching members of Halkins' staff when
Sir Lancelot called upon Dr. David Flint, and a tall spare
figure familiar to them all came into the witness-box.

David Flint's thoughtful face was grey with fatigue.
Between two hideous nights, during which the Gilbert Flint
Memorial Clinic had been transformed from a psychological centre into a casualty clearing station for the
victims of the Birmingham raids, he had travelled by
delayed, impeded trains to London and back for a
luncheon of the Industrial Welfare Society which he had
promised to address on accident prevention. For tonight,
since he wished to see Francis through to the end of the
hearing before he went home, he had left his assistant
in charge of the clinic. As he and Francis glanced at
each other, Enid perceived for the first time a strange
resemblance, as though suffering conferred actual kinship,
between the two pale faces and the two pairs of dark
weary eyes.

The witness stated that he had known the prisoner since 1924. They had met that summer while travelling on the Continent, and had finished the visit in each other's company. A month or two later Mr. Halkin was married. Shortly afterwards he had invited the witness to help him establish a welfare department at his factory, and to assume the duties of a visiting specialist. Throughout the sixteen years of their friendship, said Dr. Flint, he had never known the prisoner quarrel with his wife, or threaten to commit suicide. He was devoted to Mrs. Halkin, and always appeared one of the most keenly alive people that the witness had ever met. Yes, the witness had seen him constantly, up to September, 1938. At that time the increase of psychological disorders due to international tension had obliged the witness to devote more time to his clinic, and he had given up visiting factories, including Halkins'.

"I blame myself now for dropping that particular job, even temporarily!" exclaimed David in a tone of suppressed anguish. "My absence undoubtedly meant more work for my friend, and contributed to his breakdown. If only I had been there to observe him constantly, this tragedy might never have happened!"

Moved as he was by grief and remorse now that the hour of crisis was actually upon them, David was incapable of returning the pallid smile of forgiveness which Francis gave him. Only in response to Sir Lancelot's demands upon his professional experience was he able to throw off the burden of distressed fatigue, and to put his expert knowledge at the disposal of the Court. Replying to Counsel's questions, he testified that he had visited the accused man several times in prison, and had no doubt that the periods of amnesia which he described were genuine.

"Substantially," he said, "I agree with the explanation given by my distinguished colleague, Professor

Maclaren, of the phenomena to which my friend is liable, and the origin of their incidence."

He then described several cases at his own clinic of mental disorders arising from the long-delayed effect of explosions in battle or bombardment. It was already evident, he stated, that after this War many civilians, both men and women, would develop symptoms of a type hitherto mainly confined to men in the Forces.

" Would you, then, date back the beginning of the accused's mental disturbances to the occasion when he was blown up and buried by a bomb ? " asked Sir Lancelot.

" So far as the actual state of fugue goes, yes. But his reactions to this episode as a young officer may have been the culminating point in a long period of inward resistance to fear or stress."

" Is that equally true if, as I understand in this case, no external sign of mental disturbance had previously occurred ? "

" One wouldn't expect such a sign. In these cases of suppressed anxiety, the patient is often cheerful and courageous right up to the moment when he breaks down. He alone is aware of his constantly increasing sensations of horror. In this instance, an artistic, self-driving, conscientious temperament would make the concealment all the more determined. It's extremely significant that he refrained from relating even to me his own psychological history at the front, in spite of the years we worked together."

Again the Judge, the now copiously filled pages of his notebook open before him, took part in the inquiry.

" I want to understand this matter precisely," he said. " Was it not extraordinary that the accused's condition should have been relatively unobserved — not so much by his Company Commander, as by the battalion Medical Officer and the doctors at the Casualty Clearing Station ?

However slight his wound, he must have had some medical treatment while he was recovering from it."

"Quite so," affirmed David. "But in the last War there was a widespread failure to recognise symptoms of neurosis for what they were. The Americans were more advanced in this respect; they put each recruit through an elementary psychiatric examination. But in our own Army, manifestations of this kind were apt to be treated without sympathy or intelligence. In fact, they would never have been so universally concealed by men who wanted to act bravely, if most doctors hadn't failed to distinguish between these symptoms and deliberate malingering — which was relatively rare."

He paused, observing that the Judge was taking down his remarks verbatim, and then slowly continued.

"As it was, the period of emotional stress before the final breakdown was one of intense moral effort on a man's part to hide the symptoms — sometimes even from himself. If he complained at all, it was usually of some external physical condition, such as vertigo or sickness, and never of the underlying anxiety and apprehension."

"I see," commented the Judge. He added: "If the prisoner's loss of memory had been observed and treated at the time, would his subsequent history, in your view, have been different?"

"Most certainly," David Flint replied with emphasis. "His memory could have been restored by examination, or, if necessary, by hypno-analysis. The subconscious suppression would then have ceased to exist, and the present tragedy would have been averted."

And not only this tragedy, meditated Ruth Alleyndene as she listened, but perhaps, by similar methods, the greater one — the one that involves us all, and millions of others. She pressed her hands to her forehead, superficially dazed by the torrent of unfamiliar information, but inwardly excited by the enormous new possibilities of mental understanding and control revealed to her by the evidence of the experts.

Surely, she thought, the investigation of this vast unexplored kingdom of the mind ought to be the main purpose of science for the rest of the century if humanity is to survive? During the past hundred years, men have concentrated all their energies on mechanical development and material progress. That's why they have reached a point where they no longer possess any moral control over their own inventions. They don't understand the psychological consequences of these inventions — or even the motives which prompt their use or misuse. And the result is war. If we really saw, as I have been seeing, what it does to some of the finest people we produce, we wouldn't tolerate it for a moment longer. It's a barbarous anachronism, completely destructive of any society that calls itself civilised. But perhaps even war will be overcome when the science of human understanding catches up with material science and overtakes it.

She looked up to see that David Flint had left the witness-box. During his evidence she had observed the suppressed emotion which his testimony had produced in Francis, and had noticed one of the warders bring him a glass of water. From a slight stir in front of her, she realised that Enid Clay shared her anxiety for him. Sir Lancelot, rising to his feet, now indicated that he too perceived that his client, for the time being, had reached the limit of his endurance.

" Except for the two prison doctors, my Lord, the last witness's evidence completes the case for the defence. With your permission, I will call them tomorrow."

The Judge, his eyes also on Francis, nodded ; and the Court adjourned.

CHAPTER XVI

BEFORE THE VERDICT

IN THE LOUNGE of the Dove Hotel after dinner that evening, Ruth Alleyndene and Miriam Huntbach sat together over their coffee.

On Ruth's knee lay open a copy of the *Evening Sentinel*, with its account, at which she occasionally glanced, of the Court proceedings. Miriam was knitting ; the click of her needles seemed to emphasise the black silence of the street outside the warmly curtained room with its leaping log fire. Each woman knew that the other was instinctively contrasting this cheerful comfort with the chill bleakness of a prison cell a hundred yards away. The imagination of both shrank from picturing the agony of Francis's mind, locked in with the loneliness of its own suspense throughout that night before the verdict.

Ruth sipped her coffee, and began a conversation to make the painful image more bearable.

"Do you know anything about that young stenographer from Halkins' who sits just in front of us, and gave evidence this afternoon? " she asked, with apparent inconsequence. "She seems very much concerned by the trial ? "

"You mean Miss Clay? She's an assistant to Francis's secretary, Mrs. Rushton. The people Francis employs usually get very devoted to him, and being so young she probably finds the whole thing rather upsetting."

Ruth thought that she had perceived in Enid Clay something more significant than the orthodox devotion of a typist to her employer, but it was no business of hers to reveal an emotion which the girl probably wanted to hide. She was glad that she had not remarked on it when Miriam continued : " Francis had a great reputation for kindness with his secretarial staff, but Mrs. Rushton told me that for some reason or other he never took to this young woman. She's an intelligent girl, too — a qualified book-keeper as well as a shorthand typist. I don't know whether you realise," she added, " that she's the daughter of your brother's chauffeur."

" Is she indeed ? " commented Ruth, with increased interest. " I remember now that Clay had two or three little children, but it's literally years since I stayed with Norman. Before I bought the cottage at Fordham, I had a room at the North Stafford which I used whenever I visited the constituency. It's been a comfortable hotel since it was modernised, and it saved my Conservative brother from any feeling of obligation to invite his red revolutionary sister to be his guest ! "

At that moment the lounge door opened, and David Flint came in with Professor Maclaren. Sir Wilberforce Morley had left for London by car, but the Professor had decided to defer the long journey to Aberdeen until the morning, owing to the activity of Nazi raiders over the North and Midlands, and the consequent risk of un-suspected craters on main railway lines in front of night trains.

Ruth crossed the lounge to them, and held out her hand. " I'm Ruth Alleyndene, the Member for Witnall," she explained to Professor Maclaren. " Once or twice Dr. Flint has escorted me on a tour of inspection round Halkins' factory. Won't you both come and join us for coffee ? "

The two psychologists, who had already noticed her in Court, sat down beside the small table in front of the fire. David Flint, Ruth observed, looked less fatigued than he had appeared at the trial, and he explained that he had slept soundly for three hours before dinner.

" There's been no siren tonight," commented Ruth. " It looks as if Birmingham's going to be left alone."

" Perhaps London's getting it instead," suggested the Professor.

" I hope not," she said. " My husband's at home alone just now — not that he ever notices the bombs unless they're right on top of him. I don't mind them myself when I'm there, but the moment I go away, I begin to worry."

" You must be glad to send the children to Fordham for their school holidays," Miriam remarked.

" Oh, I am ! Halkins' occupies too much of the village to make it a really healthy spot, but the cottage is a good mile from the factory."

Inevitably, when the waiter had brought more coffee, they all began to analyse the trial. The verdict, both specialists admitted, was by no means a foregone conclusion. The jury were still an unknown quantity, and the Judge's attitude was difficult to assess, though his summing-up would probably make it clear. Ruth discussed with them how best she could approach the Home Secretary on behalf of Francis if the decision went against him. Then she spoke of her meditations at the conclusion of the medical evidence, and the conversation moved to deeper levels.

" You are, of course, correct in your assertion that the scientific advances of the nineteenth century were almost exclusively material," said Professor Maclaren. " This had its effect even on the medical profession, which came almost to despise mental and spiritual manifestations as ' unreal ' factors, to be left to philosophers and metaphysicians."

" What mattered to the doctors trained at that time," added David Flint, " were ' the facts of life ' and ' real ' disease — both of which they thought of in mainly physical terms. Hence they stopped short on the threshold of the very knowledge which might have prevented this second World War — and even the first, if scientific research a hundred years ago had taken, by and large, precisely the opposite direction from the one that it chose."

Ruth took the Professor's cup and put it down on the tray.

" A change is beginning, isn't it ? — even if only on a small scale," she remarked. " I mean, original thinkers like Adler and Freud and Jung have altered people's attitude to these problems, though their theories are all quite different, and most people don't understand them even when they imagine they do."

" You're right up to a point," the Professor said. " At least it's coming to be fairly generally accepted that the same symptoms which are produced by physical causes in one patient may be due to emotional factors in another. The treatment of the two categories should be, of course, wholly different."

" Francis Halkin himself," David Flint continued, " is typical of soldiers or ex-soldiers who broke down during or after the last War — though fortunately in most cases the results were less disastrous. Almost invariably, their collapse was attributed to the fact that the War was too much for them physically."

" But wasn't it ? " asked Miriam.

" Not as a rule. People don't often break down through purely physical exhaustion. The body is pretty well equipped with automatic mechanisms which the general public has just begun to hear of as ' glands ' and ' secretions ', and these render it capable of bearing almost any strain. No ; the real tensions come from psychological conflict. Nothing could prove that more clearly than the facts that have emerged from our friend's trial."

Meditatively Ruth poked the fire.

" I realise he's the victim of a conflict," she said, " but I don't think I quite understand its nature even yet."

" Well, to put it crudely," David explained, " it's a

tussle between the instinct for self-preservation, and the ideals of conduct that a self-respecting person sets himself to fulfil. You might call it a struggle between impulse and conscience. We know that even as a boy in the last War, Francis was already a person of proved musical talent and considerable ambition. His instinct for self-preservation would thus be reinforced by his work and aspirations. At the same time, he tended to be over-conscientious — in other words, the type driven by its own standards in the direction of self-sacrifice. These two sets of tendencies would naturally make his conflict exceptionally acute."

" I see how that links up with the War of 1914," said Miriam slowly. " But why did the conflict come back in this War ? Why, in fact, was it worse ? "

Professor Maclaren now took up the task of elucidation.

" Well, you see, the old conflict had never been recognised or resolved, for one thing. For another, it was intensified in both directions. Halkin had more knowledge of his own powers, a rising reputation, and a wife he loved ; more to live for and more to lose. And at the same time, the fear that he had to fight was a vaguer and therefore a greater fear. He wasn't afraid of something definite which *was* happening, but of a whole series of more or less unspecified horrors which *might* happen."

" As you know," added David Flint, " the newspapers, for months before this War, kept on referring to the ' War of Nerves '. The diabolical skill of those who conduct that kind of warfare lies in the fact that they don't make people frightened of the actual enemy, but of monstrous phantasies in their own minds."

" But surely," commented Ruth, " we're all frightened, more or less ? "

" That's true. Except for a few subnormal or exceptionally insensitive types, everybody's afraid. It's not the fear which matters, but the ability to control it in such a way that it doesn't interfere with one's activities or intentions. And unless the fear is localised and defined, one can't achieve this control."

From the Shire Hall the illuminated clock, now dimmed like the rest of the town, struck eleven.

" In modern war," pursued Professor Maclaren, " you get the tensions created by propaganda added to the greater range and damage-capacity of the weapons used. It's almost inevitable that sensitive, self-critical men like Halkin should suffer acutely. They haven't the outlet of the uncritical hysteria patient, who converts his conflict into some pseudo-symptom, such as deafness or paralysis. After a long period of tribulation — and the finer the human being, the longer the period usually is — the Halkin type escapes from the worst agony of its anxiety by transforming the object of its emotion into some symbolic representation. That's what we call a phobia."

Miriam Huntbach looked puzzled.

" I don't quite understand that," she said.

" I believe I do," Ruth affirmed eagerly. " What Francis Halkin was originally afraid of was death, and the end of all he could do in the world. This came to be symbolised by unconsciousness — his own or other people's — and his subconscious fear of it tended to produce it in himself whenever he had to face some unusual strain."

" Your explanation is approximately correct," responded the Professor. " It also suggests that the dream he described having in prison originated in some reality — which no doubt it distorted. My theory is that he either found his wife unconscious through some mishap, or caused her to become so — perhaps accidentally. And being already in what we call a dissociated state himself, the automatic impulse to convert the symbol into the fact became irresistible. There may even have been some deep-rooted connection in his mind between his wife's concussion, assuming it occurred, and his own, years before, when the bomb buried him. The workings of the subconscious are at present so little understood, that it is hardly possible to exaggerate their potentialities."

" But," said Miriam, unhappily, recalling the long struggle of the Quaker community for penal reforms in which she had taken a pride, " all this means that nine-tenths of the people in our prisons are still there for crimes which could have been cured by psychological treatment ? "

David Flint smiled sadly.

" Psycho-therapists have known that for years, Mrs. Huntbach. You could carry your deductions much further — to the causes, for example, of the present War. Nations are at least as liable to phobias and obsessions as individuals ; more so, in fact, because the dangerous element of the herd instinct comes into play. To ' punish ' the manifestations of these morbid symptoms by force is about as useful as shooting a so-called deserter suffering from amnesia who doesn't know why or where he has wandered."

Silence prevailed for a few moments while Ruth and Miriam sat thinking. A half-burnt log from the sinking fire fell into the hearth with a small crash.

" Then do you agree with most Quakers that this War should have been avoided ? " asked Miriam at last.

" That's a basic question," said David, " and if I tried to answer it properly, we should be here all night. But briefly, I look upon this War as the inevitable Nemesis of a long series of policies which from the psychological standpoint were completely insane. Religious people like your Society of Friends are entitled to regard it as a Day of Judgment brought upon itself by a blind and wilful civilisation."

" But wouldn't your Society be more likely to regard it as part of the cost of free-will ? " Ruth inquired of Miriam. " A Quaker M.P. said to me in the House the other day that to him this conflict was all part of the God-ordained law by which causes produce their effects. Mr. Halkin's tragedy seems to me just a smaller example of the same process — though in his case, of course, it's other people's sins that he's paying for."

Miriam stared into the fire before she answered.

" I think," she finally responded, " that for us a Day of Judgment is capable of being a Day of Redemption too. We believe that the whole purpose of Christianity is to redeem the sinner — not to punish him by some kind of retribution, but to make him a new man."

" And that, after all," said Professor Maclaren, "is the object of psycho-therapy, just as it's the principle at work in penal reform. War, needless to say, results from the exact opposite of this principle, and those who make or permit it are far in the rear of current progressive opinion. It's a method which denies the spiritual insight of the prophets as completely as it rejects the therapeutic discoveries of the few pioneer investigators in the field of the human mind."

Ruth leaned forward, her peat-coloured eyes upon his face.

" If you had a chance, Professor Maclaren, what would you do to stop it ? "

The Professor lowered his spectacles and looked benevolently upon the politician, with her idealistic belief in the possibilities of direct action.

" Well," he remarked, " it has been said very wisely that the process of mental exploration is the only means of arriving at a scientific diagnosis of the neuroses — in this case, of the morbid factors of which war is the symptom. Perhaps that gives you the clue to the future prevention of war ? One might sum up the matter by saying that all Leagues of Nations will be liable to fail until *after* mental exploration and scientific diagnosis have taken place."

" Does that give any clue to the present ? " asked

Miriam. " I mean, doesn't it suggest that in order to solve the problems we've been talking about, the first thing we ought to do is to end the War ? "

" It's certainly true," said Professor Maclaren meditatively, " that a state of war renders unattainable the minimum conditions necessary for the type of exploration which I have described. A war is apt to continue of its own momentum, just because it progressively abolishes the power of detachment and the reverence for objective truth which are essential to scientific discovery and the practical reforms that follow it. The trouble lies in the political systems which tend to give power to men of a self-interested, domineering, traditional type, with very little insight and the contempt always revealed by ignorance for innovation and experiment."

Reminiscently, David Flint cut in.

" In their particular sphere, you know, Maclaren, they're the counterparts of the medical officers in the last War, who actually hindered the process of true diagnosis, and defeated their own purpose of effecting a cure, by giving physical labels to psychological ailments. In my view, the civilisation that produced the War will be saved from complete disintegration only by the leavening effect of small groups, which insist upon keeping alive the values that the majority have progressively abandoned."

" Well, that's certainly a challenge to the politicians ! " exclaimed Ruth. The Shire Hall clock struck twelve as she spoke, and she stood up apologetically.

" I'm so sorry — I've kept you talking till midnight ! And after the last two nights you must need a long sleep more than anything in the world."

David Flint spoke gravely in reply.

" Don't apologise, Miss Alleyndene ; you've done me, at any rate, a service by occupying my mind. Francis Halkin has been one of my best friends for over sixteen years, and the thought of him in those cold cells across the way isn't exactly conducive to sleep."

" I think I can understand a little," she said. " He's certainly one of my most valued constituents. If the verdict goes against him, you can rely on me to do everything possible at the Home Office and in the House."

They shook hands again at the foot of the stairs, and went to bed to listen to the chiming hours, one after another, mark off the long night of Francis's vigil.

Next morning, before the last two witnesses were called for the defence, Ruth and Miriam observed, as they had expected, the lustreless heaviness of Francis's eyes, and the lines of strain permanently drawn upon his face by the past forty-eight hours. The trial, they all realised, would be over by the afternoon ; before that day ended, Francis would know whether life or death lay ahead.

Dr. Slaithwaite, the prison doctor from Kingsport, now entered the witness-box. The better-informed spectators realised that much weight would be attached to the experienced evidence of the prison doctors, and Enid Clay, whose sleepless night at her lodgings had been hardly less painful than Francis's in his cell, felt grateful for Dr. Slaithwaite's gentle manner and mild, compassionate eyes.

Yes, said the doctor in response to Sir Lancelot Prettyman, he had twice examined the accused at Witnall Prison. On the second occasion, Mr. Halkin told him of a significant dream which had caused him a great deal of mental disturbance.

" In your view," asked Sir Lancelot, " is it likely that this dream represented part of the facts as they actually occurred ? "

" I should say that it is not impossible. In patients of the prisoner's type, it is difficult to distinguish between genuine dreams and half-waking memories. In any case, our knowledge of the psychological borderland between sleep and waking is still elementary."

" Was this disturbance connected with anything which occurred the previous day ? "

" Yes. I had my first talk with the prisoner that morning, and during our conversation a tap was running with a splashing noise in the sink-room next door. I suggested he should turn it off, but he was unable to do so owing to some mechanical defect which had to be remedied."

Looking significantly at the jury in the hope that they would be impressed by the importance of this evidence, Sir Lancelot put a leading question.

" If the prisoner's mind was haunted by memories of water, or of drowning, which owing to his peculiar propensities had become subconsciously suppressed, would a trivial experience of this kind be liable to revive them ? "

" Yes, I should say so — certainly. Its very triviality would get past his defences, so to speak. His subconscious mind would be less on guard against the insignificant."

" What impression did you form of the prisoner's temperament when you first saw him ? "

" Very much what I expected. He struck me as a tense, highly-strung, over-sensitive type of man, liable to be carried away by ideas and obsessions."

Enid Clay felt her cheeks growing hot, as though it were her own character, instead of Francis's, that was being scrutinised. It doesn't seem to matter that he's a talented musician, a real genius, she thought indignantly. As if he could write music without being carried away by his ideas ! From the corner of her eye she glanced at Francis in the dock, but his expression of apathy, of a weariness now almost beyond conscious endurance, suggested that the Court was discussing a stranger with whom he was totally unacquainted. I don't wonder, she reflected, though she realised at the same time that her indignation with the prison doctor for this ruthless public analysis which might save her employer's life was wholly unreasonable.

" You have heard all the evidence," said Sir Lancelot, addressing the witness. " Taking into consideration what happened in the last War and at the Welbeck Hall, and recalling the prisoner's own statements about loss of memory and your knowledge of his behaviour in custody, are you able to come to any conclusion about the state of his mind on the night of the tragedy ? "

" Yes, most definitely," asserted Dr. Slaithwaite. " I should regard it as quite abnormal."

For once the jury lost their expression of bewilderment, and grasped like drowning men at this straw of recognisable information. The Judge immediately intervened to emphasise it.

" In your view, Dr. Slaithwaite, would the prisoner on the night in question have the same capacity to estimate the meaning of his actions as, say, you or myself ? "

" No, my Lord. He might be aware of what he was doing, but he would definitely have lost the capacity for moral judgment regarding its nature."

" Have you any views concerning his failure of memory at different periods ? "

" Yes. I should say that they originated in the subconscious effort of the mind to blot out a painful experience."

" And that power to blot out a memory," suggested Alaric Franklyn, " only occurs when a person's mind is deranged ? "

" Not exactly deranged. The patient is not a lunatic in any usual or permanent sense. I prefer the word ' abnormal '."

" Would you say," inquired Sir Lancelot, " that fugue, or amnesia, is not uncommon as the result of episodes experienced in war ? "

" What we call a dissociated state is not uncommon,"

replied the doctor. " These long-range results of shock, due to explosion or other forms of war injury, are far commoner than the general public allows for."

" Perhaps," put in the Judge, " you would explain to the jury exactly what the word ' dissociation ' means."

" It is the technical term for describing a condition in which communication is severed between the higher mental faculties and the lower executive of the brain," said the witness. " One can explain it best by saying that a man acquires, as it were, two personalities — one his usual self, with its normal ideas and values, and the other quite a different self, which is more often foolish or eccentric than criminal. The second self may alternate frequently with the normal personality ; or its operation, as in this case, may be intermittent and infrequent."

" And you say," the Judge continued slowly, " that these abnormal conditions are not uncommon as the result of war shock ? "

" That is so, my Lord. If every criminal case in our prisons could be traced back to its origins as exhaustively as this one has been traced, we should probably find war shock, or war anxiety, at the root of many."

The Court stirred uncomfortably, and Mr. Franklyn resumed his cross-examination.

" Do you attach any importance to the fact that the prisoner composed a piece of music, and wrote a letter to his solicitor, both of which suggested the expectation of early death ? "

" I think I cannot ignore that altogether. It is difficult in such cases to distinguish between general apprehension and half-concealed intention without an intimate know-ledge of the person concerned."

" And the same would apply to the indications that he expected his wife to share his fate ? "

" Yes."

" Then," pursued Alaric Franklyn, " do you find it

difficult to accept the fact that there was a complete break in the prisoner's consciousness between the disaster that he prepared for, and its immediate precipitation ? "

" It is somewhat difficult to estimate the period of massive dissociation," said the witness.

Ruth Alleyndene turned to Professor Maclaren, who was now sitting beside her.

" What does that mean — massive dissociation ? " she whispered.

" It means," he replied, " that the reasons for the amnesia, or abnormality, lie deep in the type and character of a man, as well as in the events of the War."

Alaric Franklyn continued, with dogged persistence, to hammer on his point.

" Do you find it difficult to agree that a man who is found in the same river as that in which his wife's body is later discovered, had no idea when he jumped in of his reasons for doing it ? "

" Yes ; but it might still remain true that he had no coherent idea whether what he was doing was right or wrong."

The last witness, Dr. Brampton of Witnall Prison, supported Dr. Slaithwaite's conclusions with some modifications. He believed, he said, in reply to Sir Lancelot Prettyman, that in Mr. Halkin's case there had been a limitation of awareness, rather than a severance of the higher realms of consciousness from the lower.

" Do you believe that his dream in prison was genuine ! It was not an invention ? "

" Oh, no. It was a genuine impression, whatever its real character. He was not in a condition to carry through any pseudo-manifestation."

On this quietly scientific note the evidence for the defence ended, and Sir Lancelot rose to address the jury. They listened to him with a variety of expressions, of which the sum-total suggested their hopeful anxiety to do the right thing, and their bewildered uncertainty whether they would ever know what the right thing was.

This case, began Sir Lancelot, was a very unusual case indeed, which had presented the new but developing science of psychology with ample material for investigation. Here was a well-known and responsible man, a conscientious employer and a composer of rising eminence, in whose mental history since the last War there had been strange episodes of disturbance and unconsciousness. During these periods he was unable to estimate the nature of his actions, and when they were over he could not remember anything that had occurred. On one thing, at any rate, the experts appeared to be unanimous ; they agreed upon the scientific truth of Mr. Halkin's statement that he did not know what had happened from the time that he heard a certain piece of music on the wireless, until he reawakened to the belief that his old pianoforte teacher was standing beside him in hospital. This excused the prisoner from accounting for anything that he did on the night of June 14th.

The injury to Mrs. Halkin's head, he continued, was a confusing feature. There was no evidence that it had anything to do with her death. Why should Mr. Halkin strike her down in anger, when the couple were on most affectionate terms, and had apparently had no quarrel ? The prisoner could not tell the jury how this injury had occurred.

" My friend suggests," Counsel went on, " that there may have been a suicide pact, by which this couple decided to drown themselves. In such conditions the essential feature would surely be that the husband and wife, agreeing to die, would die side by side at the same time. But that did not happen. What evidence is there that the wife, depressed by the fear of invasion, and under the influence of the unusual quantity of spirits which the post-mortem established that she had taken, did not spontaneously throw herself into the river? What evidence have we that the husband, witnessing this desperate act and perhaps attempting to restrain her from it, did not also endeavour to rescue her, and in despair at his failure, attempt self-destruction? Is not that theory as consistent with the evidence as any other?"

The assiduous pencils of the reporters, whose contingent was today increased by the cohorts of the Sunday Press, followed briskly in Sir Lancelot's wake as he developed his argument.

"I do feel," he admonished the jury, "that owing to the rare and interesting problem which this case has presented to the scientific world, you may be in danger of forgetting that there is no proof that Mr. Halkin had anything to do with the termination of his wife's existence. But even if some action of his contributed to the tragedy, you do not convict a man of murder unless he consciously performs an act which he knows to be evil. The essence of murder is that a man does something he knows to be wrong, by which he takes away human life."

Sir Lancelot went on to explain that if a man was incapable of knowing that his actions were wrong, he could not be convicted of murder. But if his failure to recognise the nature of his actions arose because he was insane, then the jury should find a verdict that he was not guilty of murder, but that he was guilty of the acts alleged against him whilst out of his mind.

Enid Clay observed that Francis was listening to his Counsel's concluding speech with careful attention. Anxious and exhausted though he was, his eyes had recovered something of the tender, luminous quality which always seemed to set her heart beating and turn her limbs to water. Nobody, she thought, could have looked more sane than he, with his dignified air of intelligent vigilance.

"The contest between myself and my colleague," said

Sir Lancelot, "is this : Was Mr. Halkin insane when he committed his act, assuming you find that he did commit it ; or was he, according to the theory of the defence, an unconscious automatic instrument, which was not controlled by his mind or his personality ? "

He turned and squarely faced the jury, speaking slowly and emphatically.

" I suggest that insanity means this — that a man retains his memory but it is abnormal, and instead of telling him that he is himself, convinces him that he is Shakespeare, or the Duke of Wellington. He has an abnormal, perverted memory, but it is still his own memory. The defence is that the personality of the accused was not operating during the period between June 14th and June 17th ; that to all intents and purposes Francis Halkin, whom you now see in the dock, was not there at all. The expert testimony indicates that there was no vicious operation of the higher consciousness. Its functioning was suspended, and the phenomenon was one of true dissociation, in which the accused's actions were governed by another personality operating as his own."

Impressively he concluded.

" As Professor Maclaren told you, the man whom the world knows as Francis Halkin, and better still as Francis Keynsham, was not capable of appreciating the nature of his actions on the night of the tragedy. I therefore urge you, ladies and gentlemen of the jury, that your verdict should be one of ' Not Guilty '."

Alaric Franklyn now rose to complete the case for the Crown. His duty seemed to him self-evident, but he was fully aware that it was neither easy nor popular. The Senior Counsel who had conducted the defence was supported by some of the most distinguished specialists in their own field of science ; and their sympathies — like that of the M.P. for Witnall, whose grave statuesque beauty he knew well by sight — were obviously with the prisoner.

He recognised, moreover, a sinister quality in much of the support for the prosecution on the public benches which made him wish that he and Sir Lancelot could have changed places. Glancing hopefully at Mr. Justice Dannefroy, whose impartial interpretation of the law had become as celebrated as his humane wisdom, the young Counsel plunged into his task.

"There are facts in this case," he began abruptly, "from which — regret it as we may — no other inference can be drawn than that Mr. Halkin was responsible for the death of his wife. The prosecution suggests that the prisoner, faced with the threat of invasion, and overwhelmed by the thought that the wife whom he loved might be shattered by bombs, or perhaps taken prisoner by the enemy and misused or slain, persuaded her to die with him by drowning in the River Checkley. We believe that, desiring to fortify their resolution for a period sufficient to carry out this desperate act, the couple took the unusual course of consuming a large quantity of spirits — a proceeding which, believing that they would not survive to face the consequences of their deed, they made no attempt to conceal.

"You may perhaps attach some importance," he continued, looking at the jury, "to the dream which the prisoner alleges he had in prison, and which Dr. Slaithwaite has stated that he regards as genuine. In this case you may feel that the prisoner and his wife had some kind of quarrel while in a state of intoxication, and that he inflicted a blow which damaged her head, and perhaps reduced her to unconsciousness, before she was put into the water. But whichever theory you accept, the fact remains that Mrs. Halkin's death was due to some action by the prisoner. From the facts you have heard, I suggest that this is the only inference you can draw."

Counsel went on to review the evidence again in all

its grim completeness, from the time that Francis accompanied the Kiddemores to the door, until Kiddemore's discovery of his half-drowned body in the river, and the finding of incriminating documents by the police. His Will, the letter to Mr. Fontaine, and the newly composed funeral march, taken together, made it impossible, Counsel submitted, to avoid the conclusion that Mr. Halkin had been contemplating the act which he performed.

"It has been suggested to you," he continued, "that Mrs. Halkin, in a fit of depression or intoxication, jumped into the river, and that the accused, failing to rescue her, in desperation tried to commit suicide himself. Ladies and gentlemen of the jury, I ask you to consider that there is no evidence to show that this lady was subject to such hysterical impulses. On the other hand, you have heard from the accused himself that he showed his wife the letter, signed on June 14th, which made Mr. Huntbach, instead of herself, his executor as regards his musical compositions, and left instructions for her own funeral as well as his."

The spirits of the listening witnesses sank a little as he expanded his theme.

"What point was there," he inquired, "in the prisoner leaving these instructions about the two of them, and even composing a march for the funeral of someone whom he appropriately described as 'a failure', if his reaction to his wife's death was one of horrified surprise? In the circumstances, I suggest that the prisoner was not only aware of what he was doing, but that he had contemplated these or similar actions for at least several days.

"It may be," he added, and the witnesses looked at each other more hopefully, "that the control which operated at the time of the tragedy was due to some form of abnormality, and that this may even have influenced the prisoner's acts of apparent premeditation. As Dr.

Flint has told us, in cases of suppressed anxiety the patient goes out of his way to conceal all signs of impending calamity up to the moment when he breaks down. But " — he paused and confronted the jury — " there is nothing to prove that this man's behaviour was not directed by any control at all. Therefore I suggest you cannot find that he was not guilty of the death of his wife."

He sat down, and in the silence which followed his speech Enid saw Francis close his eyes, as though the momentary hope which Sir Lancelot had inspired was once again dead. Then the Judge rose.

" It is now twelve-thirty," he said. " I suggest that the Court adjourns for luncheon, and I will give you my summing-up this afternoon."

Enid, her nerves near breaking point, turned to Ruth and Miriam with a gesture of despair.

" *Another* meal ! " she exclaimed. " Oh, I did think it would finish this time ! Why can't they get it over ? "

" He must be going to give us a fairly long summary," said Ruth gently. " That's all to the good, I think. Why not come along to the hotel with Mrs. Huntbach and me ? That won't be quite so bad as having your lunch all alone, will it ? "

She took Enid's arm, and they left the Court together.

CHAPTER XVII

JUDGMENT IS GIVEN

WHEN THE LUNCHEON interval was over and the Court met to hear the summing-up and the verdict, Walter Welland arrived at the Shire Hall in an unusual rage. Abandoning for once his self-imposed isolation, he sat down beside the Member for Witnall and began to tell her of an episode at the Dove Hotel in which he had just taken part.

" I was coming down the staircase, when a fellow exactly like the typical shootin' and huntin' squire stopped me on the landing."

" Colonel Blimp ? " suggested Ruth with a smile.

" Precisely. The chap said to me, ' You've got something to do with that case being heard at the Assizes, haven't you ? ' I told him I was one of the witnesses, and asked him what business it was of his. And he said, ' Well, I hope the fellow swings for it. He's nothing but a Nazi ; I'm told he was always going over to Germany before the War. The sooner we get rid of that sort, the better ! ' "

" And what did you say ? " Ruth inquired.

Welland judiciously refrained from telling her exactly what he had said. Still spluttering with fury, he replied, " It was all I could do not to knock the blighter down ! I told him what I thought of him, and suggested he went back where he belonged ! "

" I had rather a similar experience yesterday," commented Ruth. " A woman — a complete stranger — came up to me outside the railings and asked me what I thought the verdict would be. When I told her I hadn't the slightest idea, she said quite savagely, ' Well, if he doesn't hang, I hope they'll give him at least ten years to keep him out of the way '. It's odd how some kinds of human nature make up in vehemence for their deficiencies in charity."

" What *do* you think the verdict will be ? " Welland asked her.

" I really haven't any idea," she said. " And so far I don't believe the jury has either ! I think everything will depend on the Judge's summing-up."

Enid Clay, now sitting a little apart from them all,

listened to the conversation, and then looked apprehensively at the Judge upon whom so much would depend.
But his calm inscrutable face told her nothing, and as she
watched Francis come up into the dock, an almost un-
controllable emotion seized her.

" Oh, my love, my love, my love ! " she found herself
crying silently as she looked at his face, its vitality all
but extinguished by the racking anxiety of suspense.   " I
oughtn't to call you that, I know, but you may be at the
end of your life, and perhaps I shan't have the chance
much longer.   Anyhow, you never needed love more than
you do now, and there's no one else to give it you, except
perhaps Dr. Flint.   Mrs. Huntbach and Mr. Welland like
you very much, and Miss Alleyndene and Professor
Maclaren are sorry and sympathetic.   But I'm the only
person who actually *loves* you, as men and women love
each other.   And though you wouldn't want my love if
you knew of it, I'm sure I can give you a little more
strength just by feeling it and sending it out to you as hard
as ever I can ! "

But Francis gave no sign that he was even aware of her
existence as the Judge spread his notes carefully before
him and began, with slow deliberation, to review the facts
of the case.   Every few minutes he looked at the jury to
make sure that they understood his analysis.   Finally,
having summarised the whole story in detail, he returned
to the complicating factor of the injury to Sally Halkin's
head.

" That circumstance," he said, " suggests a variety of
possible explanations which we are bound to consider,
even though the prosecution has stated its belief that, since
it is definitely known that Mrs. Halkin died from drowning, the alternative possibilities are immaterial.   I suggest
to you that the prisoner's position is not the same if
we accept the view that the wife became unconscious
from some cause and was put into the river without her

knowledge or consent, as his position if we believe that, before the alleged period of amnesia began to affect him, there was a concerted agreement between the two to die together.

"Let us consider the possible occurrences in succession," the Judge continued. "The only one which appears to be ruled out by the evidence is the theory that the wife deliberately injured her own head, and produced unconsciousness in herself. In the first place, the accused may have struck her in a fit of anger due to intoxication, or to the operation of what has been referred to as his alternative personality — his abnormal control. You will of course bear in mind that in such a case one would expect to find some evidence of a struggle, though one cannot exclude the explanation that Mrs. Halkin may have been taken by surprise. In the second place, the wife may have been rendered unconscious by some mishap, or accident, and then put into the river by her husband, though here again it is reasonable to expect that some evidence of disturbance — a broken window, perhaps, or bloodstains in a room or on an article of clothing — would have been forthcoming. Thirdly, the husband, being stronger than his wife, might have pushed her into the water against her will, and her head might have been injured in the act of falling. This injury could also be presumed in the fourth and final possibility, which is that the husband and wife agreed to drown together, even though the agreement was not fully carried out."

On the faces of the jury, varying in successive degrees from stolidity to perturbation, the expression of puzzled uncertainty still persisted. Mr. Justice Dannefroy consulted his notes again.

"You know," he reminded the twelve men and women, "that the husband was found half submerged in the River Checkley the following morning. Whether he had been in and out of the water several times, or whether he entered it for the first time when his cook heard a distant splash, there is no means of knowing. One would suppose that if he had gone into the river at the same time as his wife and remained there, he would have been dead long before Kiddemore found him in the morning. But in a case of this description, who can tell precisely what occurred? The only surviving party is the prisoner, and he says that he cannot remember."

" The prosecution," the Judge went on, " has therefore taken its stand on the fourth of the four possibilities which I outlined to you just now. They urge that the evidence which you have heard points to an agreement between husband and wife to commit suicide together, and remind you that the document which appeared to contain the clearest evidence of premeditation — the letter written by the accused to his solicitor, Mr. Fontaine — was shown by him to his wife before he signed it on June 14th. They also emphasise the fact that, whereas the accused's Will had left instructions only for his own funeral, the later letter gave directions also regarding the burial of his wife."

He uttered the next words more slowly and with emphasis.

" Suppose that there was an agreement between the two to commit suicide together, then in similar cases it has been decided that the survivor is guilty of murder. But is it proved that there was any such agreement? You have to ask yourselves whether any of the evidence points to that, or merely to a somewhat excessive state of the anxiety which was present in all of us during the events of last summer."

Turning over his notes, he referred again to the various explanations of the tragedy put forward by the expert witnesses.

" No doubt," he said, " you found this part of the evidence difficult. It dealt with matters which are unfamiliar to most of us, though you may think that some

of these were relevant to the present situation. Dr. Flint,
for example, gave us an interesting description of neurosis
cases in the last War, and referred to the comparative lack
of intelligence with which these were treated. I suggest,
however, that you will only confuse your own minds
if you try to judge the prisoner's conduct in the light of
other cases of shell-shock, or war hysteria, with which you
may be acquainted, but in which the phenomena arose
from circumstances of quite another kind. In such cases
as this, it is wisest for juries to confine themselves to the
evidence."

The Judge paused for a moment while the large
contingent of reporters round the lighted table caught
him up with their shorthand interpretations. Then,
looking at Francis with keen appraisement, he went on.

" You have here the story of a man who fought in the
last War and displayed courage — up to a point." His
glance fell upon Walter Welland. " This man's Company
Commander has told you that as a young officer he was
conscientious and plucky. But because, in Dr. Slaithwaite's words, he was tense, highly-strung and over-
sensitive — or because, as you may prefer to put it, he had
the so-called artistic temperament which is traditionally
unstable, and hence more consistent with musical composition than with leadership on the battlefield — his
experiences had certain effects. Both Professor Maclaren
and Sir Wilberforce Morley have suggested that he was
subject to a mental disorder, or abnormality, which one of
them described as 'suspended awareness'; but Dr. Slaithwaite has given it as his opinion that though the accused
might have lost the capacity for moral judgment when his
abnormal control was operating, he would still be to some
extent aware of his own actions. A person who retains a
measure of awareness cannot justly be described as an
unconscious instrument, even though he subsequently
disclaims all memory of what has occurred. Ladies and

gentlemen of the jury, your own rational judgment is capable of deciding this matter."

Now, looking up, the Judge gave the jury the plainest direction that they had yet received.

" Supposing that the contentions of the defence are right," he said slowly, " it might strike you as somewhat extraordinary if a man said to be subject to abnormal control, and to have killed someone under such an influence, should be allowed to leave the Court unconvicted — possibly to cause another tragedy the same afternoon."

The anxious expressions of the jury lightened. One difficult alternative, at any rate, appeared to them to have been cleared out of their way. In the body of the Court, Francis's friends exchanged significant glances. Not one of them looked at Francis himself, for they knew that all hope of an acquittal had been removed.

" It has not been said of Mr. Halkin by anyone," the Judge went on, " that he, the man here in Court, is now in an abnormal mental condition. But you may think that there is evidence on which you can find that at the time when he carried out his deed — assuming that he did carry it out — he was insane in the sense that he was not responsible in law for his actions."

Opening a volume which lay on the desk before him, containing the Public General Statutes passed in the forty-sixth and forty-seventh years of the reign of Queen Victoria, the Judge read to the jury some words from the Trial of Lunatics Act drawn up in 1883 : "'Where in any indictment or information any act or omission is charged against any person as an offence, and it is given in evidence on the trial of such person for that offence that he was insane, so as not to be responsible, according to law, for his actions at the time when the act was done or omission made, then, if it appears to the jury before whom such person is tried that he did the act or made the omission charged, but was insane as aforesaid at the time when he did or made the same, the jury shall return a special verdict to the effect that the accused was guilty of the act or omission charged against him, but was insane as aforesaid at the time when he did the act or made the omission ' ".

He closed the book, and continued.

" Sir Lancelot Prettyman has submitted to you that the only contest between himself and the prosecution is whether you should return a verdict of Not Guilty, or whether the verdict should be that the accused was guilty in fact but insane in law, at the time when he committed the act of which he is accused. I would remind you, however, that every man must be regarded as sane until the contrary is proved."

A little shiver seemed to pass over the crowded Court. Mr. Justice Dannefroy went on.

" But, in a case of this kind, you have found a number of expert witnesses agreeing to a large extent on some kind of mental abnormality, and all maintaining that this man, during the events of the night of June 14th, had lost the power to judge his actions by normal standards. It may be, therefore, that you will be satisfied that if the prisoner did the act he is charged with, he was insane in the sense that he was not reponsible for his actions in law. Sir Lancelot has referred to this case as being of great interest from the scientific standpoint, but I ask you to consider it as juries have considered cases in this country year after year — upon the evidence, and upon nothing else. There are three possible verdicts before you — ' Not Guilty ', ' Guilty but insane at the time when the act was done ', or ' Guilty '. I suggest you now retire to consider them."

Slowly the jury filed out. The warder beside Francis touched his arm to rouse him from the stupor which seemed to have enveloped him, and led him down the steps of the dock. For a few moments a little buzz of conversation broke out among the spectators on the public benches, and the reporters scribbled busily, completing their summaries. Then, as the period of uncertainty lengthened, discussion died away to a whisper. From the main-line railway through Staffordshire sounded the piercing screech of an express train, travelling north.

The jury had been absent for over an hour.

In the tense gloom of the Assize Court, the waiting anxiety of witnesses and spectators had deepened into silence. Already the November afternoon was drawing towards twilight ; in forty minutes it would be time for the black-out.

Through the stillness echoed the distant voice of a boy selling the evening paper.

" La-ate Extra ! Grea-at Greek victory over Wops ! Two night raids on north-west coast ! La-atest noos of Stafford tri-al ! "

Outside, through the cobbled market square, passed a little company of soldiers, whistling and singing :

> " *There'll always be an England*
> *Where there's a country lane. . . .*"

Their confident voices sank and faded, leaving the tautness of suspense more rigid than before.

Suddenly there was a stir in the Court, followed by the clatter of the jury returning to their seats. The three women sitting together among the witnesses looked intently at one another. Then, like everybody else, they turned their eyes to the prisoner now standing again in the dock with bowed head and hands clasped behind him, his ravaged face contrasting strangely with his sensitive musician's fingers and his immaculate clothes.

" He must be seeing all his past life now, like a drowning man," thought Enid Clay. " I wonder if he's thinking of . . . her. Oh, my love, how can you bear it ! "

" If it's the worst," meditated Ruth Alleyndene, " I

must get up a petition for a reprieve at once, based on the scientific evidence. . . ."

But Miriam Huntbach heard only the excited murmur from the crowd at the back of the Court, which seemed to her to have cried for the past three days : " Crucify him ! Crucify him ! "

The Judge turned to the ten men and two women in the jury-box.

" Ladies and gentlemen of the jury, have you considered your verdict ? "

" We have, my Lord."

" And do you find the prisoner Guilty or Not Guilty ? "

" Guilty," said the man with the white hair and the black spectacles. He made a dramatic pause, and in that moment of palpable silence Ruth saw the sudden stiffening of Francis's figure and the agonized whiteness of Enid's face. Then she realised that the foreman of the jury was continuing the verdict.

" But we find 'e was insane at the time 'e committed the hact."

The Judge looked at Francis.

" The order of the Court is that you be kept in custody as a criminal lunatic in such place and such manner as shall be directed until His Majesty's pleasure is known."

An audible sigh rose from the spectators. The tears that Enid had so long restrained were coursing down her cheeks unheeded now, and she gazed at Francis with the undisguised passion of her adoration shining from her eyes.

But Francis did not see her. The colour had returned to his face ; with his head characteristically thrown back and his hands folded behind him, he was silently but resolutely facing the Judge.

For a few seconds of profound stillness he remained on his feet, confronting the man who had summed up his character and directed the jury to find him insane. He was a lunatic, perhaps, but he was not a felon ; and so long as he was permitted to live, mental illness could be analysed and cured. It could be cured and at last surmounted, for the sake of other lost men and women who could still take comfort from the inspiration of his music, and find hope in his understanding deepened by humiliation and pain. Beyond the rocks and shoals before him the sun seemed to shine clear on the distant ocean of life, and the cloud pinnacles, climbing heavenward, to point the way to renewed achievement.

Part IV

CHAPTER XVIII

THE PAUSE PROLONGED

On the last day of April, 1942, Francis Halkin paced up and down the gravel drive of Redhurst Asylum, waiting for Enid Clay to come to tea.

It was now nearly eighteen months since he arrived at Redhurst, and there still seemed to be no prospect of his early release. His dark wavy hair, which had begun to turn silver at the temples during the weeks preceding his trial, already contained as many grey strands as black. For the first time in his life, he looked older than his age.

Redhurst Asylum stood in a spacious hillside clearing in the depths of the New Forest, its back entrance and high encircling walls half concealed by trees from the distant main road. Round these walls at night scampered the forest ponies, their graceful antics reminding that strange, insulated community of a world where freedom still existed. The larger part of the institution, which housed ordinary mental cases, was divided by a thick fir plantation from the small ' criminal ' section used for inmates who found themselves there through a verdict of the Courts. In front of the series of five ' Houses ' which accommodated these prisoner-patients ran a crescent-shaped drive of red gravel, marked off into five divisions for different categories of occupant. This drive looked over a wide expanse of rough heath and lonely moorland, sloping down into a deep valley and climbing up to the beech-crowned summit of the opposite hill. The peaceful view gave a sense of space, and, for those sufficiently composed and intelligent to appreciate it, counteracted the feeling of imprisonment.

Today, for the first time since the beginning of that cold winter — the third bitter winter of the War and to Francis, it had seemed, the longest — the sun was warm, though a treacherous wind still lingered. On the banks of the primeval stream which ran through the valley, bluebells were coming out beneath late-budding wild rhododendrons, and the scent from the orange wall-flowers which bordered the drive travelled like a gentle benediction along the breeze. If he took possession of a sheltered spot, Francis calculated that it would be warm enough to give Enid tea out of doors.

During his first weeks at Redhurst, her offer to pay him regular business visits had aroused in him a measure of mild and weary surprise, but by now he had come to take her usefulness for granted. Under a régime in which visits were rationed to six per month and outgoing letters to three a week for each patient, it was difficult to keep in touch with his friends, let alone carry on persistent prepara-tions for his own release. That he had been able to do these things at all was wholly due to Enid's secretarial efficiency and her indefatigable services. It would have been against the rules for him to dictate to her, but he told her what he wanted to say, and, carefully carrying each letter in her retentive memory, she made shorthand notes in the train and then transcribed them. Occasionally he thought with remorse of the sarcasm that he had vented upon her at Fordham, and still found, when her visit happened to coincide with one of his pessimistic moods, an inexplicable temptation.

Francis had been sent to Redhurst from Witnall Prison as soon as he had recovered from his trial sufficiently to travel. There he had been handed over to a resident Medical Officer in a small reception office, and sent for three weeks to the Sanatorium some distance from the main block of buildings. His own clothes were taken from him, and he was supplied with an ill-fitting calico nightshirt to replace the well-cut coloured silk pyjamas in which he had taken so fastidious a pride. To his surprise, the music-loving steward who served him greeted his expression of dismay with a sympathetic and friendly smile.

" It's regulations, Mr. Keynsham," he said kindly. " You'll get your own clothes back in a day or two."

This method of address forewarned him that he would not be able, as he had half hoped, to relapse into immediate obscurity at Redhurst. The admission of a new patient was the only break in the monotonous lives of the Sanatorium inmates, who were mainly the aged and infirm, with a few epileptics included by way of variety. Many of them, he discovered, had read and discussed the newspaper accounts of his trial. At the very time when he most needed rest and quiet, he found himself obliged to live down the nine-days wonder aroused by the appearance among them of a well-known musician, and to adapt himself, after years of public eminence and comfortable privacy, to the melancholic existence of a numbered man in a dormitory filled with eccentrics.

On the third morning after his arrival he was allowed to leave his bed, and his own clothes were restored to him. But like the rest of the patients he was permitted to keep no knife, razor or scissors amongst his possessions. This deprivation, and the consequent need to shave with hair-clippers, irked him more than any other Redhurst regulation, though he understood its necessity. The sense that his face was never quite clean brought back uncomfortable memories of the Western Front, and embarrassed him more in the presence of his first visitors, Alfred and Miriam Huntbach, than the deep psychological factors in his changed position which he did not yet feel able to discuss.

In spite of the permission given him to get up, he spent

much of his three weeks in the Sanatorium lying on his bed with his eyes closed in self-defence, and his mind automatically revolving round the events that had occurred since the 14th of June. If for weeks after that date he had not still been living in a half-dream, possessed by the sense that his surroundings were unsubstantial and about to dissolve, the three hearings before the Stipendiary Magistrate at Witnall might well have been worse than the trial itself. He recalled the journeys there from Witnall Prison in a private car accompanied by a warder, and the small crowds of sensation-hunting sightseers outside the door of the Court. He remembered the initial distress of the faithful Kiddemores under cross-examination and the sorrowful gravity of his old friend Alfred, while the Court itself, like a Circle of Dante's Inferno, seemed filled with the craning heads of Witnall acquaintances and Fordham employees. In Stafford, at least, the spectators who came to revel in his agony had been strangers; the few familiar faces were those of friends and supporters.

During the weeks in prison and throughout his trial, the feeling had persisted of being in a nightmare from which he was bound soon to awaken. Sometimes, tense with fear and incredulity, he would start up sweating from his prison bed.

" Sally ! " he would cry, " Sally ! "

And then the torch of a prison officer, flashed through the peep-hole of his cell, would recall him to his surroundings and the intolerable truth.

Yet even after several such experiences, he could not adjust his mind to the idea that he, Francis Halkin, was a prisoner, a criminal awaiting trial, a man regarded as the murderer of his beloved wife by the millions of strangers who had read his story. He had been too distinguished, too conspicuous in both aspects of his double career, to recognise immediately his kinship, through sorrow and degradation, with the human derelicts whom he encountered at exercise or in chapel. Only one period in his life had borne the slightest resemblance to this : the week that had followed his collapse at the Welbeck Hall. In the Army his periods of amnesia, though strange and disturbing, had involved neither failure nor disgrace ; his automatic personality had then, it seemed, behaved quite creditably. He felt as though he were watching someone else who was the central figure in a long series of impersonal disasters.

Right up to the time of the trial, he had remained only half aware of his own existence. When he thought consciously of his personal ego, it was still as that of the rising musician, the moulder and benefactor of his employees' lives at Fordham, and never as the ' number ' herded with other ' numbers ' from the underworld of humanity. Even his grief for Sally came upon him gradually, like the pain of an operation wound making itself felt as the effect of the anaesthetic wears off. Sometimes an unbearable anguish, a nausea of realisation, seemed to well up from the depths of his being and gradually flood his consciousness. In the midst of a period of thought on habitual preoccupations, he would awaken with a shock to awareness that Sally was dead — and then with another and worse shock to the knowledge that he had killed her. At first this awareness was not constant, for it seemed too incredible. For weeks the shocks of recognition were daily agonies, sometimes repeated two or three times in each twenty-four hours.

In spite of them, he had struggled to retain his personality; to remember that the past was his, and that nothing could take it or its triumphs away. He might now be a potential felon remanded in custody, and later, perhaps, a convicted criminal ; but he was also the man who through his music had interpreted the life of Staffordshire to England, and thence outward to the international world. Even if he were hanged, those operas and concertos would

remain his handiwork. Again and again, in the struggle
to retain self-esteem despite loss of freedom, close con-
finement, the degrading routine of prison discipline, the
callous cruelty of public curiosity, the dissection of his
personality at the trial and the final hours of drawn-out
suspense, he had gone over the achievements of the past
sixteen years, remembering the innovations which his
initiative had started at Halkins', the bound volumes of
his compositions, the travels to musical functions on the
Continent, the visit to America as an honoured guest.
Surrounding himself with images of the past, and after
the trial with phantasies of the future, he fought for the
surviving conception of himself as Francis Keynsham
Halkin, manufacturer and composer.

It had, therefore, pleased him the more to find, when
he left Witnall Prison for Redhurst, that the prison officials
seemed ready enough to take him at his own valuation.

" Good luck to you, Mr. Halkin ! " his warder had
said. " You mark my words, it won't be more than a year
or so before you're back at the mills ! "

These men, like their counterparts at Redhurst, were
normally tactful and self-restrained, often under continuous provocation. They reminded him of non-commis-
sioned officers in the Army, showing the same kindly
tolerance towards human failings. Constantly, at Redhurst, they impressed him with their skilled management
of the many totally insane creatures in their charge, whom
they treated as irresponsible grown-up children. The
only exception was Mitchell, a supernumerary attendant
attached to the House which finally became Francis's
habitation, who seemed to have a grievance against
humanity in general and Francis in particular. Francis
summed him up as a frustrated man who had desired
greater opportunities in life, and compensated himself by
surliness towards any patient who appeared to have
enjoyed them.

Often, during his first weeks as a criminal lunatic, Francis remembered with gratitude the stabilising presence of Dr. Brampton, the Witnall Prison doctor who had testified at his trial. When Dr. Brampton examined him soon after his arrest, Francis discovered, — as he was repeatedly to discover later — that the outlook of the prison staff was far in advance of the minds which had made or failed to change the laws regulating prison routine. If progress came, it would have to come from the top ; the lower ranks of the penal hierarchy were more than ready to accept it.

So strong now in Francis was the habit of reforming zeal which David Flint had strengthened, that even in the depths of fathomless grief he began to wonder what he could do, if ever he were free again, to focus public attention on the still urgent need for more healing and less degradation in prison.

" Why," he thought reproachfully, remembering that on every car journey to the Huntbach's house he had passed the gloomy, barracks-like building in which he was now confined, " I must have gone by this place a dozen times a week ! How could I have been so indifferent to the human beings inside ? What can be done to prevent them and others like them from being utterly forgotten by free men and women ? "

Witnall Prison, he discovered, had been built almost a century earlier ; it was old-fashioned and very cold, though the worst period of the War's second snowbound winter had not begun till after he left. But even more painful to him than the cold were the unnecessary humiliations arising from poor sanitation and inadequate cleanliness, the misery of under-garments worn too long, the delayed response to bells rung in minor emergencies, the pervasive stench due to defective plumbing in sink-rooms and recesses. How could the customary humble prisoner, already mortified by trial and sentence, avoid becoming further degraded by these unlovely aspects of prison routine ? And what could the friendless man without money or influence do to publicise the need for improvement even when he recognised it ?

Only, thought Francis, by actually going to prison was it possible for one of the privileged, like himself, to perceive how far civilisation depended upon personal cleanliness and efficient engineering — advantages which he had striven, certainly, to obtain for others in his factory, but had always taken for granted as inseparable from himself. If ever he were again permitted to assume a responsible rôle, he would now know that protection against dirt and neglect was even more necessary for the bound than for the free.

When Francis first emerged at Redhurst from the pulverising after-effects of his trial, he was surprised to find that by no means all his fellow inmates were persons upon whom a jury had pronounced the verdict of " guilty but insane ". Some had lost their mental balance while serving a prison sentence ; others were convicted men and women upon whose sanity doubts had been cast at their trial. But those who shared with Francis the description " criminal lunatic " were by far the most numerous in the penal section of the Asylum. Though some were homicidal maniacs, who could not safely be left for a moment unguarded, many had been tried and convicted of lesser offences than murder. One engaging Cockney was harmless except for an incurable propensity, aggravated by the War, to blow up uninhabited dwelling-houses with home-made explosives. Another patient, a bearded ex-clergyman, suffered from the delusion that he was the prophet Jeremiah, and spent interminable hours and innumerable reams of paper writing long letters of denunciation to everyone in authority from the Prime Minister to his local Mayor.

One day early in 1942, when David Flint was visiting him, Francis drew his attention to the passionate parson walking restlessly up and down the gravel drive, his sombre eyes fixed on the ground, and a pencil and note-book firmly clasped in his hand. For a few moments David watched him without speaking, mentally recon-sidering the spread of war across the world, and the catastrophes which had followed complacency and inertia at the top of numerous ladders.

" I can't help wondering," he remarked at last, " whether our clerical friend isn't perhaps the only sane person left, and it's the rest of the human race that has gone mad."

" Yesterday," said Francis, " he told me he'd written to Churchill denouncing the fall of Singapore, and explaining how easily it could have been avoided by prayer and reflection."

" I think," commented David, " we should be justified in giving his sanity the benefit of the doubt."

But by the time that an Empire over-confident of its impregnability was compelled to adjust itself to the loss of Singapore, Francis had become convinced of his own recovery and was beginning to explore roads to release. He had still been a sick and sorrowful man when, after three weeks' rest, he was permitted to leave the Sanatorium and occupy a small ground floor cell in House No. 1.

At the farther end of the long succession of buildings stood a fortress-like erection, bolted and barred, which with grim irony was described as " the Madhouse ". It contained a number of padded cells, and was used for violent, refractory patients who never outgrew their liability to assault the warders and one another. Often, when Francis first came to the Asylum, he would lie awake in the Sanatorium listening to the howls of these demented creatures competing with the air raid siren through the sombre stillness of the long winter nights.

But in House No. 1, which was further away, he could seldom hear them.

So modest, already, had grown his demands upon life and happiness, that the privacy of his little room after the fatiguing gregariousness of the Sanatorium seemed to symbolise the beginning of a return to normal civilisation. He was permitted to furnish this room with some strong and sober-hued curtains and cushions selected by Miriam Huntbach from his now dismantled house in Dene Terrace ; to hire a portable gramophone for occasional use ; and to import a number of his own books and music manuscripts in a small corner bookcase. The regulations even allowed him to engage one of the poorer patients to keep these modest quarters clean and tidy. From a list submitted to him he selected Harry Higginson, a short, sturdy ex-potter from Stoke, who five years earlier had 'done-in' a local prostitute during a drunken quarrel, and was ready, if desired, to discourse by the hour on the habits and customs of the Staffordshire underworld.

Between the bars of his tall narrow window, Francis could look across the drive to the heath-covered valley in the Forest. The sight of the young chestnut-coloured ponies prancing up and down the opposite hill gave him a hopeful sensation of freedom. To the end of his life they remained in his mind as symbols of liberty, which gradually became identified with the consciousness of healing that began as soon as he was left alone to read, write and think. For the first time in many years he learned to sit quietly and relax, giving full play to the train of thought, often transmuted into sound, which his reading had started, and allowing the deep peace of the countryside to soften the sharp edges of his lacerated nerves. He even became accustomed to the constant locking and unlocking of doors which at first had preyed upon his mind, and to the perpetual counting of 'heads' and shouting of numbers which rasped his sensitive ears.

Except for the outdoor hours of regular work with a forestry unit in an adjacent pine-wood, this disciplined quiet, and relative segregation with the few patients of his own type, represented the only institutional treatment that he received. But, for the time being, it was enough. Every hour that he could capture for his own use he spent in thought, inspired by the reading of musical biography or the study of philosophy, history and politics. When he had been at Redhurst for a year, he saw the two Great Wars of his lifetime and the events which had led to them in a truer perspective than the majority of overworked politicians, who had no time to understand the situations which they were compelled to administer. But what use could he make of this knowledge ? How, when and where could he interpret it through his own medium of music ?

Soon after his arrival, he had realised, to his dismay, that the acknowledged restoration of a patient to sanity did not automatically bring release. A man whose mental stability had once been suspect was not returned to normal life unless he possessed friends who would guarantee his good behaviour and undertake to find him employment. Francis came across several men who had long been qualified to live as well-behaved citizens in the outside world, but who were in effect serving terms of imprisonment more protracted than those given to habitual criminals because they were penniless and friendless. The main disadvantage of Redhurst did not lie, he perceived, in its administration, which was humane and kindly, but in public indifference to the fate of its inmates, and the risk that their very existence might be forgotten.

For himself, at first, that risk seemed negligible. In addition to his former responsible position and his great potential value as a relatively young composer, he could count, he knew, upon the loyalty of intimate friends like the Huntbachs, and the readiness of influential colleagues, such as David Flint and Ruth Alleyndene, to act as his guarantors. But he soon learned that the petition to the Home Secretary which normally preceded a patient's discharge could not even be dispatched, however eminent its supporters, until the Chief Medical Officer at the Asylum had endorsed it. Moreover, the experience of ' old hands ' was not reassuring ; they seemed to enjoy recounting to him their vain efforts to secure release.

"What you're lookin' for, lad, is some rare bit o' luck," a sixty-year-old forger who had spent twenty years at Redhurst assured him with cheerful pessimism. "Mebbe somethin' 'll happen as you've got nowt to do wi' — an act o' God, like. But it's that or nothin'."

Disregarding these insidious voices which whispered repeatedly " All hope abandon ! ", Francis began, with Enid's help, the prolonged task of collecting a number of noteworthy and independent sponsors for his appeal. As soon as his period of conscious recovery started, he had determined to concentrate upon the future in spite of its uncertainty, and, alone in his room, tore up scores of letters and papers which reminded him of the trial and the weeks before it. When this holocaust was complete, he found that he had kept only five of the letters — two from David Flint, two from Ruth Alleyndene, and one, strangely enough, from Enid Clay. There was really no reason why he should keep it, but he felt, as he re-read the short letter, that there was something unusually touching in its childish sincerity.

To begin with, this systematic destruction had seemed to him to symbolise a salutary dismissal of the past. But sometimes, in moments of illumination which he was tempted to resist because of the pain that they brought him, he perceived that he would only be really cured when he was able to confront the worst of that past without shrinking, and accept it as part of experience. Somewhere behind his tragedy there was a compensation to be found, a reconciliation to be achieved ; and that reconciliation must be not only with his own downfall, but with the society and the epoch which had compelled him to pay the price of its innate delinquency. As for the compensation, it would arise from his power to understand the conflicts of men and women who had trodden the same desolate road as himself. Only those who had known the utmost humiliation and accepted it as part of life's pattern, were fully qualified to interpret as artists the suffering of the stricken and oppressed.

By the time that he was able, intermittently, to reach this conclusion, he realised that the character of his grief for Sally had also changed. At some moments it still seemed all but unbearable, yet at others he felt that the tragedy of her loss had so purged him of horror and fear that her memory, as of one who had died for him, would provide the stimulus and inspiration of whatever future work he might be called upon to do.

" Once one has touched the depths," he wrote to David Flint, " there comes an indescribable sense of release. Nothing I have ever known before has produced the same unexpected catharsis. Perhaps it is what the churches call a spiritual experience. Someday — not yet, because this place provides the wrong kind of background, and anyhow I am not ready — I shall try to embody this experience in music. If it is not what Christians mean by resurrection, I don't know what is. In some curious way Sally's life and death are both part of it, and when the full return of my creative powers enables me to rise from these depths, I believe that the love which always existed between us will find resurrection too."

How long he would be segregated from his fellows he could not calculate, but he felt certain that the deep waters of experience through which he had passed would enable him to live a life in which all his suppressed fears and memories would be exorcised for ever. He knew now that if only he had realised his need of the treatment so readily available, his own friend David Flint could have penetrated into the dark recesses of his mind, as now, with Professor Maclaren's help, he was penetrating, slowly rebuilding in his memory the events of the June night on which Sally had died and he had so nearly followed her. They could even have restored to his recollection the lost three days on a long-ago battlefield, thereby giving him an immunity which would have saved Sally as well as himself. As it was, he had achieved self-knowledge, but Sally had bought it for him at mortal cost. Now that the indefinable horror once associated in his mind with war and unconsciousness had been brought to the surface and annihilated, the cruel irony of Sally's vicarious sacrifice was the bitterest memory that he had to bear. In spite of this, he felt a confidence in himself and his capabilities that he had never experienced since his early days at the Royal College of Music. Could he convince others that he had it? He did not know ; but he was determined now to try in earnest, and to put the fear of failure behind him.

As the warm sunshine of the April afternoon grew stronger, Francis stopped pacing the drive and sat down on the warm stone of the low wall which divided him from the occupants of House No. 2. The tranquil scene before him was now identified, in its incongruous loveliness, with the successive fantastic events of the War, for so much of which it had provided a background. Today's pale golden light recalled to his mind that first incredible spring before the culmination of his tragedy, when the trusted bastions of Europe had tumbled like card castles through a long-drawn series of cloudless days. At the time, he remembered, it had brought back to him the perfect summer weather of August and September, 1914, when he was a boy at school.

" Fancy such a thing impressing itself on a kid of fifteen ! " he mused. " I never thought I'd be damaged by one war then — let alone by two. All the same, I must have been wrought up by the news at the time, to remember that weather after all these years ! "

Recalling the next few weeks, when the sign-posts were hurriedly removed from the country lanes and wooden blocks hastily flung into empty fields to prevent the landing of hostile aeroplanes, Francis wondered what fate would have befallen the occupants of such places as Redhurst if the Nazis had indeed carried out a successful invasion. Would they all have been shot by their captors, as cumberers of the ground and consumers of supplies ? Or would they have been released and permitted to defend themselves as best they could against this fate of mass execution ?

But the Nazis had not landed. Instead, he had been tried for murder during the critical days of the period, never to be forgotten in Britain's history, when the air raid siren sounded perpetually in London, and from one end of the country to the other the fires spread, and bomb explosions destroyed the silhouettes of cities. Throughout the nights of that perilous winter, the Nazi bombers had bumped and roared above the New Forest, with the sound of an overhead railway perpetually in motion which had first penetrated his stupefied consciousness in Witnall Prison.

Alone in his room at Redhurst after the period in hospital, Francis lay awake and listened to them, realising that the onslaught which he had so long dreaded was being directed against England as it had previously been directed against the countries across the Channel ; and that now, too late to bring Sally back, he was not afraid. It had been, indeed, the clatter of the hostile bombers which had first restored his habit of thinking in terms of musical themes. One midnight, when he awakened to the distant thud of heavy bombs falling upon the South Coast ports a dozen miles away, he had imagined for a moment that he was again a Royal College student, wandering round Chelsea in the darkness with the dramatic *Allegro agitato* from Verdi's *Requiem* crashing in his ears :

> " *Dies irae, Dies illa,*
> *Solvet saeclum in favilla,*
> *Teste David cum Sibylla.*" [1]

Often, in the December darkness, he had seen the horizon red from the flames which consumed Southampton, and next morning listened gratefully to the scampering ponies, a symbol of persistent life triumphant over death. That spring his visitors from London had reached him by circuitous routes because the main line trains were temporarily affected by air raid damage. Ruth Alleyndene, apologising for the infrequency of her visits, explained that she and Denis had now been obliged to evacuate their house in Westminster owing to a bomb which tore out its doors and windows, and move into a flat. A few weeks afterwards, she told him that the debating Chamber of the House of Commons itself had been demolished. But before this historic disaster, on a January evening, had come the isolated raid on Fordham which destroyed Francis's office at Halkins' and killed Mrs. Rushton. And Enid Clay, after saving all the firm's records and then helping the First Aid team to attend to the injured, had been presented by Halkins' with a gold and platinum wrist-watch, and an illuminated testimonial designed by Fred Warrington, the factory artist.

He had heard all about it the following week from Walter Welland and the Huntbachs, who journeyed from

---

[1] " Day of anger, day of trouble,
Time shall perish like a bubble,
So spake David and the Sibyl."

Staffordshire to give him the detailed news. The presentation to Enid had not then actually been made, and neither at the time nor later did she mention the episode unless he introduced the topic himself. He recalled clearly the spring day a year ago when she first came to see him after the description of her courage and its recognition had appeared in *The Sentinel*. The fact that she had behaved calmly and bravely did not astonish him ; he had always perceived a sacrificial quality in the quiet intensity which had so often exasperated him. That day the contrast between her newly acquired reputation for heroism, and the enforced immunity of a man who had automatically played the part of a criminal, moved him to bitter words of which he still felt ashamed. It was only after he had apologised and she had gone, that he appreciated the comprehending tact which had led her to visit him without wearing the elegant little watch of which her admiring family and the workers at Halkins' had been so proud.

She had continued her visits without any reference to his sarcastic outburst ; and here, a year later, he still was. Except for sporadic raids, the long aerial Blitzkrieg had ceased at last. Hitler had plunged Germany and Russia into the costly campaigns of totally total war ; the Japanese had attacked Pearl Harbour and brought in America ; Malaya and Burma had been taken from the British Empire, the East Indies from the Dutch, and the Philippines from the United States. Day after day, events comparable to the clash of planets brought suffering to millions and sorrow to many more. A musician could embody that suffering in beauty and thus comfort the afflicted ; a manufacturer could arrange practical compensation for the victims of war amongst his employees. Yet he, Francis Halkin, who answered to both descriptions, remained a prisoner, excluded from the tormented, bewildered society which had never been more in need of his artistic creativeness and benevolent authority.

Surely it was time for his restoration to normality to be recognised, his petition for release to go forward ? Why, at any rate, should he not draw it up, ask leave to submit it to the Chief, and request him to send it ?

Ideas sprang into Francis's mind, arguments to his lips. Jumping off the brick wall, he walked rapidly in the direction of the entrance at which Enid Clay was due to appear.

CHAPTER XIX

TEA-TABLE TOPICS

At Redhurst Station Enid Clay alighted from the London train, and set out briskly to walk the three miles between the railway and the Asylum.

The weather was still cold, and a sharp wind met her as she hurried along the open road which crossed the common on the edge of the Forest. But the bright sunshine showed her the lurking yellow of primroses in the ditches, and since her last visit a thin veil of verdant green had been flung over the late budding oaks and beeches. At her approach the shy ponies feeding by the roadside plunged into the undergrowth, followed unsteadily by their red-brown, spindle-legged foals.

As she walked through the outskirts of Redhurst village, Enid's young blood throbbed with the excitement always roused by her visits to Francis. Nothing could ever diminish it ; not even her advance knowledge of the frustrated longing which each visit left behind. She had no illusions about Francis's attitude towards her and the need to restrain every outward sign of an emotion which, once expressed, would have brought these monthly expeditions to an end.

When she first offered to visit him periodically in order to write letters on his behalf, and to carry his behests into that outer world where he no longer had access, she had been agreeably astonished by his ready acceptance. She could only suppose that she fulfilled, adequately enough, his practical need of a link between the inmate of Redhurst Asylum and the Francis Keynsham Halkin whose reputation survived with the tenuous persistence of a disembodied ghost. Now, after a long series of visits, she wrote his letters regularly, managed his private accounts, corresponded with his music publishers, and supervised his possessions stored in Witnall. Earlier, at Fordham, she had made neat copies of his still unfinished manuscripts, and left them for safety with her family on her departure for London at the height of the air raids. When Francis once tentatively suggested that his firm should continue her salary, she pretended not to hear.

Steadily, persistently, she had made herself indispensable to him, though she realised that he probably did not know it. If anyone had told her that, in unstinted devotion to human life embodied in an individual, she represented the most effective antidote to neurosis, to war, and to modern competitive industry, she would not have understood. She only knew that she had always been troubled by the conception, even in an enlightened factory, of human beings in the mass, coupled with the deeply pathetic personal stories which lay behind that economic façade. In war this contrast, with its negative cruelty, became actively brutal, remorseless, monstrous, sweeping away to destruction such valuable lives as Francis's in its Juggernaut progress. She saw the positive cruelty as the inevitable consequence of the negative, and never dreamed that in so doing she was wiser than the politicians.

As she passed through Redhurst village where the shops, closed for the lunch hour, drowsed in an early afternoon quiescence which even the greatest War in history could not shake, it seemed to her much more than a year and a half that she had been coming, month by month, along this now familiar country road. So much had happened that a whole decade might well have vanished since Francis's trial, though she still recalled its last day as graphically as if it had occurred only a few hours ago. She had left the Court with a deep respect for British justice and a more limited esteem for some members of the British public. This last impression arose from a fragment of conversation which she had overheard between the Huntbachs and Claude Fontaine.

" Surely," Miriam had remarked as she and Alfred waited for a word with Francis before he was taken away, " the back of the Court wasn't quite so crowded this afternoon. Doesn't it seem odd that people didn't wait to hear the sentence ? "

" No, Mrs. Huntbach," was the rueful response, " that really isn't odd at all. A good many of these people aren't local ; they're habitual trial-goers from all over the country, and they didn't turn up this afternoon because they judged from the evidence that our friend wasn't going to get a straight verdict of ' Guilty '. Some of them move from one Assize Court to another entirely because it gives them a thrill to hear a man sentenced to death ! "

While Alfred and Miriam went down to the cells below, Enid found herself waiting for their return with Ruth Alleyndene. She was encouraged to find that Ruth, from the standpoint of disinterested experience, shared her own opinion of Francis's conduct throughout the trial.

" Some day," Ruth said, " because he's fundamentally a man of courage, I believe he'll be able to face everything that has happened to him, and regard it as part of the sum of his experience. It won't be yet. He'll need a long period of recovery and preparation. I should guess that, to begin with, he'll try to put the past behind him and forget it. But in the end he'll realise that until he has accepted it and got the better of it, he won't be ready to face the future."

She spoke positively, and Enid remembered how Mrs. Rushton had once told her that Ruth Alleyndene had been through much tribulation before she became the Member for Witnall. Ruth added, before Enid could reply, " Meanwhile, I'm sure that rest and detachment are the right prescription. If this comfortless world is ever to be put right again, it'll need a few people who've been able to stand apart from the turmoil, and give themselves a chance to think."

The Huntbachs returned as she finished speaking, to report that Francis, in spite of his fatigue, was relieved by the verdict and seemed almost cheerful. But he had been anything but cheerful on the bleak December day that Enid first went to Redhurst to see him. Perhaps it was the depressing effect of the falling thermometer ; perhaps he was down in the deepest trough of despair after the first glow of relief that another chance of achievement might be given him. At any rate, he had begun by speaking of himself with bitter derision, and then proceeded to tell her harshly that he needed no pity.

" It's the most insulting of all the emotions — and the most enervating. I can do without it ! "

" But surely there's no question of that, Mr. Francis," she had asserted. " We felt *with* you, not for you. Nobody could feel pity for a person who stood up so grandly to such an ordeal."

" Well," he said more quietly, though his tone was still sharp, " I wouldn't exactly recommend the experience to anyone who needed a rest cure ! There's only one thing to be said for it ; it does show you who your friends are — and who they're not."

" Yes." She did not comment on the attitude of her

father's employer, Norman Alleyndene. But they both knew that Ruth's public support and sympathy for a man facing a capital charge had widened, in the eyes of her brother and his wife, the gulf already created between them by her Socialism.

" It's good of you to offer to help me, Miss Clay." He did not add : " After the many times I've scolded you," but the words remained unspoken in the air between them.

" I'm very glad to," she said hastily. " Most of your friends are so busy, they just haven't time to do the routine things that are easy for anyone young and energetic."

Francis glanced round, but the warder sitting at the back of the waiting-room where they were talking was tactfully engrossed in a magazine.

" By the way," he said, " I've made a list of all the expressions that were used about me at the trial."

" Oh — you did hear them, then ? "

" Hear them ? A man can't very well have his personality dissected in front of him without even noticing it ! "

He pulled out a slip of paper, and began to read :

" Tense, highly-strung, over-sensitive, ' the so-called artistic temperament which is traditionally unstable ' " . . .

" Don't, Mr. Francis ! " begged Enid. " Don't pay too much attention to criticisms like that ! Most people only used them because they thought it would help to get you off."

" On the contrary," he said, putting the paper back into his pocket, " I must pay the utmost attention to them. A man can conquer anything, even himself, when he once knows the truth."

A deep silence fell between them, but now it seemed a hopeful silence. Enid stared into the small fire burning in the grate as she committed his final remark to memory.

At last she said, " Then you do think the trial established the truth ? "

" More or less," he answered. " The law's a long way behind psychological truth, of course, and so is ordinary medicine, as Flint pointed out. But all the legal pundits struck me as just and chivalrous, not even excluding the prosecuting Counsel."

" Yes — he was really quite fair, wasn't he ? — especially in his speech at the end. The only time he got really annoyed was with the expert witnesses."

For the first time, Francis smiled.

" Well," he said, " you must admit that Maclaren treated him rather like an impudent boy in a school class-room ! As for old Morley, he wouldn't let him get a word in edgeways. I almost forgot I was a criminal attending my own trial when I watched poor Franklyn unsuccessfully trying to dive into the flood of eloquence ! "

Immersed in her thoughts, Enid walked on past the conspicuous church with its tall spire of red sandstone, and started up the hill which led to another part of the Forest. With that first awkward conversation behind them, her regular visits — mostly dedicated to the discussion of Francis's business — had gone smoothly enough. At the beginning Mrs. Rushton, sympathetic and benevolent, had made it possible for her to have the two consecutive days' leave which she required to visit Francis. Even though the air raids had caused a dislocation of transport, Enid somehow managed to get to Redhurst in time for her appointment, and return punctually to duty.

On that occasion she had taken nine hours to travel from Stoke to London, and had spent a terrifying night in a small hotel near the main line terminus, where the shuddering of the bombed earth and ceaseless rattling of the windows suggested that at any moment the roof would crash on her head. When the visit to Francis was over, the still delayed trains had compelled her to travel back to Staffordshire through an interminable night in which she seemed to pass from Alert to Alert, and lifting the corner of the railway carriage black-out, saw the blaze from some unidentified city provide a flaming signpost to the enemy. But she never mentioned these experiences to Francis, and he seemed unaware of them. Their relationship had remained business-like and externally superficial — until after the air raid on Fordham.

Even now, the events of that winter evening never seemed quite credible to Enid. She had been putting away the files in the outer office while Mrs. Rushton signed the letters in her own room, when it happened. The factory siren had not sounded and she did not consciously hear any noise ; she was only aware of a sudden indescribable convulsion, which left her standing choked and blinded with dust on the edge of a dark abyss. It took her some seconds to realise that the bomb had sliced the building in two, blowing Mrs. Rushton's room and its contents into annihilation, but leaving intact the outer office and half the staircase leading to the ground floor.

Her first coherent thought was for Mrs. Rushton ; but one shocked glance at the smoking void where the secretary's room had been indicated all too clearly that no living thing was left there to be helped by another's courage. Almost immediately, the realisation penetrated her bewildered consciousness that she, and she alone, was now responsible for the rescue of the firm's files and documents, and the unfinished manuscripts that she was copying. For Francis's manuscripts, insisted the voice of her adoration, drowning the crash of brickwork and the roar of further bombs. When the squad of firemen whom Francis had appointed and helped to train finally discovered her, she was climbing down the wrecked staircase for the third time with an armful of files and account-books wrapped in the torn remnants of a window curtain. It seemed to her afterwards, when the First Aid team which she joined had finished its gruesome work, that she had behaved like a person in a dream whose actions were controlled by some external authority.

Neither then nor later, when Wesley Bates sent her home for a week's rest, had she felt afraid. The disaster had come so swiftly that it had left no time for apprehension or alarm. She was filled only with a fathomless, incredulous depression by the knowledge that Mrs. Rushton — the kindly, solid embodiment of reassurance who was 'missing' after the raid — had disintegrated into nothingness through the material action of fire and steel. Until the Nazi bombs so ruthlessly removed her, Enid hardly realised how much she had been comforted and sustained by the warm-hearted middle-aged woman who had known Francis for so many years. Now that she, as well as Francis, was gone, Enid determined to leave Halkins' and find work nearer to Redhurst. Still overwhelmed with remorse owing to the incalculable chance which had destroyed Mrs. Rushton while leaving her uninjured, she decided to seek her next post in a permanently dangerous area. So she wrote to Ruth Alleyndene, asking if she knew of any work available for her in the East End of London.

Ruth, as her habit was, wrote sympathetically and constructively by return of post. A Settlement in which she was interested, Alton Hall in Poplar, was looking for a full-time secretary. Although the children and invalids on whose behalf the Settlement's peace-time work was mainly done had nearly all been evacuated, many inhabitants of the borough were unable to leave, and air raid casualties were frequently brought to the Settlement for attention. It also acted as a kind of clearing house for

the problems of people bombed out of their homes. The
work was hard and often dangerous, Ruth explained, and
someone youthful and courageous was needed for the
job. She felt sure that Enid would fulfil the requirements
of the intelligent and unconventional young clergyman,
Philip Faulkner, who acted as Warden.

So Enid went to London at the end of January, 1941,
and joined the staff of Alton Hall on the resounding battlefield of Bromley-by-Bow. Freed at last from the immunity
of Fordham which for one solitary evening had been so
suddenly broken, she found relative peace of mind with a
cheerful group of young men and women united by the
stimulating consciousness of perpetual danger — " safe
where all safety's lost ".

Here, twice a week, the hard-worked local women
carrying on in their battered homes met for counsel and
inspiration. To the upstairs clubroom the boys and girls
of this maximum danger area came for games and
conversation as exuberantly as though no German pilots
threatened their youth with premature extinction. Every
evening after the nightly Alert, the older women and the
few remaining children sought refuge from bombs in
flooded trench-shelters, where the duck-boards squelched
in the liquid mud, and large drops of water from the damp
roof fell upon them as they slept huddled along hard
wooden benches. In the evenings, and again in the early
mornings, Enid and her fellow-workers served these
miasmic shelters with tea, cocoa and soup. She became
accustomed to carrying her steaming dixies through pitch-
black debris-strewn streets, with the Nazi bombers whin-
ing overhead, and distant fires from incendiary bombs
glowing through the hollow ruins of buildings like a
truncated dawn.

Before she went there she had received her watch,
presented after an appreciative little speech by Wesley
Bates at a ceremony which all Halkins's employees had

attended. But she derived no satisfaction from her pictures in the local press, nor even from her parents' excited pride in the long eulogistic column which appeared in *The Sentinel*. It seemed to her that Mrs. Rushton, whose life had been forfeited, should have been rewarded, and not herself who was still alive to stand in the sunshine and walk through the fields. Filled with remorseful compunction, she had tried to seem glad and responsive when the friendly voices of her fellow-workers at the factory congratulated her, and their eager fingers fastened her watch round her wrist.

But not until she was in the train a fortnight later for her periodic visit to Redhurst, did she realise the effect that her presentation might have on Francis. It was no use hoping that he had not seen the account, for she knew that he regularly received and read *The Sentinel*. In the waiting-room at Southampton, where she had to change trains, she removed the watch from her wrist, and carefully placed it in the inside pocket of her handbag.

She had already seen Francis since the bombing of Halkins', but he had not asked her — naturally enough, she thought — for any details. At her January visit, after a few words of conventional regret on the death of Mrs. Rushton, he had passed straight to their usual business. She hoped that perhaps, on this February afternoon, he would similarly ignore the ceremony of which she had been the centre ; but from the first moment that she saw him, she realised that her apprehensions were well-founded. Though he began immediately to summarise the letters that he wanted her to write, his manner was marked by the same harsh constraint that had made her first visit so painful. When his instructions came to an end, she found herself confronted by the moment that she had dreaded.

" You're not wearing your watch, Miss Clay," he remarked as she rose to leave.

" No."   She looked at the floor.

" Unnecessary modesty, surely, for one of England's girl heroines who know how to ' take it ' ! "

She did not reply or look up. The bitter irony of his tone had not hurt her as she had once been hurt by sarcastic scoldings at Fordham, for beneath it she perceived the agony of self-depreciation, the burning consciousness of inferiority. But she could not prevent the colour from flooding into her pale face, nor the pricking of tears always too near the surface behind her eyes. That damned presentation, she thought, hating herself and the wrist-watch. It's only made the artificial gulf between us wider than ever.

Trying to prevent the tears from splashing down her cheeks, she lifted her head and faced him. Suddenly he held out his hand.

" Forgive me," he said. " That was a brutal thing to say. It was prompted by sheer naked envy — or perhaps jealous admiration would be nearer the truth. Will you allow me to congratulate you ? "

She put her hand into his then, and he gripped it tightly, looking into her face.

" You're a brave girl, Miss Clay," he went on slowly. " When you go home tonight, thank the Providence that made you for the comfortable gift of natural courage."

As she turned down the hill which marked the last lap of her journey, Enid jerked herself back into 1942. Although Francis never mentioned her reward again, he had ceased from that time to speak to her harshly. It was not, she thought, only in her imagination that his health and outlook had improved so fast since the day last year that she had been remembering. Each time she came now he seemed really glad to see her, though she told herself that this was only because she had become so useful to him, and had lately been collecting supporters for a petition for his release which began to seem fully justified.

This time her anticipation of a welcome was amply fulfilled. At the now familiar entrance to the drive he was waiting for her, and with the eager expression that he had always worn when a musical composition was going well, he escorted her to a table in a sheltered corner which he had already laid for tea.

" How lovely the wallflowers are ! " she said, bending down to smell the orange petals.

" Yes ; the sun's come at last. I thought it would be warm enough to have tea out of doors. And I've got you some chocolate biscuits from the canteen ! "

" You're spoiling me, Mr. Francis. I haven't seen a chocolate biscuit for at least a year ! "

" Sit down," he told her, " and I'll fetch the things."

In a moment he reappeared with the tea-pot and a jug of milk, and poured out the tea while she removed her gloves and loosened her coat.

" You're looking very fit," she told him. " Even better than when I was here last month."

" I *am* very fit. I haven't felt so well for at least five years. In a word, Miss Clay, I'm cured, and ready for anything. If only I could convince the powers-that-be that I'm really normal, I know I could still do valuable work. I've got ideas in my head for a Choral Symphony and one or two anthems, though this isn't the place to write them. But how can I convince people that my recovery is genuine ? There's nothing to prove it here, and others, just as sane as I, have been in this place for years — till they've lost all hope. . . ."

" Don't lose hope, Mr. Francis ! Ruth Alleyndene's working for you all the time. I saw her in the House the other day, and she said she was going to make a special effort as soon as Parliament rises and she has more time."

" I know. She was here about three weeks ago. I

told her then I was sure I could fly a fighter if I had to !
I believe I could even face a raid as bad as the ones on
Bath and York."

" The Baedeker raids ? " She referred to the German
threat, after the destruction of historic buildings by the
R.A.F. at Lübeck and Rostock, to attack " every place
with three stars in Baedeker ". " There was another raid
on Norwich last night," she added. " But Winchester or
Salisbury are the nearest they're likely to come to you."

He glanced up at the forbidding outline of the gabled
Victorian structure above them.

" Yes," he said, " I shouldn't think this architectural
excrescence exactly features in any of old Baedeker's
' Guides '. The only thing that might bring bombs here
is a new camp on the other side of that hill."

" Oh, is there a camp over there ? You can't see it
from here, can you ? "

" No. Gibbons, the Chief Attendant in charge of our
House, told me about it the other day. He says it's an
American camp and quite sizeable."

" I suppose the Nazis might mistake one hill for another. But it doesn't seem likely they'll try at all when you
consider the size of the Forest."

" It isn't likely. Neither bombs nor invasion nor any
other act of Hitler will get me out of this place. I've got
to use my intelligence."

He glanced up, to see that they had been left relatively
alone. Their nearest neighbours were a group of patients
playing clock-golf, with a warder in charge.

" When you've finished your tea," he continued, " I'm
going to take a chance and dictate to you the words of a
petition about my release that I've drawn up for the Home
Secretary. I've decided to get it down in black and white
and then show it to the Chief, instead of waiting for him
to tell me when I'm fit to prepare it."

" Why don't we do it while tea's still here ? " she

suggested. " I can easily keep my notebook under the table. When I get back I'll type it out tonight, before I go home, and send it to your next visitor to bring you."

" You're going home — to Witnall ? "

" Yes. I've got a fortnight's leave. It's the first I've had since I came to Poplar. Things are fairly quiet there at the moment. We're no more likely to have Baedeker raids in the East End than you are here."

" I tell you what," he said. " When the petition's typed, you might send it on to Ruth Alleyndene. I'm not sure whether she's actually my next visitor, but she said she'd be back in about a month to discuss what we're going to do. Anyhow, I'd like her to see it and tell me what she thinks."

" Very well, Mr. Francis. I'll send it to her with a covering letter." Enid extracted a notebook and pencil from her coat pocket. " I can take it down now, while there's no one about."

" All right. I'm quite ready."

Leaning across the table, he rested his head on his hands as though in conversation, and in a low voice began to dictate :

" I, Francis Keynsham Halkin, present my humble petition to His Majesty's Secretary of State for Home Affairs . . ."

CHAPTER XX

NO BLAME TO BAEDEKER

FIVE EVENINGS afterwards, Francis sat alone in his room at twilight with a book and a letter in his hand.

The letter was from Ruth Alleyndene. It stated discreetly that she had been much interested in the document forwarded by Miss Clay, and thought that action along the lines suggested might be advisable. Next week, when she was due to visit him, they could discuss the matter together.

Reading hope and help into her cautious phrases, he watched the spring sky deepen to indigo between the iron bars of his narrow window. Though black-out time was overdue he now had many unofficial privileges, and was permitted to darken his own windows and even to go on reading after " Lights Out " if he felt so inclined. Often, on these long evenings of Double Summertime, he never pulled the black-out curtains at all, but undressed in the dark and lay staring at the vertical oblong of starlit sky until he fell asleep.

But tonight, after some moments of meditation, he felt moved by a desire to begin the book, Nicolas Berdyaev's *Freedom and the Spirit*, which Alfred Huntbach had sent him by the afternoon post. Pulling the thick curtains across the bars and switching on the light, he lay down, still dressed, upon his bed, and glanced with interest at chapters headed " Spirit and Nature ", " Revelation and Faith ", and " Redemption and Evil ". Then, turning back to the beginning, he started to read the first page of Berdyaev's Introduction.

" As Leon Bloy has well said in *Le Pèlerin de l'Absolu*, ' *Souffrir passe, avoir souffert ne passe jamais* '.[1] This is a remarkable aphorism demanding the broadest possible interpretation. Victory may indeed be achieved over what has been experienced, and yet that experience is still in our possession as a permanent enhancement and extension of the reality of our spiritual life. What has once been lived through cannot possibly be effaced. That which has been continues to exist in a transfigured

[1] " Suffering disappears, but the fact of having suffered remains always with us."

form. Man is by no means a completely finished product. Rather he moulds and creates himself in and through his experience of life, through spiritual conflict, and through those various trials which his destiny imposes upon him. Man is only what God is planning, a projected design."

Blessings on Alfred! thought Francis. We must have established a kind of telepathy. This is exactly the book I need, to explain my thoughts to myself.

He went on reading.

"Victory can indeed be won over the past, and Christianity teaches us that it can be redeemed and forgiven. Rebirth into a new life is possible, but into every new and transfigured life there will return those former experiences which cannot disappear into oblivion without leaving traces behind them. A period of suffering can be overcome, joy and happiness can be born anew, but into every fresh joy and happiness there will enter again, in some mysterious way, that suffering which has already been endured. Joy and happiness will henceforth be different."

He put the book down for a moment, and lay thinking. From the depths of his mind emerged the memory of a long-forgotten conversation with his mother about Robert Browning's poem, *Abt Vogler*. He could not recall the exact discussion, except that it had centred round music ; and superficially there did not appear to be much in common between the Victorian English poet and the twentieth-century Russian philosopher. Yet the paragraphs which he had just read brought back the very verses that his mother had quoted :

" *All we have willed or hoped or dreamed of good shall
        exist ;
    Not its semblance, but itself ; no beauty, nor good, nor
        power*

*Whose voice has gone forth, but each survives for the
   melodist*
When eternity affirms the conception of an hour.
*The high that proved too high, the heroic for earth too
   hard,*
The passion that left the ground to lose itself in the sky,
Are music sent up to God by the lover and the bard ;
Enough that he heard it once ; we shall hear it by and by.

" *And what is our failure here but a triumph's evidence*
*For the fullness of the days ?   Have we withered or
   agonised ?*
*Why else was the pause prolonged but that singing might
   issue thence ?*
*Why rushed the discords in but that harmony should be
   prized ?*
Sorrow is hard to bear, and doubt is slow to clear,
Each sufferer says his say, his scheme of the weal and woe :
But God has a few of us whom he whispers in the ear ;
*The rest may reason and welcome : 'tis we musicians
   know.*"

Did my mother intuitively understand me better than
I have ever understood myself until lately ? he meditated.
Did she foresee that I should be a conspicuous failure, and
require the courage of a Browning, or a Berdyaev, before
I could make good ?

Picking up the book, he continued the Introduction.

" The torments of doubt may be defeated, yet even
in the new-found faith the depths of previous uncertainty
are revealed.   Such a faith will possess quite a different
quality from that belonging to those who have not had
these doubts, and who have inherited their beliefs from
tradition.   The man who has travelled far in the realms
of the spirit, and who has passed through great trials
in the course of his search for truth, will be formed
spiritually along lines which must differ altogether from

those pertaining to the man who has never shifted his position and to whom new spiritual territories are unknown. Man is tied to his destiny and has no power of renouncing it. It is in what I experience of life, in the trials I suffer, and in my search for reality, that my spirit is formed and moulded. Everything I have lived through is part of the highest acquisition of my spiritual life and of the faith and truth which I possess. I am enriched by my experience even if it has been fearful and tormenting, even if to cross the abyss which lay before me I have been forced to address myself to powers other than human. . . ."

From Redhurst village, rising and falling like the wail of a soul in torment, the air raid siren interrupted his meditations. He lay and waited, expecting the familiar sound of heavy traffic overhead, then silence, and after twenty minutes the All Clear. But this time the expected did not happen. A sudden thump shook the building, followed by a long descending scream and a crash which he felt rather than heard. Too astonished even for fear he found himself lying on the floor, blown from his bed by a force that resembled the rush of a hurricane. For a moment he was puzzled by the cold night air cascading into the room, and the sight of the dark sky strangely illuminated by a sudden flickering glow. He had barely taken in the fact that his whole window, frame, panes and bars, had vanished, when he heard the noise of running feet and a series of shouted, unintelligible commands. This sound was immediately succeeded by a long succession of blood-curdling subhuman howls.

Shaken but unhurt he scrambled to his feet and climbed through the cavity where his window had been on to the drive, now thickly strewn with bricks and glass. The waning moon had not yet risen and the air seemed to be filled with revolving fragments, like a restless curtain

obscuring the geometrical pattern of searchlights inter-
secting the sky from the coast. But as he rubbed his
smarting eyes he saw, in the glare of a fire spreading across
the heath before a sharp wind, the most grotesque and
horrifying sight of his experience. At the far end of the
drive, shrieking and gesticulating, a number of semi-clad,
half-human figures capered and danced amid fantastic
heaps of masonry. He realised that the bomb had fallen
in front of the Madhouse, and tearing down doors, walls
and windows, had liberated some of the most dangerous
lunatics in the country as surely as it had freed himself.

Whether sufficient officers were on duty to capture
and restrain these terrified madmen seemed problematical,
and the rest were probably as far away as Redhurst village
or even Southampton. Without a second's hesitation he
began to run along the drive towards the dancing figures,
guessing that the Nazi raiders, looking for the American
camp, had mistaken the Asylum for a barracks. They
must have swooped quite low, for he could hear the clatter
and drone of machines above his head ; yet he felt no
fear. For a moment he wondered whether he would be
able to scale the walls or batter down the doors which
divided the farther sections of the drive, but immediately
he realised that the Nazis had saved him the trouble.
Doors formerly locked had fallen flat, or gave way at a
push ; complete window frames with their bars attached
had crashed from end to end of the Asylum. The raiders
had blasted away Redhurst's precautionary barriers as
effectively as though their sole purpose had been to defeat
Home Office regulations.

Scrambling over the final heap of bricks, Francis
plunged into the shouting, struggling mêlée. A second
loud crash had sounded behind him as he ran, followed
by another spattering of debris and a cloud of acrid dust,
but he hardly heeded it. Side by side with his official
gaolers he wrestled with crazy lunatics, half-consciously

surprised as he caught, tripped, and pinioned these howling travesties of humanity, by the muscular strength which two years of lumber work in the Forest had developed in his slender body. As the heath fire spread and brightened until the macabre scene resembled a Gustav Doré illustration of Dante's *Inferno*, he completely forgot that he was a fellow-patient with these demented criminals, a man normally confined, as they were, behind bolts and bars. The habit of authority, acquired over many years, automatically reasserted itself. Not only was he ranged on the side of sanity and order against insanity and chaos ; he found himself directing the warders with a resourcefulness which they spontaneously obeyed. Fastening a raving giant to one of the stretchers which he had sent two young gaolers to fetch from the Sanatorium stores, he realised that the man assisting him was his own Chief Attendant from House No. 1.

"What some of these fellows want now is a shot of morphia to quiet them," Gibbons said to him when the straps were secured.

"Right ! " responded Francis. "I'll cut across to the surgery and see if I can get a syringe."

He was hurrying along the littered drive to the medical offices in House No. 3 when he almost cannonaded into Dick Waterhouse, an ex-taxi-driver from his own House who had once 'done in' a troublesome fare after a drunken argument. Waterhouse, pale and scared, caught and stopped him as a third shattering roar sounded from the direction of the canteen behind the Asylum.

"Our House was hit by the second bomb, Mr. Halkin," he gasped. "It's on fire at the back, and Mitchell's underneath ! I've tried to get help but I can't find a soul, and he's groaning something awful."

"I'll come," said Francis. "Show me where he is ! "

Through the dust and debris they ran together to the pyramid of rubble which had been the day-room of House

No. 1. From beneath a pile of masonry where a dangerous chimney of wall, propped up by a billiard-table blown on its end, overhung an artificial cavern, Francis heard the sound of stifled moans. Dropping on his hands and knees at the entrance to the cavern, he could see between huge indistinguishable fragments of brickwork and stone the head and shoulders of the surly warder, whose legs were trapped by a large section of coping. Through the crevices, alarmingly near him, flickered a hot, sultry glow.

" Stay with him ! " Francis urged Waterhouse. " I'll be back in a moment."

Again he hurried through the smoke along the drive to the surgery, where the Second Medical Officer and an orderly knelt beside a piece of human wreckage on a blood-soaked stretcher. Here was indeed a war casualty that was more damage than man, but Francis hardly observed the gruesome spectacle.

" Our House has been hit, Dr. Pilkington," he said. " One of the warders is pinned under a dangerous wall. I think I can get him out, but I ought to give him something to dull the pain. Have you any tablets ? "

Dr. Pilkington looked up from the patient on the stretcher to realise that another was addressing him.

" You'd better leave it to the officers, Halkin," he said, uncertain amid the shock and confusion whether Francis was an asset or a further liability.

" I can't. The place is on fire and it's almost got to him. The officers have all they can do at the Madhouse; half the windows there are blown out."

" If the wall's dangerous, it may collapse on top of you."

" Oh, to hell with that ! " cried Francis. Never before had he known an emotion comparable to this surging exultation of confidence, this exciting conviction of in-vulnerability. " We've got to get him out ! Are there any tablets ! "

Dr. Pilkington confronted a dilemma. A patient who

had occupied a responsible position was acting responsibly instead of behaving like a patient. Then the dying man on the stretcher choked and gurgled, and the Medical Officer decided to take a chance. This, after all, was an emergency for which the regulations had not allowed, except by the provision of shelters which no one had been able to reach owing to the suddenness of the attack. To overcome their problems without further catastrophe, they would need to use all the resources they had in the place.

"Top of left-hand cupboard," he said. "Morphia tablets. Here's the key. Don't give him more than two."

Francis opened the door indicated, and took out a tiny red-labelled box from the corner of the shelf. Carefully guarding it between his hands he picked his way back to House No. 1, cursing the few seconds lost by the argument. He found Waterhouse still there but on the verge of panic, for Mitchell was groaning louder than ever, and flames from the fire which they could not reach were filtering ominously between the stones.

"Hold on, Mitchell, I'm coming!" called Francis through the debris.

For a moment the groans ceased.

"I'm finished," said a thick voice. "Oo's that?"

"It's Halkin. You're all right. I can get you out. But I'm going to give you a couple of tablets first. Dr. Pilkington sent them."

Still guarding the box, Francis insinuated his slender frame into the cavern beneath the overhanging wall propped up by the billiard-table. Already the hot breath of the fire was sucking the air from the perilous trap. By lying flat and stretching his arms to their full length, he found he could now reach Mitchell. Just as he managed to give him the two tablets another bomb fell, rocking the ground and shaking bricks from the tottering wall upon the helpless man. Dragging himself forward to pull them off him, Francis found that the bricks were already warm. He was struggling to move the section of coping which fastened Mitchell to the ground, when a long tongue of flame penetrated through a crevice just above the warder's head.

Unaware that rescue workers, summoned by the shouts of the frantic Waterhouse, were now racing to the scene, Francis fought the encroaching fire with bricks and dust. Desperation and excitement made him indifferent to pain as he crawled over Mitchell, beating out the flames with his bare hands until he had subdued them, and dragging away smaller stones to get a firmer hold of the coping. Using all the strength available in his recumbent position, he had just managed to raise it from the pinioned leg when the last bomb fell in the soft ground to the right of the House. The convulsion that followed brought down the toppling wall, and with its collapse, darkness descended upon him.

Francis returned to consciousness to find himself being carried on a stretcher through a clearing in the Forest. The stillness was so profound after the clamour of guns and bombs, the sky so softly dark and the stars so clear now that the lurid glow of the fires had died away, that for a moment he wondered if he had died in the raid and passed into some incomparably serene hereafter. Then, suddenly, he became puzzled by the peculiar conduct of a huge red planet just above the black silhouette of the trees. As he stared at it, it stopped spinning, and he realised that the strange phenomenon, like a Chinese lantern turned sideways, was only the waning moon.

" Well, I'm damned ! " he said to himself. By its light he perceived that one of the two men carrying him was his batman, Harry Higginson. Gradually he became aware that his head ached intensely, and a molten skewer had apparently been thrust through his left eye. His hands, too, seemed on fire, and he could not move them.

"What's up with me?" he asked, in a voice that emerged only as a whisper. His throat was very dry, and except for his hands he felt cold all over. But the queer elation that had carried him through the raid still possessed him.

"Feelin' better, Sir?" asked Higginson, turning his head when Francis spoke.

"I'm O.K. What happened — where's Mitchell?"

"Leg smashed up; otherwise all right. When they dug you out, you was on top of him."

"Dug me out . . .?"

"Yes. Th' wall collapsed and buried you. It took us two hours to get at you after we put fire out."

Francis laughed — a strange sound from his parched throat.

"Good Lord — I seem to make a habit of it! Any bones broken?"

"Don't think so, Sir. Your 'ead was knocked about a bit, but the bloody table fell over you and kept the 'eavy part of th' wall off you."

"I see. Otherwise I'd have been done in?"

"Mebbe. Now you just lie quiet for a bit. You did a fine job, savin' Mitchell from bein' roasted alive. You're due for a good rest in hospital."

"Is that where we're going? We seem more like half-way to Southampton."

"Ay, I know; but we can't get along drive; it's covered with debris. And there's a crater like a young quarry just beyond your 'Ouse. We've got to go round it, and get in at back."

"The Sanatorium wasn't hit, then?"

"No; and a good job too. There'll be plenty of work to keep doctors busy tomorrow!"

Two hours later, completely exhausted, his badly

burned hands dressed and his head stitched and bandaged, Francis lay awake thinking. A sedative had quietened him, just as it had stilled the groans of other injured men, but the pain in his hands and eye was too persistent for sleep. Yet, abominable though it was, he gloried in it, for it seemed to him the token of freedom, the emblem of release from the terror of years. No one, he thought, could now argue that he was not cured. In a fashion which he himself had described as wholly improbable, the proof of which he dreamed had been vouchsafed.

Kept for the next few days under drugs which dulled his pain but left his mind relatively clear, he went on meditating in a timeless quiescence, disturbed only by the agony of his periodic dressings. He hardly noticed the intermittent sounds of knocking and hammering from the Asylum buildings ; for him they were quenched in the private strains of music which he sometimes recognised as Bach and sometimes as Beethoven, but more often heard as a distant exquisite paean which strangely combined all the writers of music whose work he loved best. Once only, it took the form of words from a familiar Requiem — not Verdi's this time, but the immortal memorial of his favourite, Brahms.

" *Yea, I will comfort you . . . as one . . . whom his own mother . . . comforteth. . . .*"

From the amount of attention that he received and the treatment given him, he guessed that he might be dying. But the fact troubled him not at all ; not even though it would end the prospect of future creativeness on which he had counted. He had, after all, tried to dispose of himself although the attempt had been made involuntarily, and might have been dead for nearly two years. If the respite granted him had meant an anguish and humiliation such as he had never calculated on as possible for himself, it had been worth while because it enabled him to quit creditably, secure in his own self-respect and in the memory which he would leave to the few who cared for him.

Sentences which had recently been in his mind came and went : " *Souffrir passe, avoir souffert ne passe jamais* " . . . " *And what is our failure here but a triumph's evidence For the fullness of the days?* ". . . . And finally — perhaps from a chapel service at Redhurst or from some Lesson heard long ago at St. Andrew's, Fordham — " *Fear not them that kill the body, and after that can do no more* ". . . . After that ? Would he see Sally again, and ask her for the forgiveness which he knew he would have in advance ? He was less interested in this possibility than in the thoughts and conclusions that passed through his mind, gradually growing more connected as his pain diminished, and the drugs given to him became less potent.

This time, at last, his peril had been real. It was specific, and therefore limited ; it had nothing in common with the vague, huge terrors that had possessed him before the fall of France. The acute external danger that he had just faced had released him, once and for all, from the twenty-year-old conflict arising from another acute external danger the memory of which he had tried to suppress. He realised that henceforth security, for him, would lie in confronting both the past and the future, and shrinking from nothing that he found there.

Sorrow and humiliation, it now seemed to him, were part of the fullness of living, and could not be eliminated. They were especially typical of his generation, the generation which had known two great wars ; and because they were typical, his understanding of his own age would be heightened by the grief that he had known. Pain, he perceived, was harmful when resented and futile when merely endured, but it became a cathartic experience, capable of releasing not only himself but others from spiritual bondage, the moment that it was accepted as a contribution to the richness of life.

Sometimes, meditating upon the paragraphs from Berdyaev's book which he had been reading when the raid began, he felt that he was justified in going even further and accepting the fact that a man or woman who fails and suffers may be the unconscious instrument of a higher purpose, by which the individual is used as an example to enlighten others who may still be astray. His conception of himself as a servant of society was thereby restored. The loss of his dignity, the blow to his love, the downfall of his self-confidence, the humbling of his creative pride, would only make him of greater value to those who had experienced similar losses and suffered similar blows. Redeemed from egotism and fear he was indeed a new man, mentally and spiritually born again.

In another week he was off the danger list, and able at last to receive Ruth Alleyndene when she came to visit him.

By now, with the peculiar rapidity with which towns, villages and even asylums had accustomed themselves to return to normality after air raids, the drive had been cleared, windows and doors replaced, roofs mended, and walls partially rebuilt. Except for a gap in the middle of House No. 1, and an erection of scaffolding round the Madhouse whence the inmates had been temporarily evacuated, Redhurst Asylum looked almost itself again. As Ruth walked along the drive to the Sanatorium, the patients replacing panes and bars smiled at her cheerfully. They knew her well by sight, and they were proud of Francis. Again, as in the Assize Court at Stafford, she felt stirred by the gallantry of human nature under the shadow of degradation ; by its astonishing resilience in the face of utter defeat.

At the door of the crowded ward where those air raid casualties who had not been removed to the mortuary were now recovering, she stood for a moment trying to find

Francis. Still intoxicated by the victory won over imaginary nightmares through a real one, Francis forgot his discomfort and gaily waved the large bandaged wads which covered his hands.

" You didn't know I'd become a boxer, did you ! " he called to her exuberantly as she came to his bed.

" Well, you *do* look a wounded hero and no mistake ! " she cried, with a buoyant emphasis which concealed her emotion. But it was not the bandaged head and hands, nor the pallid face which moved her ; nor even the danger, of which she had been warned, to the sight of the covered eye. It was the look of delirious happiness in the eye which could see, the mouth which smiled even when twisted with pain. She realised that never before had she seen Francis so gay, high-spirited and carefree. The composer struggling to emerge from the overburdened manufacturer and air raid warden, the murderer, the prisoner, the criminal lunatic, all had vanished. For the first time she was seeing Francis Halkin, the man whom God made.

Sitting beside him, speaking slowly and quietly so that he would not be tempted to talk and tire himself, she reviewed the petition that he had drawn up. She approved of its arrangement and contents, though now, she thought, it would be a mere formality. Already, she told him, she had seen the Chief Medical Officer, and had an appointment for the following week with the Home Secretary. Throughout official circles, both inside the Asylum and within the Home Department, Francis's courage and self-possession during the raid were well known. Gibbons, the Chief Attendant at his House upon whose judgment the release of patients there largely depended, had reported on his prompt and valuable assistance in capturing the homicidal lunatics from House No. 5, while Mitchell and Waterhouse had described his subsequent exploits that night to anyone who would listen. His release, she thought, would be arranged in a matter of weeks.

They were discussing the prospect as a foregone conclusion, when a small figure in a dark-blue coat hurried up the ward. It was Enid Clay.

" Why, Miss Clay," Francis exclaimed. " I thought you were in Witnall ! "

" So I was, Mr. Francis. But as soon as I heard about the raid from Mrs. Huntbach, I came back," Enid explained breathlessly. " I rang up every day till they said you were out of danger and could see visitors, and then I took the first train I could get. I . . . I thought you might have a good deal for me to do." She added, trying to combat the sudden threat of tears due to his damaged appearance, " There wasn't anything about you in any of the papers, but I told everyone at home who mattered."

Francis had already realised that the raid and his part in it would not be publicly reported. When Enid Clay, young and unknown, received her presentation, she could be publicised safely, but he, Francis Keynsham, first famous and then notorious, could not have his efforts at atonement recorded without telling the Nazis where their bombs had fallen. There would be no ceremony for him ; but he did not care. If what he had done brought him freedom to make his music and serve his generation, it was more than enough.

" I'm glad I've managed to keep out of the papers this time ! " he remarked cheerfully. " It's quite an achievement for me."

Ruth silently watched them, observing Enid as Francis spoke. Looking at her pale face, the shadows under her eyes and the mingling of tension and triumph in her expression, Ruth felt an earlier intuition grow into certainty. If I'd had a child after Eugene and I went to the forest at Hardelot, I might have a daughter almost her age, she thought, recalling the young American and the weeks of glory and anguish which she had spent with him at the back of the front in France.

The beginning of her talk with Miriam at the Dove Hotel on the second evening of the trial came back to her mind ; she also remembered a conversation over tea there with Walter Welland and the Huntbachs after the verdict. They had all expressed the hope that Francis's detention at Redhurst would not last long, when Walter suddenly added : " You know, in spite of everything, I shouldn't be surprised if Francis were to marry again one day. He's an attractive fellow, and you women seem to be fascinated by misfortune ! "

"Women vary, like men," Ruth had said, thinking of her sister-in-law, Jennifer Alleyndene. " Anyhow, I don't think it would be remarkable for somebody to marry Francis Halkin. Even this terrible experience hasn't destroyed that peculiar quality of distinction which made our discussions at Fordham so stimulating. If I were five years younger, and unmarried, I'd almost take him on myself ! "

" And if I were ten years younger, and hadn't got Alfred, I'd certainly do so ! " affirmed Miriam emphatically. " I'd make a good job of it, too ! "

They all laughed, and for the first time in three days the look of distress lifted from Walter's face.

" I'll remember that ! " he exclaimed. " When poor Francis is free again, I shall relay it to whomever does take him on ! "

I wonder if you will, thought Ruth, with her eyes on Enid. She got up suddenly.

" Look here, Mr. Halkin, I've been with you nearly an hour. One visitor at a time is enough for you just now, and it'll suit me very well to catch the early train back to town. So I'll leave Miss Clay to give you your tea, and come again when I've seen the Home Secretary."

Disregarding Francis's vigorous and Enid's less

emphatic protests, she said goodbye, picked up a car at the village garage, and sat down to a scanty tea in the bleak dining-room of the station inn. There she waited patiently for the train which she knew that Enid would take as soon as visiting hours at Redhurst were over. The dreariness of the room and the staleness of the bread and margarine did not trouble her, for her mind glowed with the satisfaction that she always felt when people whom she liked behaved creditably. She found herself repeating some words which Robert Louis Stevenson put into the mouth of a fiction character, Alan Breck Stewart : " To be feared of a thing and yet to do it is what makes the prettiest kind of man."

Ruth's calculations were correct. Enid Clay ran into the station just as the 4.45 appeared on the horizon. The preoccupied expression of joy and misery which Ruth had noticed at Redhurst was still on her face.

" Why, Miss Alleyndene ! " she exclaimed, " I thought you'd gone by the earlier train ! "

" I just missed it," said Ruth, hoping that the Power who presided over human affections would pardon this unwonted mendacity. " It didn't matter. I had quite a decent tea at the inn."

There was actually an empty carriage on the local train, and they got into it together.

" How do you think he's looking, Miss Alleyndene ? " Enid asked, as the engine puffed slowly out of the country station along the outskirts of the Forest.

" Another man altogether," Ruth replied. " The raid confirmed what he's known for a long time — that he's lost all his fear. Even the injuries help ; they add to his self-respect and the recovery of the person who partly died in 1918." She paused ; and continued abruptly, " You're in love with him, aren't you, my dear ? "

Enid's face turned scarlet and then white. After a moment's silence, she jerked out : " Is it as obvious as all

that ? I've loved him as long as I can remember — ever
since my father talked to me about his work at Fordham
when I was a little girl. I took my secretarial training
because I wanted to join his staff. But I didn't think
anybody knew. I did think I'd managed to hide it."

" It wouldn't be obvious to most people," said Ruth.
"But it just happens that I once went through what you're
going through now — when I was nursing in the last War,
years before I met my husband. I know what it means to
love someone like that — to feel unfulfilled and uncertain."

" Was he killed, Miss Alleyndene ? "

" Yes." She added thoughtfully : " But we were
lovers before he died."

" I'm so glad ! " cried Enid eagerly. " I couldn't bear
to think you'd gone on feeling — well, what I'm feeling
now, and shall have to go on feeling for years, I suppose."

" Why for years ? I really don't think there's much
doubt of his early release. I'm seeing the Home Secretary
about it next week."

" But what difference will his release make ? He'd
never want me — either as wife or mistress. He's still
really in love with Sally."

Ruth looked meditatively at the late spring landscape,
the delicate green of suburban trees and the tulips in the
back gardens of railwayside villas.

" In a way you're right, of course," she said. " I don't
say that a second wife would ever be the same to him
as Sally Halkin. He's the loyal and faithful kind, that
doesn't forget, and the happier he felt, the greater his
remorse and compunction for her would be. But I don't
think, you know, that Sally's really a person to him any
longer. I believe she's become a kind of symbol — the
symbol of his recovery and re-conquest. A man of flesh
and blood can't spend the rest of his life with a symbol —
but of course, with his history, he might find it difficult —
. . . Look here, why don't you ask him to marry you ? "

Enid confronted the unimagined possibility with a sense of shock.

"But Miss Alleyndene, I couldn't do a thing like that!" she exclaimed. "Even if he cared about me I'm not good enough for him — my father's only a chauffeur, as you know. . . ."

"Nonsense!" said Ruth. "I don't think in those terms. Neither does he."

"But he hasn't any use for me at all, not in that way. He never has had. Something about me has always annoyed him."

"He may feel differently now. Suffering does change people, you know. If they're courageous they get over it, and even find value in the experience. But they never go back to being just what they were before they suffered."

The train slowed down as it ran through the battered outskirts of a city, passing the wrecks of houses without roofs or windows and the weed-choked travesties of gardens once carefully tended.

"Here's Southampton," commented Ruth. "We shan't be able to talk in the London train; it's sure to be crowded. So don't forget what I've said! True happiness is a rare thing in this grim and shattered world. If you see any chance of it, take it — and give it to him. He needs it, Heaven knows; and so do you!"

CHAPTER XXI

HARMONY EMERGES

ON ENID'S next visit to Francis at the beginning of June, she found him sitting in a wheel-chair on the drive, with a suitcase half-filled with papers on a garden table beside him. His hands were still covered, but except for a shade over his left eye the bandages had been removed from his head, leaving exposed the long stitched scar from the wound made by a jagged brick.

The train had been very hot owing to a sudden early heat wave, and the papers were filled with information about a mammoth R.A.F. air raid two days earlier on Cologne. Enid felt tired and depressed ; the news sickened her with its indications of superlative civilian suffering and the complacent indifference of war-makers to the once paramount claims of young and helpless human life. It all comes back in the end, she thought ; if not to this generation, then to the next. Our children pay for their children, our sick and aged for theirs. Nobody who knows, as I know, what these raids mean to the poorer sections of crowded cities, could want them to go on. Haven't we hurt each other enough by now ? Surely it's time to cry quits !

But her spirits rose in spite of herself when she saw Francis out of doors, still pale and ill, but alive and wearing the same vital expression of happiness that he had worn since his narrow escape.

" They let me get up two days ago," he told her. " It was about time, after being in bed nearly a month. But I'm supposed to stay in this wheel-chair because I'm still rather wobbly on my feet and I can't hold a stick. Apparently something awful would happen if I came down on my head in its present state ! "

" Are you still in the Sanatorium ? " she asked him.

" No, thank goodness ! They've let me out into a room of my own again. The one I had is uninhabitable — in fact the whole of House 1 is still out of commission. So they've given me an empty staff room for the time being. And another concession — if you can manage it I'm allowed to have you till five o'clock ! "

" Of course I can," she said, glancing at the suitcase.

" You look as if you've got plenty of work for me ! "

He smiled at her apologetically.

" I'm afraid I have. It's appalling the way these letters have accumulated while I've been in bed. I don't know whether you'll be able to do them all."

" I shall be, I'm sure. The Settlement's rather quiet just now. People don't come in so much during these long warm evenings, so I've got plenty of time. Is there any further news of your release ? "

" Yes. Entirely good. The Home Office is in communication with Claude Fontaine. I gather from him that I may be allowed to leave as soon as I'm fit. Ruth Alleyndene will tell me definitely when she comes next week."

" That's splendid ! " cried Enid, and tried to feel that indeed it was. She looked across the valley at the ponies sheltering in the shade of the sunlit trees, and faced the fact that once he was free, his need of her would cease.

" Where do we begin ! " she inquired, lifting the suit-case on to her knee to sort his correspondence.

" I'm afraid it's in rather a muddle," he said, his characteristic dislike of untidiness expressing itself in an attempt at a frown which his scars defeated. " I haven't been able to arrange anything. It's incredible how help-less one is without hands."

" There are letters here from Mr. Welland and Mrs. Huntbach. Do you want to answer those ? "

" No, there's no need. Walter and the Huntbachs were down here last week. But there's an interesting letter from Professor Maclaren and a most charming note from Flint, saying that as soon as I've had a period of freedom he's going to look out for something useful that I can do. I've been thinking it over, and, as things are, I don't believe I should ever feel justified in working at music alone."

" I should think he'd be the right person to help you, if you feel you must do something of that kind."

" He certainly would. He's working for just the people I'd most like to look after — men and women who suffer from various kinds of neurosis, and sometimes don't even realise it. There'll be a good many of them, after this War."

" I'm afraid there will," she agreed, thinking again of the thousands of terrified children crying in shelters beneath the world's raided cities. She looked through his papers until she found the letters that he had mentioned. " Here they are. What else ? "

" There's a whole series of inquiries from Fontaine's clerk about my investments, and a letter from Vesey's about publishing a new edition of my *Old Wives' Tale* opera. Then I've had a note of congratulation from Sir Lancelot Prettyman. It came about a week ago."

" I wonder how he heard ? "

" Fontaine told him, I imagine. I know the Chief wrote his office immediately after the raid. I believe they thought for a day or two that I might pass out altogether, though I was blissfully undisturbed about it at the time."

Blissfully ? Yes, she thought, imagining how it must have felt to overcome the very fear which had been responsible for his tragedy, perhaps that *is* the right word to use. If so, he was luckier than some of us who also knew — and waited.

" What did Sir Lancelot say ? " she inquired.

" His letter was very encouraging. He said he always felt sure I shouldn't be here long. It was good of him to write, wasn't it ? " . . . Francis paused, and added more slowly, " He also told me that Franklyn, the prosecuting Counsel, joined the Navy soon after the trial — and went down in the *Repulse*."

" I'm sorry to hear that. I suppose he had to try to

get you convicted, but he really was quite decent."

"Very," said Francis. "In the end he went for the same verdict as the Judge — the one I actually got. Poor Franklyn ; he was a brilliant fellow ! I'd have liked to meet him again on rather more equal terms."

For an hour they sat together over Francis's letters, Enid in the warm sunshine and Francis, because of his injured head, beneath the shadow of an awning fixed by Higginson on the back of his chair. Later Higginson brought their tea, waiting on Francis with a respectful devotion which proclaimed the added status that the raid had given him among his fellow-patients. To Enid, the long and lovely afternoon seemed hardly to have begun before it was over, and Francis told her that he was under instructions to return to his room.

" I'm still supposed to retire to bed after tea," he explained, " and Harry seems to have vanished with the tea-things. Would you be good enough to take me back ? It's on the second floor, but there's a lift and the chair fits into it."

" Of course," she said, pushing him along the drive and through the tiled entrance of House No. 3. She steered the chair into the lift and out again, wheeling him into his room. The staff quarters were quiet and empty ; officers and patients alike all appeared to be out of doors enjoying the warm golden evening.

" I shall be all right now if you wouldn't mind helping me out of the chair," he told her. " I can lie on the bed till Harry or one of the officers comes up. You mustn't stay any longer, or you'll miss your train."

" This is where First Aid comes in useful ! " she said lightly, trying to conceal her desire to stay, to help him into bed, to take the place of Higginson and the warders. Linking her arms in his, she lifted him quite easily on to the bed from the chair. Except for their customary formal handshakes, she had never touched him before, and her

heart began to beat so fast that its throbs made her breathless.

" Where are you going when you're released, Mr.
Francis ? " she inquired abruptly, mechanically putting
the letters that he had given her into her handbag.

" Alfred and Miriam Huntbach have promised to put
me up for a time," he replied. " It won't be for long,
because I want to find some place where I can get to
work on my Choral Symphony." He added slowly :
" For many reasons I'd rather not have gone back to
Witnall just yet, even to them, but I've got to get used to
present conditions. I know things have changed out of
recognition in the past two years — and criminal lunatics
can't be choosers."

" Oh, Mr. Francis, don't ! " She looked at the floor,
her heart thumping harder than ever. If Ruth Alleyndene
were here, she thought, I know what she'd tell me to do.
And after all, there couldn't be a better chance than this.
I might as well know. If it means goodbye from today,
it'll only be a few weeks sooner. . . .

Still looking down, she began to speak in a voice that
she hardly recognised as her own.

" Mr. Francis, I just wanted to say . . . if I could ever
be of any further use to you . . ."

" How do you mean ? " he asked, puzzled by her
sudden change of manner. " You've been splendid, the
way you've come down here — but what can you do for
me once I'm released ? "

She lifted her head then, and looked at him proudly.

" There are quite a number of ways in which a woman
can be of use to a man — even when she's his inferior ? "

When Francis spoke again, his voice too might have
belonged to someone else ; its pain was so acute.

" My inferior ! My God ! "

" Of course I'm your inferior. You're a fine musician
and a wonderful employer. If only there were more

ability like yours in the world today, things wouldn't have gone so wrong." She continued firmly : " I know you can never stop loving Sally, and I wouldn't want you to. You wouldn't be you if you did. But if you need me — if you can use me in any way — please do."

Again there was a long pause. Into Francis's mind had flashed incongruously the spectacle that he must present as he lay there ; the shade over one eye, the long scar from his brow to the top of his head with the hair shaved round it, the colourless cheeks, the bandaged hands. Did ever a woman, he thought, declare her affection for such a damaged piece of human wreckage ?

" Look here, Enid Clay — are you proposing to me ? " he said at last.

She looked at him with resolute dignity.

" No, no ! I'm not asking you for marriage. I'll be your friend, your mistress, anything you choose, so long as I can serve you in some way, and look after you when you leave this place."

Francis struggled off the bed, and supporting himself against the wheel-chair, stood up and faced her, astonished and incredulous. He spoke very quietly now.

" Do you really mean you'd consider marrying me — you, whose courage has been proved and rewarded, marrying a criminal and an ex-lunatic — after all that has passed ? "

She fell on her knees before him then, gently holding his bandaged hands and pressing her lips against them as the emotion that she had restrained for years poured out in passionate words.

" Consider it ! Why, Mr. Francis, there's nothing more I could ask of life ! I've loved you as long as I can remember — ever since my father told me stories of your work at Fordham when I was a child ! I went to Witnall Polytechnic and trained as a stenographer so as to join your staff . . . and then I felt sick to the depths of my soul because I was so stupid, so awkward, and could never please you ! . . . And after the tragedy happened . . . and we thought things might go wrong, that you might be sentenced to death . . . I'd have wanted nothing better than to be allowed to die instead. And when Halkins' was bombed, that's what I thought I was going to do. I'm not at all brave really — not half as brave as you are ! I only kept my head because it was your factory I was in, your things I was saving ! Oh, Mr. Francis, let me . . ."

Her voice failed, and she hid her face in the rough blanket on his bed, her shoulders shaking. Francis stood looking down at her, emotionally moved to a degree that astonished him, but intellectually capable — as he had always been capable when his nervous reactions were under control — of viewing both her and himself with complete detachment.

Weak though he was, he became conscious of a stirring in his blood, long forgotten, but once very familiar ; of a physical urge which excited even while it shamed him with a remorse that was strangely divided between Enid and Sally. In a flash of intuition he realised that there were still some facts about himself that he had not understood, and perceived the significance of the exasperation which he had so often felt in her presence. He knew now that it had originated, not in her, but in himself ; it had been his automatic safeguard against the strong sexual response to which, if he had once permitted it, she could always have moved him. Was it really possible that she meant what she had said ; that he — the murderer, the outcast, the man whose impending release would have embarrassed his relatives if there had been any left to embarrass — had it in his power to give so much happiness to a courageous and intelligent human being ?

Still supporting himself against the chair, he put one arm beneath her elbow, lifted her to her feet, and held her close to him.

" I understand now . . . my dear. And I'm not ' Mr. Francis ' to you any more. Just ' Francis ' — and your future husband."

A week later, Ruth Alleyndene brought him the news that his release had definitely been granted, and would take effect as soon as he was well enough to lead a normal life.

" If we really made a fuss, you could probably be transferred to a nursing home, or another hospital," she said. " But is it worth while to move just for two or three weeks ? They say you'll be fit to leave by then."

He held out his still covered hands.

" The bandages are coming off tomorrow," he told her. " Do you know, I've become almost fond of this place in the last few weeks ! I daresay I can stick it a little longer."

She stood up, looking out of his window at the valley. The heat-wave had broken, but on the heath the wild roses, brought into full flower by the warm weather, blossomed starry and pale. There was a hardy youth about them, a delicate proletarian strength, which made her think of Enid Clay.

" At any rate," she said nonchalantly, " it'll give Enid time to make plans for your wedding, and find you somewhere to live."

" She's told you, then ? "

" Yes. But I wasn't . . . exactly surprised. I've had a feeling for ages that you'd marry her in the end."

He moved to the window, and stood beside her.

" You knew me better than I knew myself, then. It never occurred to me that a woman could fall in love with me again — especially a young one."

" Why did you imagine she came and worked for you here month after month, for nearly two years ? Sometimes I think the most intelligent men are the blindest !

She told me the other day that she'd loved you since she was quite a child. You've been through more than most people, Francis Halkin, but at least you have something to thank God for. Not many men get devotion like that offered to them twice in a lifetime."

"That's just it," he said slowly. "Ought it to be accepted twice? That's the one thing that troubles me, Ruth Alleyndene. The only person who gets nothing out of all this is . . . Sally."

"I know." She was silent for a moment. Then she went on : "The one time I saw her, it seemed to me that you were literally everything to her. If she had known what was to happen, I believe she would willingly have laid down her life to give you peace and fulfilment."

"And," he added, with a touch of the old bitterness, " to see herself replaced ? "

"Yes," she said gravely. "A person who really loves is prepared even for that."

"But surely it's a kind of disloyalty — particularly when I was responsible for her death ? "

Ruth's mind went back, as it had often gone back since the return of war, to a grave in the American military cemetery at Romagne, now in enemy-occupied territory no longer accessible to the women who had once loved the men who lay there. Then she thought of her husband Denis, of her twin son and daughter, Jack and Jill, and her youngest child Timothy. Taking Francis's arm, she led him back to his chair.

"Sit down, Francis Halkin. I've got to talk to you. You're still a comparatively young man, and I don't want to see you lose a chance of real happiness — or make Enid lose it — by over-cultivating your conscience."

Looking out at the Forest dark beneath the summer clouds, she continued.

"You won't ever forget Sally — and being you, I don't suppose you'll ever cease to feel compunction for her. But can't you just accept her now as part of your life and experience? To do more than that is to make Enid pay as well as yourself." She stood still a moment, remembering, and then continued. "Don't you see? — we've got to be unfaithful to the dead, we who go on, in order to have strength enough for the larger loyalties. I didn't realise that myself after my brother and my lover were killed in the last War. For years I went on trying to make up to *them* for the fact that I was still alive, instead of to life itself. It wasn't till I met Denis, when we were both working for the Quakers in Russia at the time of the famine, and he persuaded me to go home and get back into the main current of things, that I realised we don't serve the dead best by destroying the most vital parts of ourselves."

He did not speak, and she resumed with the sense that never in her life had she worked harder to establish a point of view.

"What you did to Sally may have been legally the worst you could do to her, but morally men have done crueller things to their wives all through the ages, and in some periods have been praised for it too. Look at the Victorian epoch, with so many of its women dead from too much child-bearing! Think of all the families in which wives have been worked or nagged into their graves — or deserted and left to fade out in desolation. You treated Sally with kindness and compassion. You tried, as you always had, to spare her suffering — and may actually have done so, even though you didn't intend the way you took. And for any wrong there may have been, you've more than paid the penalty."

"Perhaps I've done that," he said, almost inaudibly. "But it doesn't change the consequences of my crime, or alter the fact that I'm still here to accept love when it's offered me, and she isn't."

"Don't think of it any more as a crime, Francis. Call

it rather a part of the evil done by societies that go to war. After all, the whole definition of crime is due for revision in the light of modern psychological knowledge — and so is the definition of insanity. To my mind, there are people in the present government who would benefit by a spell of detention at Redhurst ! "

" You mean that the discipline here would do them good ? "

" I meant much more than that. When so-called statesmen pursue policies that lead to international catastrophe, and then have neither pity for the human suffering that results nor even an imaginative understanding of what it means, the category of criminal lunatic seems far more appropriate to them than it ever did to you ! To my mind, there ought to be a special section of this Asylum for all the people on both sides who are responsible for starving children to death or annihilating great cities by bombs, and who care nothing for the holocaust of innocent human life or the destruction of irreplaceable historic treasures ! "

In spite of the sorrowful memories which had crowded upon him, he smiled at her vehemence.

" You know," he said, " most of them are probably more stupid than base, and simply don't see the ultimate consequences of their actions. There's not much intelligence in this distraught world, after all. And I daresay very few of them have learned from the depths of experience, like you and me."

" Not like me, Francis — only like you. I've been pretty near the depths, but I've never touched bottom in the sense that you have. Since I first knew you, I've realised afresh that grief in itself is not the worst and final pain. That comes only when one endures remorse and humiliation as well. And it's those things, and the understanding of them which comes by sharing, that carry a man or woman to adulthood." She sat down on the bed, and laid her hand lightly upon his. "So in the end, Francis Halkin, you'll be able to do more for people who suffer than those of us who have never quite descended into the utmost pit of hell. And because Sally, by dying, at last brought you salvation, that will be her achievement too."

He stood up then, and took her hand.

"Thank you, Ruth Alleyndene. Quite apart from what you've done to get me back my freedom, you've helped me more than you probably realise. Oddly enough, you've put into words some of the very thoughts that passed through my mind while I lay in bed here in the Sanatorium. At least I know what to do with my salvation now it's been won for me."

"I'm sure you do. Tell me."

"Well," he said slowly, "while I've been here I've often thought that, supposing I hadn't been a composer and a man of substance, but, say, a bricklayer or a rag-cutter at Fordham, would any experts have been brought in to give evidence about my mental idiosyncrasies? Mightn't I have died on the gallows long ago — or at best be facing interminable years of death-in-life in this place?"

He held both her hands now, and spoke quickly, resolutely. "When I get out, I want to put all the resources I have — time, financial backing, the power of music to interpret and heal — at the disposal of specialists like Flint, who are studying in others the thing that destroyed Sally and so nearly destroyed me. I want to help them to cure this thing before it leads people to catastrophe — and, at the very least, to see that every criminal awaiting trial, rich or poor, eminent or unknown, gets the same sort of careful examination as I received."

She nodded. "You're right there. There's no equality before the law in that respect. The need for a thorough examination of all prisoners — their minds as well as bodies — is something which so far our whole penal system ignores."

" Flint says," Francis continued, " that after the last War the number of shattered lives was appalling — largely because their trouble, like mine, was never understood. He thinks that this War will probably leave even more neurosis cases behind it — but if he and I have any say in the matter, there'll be a few less who meet with disaster. Anything I can do to help them will be part of my life's work from now on."

" You'll be able to help them, Francis," she said with conviction. " Your suffering, and Sally's, has been part of the price paid for war by those who are least to blame. For that very reason, you're specially qualified to work with the people who are seeking peace through human understanding."

" Yes," he agreed. " If we understood individuals more radically, we should be better equipped to analyse the motives which drive countries into war, and make the ordinary citizen so blindly ready to accept it."

" I know. I began to think along those lines myself during the scientific evidence at your trial. After that, Miriam Huntbach and I had a most enlightening conversation with Dr. Flint and Professor Maclaren at the hotel in Stafford, the night before the verdict. Since then I've realised that although wars may appear to begin in economic or political conditions, they can only be abolished in terms of the spirit. The peace that some of us are seeking lies in the creation of a new state of mind."

She gathered up her coat from the bed, and turned to go.

" It's men and women who have suffered as you have, Francis Halkin, who can help most to create that state of mind. After all, nations respond to challenge and provocation in just the same way as individuals, and, like individuals, they can be healed by pity and understand-

ing." She opened the door. " Next time we meet, you'll
be a free man. And when I'm struggling in Parliament
against heavy odds for a modicum of sanity in international
affairs, I shall often think of you on your particular
battlefield, working through your friends and your music
for a similar end."

On the day of Francis's release from Redhurst, he
dressed himself carefully in the best of his pre-war suits
and brushed the thick waves of his greying hair over the
scar on the top of his head. That July afternoon, as soon
as they arrived in London, he and Enid were to be married.
Later they would go home to the flat which she had made
ready for them just below the summit of Richmond Hill.

He wasn't much of a bridegroom for a young girl, he
thought, adjusting his tie in front of the shaving mirror
borrowed from Gibbons. But at least he had given himself
a decent shave, the first he had been allowed since he came
to Redhurst, and though the sight of his left eye was still
poor, he had been permitted to remove the shade which
covered it. The Birmingham eye specialist who had come
to Redhurst at David Flint's request to examine him and
prescribe treatment, had guaranteed that he would be
able to see normally in six months' time. His hands, he
realised, would always be scarred, and the left one was
still covered by a glove, but the use of the right had fully
returned, and with time his musician's delicacy of touch
would be restored.

The day that he faced inspired him with mixed feelings
of excitement and apprehension. He longed for freedom
now with an impatience that for the past few days had
become almost unbearable. The thought of making Enid
his wife awakened in him a renewed sense of physical
anticipation, mingled with remorseful gratitude that he
was still alive to play the part of a husband, and perhaps
even to beget the children of whom he had once aban-

doned all hope. But he shrank from the prospect of the marriage ceremony at the Poplar Settlement to which, in order to satisfy Enid, he had reluctantly agreed.

" Surely," he had protested, " a registry office would be more appropriate — particularly for me, of all people ? Anyhow, I usually loathe parsons."

" You wouldn't loathe Philip," she said. " He's not a bit like the Rector at Fordham."

" I didn't so much mind the old Rector. He was what he pretended to be, and nothing else. The padre here is a decent chap too. It was the one at Witnall Prison that got me down. He treated us all as though only his intervention could save us from utter damnation."

" If you really hate the idea, we won't go to the Settlement. But it isn't a bit like Witnall Prison — and everyone there wants to see you so much."

Oh, well, he thought, I may as well go through it to please her. After all, it's her first wedding, if it isn't mine, and I'm sure her parents are good chapel-goers. She probably wouldn't feel properly married if we went to a registry office.

" All right," he capitulated. " But I shall trust you to take me away the moment it's over ! "

He had hardly finished his breakfast and collected his possessions, packed the previous day in Gibbons's presence, when Enid, who had spent the night at the village inn, came to the Asylum to fetch him. With her slim figure dressed in a neat navy coat and skirt, adorned with two flame-coloured rosebuds fastened to the lapel, she seemed to him to be hardly more than a child. She never had been and never would be pretty, but the soft fair hair left uncovered by her little halo hat was the colour of pale daffodils, and her expression of happiness enhanced the vital intensity with which his repressed sensual self had done such persistent battle. Her youth filled him with a sudden poignant compunction.

" I'm not sure you're old enough to commit your life to me," he told her ruefully. " After all, there are eighteen years between us. You just might be my daughter ! "

" That would be very nice, of course," she said, smiling. " But I'd much rather be your wife. And since I've known my own mind about you for fifteen years, I'm surely entitled to say so ! "

In the entrance yard where the Asylum car was waiting, a group of friends had assembled to bid Francis farewell. He had said goodbye the previous day to the Chief, the Chaplain, and the Medical Officers ; the men gathered to watch him depart were the supervisors and participants of his daily life for nearly two years. Gibbons, the Chief Attendant, was there, and Mitchell, the once churlish warder, now walking with a stick, whose life he had probably saved. But even their obvious pleasure in his regained freedom did not move him so much as the generous satisfaction of Higginson and Waterhouse, and the cordiality of his constant companion Adrian Farraway, the notorious murderer of his fashionable mistress, who would not leave Redhurst this side the grave. In the peculiar fashion by which information never actually imparted becomes common knowledge, they all knew that Francis was to be married that day to the young secretary who had visited him so faithfully. No sign of envy diminished the heartiness of their handshakes or impaired the warmth of their discreet congratulations.

" So long, Sir. Maybe you and the wife will come back and visit us one day ? "

Francis shook Higginson's hand. A sudden uprising of emotion choked him, making it difficult to speak.

" Goodbye, Harry. I can never thank you enough for the way you've looked after me the last few weeks. We shan't forget any of you. We'll come back and see you, of course ! "

All the way to the station Francis was immersed in a remorseful silence which Enid respected and shared, understanding his pain in being, for once, more fortunate than others ; in accepting the magnanimous wishes of men who would never be free, or marry, or have children. It was not until the compartment reserved for them was transferred to the London train at Southampton that he threw off the burden of compunction and put his arm round her, silently drawing her to his side. As though he had never seen England before he gazed entranced at the open fans of the elms above the hedgerows, and the fragrant clusters of meadow-sweet in the summer fields between Winchester and Basingstoke.

At last, when he had looked long enough at the fair face of freedom and turned from the window, Enid hesitatingly put to him a question which had long troubled her.

" Don't tell me if you'd rather not, Francis, but sometimes I do still wonder why I used to annoy you so much at Fordham. It's only that I'm afraid of making you feel the same again without knowing why."

" I don't think you ever will," he told her. " To be honest, I suppose I was subconsciously afraid that you might have a sort of attraction for me. Call it lust at that stage, not love — which I couldn't have felt for anyone but Sally so long as she was alive."

He was silent for a moment and then continued slowly, feeling that though he might be betraying Sally, he owed Enid the explanation.

" You see," he said, " although I may have been abnormal in some ways, I'm entirely normal in others — and those rather vital ones. But Sally didn't care for that side of life after a few years of marriage. She dreaded having children too much."

" That's something I don't understand, Francis. Didn't you mind at all ? "

" Yes ; a great deal. I lost my only brother when he was quite a baby, and perhaps for that reason I'd always counted on having a family. It was difficult to subdue the desire for one at first, though I used to pretend I didn't care. Finally I became so busy that sublimation was easy."

" Don't you think it made the thing you were fighting more difficult to overcome ? "

" I'm sure now that it did. Wasn't it Bacon who said : ' One may trust his victory over nature too far ; for nature will lay buried for a great time and yet revive upon the occasion of temptation ' ? I think that explains why I treated you so roughly. I was really afraid of you all the time."

A secret triumphant relief flooded Enid's heart. She had known that she could take care of Francis, and already she had made herself indispensable ; she had doubted only her ability to hold him physically after Sally's remembered beauty. It seemed evident now that even this doubt was superfluous ; that she could speak to him with the uninhibited frankness of her young generation.

" Well, I shall never be good enough for you, Francis, but at least I'm not the withholding sort ! If I could give you children, I should be prouder and gladder than I can ever tell you ! "

" In spite of everything ? " he asked rather sadly.

" There's no ' in spite ' about it," she said. " Your child would be yours."

At Waterloo Enid steered them competently through the crowded noisiness of a wartime terminus, which bewildered Francis's long-secluded eyes and ears. Leaving his possessions in the Parcels Office to be picked up later on their journey to Richmond, they took the Underground Railway to Bow Road Station, and emerged half an hour later on the wide East End thoroughfare which led straight to the heart of raided Poplar.

It was a cool day for July, with low clouds occasionally penetrated by Jacob's Ladders of sunshine. The glancing yellow light fell impartially upon the dusty remains of burnt-out shops, with their windows boarded up or left altogether uncovered, showing bits of broken glass still clinging to their frames. In the corners of the deserted interiors, little piles of bricks and paper had lain unremoved for over a year. Close to the grass-grown fragments of grey masonry which had been Bow Church, they turned off the high road into a side street where the houses, windowless and often roofless, were completely uninhabited. Sometimes the furniture had been taken away ; sometimes it had been left as it stood, with cups and saucers, now smothered in dust, still standing on the table. In the more damaged houses the inside walls, though exposed to the weather, exhibited the original colour of paint or paper. Francis and Enid walked by a ruined church with the windows shattered and the tiles blown from the rafters ; the door hung loosely from a broken hinge, and a notice board outside announced, somewhat superfluously, that it was dangerous to shelter in the basement below. Over the whole street hung the strange silence of deserted cities.

Now and again they passed huge clearances where whole blocks of buildings had been destroyed and removed. On one had stood a workhouse in which many aged men and women had perished during a night of heavy raids. On another a fire station had received a direct hit when half Poplar was blazing, and a squad of firemen from a neighbouring borough arrived just in time to meet their death. One such wide gap adjoined Alton Hall, where an aerial torpedo had destroyed half a street in September, 1940. The Settlement itself looked the worse for wear ; its doors and windows were obviously temporary, and the china angel which stood above the entrance was cracked from head to foot.

Francis looked round astonished upon this battered unfamiliar London.

" At night," he said, " when you can't see how mean the houses were, it must be like walking through the ruins of Pompeii. . . . You know, Enid, I oughtn't to go to Richmond. I ought to stay here and work for these people ! "

" Oh, dearest, not yet ! " she cried, smiling at his characteristic desire to do everything at once. " Give yourself a chance ! Perhaps someday we'll get Dr. Flint to start another clinic in the East End, and run a special concert hall in connection with it. I'd like that more than anything, I think. But first you must get adjusted again." She added gaily : " Don't imagine you'll find complete immunity even in Richmond ! It had a Blitz of its own one night, and there's quite a fine collection of ruins about the town ! "

At the door of the Settlement, Alfred and Miriam Huntbach stood waiting for them with the Warden, Philip Faulkner. Like other friends of Francis they would gladly have gone to Redhurst to welcome him back into the world of free men and women, but had spontaneously given way to Enid's prior claim to have him to herself for those first few hours. While Alfred took Francis in charge, Miriam now accompanied Enid to the small bare dressing-room where she removed her hat and tidied her hair for the ceremony.

" My dear," she said, taking Enid's hands and kissing her, " I'm so glad for you both ! Sally would be very grateful to you."

In the clubroom of the Settlement they all gathered for a modest meal of tea and sandwiches, held before the ceremony because the workers there knew that Francis was not yet strong and would probably be tired by his journey. Sitting in an armchair with a cup of tea in his hand, he felt confused by the interested group of local helpers who addressed him as " Mister " and called Enid " dearie ". But almost immediately they gave way to Walter Welland, who had managed for one day to discard the wartime responsibilities of a pottery owner, and to Ruth Alleyndene, who told him how glad she was that the House was not sitting and she had been able to come.

She was not sufficiently interested in her brother's wife to have telepathic knowledge of the comments made on her visit to Poplar by Jennifer Alleyndene to a Witnall friend in a coffee shop that morning.

" It's absolutely typical of Ruth — going to the wedding of our chauffeur's daughter with that Francis Halkin, of all people. Of course Clay isn't our chauffeur any longer ; we had to let him go when we laid up the car, and he's making munitions. But everybody identifies him with us, and the whole story's all over Witnall. Whatever Ruth does seems to get into the papers, and it makes things very difficult for Norman — as if her politics weren't bad enough ! "

But to Ruth it appeared the most promising wedding that she had ever attended since her own to Denis Rutherston — who was at the Settlement too, a little vague about the respective histories of the bride and bridegroom, but quite prepared to rejoice in an occasion with which his wife was obviously pleased. They watched Enid's parents being introduced to Francis, who was meeting them consciously for the first time.

The warmth of their hand-shakes and the look of pride with which they regarded both him and Enid betrayed no awareness of the fact that he had ever committed a crime or been in prison ; much less that he had left an asylum only that morning. Confronting their benevolent, well-satisfied expressions, Francis understood better the attitude of Enid herself, to whom it had not seemed in the least strange that her wedding day should begin within the shadow of imprisoning walls. A deep gratitude filled his heart towards the poor and the humble, whose habit was to stand beside the sinner and the sufferer, and not above or against him. Now, on his own behalf, he was reminded that, among people not endowed with privilege or security, to fall foul of the law and get into trouble with the police was just one misfortune among many others, to be shared and carried between them. They showed no censoriousness towards their unlucky neighbours. They judged not, and they were not judged.

When the informal meal was over the little gathering of friends prepared to go down to the chapel, and the tall young clergyman from whom Francis had anticipated patronage approached him with an air of respectful diffidence.

" Won't you take my arm, Sir ? These steps are rather tricky."

He treats me as if I were his Commanding Officer, thought Francis, converted in spite of himself to Enid's opinion of Philip Faulkner. " He comes, the prisoners to release. . . . The bleeding soul to cure . . ." Where on earth had he read those lines ?

" Thank you," he said, and they went down the worn staircase together.

In the small shabby chapel with its damaged ceiling Francis and Enid stood before the altar, and their friends sat behind them on the scarred wooden benches. Francis looked up once, to see the beauty of flame-coloured roses in a copper vase beneath the cracked window-panes, as the Warden pronounced the words of the marriage vow.

" I, Francis Keynsham, take thee, Enid Irene, to my wedded wife . . ."

Francis repeated the words after him in a low, inaudible voice, stumbling as he went. Was he remembering the last occasion on which he had uttered them nearly twenty years ago, at a wedding which had been a complete contrast to this ; a fashionable wedding in a Staffordshire church, with flowers and a choir, followed by a crowded reception at a country manor, and speeches, and local reporters, and a wedding-cake, and champagne ? Enid knew, at any rate, that he was recalling a very different bride from her plain, insignificant self — a tall, lovely bride in a long satin gown and a veil crowned with orange blossom ; a graceful, elegant bride, who had vanished . . . where ?

" Sally would be very grateful to you," Miriam Hunt-bach had said. Taking Francis's hand in hers, Enid repeated the words of her own vow after Philip Faulkner in a firm, clear voice.

" I, Enid Irene, take thee, Francis Keynsham, to my wedded husband, to have and to hold from this day forward, for better for worse, for richer for poorer, in sickness and in health, to love and to cherish, till death us do part, according to God's holy ordinance ; and thereto I give thee my troth."

CHAPTER XXII

THE END OF THE BEGINNING

One afternoon in the third week of March, 1943, Francis Halkin walked rapidly up Richmond Hill. He had information for Enid which he was eager yet reluctant to give her. Half of him felt satisfaction in a consummation which he had long desired. But the other half wished that its coming could have been delayed another six weeks, for Enid was expecting a child at the end of April.

Passing hurriedly through an outer courtyard he

pressed the button of the lift with vigour, and arrived at their third-floor flat an hour before she expected him.

" I've got some news for you," he said, the moment that she heard him and came into the small lounge hall.

She guessed it immediately. " You're going to do a war job ? "

" Yes." He went on slowly : " David Flint's been asked to take a field hospital out to Tunisia at once. An advanced psychiatric centre is its official name. . . . He wants me to go with him as an ambulance driver."

If she had counted on his remaining in England, not a muscle of her face betrayed the fact.

" You'll go, of course."

He looked at her ruefully. " Yes. I'd have given anything for this to come six weeks later. I did want to see you through — and to see my child. But . . ."

" But the Axis may be cleared out of Tunisia by then ? Anyhow, it's now the campaign's at its height."

" That's the point. It's a god-sent chance of getting close to the kind of work I've been thinking about so much. David will get men immediately after they've been blown up, or buried. He'll be able to treat them for the thing that did me down before they even know they've got it."

" I'm glad it's Major Flint you're going with, anyway."

" He's Colonel Flint now. It was gazetted yesterday. As a private in ordinary battle-dress, I shall have to salute him. You can't call that unrestricted ambition, after twenty-five years ! "

She put the next question without flinching.

" When do you have to leave ? "

" Almost immediately. Probably at the end of next week. I've got to get my tropical kit at once."

" That's splendid. I shall be able to help you better now than I could a month hence."

" I can manage most things all right without you. I won't have you tiring yourself." He paused. " Enid . . .

you do realise this trip won't be a picnic ? Ships get
bombed and sunk nowadays ; field hospitals can be blown
to smithereens, however many Red Cross flags they fly.
I may be leaving you alone — for good."

" Dear Francis, I do realise that," she answered quietly.
" I'm not afraid for myself — or the next generation. And
I'm afraid for you least of all."

" I daresay we shan't be in Tunisia long. As soon as
the Second Front starts, we shall probably follow it. That's
when our worst cases will come in."

" Yes," she said.

" Before you know where you are, Enid Halkin, you'll
be hearing that your husband's landed among the troops
from a parachute, like some of the M.O.s in North Africa.
I'm sure I could easily learn to jump. So far I've managed
to avoid a middle-aged spread ! "

" I'm sure you could," she agreed, smiling a little as
she looked at his light athletic figure and eager luminous
eyes, their sight now fully recovered from the injury
caused by the raid. His suggestion did not seem to her in
the least fantastic. For the rest of his life, she knew, he
would seize every available opportunity of proving his
courage.

" We must talk about the things you need, but I'll get
tea first," she said, knowing that she would not be able to
realise the fact of his imminent departure until she was
alone again.

The next morning, when her work in the flat was done
and the day's meals prepared, she went across the road
to the Terrace Garden, sloping downwards towards the
river from the brow of the Hill. It was getting difficult to
walk now, and she was glad to sit down on a wooden seat
in the warm sunshine of that exceptional spring. Surely
this must be one of the most beautiful gardens in the world,
she thought, looking at the daffodils under the trees amid
the wide open purple crocuses, and the vivid beds of

brown and orange polyanthus. I was right to bring
Francis here. I don't believe there's a place in England
where he would have become himself again so quickly,
and yet have been within easy reach of his work at the
Royal College.

Their life in Richmond, she felt, could not in any case
have lasted much longer; it had been too deeply and
quietly happy for them to be entitled to it indefinitely in a
world overshadowed with suffering. Neither he nor she
wanted permanent immunity from that suffering, even
though he, perhaps, had already endured more than his
share. Nothing, at any rate, could take away their months
together. Nothing could blot out the memory of those
first weeks of marriage, when she knew that with her young
body — so much more articulate than her vocabulary in
its passionate response — she had comforted and compensated him for the physical deprivations of many years.
She was glad that their child had been the outcome of
those weeks. Whatever else that future personality might
inherit, it could hardly lack affirmativeness and vitality.
It would crown the love that she had given to Francis even
though he might never see it.

A poem by William Soutar came into her head which
Francis had read to her recently from the Sunday *Observer*.
She had cut it out afterwards, and put it into her old
school prayer-book between the pages setting forth the
ceremony for the Publick Baptism of Infants.

> " *Wombs are not withered by decrees*
>   *Of tyrannous assize ;*
>   *On life's unconquerable knees*
>   *The child triumphant cries.*
>
> " *Centred in riots and alarms,*
>   *And Stratagems of State,*
>   *He holds tomorrow in his arms*
>   *Beyond Herodian hate.*

" He is the dedicated bud
Upon the desolate bough :
The April which is unsubdued
Within our wintry woe."

Except for the steady development of the baby towards that future April day of birth, she would hardly have realised that it was eight months since she and Francis arrived at the flat on the afternoon of their wedding. It had seemed unbelievable then that they were really alive, and together, and married ; two people who, like a large proportion of Britain's population, had been nearly but not quite killed in air raids. She had struggled to hide her emotion as she watched him move, half dazed and wholly incredulous, amongst his possessions as though he had never seen them before. He touched the silk curtains with a wonder which suggested that the feel of silk was some astonishing novelty ; he tried, half unbelieving, the softness of the cushions ; he walked up and down the thick carpet instinctively testing its pile with his feet. When she brought in the tea he had caressed the delicate egg-shell blue cup with his fingers, holding it carefully as though at any moment it would evaporate and vanish.

Throughout that autumn and the winter that followed it — a winter so mild and sunny that it seemed to have turned into spring before they even realised its presence — Francis had gone back to the Royal College of Music to refresh his technique. After the two uncreative years of imprisonment, his talent had flowered again, as he had foreseen that it would. Seeking to embody in music what those years had taught him, he was working at a Choral Symphony called "The Resurrection". In the intervals of that massive composition, he had begun three anthems — "He was despised", "I saw a new Heaven", and "The earth is the Lord's".

The young men and women with whom he studied paid

little attention to him, and few even realised that he was
Francis Keynsham. To them he represented merely a
fellow-student, conspicuous only by his maturity and his
greying hair. Most of them had been at school during
the *cause célèbre* in which he had figured, and even when
they heard his name, connected it only with his musical
compositions.

"That's one advantage of living in an over-eventful
period of history," he thought. "Honourably or dis-
honourably, we occupy the limelight only for a second —
and then we move off the stage."

But, well though his work on the Symphony was going,
for the first time in his life his music, as he had foreseen, did
not wholly satisfy him. As the weeks and then the months
went by, he seemed to be watching for something, and
waiting. Although he never put this slight restlessness
into words, Enid knew that he was looking for an opportunity to get close, once again, to the grimmer realities of
active service, and to prove, in caring for those afflicted
as he had been, that war had no longer the power to
overcome him. Only, she realised, when he had thus
finally proved himself, would he be able to give his whole
mind and spirit to his music.

His work at the College seemed hardly to have fallen
into a regular daily routine, when they realised that their
desire for a child was to be fulfilled.

"Do you mind which it is ? " she had asked him, and,
still deeply stirred by the prospect of fatherhood, he
replied : "Not a bit ! After giving up hope of children
for so many years, the very thought of somebody of my
own flesh and blood is like a miracle."

"Well, then, I want a daughter," she asserted. "She's
more likely to take after you ! "

"I'll put up with that," he said gaily, "so long as she
inherits your courage."

With the life of the child, a new and confident vitality

seemed to enter into him which was linked in her mind with a small but significant episode that had only recently occurred. One evening, after his return from the College, he had been looking through a cabinet which had belonged to his mother for some old notes made during his student days, when he came to her with a piece of music in his hand and a curious expression on his face.

"What's that?" she asked, and he replied: "It's my mother's copy of the *Morning Hymn*. . . . I'd no idea we had it here."

"Isn't that the piece that was mentioned at your trial?"

"Yes. In some queer way, it came to be connected with my periods of unconsciousness. My mother adored it — and yet the thing seems to have haunted my life like an evil spirit."

"The only thing to do with evil spirits is to exorcise them," she said promptly. "How can we exorcise this one?"

"Play it to me, Enid. If it has any kind of . . . devastating effect, you can always ring up David — or send for the porter!"

"That's just absurd," she told him resolutely. "It won't affect you at all. The one disadvantage is, with my school-girl strumming it probably won't even sound like the piece you knew."

She sat down at the small upright piano, thankfully exchanged for Sally's baby grand by an instrument-seller now unable to obtain appropriate pianos for concert platforms. As she struck the opening chords of George Henschel's music, he sat down on the couch with his face hidden in his hands. He remained in this attitude until she had played the piece through. Then he got up and stood beside her.

"Would you mind playing it again?" he said, and as she obeyed he quietly intoned the words.

> " *Bald ist der Nacht ein End' gemacht,*
>   *Schon fühl ich Morgenlüfte wehen . . .*"

"These words are in English, and you're singing them in German ! " she exclaimed.

"Reinick wrote them in German, and that's how they always came to me. Why not ?"

She went on with the song, and he murmured the second verse.

> " *Vom Himmelszelt durch alle Welt,*
>   *Die Engel freude jauchzend fliegen ;*
>   *Der Sonne Strahl*
>   *Durchflammt das All.*
>   *Herr, lass uns kämpfen, lass uns siegen !* "

They were both silent for a moment, and then he remarked : "It's strange — I can't remember or so much as imagine now the incommunicable terror that conventional thing used to give me. There's even a sort of . . . constructive romanticism about both the music and the words. My poor mother — she was an incurable romantic ! "

Enid turned to him from the piano, smiling.

"And aren't you ? "

He smiled back ruefully.

"I suppose I am. . . . That's probably why I've had so many troubles that most people manage to avoid. It took Sally's death and a murder trial and two years of solid thinking to teach me to understand myself a little. Rather an expensive process, wasn't it ? "

"Well," she said, "at least the last line of the song has come true now, and you can forget it ! "

He meditated for a moment.

"Has it come true ? I wonder. Ask me when we've run that Poplar concert hall together for ten years, and I'll tell you."

At any rate his final fear was conquered that afternoon, thought Enid, moving from her seat in the sunshine. She walked slowly up the steps through the rock garden where the purple arabis was budding, and the grape hyacinths made vivid patches of cobalt between the stones. Unless I play that song to him myself, he'll never hear it again. He will go to North Africa unhaunted by even the smallest shadow from the past.

Three days before the date fixed for their departure, David Flint came to the flat to discuss the remaining items of equipment with Francis and arrange their final plans. The departure of the psychiatric field hospital seemed especially timely, he said, for only that morning he had received a letter from a friend in the American Medical Association, reporting that thirty per cent of the casualties returned to the United States from active war zones were psychiatric in character.

" That doesn't mean, of course," he explained to Enid, " that men are less fit for military service than they used to be. It means that cases of this kind are now detected and rightly diagnosed, whereas in the last War they weren't."

" Did you see the letter in _The Times_ this morning about the McNaughton Ruling? " Francis inquired, referring to the legal precedent upon which the conduct of his own case had rested.

" No. I haven't had time to look at a paper today; I've been rushing about all over London. What does it say ? "

Enid opened the newspaper.

" It's a letter from someone called Ivor Back, about the case of the unfortunate boy who killed his mother." She read the letter aloud :

" The MacNaughton Ruling is a hundred years old. It was formulated at a time when the science of psychiatry was in its infancy. Much progress has been made in the study of mental diseases since then, and I suggest that the appointment of a Royal Commission of judges and doctors to clarify the position would be opportune."

" A Home Office Committee considered the question in 1924," said David. " But even that's nearly twenty years ago. I should say there's a case for a Royal Commission myself."

" Perhaps I shall be back in time to appear before it," suggested Francis. " You could hardly have a better witness than an ex-lunatic. . . . Look here, David, have you time to go through the complete list of equipment now ? I've got it next door."

" You'd better bring it along, then. I'll make time. I can't see what other chance there's likely to be before we go."

As Francis left the room, Enid turned to David.

" I'm ever so glad he's going to do this job, and with you," she said.

David Flint looked at her remorsefully. He had known that she was expecting a child and had felt glad, for anything that added stability and a reason for endurance to Francis's background seemed to him to be all to the good. But now, when he saw her, she appeared so young, and the birth of her child was evidently so near, that compunction seized him.

" I'm awfully sorry to take him away just now," he said. " It's pretty rough on you."

" Not more than it is on hundreds of women, Colonel Flint. When men like you and Francis are sent to dangerous places and we're not in a condition to go too, the least we can do is to carry on and have our children without making a fuss ! "

" I'm not surprised Halkins' rewarded you for your

courage," he said, moved by her refusal to contemplate self-pity.

" Oh, that. . . . Really, I was a fraud.   It's Francis who ought to have been rewarded, not I ! "

" Well," said David Flint, " perhaps he will be."   He added thoughtfully, " I'm sure he'll deserve to be, if we give him half a chance ! "

It was Saturday evening, the 27th of March.   In the flat Francis fastened the straps of his kit-bag and moved it into the hall.   He was in uniform now, with the insignia of a driver in the Royal Army Medical Corps on his shoulders.   In some curious fashion the khaki seemed to take the years away, and Enid could imagine that she saw standing there the boy of nineteen who had fought at Arras.   Following him, she continued the conversation begun while he finished his packing.

" It's tremendously lucky you were just able to finish your Symphony.   I'll register it and send it to Vesey's on Monday."

" I wish I'd had time to do a bit more to it.   But I don't believe it's too bad.   At the College they've promised to try it out at one of their summer functions.   If you feel fit enough by then, perhaps you could go along and let me know what you think of it."

" Of course I shall go.   You needn't worry about next month — or after.   Everything's fixed up.   It's difficult for Mother to leave the boys for long, so Miriam's coming to stay here tomorrow, and Mother will follow later."

" I wish Miriam could have come today," he said, his heart wrung by the prospect of Enid's loneliness after he had gone.

" She could have.   I thought I'd rather be alone tonight. . . . She'll be here by lunch-time tomorrow. It's easy for her to get away now, with Jane nursing, and Anne in the Friends' Ambulance Unit."   She added :

" I had a note from Ruth Alleyndene this afternoon. She says she'll come and see me every Sunday till the baby arrives, and oftener when I'm in hospital."

" That's just like her," he said. " I was discussing your career with her the other day. You needn't worry about finances, anyhow. I've settled enough on our child to fix her up till she's old enough to stand on her own feet. And I've deposited a separate sum for your legal training. By the time I come back, I shall have a private barrister at my disposal if ever I get into trouble again ! "

" You never will. But plenty of others will need me. I'm going to begin reading as soon as I'm fit. Miss Alleyndene's promised to help me. She's bringing a woman solicitor to tell me all about it when she comes tomorrow week."

She would, thought Francis. A glow of warmth towards his loyal friends irradiated his heart. They had stood by him, and now they would stand by Enid. They loved and admired her, and there was every reason why they should.

The clock in the sitting-room struck half-past six. At seven he must leave, for he had promised to join David at Paddington by eight o'clock. With a feeling that he would remember everything he wanted to say to Enid only after he had left her, he took her hand, and spoke insistently.

" You will take care of yourself, won't you, dear heart ? I shan't have a moment's real peace till I know that she — or he — has arrived, and you're safe."

" But you mustn't worry like that, Francis. There's absolutely no need. Dr. Maddison says I'm normal in every way, and she's promised to see that I go to hospital in plenty of time."

" I know she'll look after you. She's first-rate at her job. I only hope there'll be no more air raids between now and then."

Enid smiled at him tenderly.

" You're as bad as ever you used to be, where someone else is concerned ! You mustn't trouble yourself about the air raids either. That one the other night was more noise than anything else. Nowadays, the louder they are, the more confidently I think, ' It's only our guns.' "

" Well, there's some reason for that," he admitted. Letting go of her hand, he walked over to the window and looked at the spring beauty of the Thames Valley as though he were memorising it for the months, and perhaps years, when he would be far away. The view from their flat always reminded him of a tinted lithograph in a series called " Beautiful England ". Glistening amid the trees lay the river, a crescent-shaped mirror reflecting the pale carmine of the western sky. Beside it the towing-path curved towards Kingston, fringing the wide emerald meadow between the river-bank and Petersham Church.

" You know," he said, " that valley makes me think of some lines from Euripides which Gilbert Murray translated. I wonder if I can remember them ? "

He paused for a moment, and then repeated the verse.

> " *What else is Wisdom ?   What of man's endeavour,*
> *Or God's high grace, so lovely and so great ?*
> *To stand from fear set free, to breathe and wait,*
> *To hold a hand uplifted over hate,*
> *And shall not loveliness be loved for ever ?* "

" ' To hold a hand uplifted over hate '," she reiterated slowly. " That's what you and Colonel Flint will do, in your work in North Africa."

" I hope so. If I get any Germans or Italians in my ambulance, they'll certainly have such care as I can give them. I haven't forgotten what it means to be a prisoner."

He turned from the window.

" Look here, my dear, I don't want you to come to the station. One can't ever talk at stations, and anyhow crowded places aren't good for you at the moment. Let's say goodbye on the Terrace. Somehow I feel I'd like to remember you standing there, in case it's a long time before I see you again."

" All right," she said. " I don't like stations either. Most of the Saturday visitors have gone now, anyway. We shall probably have the Terrace to ourselves."

She put on her coat as he picked up his kit-bag, and without looking round at the flat which had been their home for eight months, they crossed the road and walked a little way to the summit of the hill where a high wall concealed them from the houses opposite. Standing hand in hand on the edge of the sloping garden and the wide green valley, they saw the descending sun, a huge blood-red disc, on the verge of sinking into a purple bank of cloud above the faint outline of Windsor. In the garden the chestnut trees were budding, and the pale yellow stars of daffodils gleamed through the wood. From the rockery glowed patches of vivid colour where golden forsythia and magenta plum-blossom had burst into flower. On the slanting lawn the magnolia branches, like graceful candelabra, were adorned with waxen pink and white petals which the previous year had only reached perfection in May.

" Last week, do you know," Enid remarked inconsequently, " I actually saw a tortoiseshell butterfly sitting on a crocus ! I wonder how often that's happened before ? "

" It's been a miraculous early spring," he said. " I couldn't wish for a better if it were to be my last."

Was it his last ? She faced the fact that it well might be. Francis, she realised, would do nothing now to safeguard his life. His tendency to take unnecessary precautions had been permanently exchanged for a readiness to confront excessive risks. And she knew that she would not have it otherwise. Even if the very worst occurred, he

would always live for her in his music.   For her and their
son or daughter.

"Yes," she answered.   "This spring has been a kind
of symbol of our life together, hasn't it ?   Everything
renewed and reawakening. . . . No matter what happens
now, we've had these eight months.   Nothing can ever
take them away."

"It's certainly more than I asked or expected of life
two years ago," he admitted.

"Or I, Francis.   In all the years I've loved you, I never
thought that anything like these months could happen to
me. . . . And, of course, they're not over.   They never
will be.   They'll go on indefinitely in the life of our
child."

"Yes," he said, "that's the only immortality we can
be sure of — life itself, and its unconquerable continuation."

They were both silent for a moment, and then he
glanced at his wrist.

"It's time, my dearest. . . . Don't watch me going
down the hill.   Look at the sunset instead."

"Very well, I will.   It's certainly remarkable enough
to hold my attention."

On the enclosed pavement where they were now alone,
he took her into his arms.

"Goodbye, then, my beloved wife !   You'll never know
quite what you've meant to me. . . ."

"Nor you to me, my own dear love."

For the last time — was it for years or for always ? —
she felt his lips pressed upon hers, his fingers moving
tenderly against her breast.   Then he was gone ; and
without a glance down the hill, she moved to the low
balustrade and looked over the darkening garden to the
bright feathers of luminous cloud, drifting unsubstantially
across the crimson and purple of the sunset.   Above the
dark dramatic boughs of the cedar on the hillside the first

star appeared, a yellow pin-point of scintillating light.

Whatever might happen in the years before her, this was not a moment for grief. Her mind was at rest about Francis's future, and her body itself carried the proof that human vitality is indestructible and the human spirit immortal. As she turned to go home the child stirred vigorously, and she rejoiced that out of death and sorrow, new life had come.

OTHER BOOKS BY VERA BRITTAIN

TESTAMENT OF FRIENDSHIP

In *Testament of Youth,* Vera Brittain passionately recorded the agonising years of the First World War, lamenting the destruction of a generation which included those she most dearly loved – her lover, her brother, her closest friends. In *Testament of Friendship* she tells the story of the woman who helped her survive – the writer Winifred Holtby. They met at Oxford immediately after the war and their friendship continued through Vera's marriage and their separate but parallel writing careers, until Winifred's untimely death at the age of 37.

Winifred Holtby was a remarkable woman. In her short life her generous, loving, talented nature shed a special light on all who knew her, on the many causes and campaigns for which she worked. When she died her fame as a writer was about to reach its peak with the publication of her greatest novel, *South Riding.*

Vera Brittain's life was marked by the tragic loss of those she loved, but in this portrait of her friend a spirit of love and confidence shines through. *Testament of Friendship* records a perfect friendship between two women of courage and determination, a friendship which transformed their own lives and illuminated the world in which they lived.

'An intense account of the love between two women writers...vivid glimpses of literary journalism of the period' – *Sunday Times*

Already published

TESTAMENT OF EXPERIENCE

In this her third testament Vera Brittain continues the story of those who survived the devastation of the First World War. Once again Vera Brittain interlaces private experience with the wide sweep of public events. Personal happiness in marriage and the birth of children, pride in her work as writer and campaigner are set against the fears, frustrations and achievements of the years 1925-50, one of the most crucial and stirring periods the world has known. The depression, the growth of Nazism, the peace movements of the 'thirties, the Abdication, the Spanish Civil War, the full horror and heroism of the Second World War come alive again through the eyes of this remarkable woman, who was herself a testament to all that is best in the times she lived through.

'A remarkable record' – *The Times*

'Lucid, intelligent, eye-witness account of events whose repercussions are as loud today, as ever' – *Time Out*

'Her record is honest and moving' – *Evening Standard*

Already published

OTHER BOOKS OF INTEREST

ANDERBY WOLD
Winifred Holtby

Mary Robson is a young Yorkshire woman, married to her solid unromantic cousin, John. Together they battle to preserve Mary's neglected inheritance, her beloved farm, Anderby Wold. This labour of love – and the benevolent tyranny of traditional Yorkshire ways – have made Mary old before her time. Then into her purposeful life erupts David Rossitur, red-haired, charming, eloquent: how can she help but love him? But David is a young man from a different England, radical, committed to social change. As their confrontation and its consequences inevitably unfold, Mary's life and that of the calm village of Anderby are changed forever. In this, her first novel, Winifred Holtby exhilaratingly rehearses the themes which come to fruition in her last and greatest work, *South Riding*.

'It is in the vividly affectionate detail with which she describes the routine of petty squabbles, small-town pride and the rhythm of the farming year that the book finds its life' – *Event*

Already published

THE CROWDED STREET
Winifred Holtby

This is the story of Muriel Hammond, at twenty living within the suffocating confines of Edwardian middle-class society in Marshington, a Yorkshire village. A career is forbidden her. Pretty, but not pretty enough, she fails to achieve the one thing required of her – to find a suitable husband. Then comes the First World War, a watershed which tragically revolutionises the lives of her generation. But for Muriel it offers work, friendship, freedom, and one last chance to find a special kind of happiness...

With the exception of *South Riding*, this is Winifred Holtby's most successful novel; powerfully tracing one woman's search for independence and love, it echoes in fictional form the years autobiographically recorded by her close friend Vera Brittain in *Testament of Youth*.

'Rather as if Jane Austen had thrown her cooling shadow a hundred years on – the same quiet humour and observation of the set stages in the social dance – but then there are bursts of Brontëesque passions stirring in an isolated Yorkshire´farmhouse...it is painfully vivid' – ALEX HAMILTON, *Guardian*

Already published

If you would like to know more about Virago books, write to us at Ely House, 37 Dover Street, London W1X 4HS for a full catalogue.

Please send a stamped addressed envelope

Book Tokens

Give them the pleasure of choosing

Book Tokens can be bought and exchanged at most bookshops